INSTALLMENT IMMORTALITY

Praise for the InCryptid series

"The only thing more fun than an October Daye book is an In-Cryptid book. Swift narrative, charm, great world-building . . . all the McGuire trademarks."
—Charlaine Harris, #1 *New York Times* bestselling author

"Seanan McGuire's *Discount Armageddon* is an urban fantasy triple threat—smart and sexy and funny. The Aeslin mice alone are worth the price of the book, so consider a cast of truly original characters, a plot where weird never overwhelms logic, and some serious kick-ass world-building as a bonus."
—Tanya Huff, bestselling author of *The Wild Ways*

"McGuire's InCryptid series is one of the most reliably imaginative and well-told sci-fi series to be found, and she brings all her considerable talents to bear on [*Tricks for Free*]. . . . McGuire's heroine is a brave, resourceful, and sarcastic delight, and her intrepid comrades are just the kind of supportive and snarky sidekicks she needs."
—*RT Book Reviews* (top pick)

"While [*Spelunking Through Hell*] veers noticeably from the urban fantasy of earlier volumes, taking place primarily in strange realms with almost no humans in sight, it still bears all the hallmarks of the InCryptid series: a clever protagonist, snarky banter, unusual creatures, and an entertaining blend of action, romance, and horror (the secret behind Alice's enduring youth and vitality is especially unsettling). At heart a love story, this entry delivers both a satisfying payoff for fans of the series and an intriguing expansion of its universe."
—*Publishers Weekly*

By the Same Author

Deadlands: Boneyard
Dusk or Dark or Dawn or Day
Dying with Her Cheer Pants On
Laughter at the Academy
Letters to the Pumpkin King
Overwatch: Declassified:
    An Official History of Overwatch
The Proper Thing and Other Stories

The InCryptid Series

Discount Armageddon
Midnight Blue-Light Special
Half-Off Ragnarok
Pocket Apocalypse
Chaos Choreography
Magic for Nothing
Tricks for Free
That Ain't Witchcraft
Imaginary Numbers
Calculated Risks
Spelunking Through Hell
Backpacking Through Bedlam
Aftermarket Afterlife

The Ghost Roads Series

Sparrow Hill Road
The Girl in the Green Silk Gown
Angel of the Overpass

The Alchemical Journeys Series

Middlegame
Seasonal Fears
Tidal Creatures

The Wayward Children Series

Every Heart a Doorway
Down Among the Sticks and Bones
Beneath the Sugar Sky
In an Absent Dream
Come Tumbling Down
Across the Green Grass Fields
Where the Drowned Girls Go
Lost in the Moment and Found
Mislaid in Parts Half-Known
Adrift in Currents Clean and Clear

Seanan McGuire's Wayward
    Children, Volumes 1–3 (boxed set)
Be Sure: Wayward Children,
    Books 1–3

INSTALLMENT IMMORTALITY

SEANAN McGUIRE

TOR PUBLISHING GROUP

New York

INSTALLMENT IMMORTALITY

Copyright © 2025 by Seanan McGuire

Chapter art by Shutterstock.com

"Mourner's Waltz" ornament by Tara O'Shea

A Tor Book
Published by Tom Doherty Associates / Tor Publishing Group
120 Broadway
New York, NY 10271

www.torpublishinggroup.com

Tor® is a registered trademark of Macmillan Publishing Group, LLC.

The Library of Congress Cataloging-in-Publication Data is available upon request.

ISBN 978-1-250-37511-7 (trade paperback)
ISBN 978-1-250-37512-4 (ebook)

Our books may be purchased in bulk for promotional, educational, or business use. Please contact your local bookseller or the Macmillan Corporate and Premium Sales Department at 1-800-221-7945, extension 5442, or by email at MacmillanSpecialMarkets@macmillan.com.

First Edition: 2025

Printed in the United States of America

0 9 8 7 6 5 4 3 2 1

For Alexea
Who well knows the glory of Turtle Boy

Price Family Tree

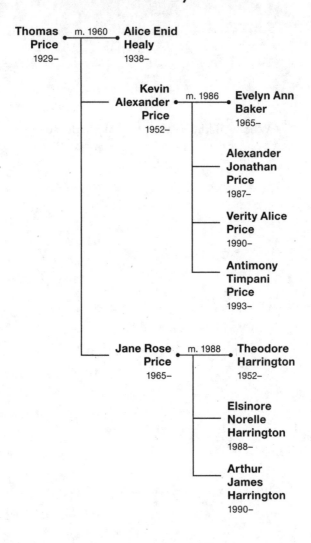

Thomas Price 1929– m. 1960 Alice Enid Healy 1938–

Kevin Alexander Price 1952– m. 1986 Evelyn Ann Baker 1965–

Alexander Jonathan Price 1987–

Verity Alice Price 1990–

Antimony Timpani Price 1993–

Jane Rose Price 1965– m. 1988 Theodore Harrington 1952–

Elsinore Norelle Harrington 1988–

Arthur James Harrington 1990–

Baker Family Tree

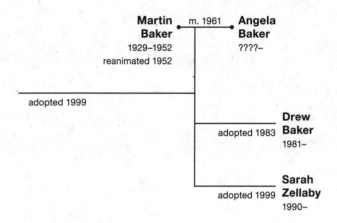

Martin Baker
1929–1952
reanimated 1952

m. 1961

Angela Baker
????–

adopted 1999

Drew Baker
adopted 1983
1981–

Sarah Zellaby
adopted 1999
1990–

Recover, verb:
1. To get back something that has been lost or taken away.

Recovery, noun:
1. The act of returning to normal.
2. The restoration of a previous state of being.
3. See also "resurrection."

INSTALLMENT
IMMORTALITY

Prologue

"It's all right, baby girl. This isn't your fault, and the best thing you can do for me now is to live your life. The world isn't your responsibility to save."

—Eloise Dunlavy

A remote crossroad in the Mojave Desert
Seventy-five years ago

THE SKY WAS THE DEEP, rich blue that was only possible miles from any signs of civilization, and it glittered with so many stars that they seemed to fill the entire world, lighting up the sand with a pale, luminous glow. The road that cut through the dunes was a scar against the flesh of the land, too dark and swallowing the starlight as nothing else in the environment did. The moon was a bleached, bloated disk, hanging high overhead like a silent judge over the scene that had yet to properly begin.

The air grew thick, and the staticky sound of a million insectile wings began to emanate from absolutely nowhere, forming an ongoing, inherently endless drone. There was something wrong with it, something unnatural in the precise timing of each individual wingbeat, like they were matched to an invisible metronome.

Overhead, a star glittered brighter for a moment, and a single gust of wind blew along the black tar ribbon of the road. A scorpion that had been lounging on the concrete, absorbing the last lingering heat of the day, rose on its segmented legs and scuttled away, vanishing into the sand.

The pale teenage girl who had appeared where the scorpion was looked around herself with disinterested eyes, long white hair ruffled by the wind. Her clothing was easily twenty years out of date, matching the age of the shadows in her graveyard eyes. They weren't gray or black or any other color that has a name behind it; rather, they were the color of a cold afternoon in an empty churchyard, when everything smells of petrichor and loam. They were impossible eyes, for an equally impossible girl. Her fingers were stained blue and red and yellow, primary colors swirled together in a formless, artless mess.

The buzzing grew louder for a moment, and then a voice spoke out of the nothingness, saying, "You know this won't do, Mary. You're not dressed for a negotiation."

"Huh, what's that?" The girl—Mary—looked down at her loose, well-worn shirt and lifted her eyebrows, white as her hair, in an expression of exaggerated surprise. "You mean this isn't what you think of as my uniform? Funny thing, that. I was supposed to have tonight off."

"You're our arbiter, and we own you," said the voice from nowhere. "Dismiss this idea of nights off and dress yourself accordingly for your position, or we'll do it for you." The threat in those words wasn't even partially veiled: it was open and direct.

Mary rolled her eyes and waved her painted hands in a sweeping gesture that managed to encompass her, the road, the fleeing scorpion, everything there was for her to encompass, and she . . . flickered, like a still from an old, well-patched strip of film. Her out-of-fashion clothing vanished in that flicker, replaced by a blouse with a deep V for a neck, colored as scarlet as her perfectly applied lipstick, a wide black belt, and a long A-line skirt that stopped just above her ankles, displaying her black Mary Jane pumps to perfect effect. Her hair remained loose and unstyled, now moving ever so slightly against the wind, like even it was running out of patience.

Her hands were abruptly clean, not a trace of paint in sight.

"Is *this* better?" she asked.

"Yes, Mary," said the voice from nowhere, mockingly. "You finally look as if you know your proper place, and won't embarrass us before tonight's petitioner. You're going to be meeting a very famous man on our behalf. A *movie star*."

Mary rolled her eyes. "I don't care. Alice is almost too old for fingerpainting, and you pulled me away from her when you knew I was supposed to be sitting tonight. This goes against our agreement."

"Do you really want to renegotiate the terms of your employment, Mary Dunlavy? Do you want to count on your connection to that mewling brat being strong enough to keep you manifest if we decide to be done with you?"

Wisely, Mary didn't answer.

The nothingness chuckled. "Good girl," it said. "He should be here soon."

Under the endless stretch of stars, Mary and the desert waited.

✦ ✦ ✦

Minutes stretched into hours, and the buzzing faded into an annoying background hum, like an overloaded power line singing to itself through the country night. Mary shifted her semi-substantial weight from one foot to the other, trying not to squirm. She wasn't physically uncomfortable—that sort of burden was no longer hers to carry unless she wanted it to be, and as she wasn't fully solid, she wasn't heir to the miseries of the flesh. What she *was* heir to was boredom, made worse by the knowledge that Alice was missing her. The girl's little voice had been tugging on the edge of Mary's consciousness for well over an hour, repeating her name over and over again. It was like having someone ringing a hotel bell every few seconds to summon a clerk who was busy with another guest.

"Are you *sure* he's coming?" she demanded peevishly, as off in the distance, the sound of an engine split the night. It was roaring, clearly pushed to its limits by whoever was behind the wheel.

"He comes," said the voice from nowhere, sounding smug. Mary caught her breath and stood up a little straighter. "Hide yourself," commanded the voice, and Mary disappeared. The buzzing stopped a moment later.

The night was silent except for the distant roar of the approaching engine, still as only a midnight desert could be. Even the wind had stopped.

With a screech of rubber tires and laboring brakes, a cherry-red roadster swept around the curve in the road and roared to a stop just shy of the physical crossroads. The cooling engine ticked almost angrily as a booted foot kicked the driver's-side door open and a short, slim man slid out of the seat. He didn't walk so much as he swaggered, like he was performing for some unseen camera. Like his car, he stopped just shy of the place where the two roads met, standing on the border of the physical crossroads.

He looked at the intersection for a moment, then up at the sky, studying the stars as the renewed wind stroked the perfectly gelled sweep of his pompadour.

"Oh, this is bullshit. This isn't anyplace special. Just another chunk of dead-end road not worth pissing on," he said. "That fucker was just saying whatever he could think of to get me out of his shit-ass trailer. Probably afraid I'd tell the fuzz where to find his little camp. Bet he's terrified someone's going to come along and sweep all his child brides away into the dark."

(Beneath his feet the road, which had been neutral a moment before, cooled and turned against him. But Diamond Bobby had never been destined for a routewitch's life, and he didn't understand how important it was to stay on the good side of the roads. He wasn't paying attention.)

He scoffed, looking down again. "This is stupid," he said. "Waste of time and gas."

He began to turn back toward his car and the wind caressed his cheek, suddenly warm and smelling of sun-sweet corn, fresh from the stalk and ready to be swallowed sweetly down. "Say what you came here to say," whispered a voice, barely audible but feminine and seductive all the same.

Bobby Cross had been a celebrity long enough to grow accustomed to the sound of beautiful women trying to talk him into things. Still, he stopped and turned once again to the intersection, taking a deep breath followed by a long step forward, past the border of the crossroads.

"The name I was given is Robert Cross. The name of my heart is Diamond Bobby. I am here tonight by the grace of the King of the North American Routewitches, who told me that if I came to the crossroads with desire in my throat, I could have what I most wish for in this world. I come prepared to pay."

The world flickered around him, and he was abruptly standing in the same spot, on the same road, but in the middle of the day, with blue skies above him and green fields all around. The desert was gone with the night, replaced by the rolling richness of some farmer's prize harvest. The corn rustled as the wind blew through it, and every leaf was like the bells of heaven, calling him home.

And then an angel stepped out of the corn. She had long white hair and a long black skirt, and the kind of figure that could have made her famous in Hollywood with a cock of her hip and a voluntary visit to a casting agent's office. She was as impossible as the cornfield all around him, and those two impossibilities somehow canceled each other out, making her an ordinary sight. Why shouldn't beautifully dressed angels wander around in cornfields? Where else did they belong?

"You don't want this," she said, and she wasn't an angel after all. Angels didn't have flat Michigan accents, didn't sound like the fields and farmlands he'd been running from since the day he realized he was too good for that life. She sounded like all the girls his mother had ever tried to force on him, and he knew in an instant that he wasn't going to listen to a damn thing she had to say.

Dress a bumpkin like a bombshell and she'll still smell like cowshit when she comes to bed.

He looked her up and down with a sneer, not bothering to hide the way his eyes lingered on her breasts, and, as he finally reached her face, tried not to flinch away from the infinite horrors in her eyes. "You don't know what I want, little girl," he said. "What are you, sixteen?"

"Dead girls don't age," said the girl. "Which is a pity, because I'm a lot older than you take me for, and I know what I'm talking about. You don't want this."

"That old fuck in his trailer tried to tell me the same thing," said Bobby.

The not-an-angel blinked. "The old . . . Did you see Big Buster?"

"Old bastard, big bushy beard, lots of young things hanging around him and batting their eyelashes like old-guy dick is something worth chasing."

"That's the King you're talking about."

"Lady, I'm an American. We don't have kings here."

"Not of America, of the— Oh, never mind. I guess now I know what happened." At Bobby's perplexed expression, she shrugged. "Time isn't always linear for the routewitches. It's just another form of distance to them. Eight years ago, he stepped down and cut himself off from the road, wandered off to die somewhere on the map of what's real. I always wondered why."

"But I just saw him."

"Eight years ago, the man you saw *tonight* stepped down. His younger self has been sharing the throne with his successor since then, getting her eased into the position. It's not important. You're not one of his people. He sent you here?"

"Yes." Bobby pulled himself as tall as he could. "I'm here to make a deal."

"And I'm here to tell you that you don't want to do that. I'm your advocate. That means I tell you how much this isn't worth it."

"How much what isn't worth what?"

"Whatever you want," she said. "No matter what you ask for, they'll charge you more than you can possibly pay. This is your chance. Go."

Bobby sneered at her. "I'm staying right here, and I'm going to get my crossroads deal. I'm not scared of any bill."

The girl sighed. "I tried. That's all they can ask of me."

A strange, heavy buzzing filled the air, drowning out the sound of wind in the corn. Bobby turned, unable to stop himself, and watched as a figure appeared out of nothingness. Only the figure *was* nothingness, nothingness given a singular form, and looking directly at it hurt his eyes, so he didn't allow himself to look away.

"A fair try, Miss Mary," said the shape of nothing, and its voice was the buzzing in the air, horrible and distorted and inhuman. "A pity that they never listen, isn't it? You can go now, if you'd like. We all know the outcome."

"No," said Mary. "You made me come here to advocate for him, and I'm going to advocate for him whether he likes it or not. You don't get to use me to follow the rules when it suits you and then brush me off like a bit of lint when you can say you've done the bare minimum."

The shape out of nothing didn't have a face, or an expression; there was no way that it could look amused. And yet somehow, impossibly, it did precisely that.

"Brave little ghost," it said. "Maybe we need to remind you

who you work for. But no matter. Fine, then. Diamond Bobby, you have come to the crossroads according to the path laid out by the routewitches. You have followed the rules, and we will do the same. What bargain do you come here to seek?"

Mary sighed, the sound soft and small and closely akin to the wind rattling the rafters on an abandoned house. Bobby shuddered. He was starting to get the idea that spending time with dead things was not in his best interests.

"I'm a star," he said. "Everyone loves me. There's not a straight bitch in Hollywood who wouldn't drop her panties in a heartbeat if she thought I wanted her, and I never need to settle for any of them twice. I'm on top of the world."

"That doesn't sound like a request," said the nothing.

"Long way to fall when you're standing at the top," said Bobby. "I saw them screen-testing this little punk last week. Face like a baby's ass, waist like one of my wrists. Big blue eyes and a girl's pout on his pretty lips. He's not going to be my replacement tomorrow, but three years from now? Five? He's younger than me. He can wait me out."

"Ah," breathed the nothing. "So you're asking for an exemption from time."

"She"—Bobby pointed at Mary—"told me it was possible. Said those routewitch freaks have a negotiable relationship with the shit. I don't want to get old. I want to be young and pretty and perfect forever. Can you do that for me?"

The air grew heavy, thick as honey, as the figure in the nothingness drew closer to him. "I can do that," it agreed. "If it's what you want, I can do that. Only say that you agree, and everything will be binding."

"There's the matter of price," said Mary hurriedly. "What will this cost him?"

"What is he willing to pay?"

"Anything," said Bobby.

Mary shot him a hard look. "You don't mean that," she said. "You think you mean that, but you don't. What if they take your talent, or your looks? Youth won't do you a lot of good without those."

Bobby looked momentarily alarmed.

"We'll have his stardom," said the nothingness. "What he's made will endure—and endure better than most of his contemporaries, we'll throw that in for free. He'll be remembered for as long as there is a record of his work, and celebrated in festivals and reviews. Retrospectives of his career will be unending."

"A retrospective isn't the same thing as a new movie," said Mary.

"No, it's not. It's better—a retrospective doesn't disappoint. He calls himself diamond. We'll make sure he shines forever."

Bobby looked between them, frowning. "I stay young, I stay handsome, and I get remembered. I'm not seeing a downside."

"What will it *cost*?" demanded Mary.

"Only his freedom. Only his place in the world of the living. He came here in a motor vehicle, and we'll give him a better one—a car forged in the depths of the midnight layer of the afterlife, where the dead hearts of stars will serve as crucibles, and the ancient souls of sleeping beasts wait to be chained. It will be our gift to him, and with it, he'll be able to drive through the twilight where the ghosts linger, and find them, and feed them into his fuel tank. As long as it never runs dry, time will never find him, and he will be eternal. Are we in agreement?"

"No," said Mary.

"Yes," said Bobby Cross, and the nothing reached out and grasped him and he screamed, the sound echoing across the desert and into eternity.

Mary, being a sensible dead girl, fled.

✦ ✦ ✦

It had been well past midnight in the Mojave Desert, and the clock on the wall said that it was almost four o'clock in the morning when Mary appeared in the kitchen of the Healy family home in Buckley Township, Michigan. She was still wearing the black-and-red outfit she had donned to appease the crossroads, and although she'd been dead for years and couldn't be physically ill, she had the distinct feeling that she was about to throw up. She clutched the edge of the sink to keep herself upright, waiting for her stomach to settle enough to allow her to change her clothes.

"Hard night at work?" asked a sympathetic voice.

Mary turned. Alexander was seated at the kitchen table with a mug of tea in front of him, looking at her kindly. She exhaled, still holding onto the sink.

"I had to broker a bargain," she said. "It was a nasty one."

"I know you can't say any more than that, but Alice missed you tonight." The crossroads had started calling her away during babysitting jobs as soon as Alice turned ten, demonstrating that their claim over her was stronger than her commitment to the child she cared for. They hadn't been able to do that much when Alice had been younger, constrained by their agreement to let her protect her family.

Eventually, they'd be able to call her whenever they wanted to. There were crossroads all over the world, and there was always someone looking to make a bargain. The thought was the last straw for her poor, unsettled stomach, and she turned back to the sink, vomiting clear slime into the basin.

"Good thing I did the dishes when I couldn't sleep, or Enid'd be furious with us both," said Alexander, stepping up behind her. "She doesn't care for ectoplasm in her teacups. You all right there, Mary?"

"All right as I ever am when I have to deal with my employers," choked Mary, spitting to get the taste out of her mouth. "Sorry. I'm sorry."

"Don't be sorry, sweetheart. This is your home and we're your family, and family doesn't get mad over a little sour stomach." Alexander put a hand on her half-solid shoulder. "Come on. Let me make you a cup of tea."

Sniffling, Mary nodded and let him lead her to the table. In that moment, the desert felt very far away, and the consequences of this night's work were something that she would never be forced to face. Even though she knew that wasn't true, as she sat and watched him fix her a cup of chamomile, sweet and comforting even to the dead.

The consequences of her actions would always come due. No matter how good her intentions had been. Someone always had to pay the piper.

One

"With the cost of childcare these days, I'm surprised more people aren't trying to get their houses haunted. Who cares if the walls bleed, as long as someone's got the kid."

—Jane Harrington-Price

*A small survivalist compound
about an hour's drive east of Portland, Oregon*

Now

ALL RIGHT, THIS IS WHERE I recap. Because we're dealing with five generations of family history here, and that's a lot, even when you've been there from the beginning. I can't count on anyone having been here from the beginning anymore, myself included, so I'll give you the basic shape of things and hope that will be enough to ground you in this glorious ghost story already in progress:

My name is Mary Dunlavy and I'm a perfectly human, perfectly ordinary teenager. I was sixteen in 1939 and I'm still sixteen today, which would be impossible if not for the small and slightly unsettling fact that I was sixteen when I died. Ghosts don't age the way the living do. We can change and grow as people, if we're willing to make the effort, but whatever age we are when our clocks get stopped is the age we're going to be forever. Sixteen then, sixteen now, sixteen in another hundred years, assuming I'm still haunting my preferred patch of humanity.

Oh, yeah—ghosts are real. Hope that's not too much of a

shock, since you're here, but it's surprising what people can and can't accept. I've met folks who were fine with the idea of shapeshifting shark-people living in the waters off Hawaii, but flipped their lids when they found out that some people treat the various laws of physics as negotiable. People who were cool with sorcerers but got big upset about the psychic ambush predator wasps from another dimension. And plenty of people who accepted everything they learned about the cryptid world, but didn't want to admit that hauntings were real. The human mind needs a few limits it can believe are absolute if it wants to stay stable, and "ghosts" is a surprisingly frequent barrier. Which isn't one that can really linger long if we're going to have a productive relationship.

So: I died when I was sixteen, in a hit-and-run accident involving someone who never even realized what had happened. By the time I realized I could go looking for the guy, it was too late; he had shuffled off his own mortal coil, blissfully unaware that he'd committed vehicular manslaughter, and he didn't hang around to haunt the joint. I never got to confront him. Even "him" is a big assumption, since women could drive even back when I died: it's just that I know it was a truck that did me in, and in the 1930s, in rural Michigan, most trucks were driven by men. Sexism can help you narrow the field, when you know how to apply it.

I died, and was immediately recruited into the service of an eldritch entity that we knew as "the crossroads," an invader from outside this version of reality that had replaced Earth's natural anima mundi and was happily playing parasite, making deals with people who asked for them and gradually destroying the magical skin of the world. It was my job to advocate for the people who came to the crossroads looking to make a deal, whether it be for fame, fortune, eternal youth, or something even less pleasant. I was never the best, which suited the crossroads well; they didn't want their petitioners to be discouraged. Hard to chew people up and spit them out when a meddling ghost can convince them not to deal with you in the first place.

Most crossroads ghosts gradually lost their humanity, fading more and more into the sort of amoral unpleasantness made manifest in the crossroads themselves. It was part of why they didn't last. Once a ghost had been too reduced to their nastier impulses, they couldn't do their job anymore, and the crossroads would devour them. I got lucky.

I got a babysitting gig.

I had posted the flyers while I was still alive, little advertisements offering my services to anyone who needed them. "Give your kid to an unlicensed teenager and I promise to give them back alive in exchange for money when you're done doing whatever it is you needed to do!" Leaving children alone with someone who's barely more than a child themselves sounds like a criminal activity, but is actually an essential part of keeping those kids alive while also holding a job, or doing the grocery shopping, or just not losing your goddamn mind in small-town Michigan. And it worked! I'd been on my way home from a babysitting job when I had my fatal run-in with the truck that killed me.

Because the crossroads had claimed me before anyone knew that I was dead and let me go home to my father with nothing to indicate that I no longer had a heartbeat, my flyers were all still up even after my body had cooled.

Enter Frances Healy.

To explain Fran, I have to explain the Healys. They were come-latelies, a family of immigrants from far-off, exotic England, their accents strange to Michigander ears and their traditions even stranger. Like voluntarily entering the Galway Woods, which every child of Buckley knew not to do. There were monsters in those woods, creatures hidden among the trees, which seemed to shift positions in the night, roots appearing in the middle of previously smooth trails while clearings vanished and the shadows grew beyond control. Enid and Alexander had been the first to arrive, and their son Jonathan had come not long after, born in the town hospital, screaming and wrinkled and already a stranger. He would spend his entire life in Buckley, and he would always be viewed as an intruder of sorts, someone who had come in from the outside.

He'd been a reasonably good-looking man, and his parents were well-liked in the town, for all of their oddities; there was a time when a lot of the local girls had hoped he might decide to solidify his family's ties to the township by marrying one of them. Instead, he'd gone on a trip out west and come home with a loudmouthed blonde who liked to wear trousers, throw knives, and ride her horse in the Galway Woods. Somehow, even though no other horse would even go near the edge of the trees, Fran's Rabbit had always been willing to trust her to protect him. He never threw her. Not even once.

Fran had been the one to spot my advertisement on the library bulletin board, and she was the one who came to ring the bell and ask if I'd consider watching her baby daughter. I'd been playing alive in those days, and a living teenager would have been happy for the easy job and extra spending money, so I said yes, of course. Yes, I'd be happy to watch her, and yes, I loved babies, and yes, I had a list of names she could call to check my references.

I'd love to be able to say that I felt something change the first time she handed me her daughter, and maybe I did, but I suspect it was like a crack in a dam: so small and so slight that it was invisible and imperceptible. The damage was done, whether it could be seen or not, and the crossroads had given me permission to care for my family when they claimed me as their own.

Alice was a year old when I met her, pretty as a picture, all golden curls and huge blue eyes and a curiosity strong enough to change the world. She was just a job like any other in the beginning, and then . . .

Then everything changed.

✦ ✦ ✦

Once Fran learned that I was dead, babysitting for Alice had become paradoxically easier. The family was strange in some ways even the town's biggest gossips had never guessed, and their relationship with the woods went a lot deeper than just walking in the trees. As a normal local sitter, I'd been too likely to turn on them to be trusted with their secrets or allowed inside their house. Once they knew I had secrets of my own to keep, everything changed.

For one thing, I'd started watching Alice at her own house, which was substantially better childproofed and equipped with things to keep her occupied. Including a colony of talking mice that had immediately deified me and worked me into their complicated religious rituals, and if that's a sentence that has ever existed before, I don't think I want to know about it.

Johnny and Fran had been out of town, visiting a family of gorgons in Chicago, while Alexander and Enid were enjoying a well-deserved date night at the Red Angel, our local hangout for people who weren't exactly ordinary. And I had been sitting on the couch in the Healy family living room, watching Alice drag her favorite stuffed jackalope around by one antler. Two of the mice were following her, their eyes bright with doting adoration. An ordinary night, all things considered.

I'd been starting to think about getting up and fixing Alice her dinner when I heard the crossroads calling for me. It wasn't a sound, exactly, more like a sensation, a prickling itch along the edge of my consciousness, discomfort in a place that shouldn't have been uncomfortable. I did my best to ignore it, even as it got louder and louder before finally cutting off, replaced by relief. I sat down next to Alice on the floor, wrapping my arms around her and letting her tell me all about the mice in her short, half-coherent sentences.

I'd had just enough time to relax and think that it was over before the crossroads called again—and this time, when I ignored them, they *yanked*.

There are rules to the way the dead can move. In my heyday, I could go from one side of the country to the other in the blink of an eye, answering the call of the crossroads. Distance didn't matter to them, and I was one of them, free to go wherever I pleased by tunneling through the top levels of the lands of the dead. But I couldn't carry the living with me. That was outside my power even when I was at my strongest. Holding on to Alice should have been a sufficient anchor to keep me where I was.

Instead, the world had warped around us, and I'd abruptly been sitting on warm concrete under a twilight-stained sky, empty fields all around us, power lines buzzing overhead. Alice was still pressed against my chest, and my brief throb of fear didn't have time to fully form before she was pushing against me, saying peevishly, "Mary, let go."

Shocked, I let her go, and she rose and toddled several feet away before plopping down and beginning to roll a rounded rock back and forth, apparently viewing it as a sufficient substitute for her jackalope, which was still back in Buckley.

"Adorable child," said a buzzing voice from behind me.

I jerked around, eyes narrowing as I took in the empty outline cut into the air behind me. "Stay the hell away from her."

"Oh, don't worry. She's too young to understand any bargain we might try to make with her, which means she's off-limits until she gets a little older. Now, once she does, we'll thank you for keeping her safe long enough to come to us. She smells of something we haven't tasted in a very long time."

"Alice is off-limits."

"Is she?" The voice of the crossroads turned sharp. "We worry that you're forgetting who you belong to, Mary Dunlavy. That you're getting distracted by these frivolous duties you perform among the living."

"You agreed that my family comes first," I said, trying to keep my voice from shaking. "If you call when I'm with them, I don't have to come immediately. I can fulfill my duties to them first. Well, Alice is my family, and I couldn't safely leave her alone in the house. That means you broke the rules of our agreement by forcing me to come here."

"You have no relation to this child."

"I didn't ask you for my relatives, I asked you for my *family*. A husband isn't related to his wife—or shouldn't be. An adopted child isn't related to any of the people they call kin. Alice is my family. She belongs to me, and I belong to her, and you agreed when you claimed me that my family would come before anything else, even you."

The crossroads hissed, a low, angry sound like a teakettle boiling over. "Semantics."

"Everything you are is built on semantics. Those deals you take so much pleasure in making, they're all semantics. You're the one who taught me to look for the loopholes. You broke the rules by bringing us here, not me."

"Do not test our patience, child," said the crossroads, voice gone cold and dangerous.

"I don't have anything else to test," I said, and moved to scoop Alice off the concrete. She came willingly, holding her rock in both hands like it was some sort of treasure.

"I keep this?" she asked me, hopefully.

Her parents let her play with taxidermy and sticks. They weren't going to object to a rock. "You can keep it," I said.

She beamed. "Thanks, Mary!" she declared, and waved her rock like a tiny orchestra conductor before squirming and saying imperiously, "Down."

I released her again, and again she ran off to examine the wonders of our surroundings. She had almost fifty reliable words at that point, and it was a matter of pride for me that "Mary" had been among her first. I was her family as much as she was mine.

"Well?" I turned back to the shape cut out of nothing. "You wanted me to negotiate something for you?"

"The child makes you less imposing and thus less effective," complained the crossroads.

"You brought me here against my will while I was babysitting," I said.

"We could command you to stop."

"You could try. I know you don't have a boss as such, but I've always gotten the impression that you have to follow the rules. What's the point of making a deal if you don't adhere to the terms? If you punish me for keeping to the rules you negotiated, you're breaking our deal, and word will get out. You want that to happen?"

Alice had found a stick and was poking it into a hole by the side of the road. I itched to swoop over and grab her before she could find some unfriendly local wildlife. Instead, I forced myself to stay where I was and scowl at the crossroads, which didn't have a face but still managed to give the impression of scowling back.

"Our rules are our rules," they said. "You aren't meant to use them against us."

"Oops."

"Perhaps we were . . . hasty in demanding your attention."

"Looks that way to me." I shrugged broadly, looking around. "I don't see anyone looking to make a deal."

"Our petitioner is on the way."

"Great. You have time to get another interlocutor on the scene."

"We will agree that the girl is your family," said the crossroads, sounding surprisingly sullen for an untouchable force of the universe. "We will extend that agreement to her blood relations. But that is the *end*, do you understand? We will acknowledge no others in such a way."

"Works for me." And it did—I'd been taking fewer and fewer jobs the longer I'd been dead. My hair had already gone from pale blonde to a bleached-out bone white that would have looked artificial if not for the fact that my eyebrows and lashes had paled to match, and my eyes were something unspeakable. Most of me could still have belonged to the living, but not my eyes. They were filled with cemeteries and screams. Adults mostly didn't notice, or didn't look closely enough to understand what about me they found unnerving, but children—I always wound up feeling bad when I met new kids. They had a tendency to meet my eyes and start wailing like they'd just seen the shadow of their own mortality and didn't quite understand what it meant.

I crossed the intersection to Alice and picked her up for a second time, resting her on my hip as I turned to face the nothingness. "You can send us back now."

"Perhaps we'd prefer it if you took her home the ordinary way."

"All right." I shrugged. "Just keep in mind that I'm a teenage girl, on foot, and I can't take any shortcuts. I don't have any money, and you've just promised not to pull me away from her when she needs me, you could be without an interlocutor for a while. You'll have to call in one of your backups. Maybe Carlton would be good for the job?"

Carlton was another crossroads ghost, based out of Wisconsin. He was a lot more experienced than I was and argued a lot harder for his petitioners. Rumor was that he'd actually won a few times, convincing them to leave without taking a deal. The crossroads didn't like that.

". . . fine," said the crossroads, sullenly. "We'll call next time you're free."

And then I was back in the Healy family living room, Alice in my arms, her new rock still clutched firmly in one hand. The mice cheered as I put her down and she ran off down the hall, presumably to do something unfathomably inappropriate with her rock.

I sagged. The mice knew we'd been gone. That meant they were going to tell Fran and Jonathan, and that meant there was no way I could get out of explaining the situation. Oh, well. It had been fun while it lasted.

Resigned to my impending doom, I followed the sound of Alice's laughter down the hall.

✦ ✦ ✦

Only I hadn't been met with doom. I'd been met with surprising understanding and a new gig as Alice's exclusive babysitter, which had suited everyone involved. More importantly, that was the moment the crossroads had come to accept Alice as my family and, through her, each and every one of her descendants. From Kevin to Olivia, they were mine, and I was theirs, and nothing was going to split us up.

Not even Alice growing up and falling in love with a man who made a deal with the crossroads to save her life after she'd been bitten by a dangerous cryptid whose venom went ripping through her body, shredding cells like they were nothing of any consequence. His name was Thomas Price, and he'd paid dearly for her life, finding himself locked in to a world growing steadily smaller while she thought he didn't care. Until finally, explosively, they'd figured out how much each of them cared, and gotten down to the business of making more kids for me to babysit.

Kevin had come first, followed by Jane, and I'd been a major part of their upbringing. The family babysitter who never had other clients, or conflicting appointments, or caught a cold. Who never got any older. I was the cool older kid when they were little, and then I was a peer, and when they looked at me and saw a child, they would graduate from my care.

The years between Kevin and Jane being too old to need a babysitter and them having kids of their own had been among the most unpleasant I'd known since I died. The fact that they were family enough to call me away from the crossroads was a source of constant irritation for my real owner-employers, and there had been a brief period when I'd been afraid that the crossroads were going to find a way to kill them both, stopping the family line in its tracks and taking away my one excuse to hold on to my humanity.

But Kevin and Jane had been born with the same bizarrely coincidence-based luck as their mother, and more importantly, their living guardian had been a woman named Laura Campbell, Alice's childhood best friend and—most importantly of all—an umbramancer doing her best to masquerade as an ambulomancer.

Both umbramancers and ambulomancers are types of road witch, close cousins to the routewitches. Ambulomancers are about half as common as routewitches, unusual enough to be worth remarking on, but not so rare as to be intimidating. Umbramancers, though . . .

There's a lot of confusion about where umbramancers get their power. This much is absolutely certain, though: they're living humans who can traverse the twilight for short distances without dying, they can see the future in limited ways, and they can speak to the dead, even the dead who are too weak and distanced from their origins to manifest visually or audibly. They're good at wards and seals. Most umbramancers will spend their whole lives trying not to be noticed. I know Laura did. She wanted to be taken for a walking witch, to be left alone and ignored.

And then she'd found herself the custodian of Alice and Thomas Price's two children, which meant she had the attention of the crossroads from the very beginning, and would have the attention of the Covenant if she wasn't careful. (We haven't reached the Covenant of St. George yet. Be patient, I'm getting there.) She'd needed to do some things she really didn't want to in order to protect herself and the children, and the whole time, Alice had been slipping in and out of our lives on her endless search for Thomas, never staying long enough for her children to know her, never slowing down enough to let herself ask what was going to happen if she failed.

It had been a dark period for all of us. Laura had been spending more and more time trying to perceive an ever-shifting future, reaching deeper into the midnight, the deepest layer of the afterlife, with every reading. And then one day she'd pulled me aside, and told me, in a voice as empty as an unfinished tomb, that she knew what had to happen next.

"There will be children," she'd said. "They're coming, sooner than you think, if not as soon as I'd like. I'll see the first born to each of them, and no more than that."

"What's going to happen to you?"

"I'll be going away. I can't tell you where, only that it's for everyone's safety, and that they'll be able to have me back someday. I'm not going as far as Tommy went, or Alice." She'd smiled at me then, and her eyes had been older than even my own. "Don't worry so much, Mary. It's bad for your heart."

"I'm dead," I'd replied. "The only good part about it is not needing to worry about my blood pressure. Where are you going?"

I would remember her sigh for as long as I lived. "Away. Somewhere you can't follow. Somewhere none of you can follow. And I'll see you when the time comes, when you have to come and find me, but if I'm still here, the future changes in some ways that it's better we avoid."

"Jane's not going to like this."

With Alice gone, Laura was more her mother than her biological mom had ever been. She even called Laura "Mom" sometimes, although Laura tried to dissuade her. Jane and Alice were never going to have a very traditional relationship, but Laura felt it was important for Jane to remember where she came from, and Laura was normally right about that sort of thing.

True to Laura's word, both Kevin and Jane had gone off to college, met the loves of their lives, and gotten married. The children had followed a respectable time later. The first, Alex, had been welcomed with a smile and a kiss on the forehead. The second, Elsie, had been met with the same, and with a slim book of predictions that related to the kids. Laura had handed it off to Kevin and returned to her trailer.

Two days later, she'd been gone, wherever it was she'd vanished to had been too far away for even me to reach. Not that there'd been a lot of time to look for her—after being abandoned by their own mother, neither Kevin nor Jane had been willing to leave their kids alone while they went on a wild goose chase. The trail, such as it was, had been given years to go cold, and by the time we started searching, it was far too late.

I had no doubt that Laura had planned it like that. She was always good at covering her bases. But there had been children to focus on and worry about—first Alex and Elsie, and then Verity, Artie, Antimony, and finally Sarah, who was older than Verity but didn't become a proper part of our family until three years after Antimony was born. Bringing her into the family had been enough to confirm that adopted children were exactly the same as biological ones in the eyes of whatever cosmic law managed my debt to the crossroads, because I'd been able to hear her calling me from the beginning.

One child in the first generation I was responsible for, two in the second, six in the third. It seemed like I would have a place and a purpose forever. The crossroads saw it too, and they didn't approve; they wanted me away from my family, fully under their control. But when they tried to press the issue by targeting the youngest of my charges, Antimony, she'd responded by tapping in to the same sort of power the routewitches used to control distance and turned time against them, going back to the point where the crossroads had entered our world and driving them away before they could take root.

Thanks to her, the crossroads had never existed. Thanks to the tangled web of reality refusing to be undone outside of the metaphysical side of things, I continued to exist. I was just defined as a full-time babysitter rather than a part-time servant to an unspeakable force infinitely greater than myself.

And the timing had been pretty good, since that was also right about when the family started acquiring kids again, both through the "make your own" method and via the "if you can't make your own, store-bought is fine" route. Antimony adopted another brother, James. Alex's girlfriend got pregnant. Verity got pregnant. Sarah's parents—who were also Evelyn's parents—adopted a little boy, and Alice and Thomas came home from the abyss with a new daughter in tow. The family had never been larger, I had never been busier, and everything would have been perfect, if not for the Covenant.

Which means it's time to explain the Covenant, because as I said, this is the recap to make sure we're all on the same page. Not easy, sometimes necessary.

✦ ✦ ✦

Just about all the legends from all around the world are true, or based on truth. True enough to chew your face off if you get too close. Ghosts are real, obviously. Exhibit A: yours truly. The latest name for all the legendary creatures and spectacular monsters is "cryptid," meaning a thing which is currently unknown to science. Dragons are cryptids. So are finfolk, and tailypo, and gorgons, and all sorts of other things that officially don't exist. Most of them are as harmless as anything that wants to stay alive—no, you probably don't want to get cuddly with a questing beast, but you don't want to get cuddly with a bear, either. That doesn't make the questing beast bad, just not domesticated or friendly toward humanity.

But some people didn't see it that way. Some people saw it as humans vs. cryptids for control of the world, and viewed the fact that not all cryptids wanted to slink off and surrender their territory to humanity as inherently evil, like protecting their homes and families was wrong just because the creatures doing it weren't the right species. And in those days, there were a lot more of the big flashy cryptids around, the ones you couldn't exactly pretend didn't exist when you were looking right at them. This was way before my time, of course, but I've heard the stories. There's a reason "dragon slayer" used to be a reasonable profession.

So the people who thought humans shouldn't have to share the world with cryptids got together, and they formed an organization called the Covenant of St. George. Now, in the beginning, maybe they were more reasonable than they sound now. Back then, dragons really did burn down villages and attack people for their gold. They were a problem. The Covenant was the solution.

Only after they solved the issue of the dragon in their own backyard, they decided to push the issue. They started solving the issue of the dragon in the mountains, far away from humans. And then they started solving the issue of the dragon that had been coexisting peacefully with the local humans, and then they started solving the issue of dragons existing at all. From there, they started on a campaign of solving the issue of literally anything they didn't think had a right to exist. Ghoulies and ghosties and long-legged beasties and things that went bump in the night. People like Alice, with her preternaturally good luck. People like Thomas, who didn't want to follow their rules.

The Covenant had the best intentions when they got started,

and they turned into the villains in their own story a long time ago. If they'd been content to stay there, we could have gone our merry way, but they wanted to be the villains in *our* story, too, and they kept pushing the issue. To them, my family is made up of monsters, traitors, and monstrous traitors, people who have no right to exist in their perfect, human-dominated world. We're a threat to be exterminated. Worst of all, we've been collectively keeping them from getting the kind of stranglehold over North America that they enjoy over Europe, the Middle East, and Asia. So after Verity accidentally revealed us to the Covenant on national television, they pretty much declared war.

The first big battle was six months ago. It ended with two members of my family dead, the rest traumatized to one degree or another, and me discorporated in a way we had all genuinely believed was going to be the end of me.

But the anima mundi, the living spirit of the Earth that had existed before the crossroads and was now reasserting its authority over the world, had gathered the motes of me that remained and reassembled them bit by bit into the spirit I'd been all along. She didn't bring me back to life or anything. She just put me back together, with a few more limitations on what I could do—which was fair, really, since there hadn't been a ghost like me before, and with the crossroads gone, there was never going to be one again.

I woke up from my six months of nothingness about an hour ago, and the first thing I wanted to do once I existed again was go home, a request the anima mundi had been kind enough to grant. Unlike the crossroads, they had no interest in forcing me into anything I didn't want to do.

And that's where we pick this back up as a "things that are happening" rather than a "things that have happened": with me following Sarah, one of my charges, into the house in Portland, finally home, finally back where I belong. Sure, we still had a war to fight, but for the moment, I had never been happier.

Two

"Home is where you go to lick your wounds, set your bones, and find the strength to wade back out into the fray. You can survive anything this world has to throw at you, long as you have your home."

—Frances Brown

Walking into the living room of a small survivalist compound about an hour's drive east of Portland, Oregon

SARAH KEPT SHOOTING SMALL, ANXIOUS glances at me as we walked, like she expected me to disappear at any moment. That, or my newly blue eyes were disturbing her more than I'd realized at first. Coming back together and no longer belonging to the crossroads had removed the empty highway from my eyes, and left me looking closer to the living than I had in a very long time.

If that was the case, it was a little hypocritical. Sarah isn't human. She's a cuckoo, a member of an extradimensional predator species that's closer to wasps, biologically, than they are to anything that evolved on Earth. She's also telepathic, and when she uses her abilities, her eyes glow a remarkably bright white. You'd think she of all people might understand that eyes change colors sometimes.

Oh, well. Stepping into the house was like waking up on Christmas morning. It was warm, and the air smelled of popcorn, coffee, and something freshly baked that I couldn't quite put my finger on. It was probably an offering to the mice. Every member of the family learned how to bake at least a few simple things as soon as it was safe for them to operate the stove, because the mice demanded baked goods on a regular basis. You could virtually set your watch by their raucous cries of "cheese and cake," and failure to provide what they were asking for could lead to disaster.

Even Verity, who could burn water if asked to boil it, knew how to turn boxed cake mix into something edible. At this point, the smell of baked goods was the smell of coming back to normalcy. I stuck close to Sarah, trying to smile every time she looked in my direction, and focused on not walking through the furniture. It was easier than it should have been.

The anima mundi had told me that I was going to be more limited now than I'd been before I toted several explosive devices to the other side of the world and blew myself up in the process of using them to demolish a major Covenant stronghold. I could tell I wasn't somehow alive again; when I focused, I didn't have a heartbeat, and when I stopped breathing, I didn't have any particular desire to restart. I was just . . . solid, unusually so.

There would probably be some sort of downside to that, but for right now, it was just nice not to worry about finding myself standing in the middle of a coffee table. I'm usually pretty good about interacting with my environment. It's just that sometimes, I forget.

"You missed the funerals," said Sarah, in a very small voice.

"I didn't mean to."

"Where have you *been*?"

"It's a long story." It wasn't, not really, but it was a complicated, confusing one, and I didn't want to tell it more than once if I didn't have to. "I'll explain once we're with the others."

She nodded minutely, irises seeming to frost over around the edges. It wasn't true frost, of course, but the delicate fractal pattern was similar enough, little spirals of white eating into the blue.

"Yes, reading my mind to get the full story would probably be faster, but counterpoint, I'd rather you didn't do that right now," I said, calmly. She jerked back, the white disappearing as quickly as it had come, and looked at me with wide, guilty eyes.

I sighed. "I'm not *mad*, sweetheart. I understand the impulse, and I know how frustrating it is when someone doesn't want to explain what's going on. I just want to get to the rest of the family. Who all's home right now?"

"Evie and Uncle Kevin, Annie and Sam, James, and Olive," said Sarah dutifully.

"And everyone else?"

"Alex and Shelby are in Ohio with Lottie and Isaac; Elsie and Arthur are in Portland, with Uncle Ted; and Grandma and Grandpa are in Michigan with Sally."

For a moment, it felt like I had swallowed a sharp rock. "Where's Verity?"

Verity hadn't been my primary charge for very long. As the family babysitter, all the kids are my responsibility, but the majority of my focus is always on the youngest. It's not fair, since it reduces all children to ages rather than individuals, but the younger a child is, the more likely they are to need constant supervision, and the little compass in my head that tells me where my family is had always seized on that need as a form of guide. Verity had been born only a little while before her cousin Arthur, and so I'd been pulled away from taking constant care of her before we'd been able to make much of an impression on each other.

To me, she'd always been one more child in a swarm of children I knew better, and to her, I'd always been something she'd been denied by the order of her birth. It wasn't fair, but it was the way it was. I still cared about her desperately, and I always would.

Sarah sighed. "She's still in New York," she said. "After we . . . after . . ."

"It's all right," I said gently. "I know what happened." Verity's husband, Dominic, had been one of the casualties of the early days of our war against the Covenant. They'd set an ambush, and Dom and Verity ran right into it. His death was quick and traumatic, and his ghost hadn't lingered, or if it had, it hadn't manifested yet by the time I got discorporated.

Sarah nodded. "She said it was better if Livvy stayed here with us until she felt a little bit more like herself, and nothing in her thoughts sounded like following Dominic into the afterlife, so we let her go. She calls every night so she can tell Liv a bedtime story, and Uncle Mike is there with her."

"All right. As long as she's not alone." If she didn't want to be here with her family, New York was a good place for Verity. She had friends there, good ones, the kind who would make sure she ate and showered and didn't jump off too many buildings. It would still have been better for her to be in Portland with her daughter, but I could understand why she wouldn't want to be. If I knew Verity at all, she was going to be struggling with her own culpability in this entire situation. She'd been the one to set the Covenant off this time, and she was the reason Dominic had been anywhere near the battlefield.

That didn't make this her *fault*. If there was any fault to be handed out, it belonged to the people who'd decided they had the holy right to assault us because we weren't all perfectly, impeccably human. But we'd all played our part in things getting as bad as they had, and Verity had always been remarkably good at dodging the consequences of her own actions. She wasn't used to things having permanent costs.

Sarah nodded again.

"Do you ever go there to see her?"

"Sometimes," she said, and looked away.

Sarah could move through space as easily as the dead did, bending the innate math of distance to wind up wherever she felt she needed to be. It had been a relatively new skill of hers the last time

I'd seen her, but she'd been getting steadily better. She referred to it as spatial tunneling, and while it had its limitations, some of the things she'd said made me suspect that those limits weren't going to exist forever.

Her steadily increasing power was honestly a little frightening, even to me—and I was already dead. I didn't have anything left to lose, not in the traditional manner. She was the most sophisticated example of her species we'd ever found ourselves dealing with, and no one knew what she was going to be capable of in the end.

Whatever it was, she'd still be our Sarah, and our ally. That was enough to keep me from getting too worked up about it.

We walked through the empty living room to the hallway beyond, from which various parts of the house could be accessed—most importantly the kitchen and the main living room. People could usually be found in one of those places, if not both of them. My family liked their coffee and their cushions when they weren't traveling, and those things could be found in the living room/ kitchen area with reasonable reliability.

As we got closer, I heard voices, and Sarah's hand closed around my wrist like a vise, stopping me before I could go any farther. I tried to go insubstantial and pull through her fingers, but nothing happened. I blinked down at my arm, staring at the place where she held me. Nothing changed.

I was as solid as a living girl, and as trapped.

Sarah's eyes flashed white, and her voice filled my head.

You weren't here. We buried Jane and Dominic, and you weren't here. If you're planning to just run off on us again, you'd better think twice, because I don't think Uncle Kevin will be okay if you do that.

I blinked at her, and thought back, as clearly as I could, *I'm not planning to go anywhere unless someone needs me. Livvy is still technically the youngest.*

The anima mundi had said that I'd still be able to be there for my family. But she could be expecting me to be there on a bus. We'd find out when someone younger than Livvy came along.

Sarah glanced guiltily away. I blinked.

"What don't I know?" I asked, aloud.

Sarah didn't look back.

"What don't I know?" I repeated, slightly louder. If she wanted to keep me quiet, this wasn't the way to go about it. "I'm warning you, Sarah, I *will* start yelling if you don't—"

"Verity was pregnant when Dominic died," she blurted. I stared in shock as she turned back to me, her pale cheeks wan in the interior light. Cuckoos aren't mammals, and they don't have hemoglobin the way humans do. Their blood is clear and viscous, like mucus. No matter how distressed Sarah was, she would never redden or blush. "She's about eight months along now. Evie's been trying to convince her to come home for the birth, but she says she wants to stay in New York, that she feels closer to Dominic there, even though he was buried here. I've been attending all her prenatal visits and holding her hands. It's a boy."

Now that I knew what I was listening for, I could hear a faint hum in the distance, like a note from a tuning fork. It would get stronger once the baby was born, and start becoming unique to him almost immediately, distinguishing itself from the rest of the family.

Hearing it was a relief. It meant my connections were still open, even if my intangibility was on the fritz. Honestly, being unable to pass through Sarah's grip reminded me of my first days among the dead, back when I'd been reasonably recently deceased and still trying to figure out how to control my various ghostly abilities. Being solid had been hard back then. Being intangible had been even harder. It was like having to focus on every aspect of my existence.

The thought was followed by another: maybe I *was* recently deceased, in a way. The blast in the basement of Penton Hall had blown me apart, scattered me across the starlight like a phantas-mal glitter bomb. The anima mundi had gathered all my parts back together and sort of glued them together to give me the time to heal.

And something about that process had shaken the cemetery sky straight out of my eyes. I was a different kind of ghost now, no longer a hybrid of crossroads and babysitter, but a caretaker from one end to the other. So maybe I needed to behave like someone who had only just died, who was still figuring things out. Maybe I needed to relax.

As if on cue, my wrist passed through Sarah's fingers, and I was free. I raised it to my chest, rubbing it with the opposite hand, and was pleased to find that both halves of me seemed to be equally solid. The last thing I needed was to be halfway walk-ing through things and halfway not, like some sort of conscious transitory state.

"I didn't run off last time, Sarah," I said, quietly. "I tried to get out of that basement, and I couldn't do it. It was like the world didn't want me to. I'd pulled all the strength I had into getting those bombs where we needed them to be, and nothing I did would let me leave. Hasn't the math ever failed you? Hasn't it ever left you somewhere that you didn't want to be?"

She flinched, and that was more than enough of an answer for me. Of course she understood what that was like. Her own abili-ties were new and still evolving; there was no way they could work perfectly every time she asked them to. That didn't mean people wouldn't blame her when they failed. That didn't mean people weren't going to blame *me*.

I leaned over and wrapped an arm around her shoulders, giving her a quick hug. "Come on, Sarah. Let's stop standing here and playing 'what if they get upset,' and go upset them instead, okay?"

"Okay," she said, voice surprisingly thick, and didn't resist as I started forward, pulling her along with me.

✦ ✦ ✦

The Portland compound was designed and constructed by Kevin, intended to serve as a permanent place big enough for his whole family to live if they wanted to. "Constructed by" is a pretty generous way to describe it, since he's not particularly handy, but he was the one who'd organized the crews, mostly sasquatch and bogeymen, who'd cleared the land and put the physical buildings up. Over two dozen groups of workers had been responsible for getting everything put together, with Kevin rotating them regularly to make sure no one knew all the details of the security system. Paranoid? Yes. Unreasonable? When we already knew that the Covenant was out there looking for us, no. Not unreasonable in the least.

Although maybe the idea that the whole family would ever come and live happily under one roof had been more than a little unreasonable. Jane never forgave her mother for missing most of her childhood, and she'd taken that resentment with her to the grave. When Alice was in the house, Jane did her best not to be, and since Kevin had always insisted that his mother would be welcome in any home of his, the happy fantasy he'd been trying to build had never come to pass.

The house was nice, though.

We followed the hallway to the living room, a well-lit, airy space with a ceiling so high that I had sometimes suspected Evelyn had managed to train songbirds to do the dusting in the corners and light fixtures. These days, she probably just has Sam do it. Couches and comfortable chairs were scattered around the space, and the lack of too many shelves kept it from feeling claustrophobic, even as a few low bookshelves stuffed with popular novels and foraging guides made sure that no one was going to forget who lived here. Family photos covered the walls.

Several had been added since my last visit. One showed Alice and Thomas sitting on the porch swing of their house in Buckley, grinning like fools with a banner on the wall behind them that said "IT'S A GIRL!" Sally was sandwiched between them, a resigned look on her face and a tailypo in her lap.

The others were less cheerful. They looked like they'd been taken at the recent funerals, and I had little doubt that they'd be moved to an office or parlor by the end of the year, replaced by fresh baby pictures and other, more optimistic images.

Kevin and Evelyn were sitting on one of the couches, clearly deep in some sort of serious discussion. For maybe the first time since he'd first brought her home, the sight of them together didn't cause me to do a double take. Kevin looked so much like his father, and Evelyn, for all that she didn't look *exactly* like Alice, was still a girl just like the girl who'd married dear old Dad.

It was mildly unsettling to see them together while Thomas was still missing. It would have been worse, if not for the fact that I'd never seen anything in their actual relationship to imply that Kevin had been trying to replace his mother. They fought and lived and loved like any couple, and they'd raised three reasonably well-adjusted children. Although I took part of the credit for that.

Evelyn was the one with a direct eyeline on the hallway door; she raised her head when she heard us enter, and froze, eyes going wide and suspiciously bright, like she was on the verge of tears. She raised one shaking hand to her mouth, and otherwise didn't move.

Kevin stiffened, head coming up before he turned. Then he joined his wife in staring, both of them focused on me in a way that might have been gratifying if it hadn't been silent and accompanied by tears. Evelyn's were the first to fall, but Kevin's, when they came, were copious and steady, running down his cheeks unhindered as both his hands were still resting on the couch between them.

"Hi," I said, with a little wave. "Miss me?"

Kevin finally made a sound—a choked gargle that sounded like it couldn't make up its mind between a laugh and a bark—and lunged to his feet before rushing over to sweep me into a hug. Or to try to, anyway. He definitely made the gesture, but when his arms closed, they passed right through me, leaving me unhugged.

"Er," I said. "Sorry about that. I'm having a little trouble with the whole 'solid, not-solid' thing right now. I probably shouldn't try to do the grocery shopping until we know what's going on."

"Mary," said Evelyn. "It's really you."

"Mary Dunlavy, at your service," I said.

"We thought you were dead," said Kevin. "Again."

"Can you be double-dead?" asked Evelyn.

"Absolutely," I said. "Ghosts can be destroyed. It's easier than we want people to think. I mean, it's still hard, but there are a lot of methods that will do it if someone is determined enough. Most of them wouldn't work on me when I worked for the crossroads, because they were a bigger, meaner boss than your average ghost hunter was expecting."

"And now?" she asked, with clear anxiety in her expression.

"Now I don't know." I shrugged. "I'm technically a caretaker—a form of nanny ghost—and we know most of what those are capable of, but I'm a caretaker who's answering directly to the anima mundi, and that could change things. It's hard to say. I'm not really in a hurry to find out, though. Six months of nonexistence was enough for me."

Kevin tried again to hug me. This time, I stayed solid as he wrapped his arms around my shoulders and pulled me against him, and I responded by turning to make the hug easier, patting his shoulder with one hand. He clung, shaking, and pressed his face against my neck.

"I know, buddy," I said. "I'm sorry I was gone for so long. I didn't mean to be."

"What *happened*?" asked Evelyn.

"When the charges went off at Penton Hall, I was already exhausted from the effort of transporting the explosive devices, and I couldn't shift myself out in time. I tried, really I tried, but it didn't work." I'd been crying blood by the time I picked up the last of the bombs—and no matter how much I wanted to call them "explosive devices" or other polite, bloodless phrases, they were bombs. They'd been designed to kill people, and that was what we'd used them to do. "One more thing to thank the crossroads for, I guess: they never bothered to tell me I was supposed to have limits, and so once I reached them, I didn't know what to do."

"So you were still there when the blast went off," said Evelyn, sounding horrified.

"I thought she was, but everything was so chaotic and there were so many minds in play that I wasn't fully certain," said Sarah. "I'm sorry, Mary. I should have found a way to get you out of there."

"Don't even start that," I said firmly. "I was intangible and incapacitated. All you could have done was put yourself and Annie in harm's way, and I'm the babysitter here. I'm the one who takes care of you. You follow me?"

"Yes," said Sarah.

"Good." I looked back to Evelyn. "The explosion was big enough to blow me out like a candle. Bombs don't normally hit ghosts that hard. I guess me transporting them through the twilight made them a little more effective against phantom targets."

Evelyn sat up straighter on the couch, eyes going bright with curiosity. "Do you think that would work with all sorts of weaponry?" she asked. "Could we enhance our bullets that way?"

"Are you planning to fight an army of the dead?" I countered. "Maybe it would work and maybe it wouldn't, but I think if I started becoming an anti-ghost arms dealer, the rest of the afterlife would get pissed at me, and I have enough problems right now without adding more to the pile."

"No," Evelyn admitted. "Sorry. That's just not an area where we know as much as I'd like, even though you've been around for all this time."

Until the anima mundi had taken over as my employer, there had been active rules against my telling my family anything the crossroads didn't want them to know—which was virtually everything. Most of what they knew about the laws that bind the dead had come from other hauntings, and it had been a bone of contention for years that I refused to confirm or deny all the details. Not pissing off the crossroads had been a full-time job in its own right, which left me with three jobs, total, and the constant desire to smack my head against the nearest wall.

The anima mundi didn't have any such rules, but looking at the thinly veiled eagerness in Evelyn's face, I wasn't sure I was going to tell them that. Evie may have married into the family, but she's still a Price, with their unending need to know *everything* about the world around them, even the things she would be better off not knowing. Even the things I didn't want to explain.

"You know why that is," I said gently.

She sighed, some of her excitement dimming as she slumped back into the couch.

"The blast shattered me into pieces and scattered me across the layers of the afterlife," I said. "Under normal circumstances, I would have dissipated completely, but the anima mundi pulled me back together and held me that way until I could heal on my own. It took the last six months. When I woke up, she told me I could move on if I wanted to. The crossroads are gone. Any claim they had over my soul went with them. She doesn't want to own people the way they did."

"I'm guessing from the fact that you're here that you said you weren't ready?" said Evelyn.

I stroked Kevin's hair with one hand. "I thought my family might still need me," I said.

He made a hiccupping sound and squeezed me briefly tighter.

"We just got Mom and Dad back, and then Jane and Dominic died, and you were gone, and I'd never had to consider a world without you haunting the house," he said, raising his head and looking at me.

I offered him a small smile. "Hey, kiddo. No one who's currently alive in this house has the authority to fire me. You're stuck with me. I'm just sorry I missed the funerals."

"They were unpleasant," said Sarah. "Everyone was trying their best not to blame anyone else, and not to project their grief too loudly, but most people aren't sufficiently practiced at controlling their minds, and it was like standing in an amphitheater full of people shouting about how unhappy they were. Uncle Ted had to leave Aunt Jane's funeral before the service was done. Everyone else's misery was too heavy, and it was smothering him. Arthur lasted longer, but in the end, he was unable to understand too many of the feelings around him, and he had to excuse himself. I managed to stay."

"I'm not surprised." I've never met anyone as good at punishing herself as Sarah is. For her, staying in a room full of people who were devastated and grieving would have been like immersing herself in a vat of lemon juice right after rubbing her whole body with sandpaper. And that meant there was no way she would have left until she'd finished soaking in every bit of blame and recrimination she could hold.

It wasn't her best attribute. It was one she'd developed to keep herself from turning into a monster, from becoming the kind of cuckoo who shrugged off other people's pain as a necessary side effect of living her life the way she wanted to. The people she cared about wished she'd stop hurting herself, but she never did. I wasn't sure she even could anymore.

"And now I'm back, and I didn't miss the baby, so we can just move forward from here, yeah?"

Kevin finally let go of me and stepped back a bit, toward the couch where Evelyn was sitting. "Sarah told you about the baby?"

"Yeah, and now that I know what I'm looking for, I can feel him. He's already family." I paused. Better to tell them now, I suppose. "Speaking of which, I can still feel you all, so I know that part of the caretaker's connection is still intact, but I don't know what I can do right now, or how any of it works. I don't seem to choose whether or not I'm solid, not really, and while the anima mundi said I'd be able to answer my family when they called for me, I don't know how voluntary that's going to be, and I don't know whether I'll be able to move between you when you're not calling. They wanted me to chill out a little with the popping all over the place."

It was a reasonable request, especially with the anima mundi trying to rebuild Earth's pneuma. The pneuma was the living soul of the world, the source of all magic—and all hauntings. As a caretaker, I was well defined and easy for the pneuma to maintain. As a crossroads ghost, though, I had been a nebulously described creature and a constant power sink. The crossroads had probably liked it that way. Let their servants weaken the world just by existing, make it less likely that the anima mundi would ever be able to re-manifest and challenge their domination.

Then the anima mundi had returned, and found themselves with custody of the strange hybrid creature that I was. They'd already been taking steps to limit what I was capable of before I'd gotten myself exploded and given them the opportunity to tinker with me. Whatever I was now, I had little doubt that it was less expensive for them to fuel.

"I can test this," said Sarah, sounding relieved. Her eyes flashed white, and then she was gone, pulling space around her like a shroud and using it to transport herself somewhere else.

I blinked. "She's getting better at that."

"She is," said Kevin. "It still makes me nervous when she does that. Living people shouldn't do that sort of thing."

"Neither should dead ones," said Evelyn. "Begging your pardon, Mary, you've always been very respectful of our privacy, and you being able to go through doors was a lifesaver when Verity was in her locking phase."

I smiled nostalgically. "That was a fun year."

When she was six, Verity had decided the best thing to do with doors was to lock them at every opportunity she had, both when she was on the other side and—in the case of doors that could be locked, then closed without unlocking them—when she wasn't. I'd been tapped to walk through doors and unlock them more often that summer than I had ever thought possible.

"You say 'fun,' I say 'periodically terrifying and definitely an incentive to handcuff my eldest daughter to things.'"

"Yes, but all that did was encourage her to get better at picking locks."

"Which has served her well in her adult life," said Kevin.

It was hard to argue with that. All three of Kevin and Evelyn's kids had gone willingly into the field once they were old enough, and they thrived there. They liked the practical side of cryptozoology far more than they enjoyed the theoretical—even Alex, who never met a research paper he didn't want to commit to memory, liked getting his hands dirty.

Kevin shot me another look, seeming like he couldn't really believe I was here and real and negotiably solid. He hadn't lost another member of his family after all.

But before he could say anything, I heard Sarah calling my name, distant but insistent, like an alarm clock pulling me up out of sleep. I blinked and turned toward the sound, which was more *of* a sound than the calling of my family had ever been. The calling didn't stop, but I was still in the living room, which answered one question: I wasn't going to find myself moving involuntarily like I had in my early days with the crossroads. I got to keep that much control.

"I need to go," I said, and I was gone.

Three

"I worry a bit about you being dead, dear. You're so young. You should be resting easy or enjoying your afterlife, not spending all your time keeping my granddaughter's total lack of self-preservation from sending her into the grave with you."

—**Enid Healy**

Appearing out of the afterlife into an unknown location, following the sound of one of my kids calling for me

ONE SECOND I WAS IN a living room, and the next I was outside under a honey-mild afternoon sky so blue that it could have been a painting, trees to my back and a long, tangled field in front of me. If the trees hadn't been enough to tell me where I was, a ramshackle house painted the color of mold growing on bone stood on the other side of the field, with windows that seemed to stare at me like furious, mindless eyes. The Old Parrish Place had a way of looming while still being completely inanimate. It was a nice trick.

So far as anyone's been able to tell, the house isn't haunted. It just doesn't like most people, and how it manages to be hostile while not alive, intelligent, or possessed is anybody's guess. But it liked Thomas Price well enough, and it liked Alice enough that when she and Thomas got married, she was able to live there without too many nightmares, and most importantly, it liked me enough to let me come in to babysit.

Any house that allows the babysitter past the threshold can't be all bad.

I looked around and, finding no sign of Sarah, sighed. I paused for the first time since my reappearance to take stock of my clothing. I was wearing faded blue jeans and a white peasant blouse with little white asphodel flowers and red pomegranates stitched around the cuffs in the sort of decorative pattern that had fallen out of favor in the late seventies. Old-fashioned, but not synchronized to any of my current kids.

At least I was decent, and should still be recognizably myself, even with the highway absent from my eyes. Before the explosion, I would have just popped myself into the house, away from the trees, which had never liked me half as much as the house did. Now, though, I didn't want to take the chance that it wasn't going to work. Instead, I took a deep, unnecessary breath and started walking.

The field wasn't that wide, but it had been so long since I actually needed to walk anywhere that I was bored before I was halfway there. Each step was a chore, and it was difficult not to think of this as a punishment rather than what the anima mundi said it was: a necessary rebalancing of the way things worked. I'd been improperly restrained for too long, and it was time I started behaving like a civilized ghost who didn't think the rules were for other people.

The back door slammed open when I was almost to the house. Alice appeared in the doorway, short and blonde and dressed in the sort of casual clothing she'd favored since her teens. At least these days, no one judged her for her fondness for shorts and tank tops. Both were easy to move in, and since she preferred guns over knives, unlike most of her descendants, the lack of places to hide thirty knives didn't really impact her much. Back when she'd been a teenager, she used to get called all sorts of name by the people in town. The good old days only were for the people who naturally lived up to society's expectations. For the rest of us, the present was a lot more pleasant. Not perfect, sure, but at least now speaking to an unmarried man without a chaperone wasn't enough to ruin a girl's reputation forever.

She stared at me for several beats before shouting my name and throwing herself down the porch steps at top speed. As she ran toward me, a tall, lanky man appeared in the door where she had been, sunlight glinting off his glasses. I thought I saw Thomas smile before all my attention had to be focused on Alice, who was pelting toward me as fast as her legs could carry her, hair streaming backward in the breeze and throat working hard as she fought not to hyperventilate.

Please stay solid for this, I thought sternly, and opened my arms.

A moment later, Alice slammed into them, and I held her close, and thought that maybe everything was going to be all right after all. She squeezed tightly, just as Kevin had, but let go a second later, stepping back.

"Are you really Mary Dunlavy?" she demanded.

"I am."

"Prove it."

I sighed. "Anything I can say as proof would have been overheard by the mice, meaning it's all circumstantial at best. You have a living Greek chorus. That makes it pretty difficult to keep secrets. Oh, how's this—you didn't speak to me for almost a year after you caught me kissing Tommy, since you thought I'd been poaching behind your back and didn't want to give me a chance to explain."

Alice paled. "Mary?"

"Yeah, kiddo," I said. "It's me."

"Sarah said it was you, but I didn't want to—I was afraid that if I hoped she was telling the truth, I'd just get disappointed again.

I don't think my heart could handle it, not after everybody we've lost this year. I thought you were on that list. Your clergy is going to be *so* relieved."

I'd been with the family for long enough to have been adopted as an honorary part of the Aeslin pantheon. They called me the Phantom Priestess, and most of their chthonic rites included me one way or another. I frowned.

"If you thought I was dead, shouldn't most of them have shifted to another branch of the faith?" I asked delicately. It was "most" because the central clergy of any given god or priestess usually didn't outlive them by terribly long. If they didn't actively take their own lives, grief would do it for them, refusing to let them keep living in a world that didn't include their divinities.

"Rules are different for your clergy, because they started worshipping you after you were already dead."

It made exactly the sort of sideways sense I had learned to expect from the Aeslin mice, and so I nodded, stepping closer to her and offering my hand. "Well, then, I'm sure they'll be thrilled when their faith is rewarded."

"Are you kidding? They're going to throw the kind of festival that means no one in the house gets any sleep for a week." She took my hand firmly in hers. "Welcome home, Mary. We missed you."

I couldn't exactly say the same, since the past six months were a gaping void for me, and so I just smiled at her and squeezed her hand, letting her lead me toward the house.

Inside, Thomas had gone back into the kitchen, and I could hear Sarah and Sally talking in the other room. Alice let go of my hand and moved to the side, letting Thomas step forward and embrace me. It was getting a little weird. I've never been the huggiest person, not even where my kids are concerned, and they generally respected that. Having everyone I knew suddenly want to hug me was jarring.

"I told Alice you weren't dead," he said, then paused, catching himself. "Well, no, I didn't say that, as it would have been patently untrue and she would have been well within her rights to laugh at me had I tried to convince her of something so ridiculous. I told her you weren't gone for good, that no matter what had happened, you'd find your way back to your family."

"That includes you, you know," I said.

He grinned in answer. "And don't think for a moment that I don't appreciate that. Welcome back, Mary. We missed you."

"I'm getting that impression," I said. I nodded toward the living room. "That Sally I hear? She still comfortable with signing herself up for this circus?"

"We're a carnival family," said Alice primly. "I thought you'd know that by now."

"Oh, very funny," I said. "That joke certainly didn't get old thirty years ago."

"I mean, I didn't, so why would my jokes?" countered Alice.

That time, I had to groan.

"What happened, Mary?" asked Thomas.

So that was how this was going to go: I was going to visit all the members of my family one by one, and they were each going to expect me to explain myself, repeating the story of the past six months over and over again until it became just so much nonsense, the words blending together to form a tapestry of sound that didn't make any sense at all. I took a deep breath, preparing to explain. It wasn't like I had anything better to do.

Instead, a small voice at the edge of my awareness said *Mary, come back. We need you.*

I held up a hand. "Sorry," I said. "Sarah can fill you in. Right now, the anima mundi needs me. I'll ask them to drop me back here when they're done."

Then I closed my eyes, and I was gone.

✦ ✦ ✦

When I opened my eyes again, I was in the middle of a field of wheat under a beautiful twilight sky, painted in a dozen shades of blue, black, and purple. That was one of the biggest changes to have come to this in-between domain since the anima mundi took it over from the crossroads: the corn was gone, taking its ergot and its whispering leaves with it. Instead, the fields grew gold with grain, and the anima mundi moved through them, reaping as she needed to reap, scattering seeds where she walked.

This was a more balanced place now than it had ever been before, and that balance was echoed in everything around me, even the sweetness of the wind and the glitter of the stars above. The anima mundi's domain was adjacent to the rest of the afterlife, not necessarily connected, but I felt like it was probably closet to the starlight, if that mattered at all.

There are three levels of the afterlife accessible to Earth's dead, even if very few ghosts can travel through them all. The twilight is the closest to the lands of the living, and most human ghosts will be found there. It's rich in road ghosts and household hauntings, specters and haints and all manner of the restless dead. Few of them linger for long, and those that do are either very powerful or very dangerous or sometimes both. My sort-of friend, Rose Marshall, is both, and she calls the twilight her home.

The twilight has never been super friendly toward the crossroads, since they used to exploit the routewitches to get their victims to them. Their servants and playthings always dwelt a layer down, in the starlight. The starlight is primarily a place for nonhuman dead to exist without needing to worry about unpleasant encounters with monster hunters. A dead monster hunter can't kill a dead dragon a second time, but they can make things unpleasant, and nobody needs that sort of thing. If I was existing in the afterlife, I was generally down in the starlight.

Below that, where no sensible ghost goes, is the midnight. That's the deepest part of the afterlife that a human ghost can hope to access, and I've never gone there voluntarily. A few times under duress, yes, but if I never have to go that deep again, I won't be mad about it.

The anima mundi's patch of the afterlife—if this *was* the afterlife; she was the living spirit of the collective world, she could just as easily have been sowing her crops on the pneuma itself—was brighter and less oppressive than the midnight, and felt comfortingly like home. It would have been easy to stay here forever, if not for the fact that my family needed me.

I turned slowly, looking around. The anima mundi themself was a short distance away in the wheat, a scythe in their hands, frowning as they studied a particularly thick clump of stalks. As always, they looked like a tall, feminine human, a composite of every woman in the world. Their skin was a brown averaged out from every skin tone among the living, and their hair was a glorious riot of curls comprised of strands in every possible color, natural or unnatural. They generally looked human, because I was looking at them with human eyes, but sometimes they would turn their head just so and I would see a streak of scales on one cheek, or the delicate tip of a horn poking upward through their hair. They were the ideas and ideals of every living, intelligent thing that lived within their slice of the universe, and sometimes I was glad they tended to wear long, voluminous skirts. I didn't really want to see what they looked like from the waist down.

They turned their head in my direction, and I raised one hand in a careful wave, staying where I was. They weren't a predator the way the crossroads had been, but they were close enough that I tried to be careful around them, when I wasn't smarting off to their face. Self-preservation has never been one of my strong suits, a tendency that's only been exacerbated by decades as an untouchable phantom. If you want to teach somebody not to be a mouthy brat, it's a good idea not to render them immune to most forms of harm.

They smiled, slight and sweet, and swung their scythe in a careless arc, much like a cheerleader might swing a baton. As soon as that gesture was complete, they were standing directly in front of me, skipping over the space between us like a bad film splice.

"Mary Dunlavy," they said, their voice a harmonic choral blend of a million voices all speaking at the same time, in virtually perfect synchronization. "We had hoped you would listen the first time we called you. We didn't want to call again."

"I try not to ignore cosmic forces when I have a choice in the matter," I said. "You rang?"

"We have need of you, Mary Dunlavy."

"I got that part. What do you need?"

The anima mundi blinked, looking momentarily taken aback. "The one who freed and restored us is one of yours, is she not?"

"Antimony? Yeah, she's one of mine."

"We thought she was the most disrespectful, impertinent child this world could ever have created, and while we were impressed by her acts and deeds, we were . . . less than charmed by her manner of speaking."

"She's always been a blunt one, our Annie. I'm sorry if she offended you. I'm sure she didn't mean it."

"No, she didn't. She asked us questions no one else had ever bothered with, and she restored us to our primacy, as we always should have been."

"So what's the problem?"

"No problem. We just see now where she gets it." The anima mundi smiled briefly. "Walk with us, Mary Dunlavy."

They turned then, and started back into the wheat at a more human pace, one foot in front of the other, the individual stalks swaying behind them with every step they took. I hesitated. Following cosmic figures into fields is rarely a good idea, and this was one that I knew had the power to hurt me. She controlled

the power that kept me stable as a haunting, and all the new limitations I was trying to learn how to live with had been handed
down by her.

Still, ignoring the requests of cosmic powers isn't a good idea
either. I trotted after her into the grain, letting her set the pace
and lead the way.

For some time, we just walked, silent, through the endless field
of wheat. Finally, the anima mundi looked at me.

"What am I going to do with you, Mary Dunlavy?" they asked.

"I thought you'd already figured out what you were going to do
with me, when you let me go home," I said. "I haven't pushed any
boundaries or broken any rules, and you said I'm allowed to go to
my family when they call for me."

"Yes. We didn't anticipate the mathematician." They sigh.
"Most of them are gone now, but the ones that remain will remain
an issue. They don't draw upon my pneuma, precisely, not as you
or the sorcerers do—they pull their power from concepts outside
my control, and I have no way to limit them, no means by which
to prevent them from running rampant over the way things are
meant to be. You've broken none of the new rules we set for you,
Mary Dunlavy. When your family comes, you may go. You will
simply stop *expanding* that family whenever it suits you."

"Verity's pregnant," I objected. "That baby is going to be a part
of my family, and I'm going to need to be able to take care of him."

"Yes," agreed the anima mundi. "Your family will expand, in
the natural ways. Birth and acquisition, bonds of affection. But
you won't go looking for people to add to the family on your own,
and you won't volunteer your services to anyone."

"As long as I still get to take care of the babies," I said.

They nodded. "You have a purpose, expensive as you are, and
we won't forbid you to fulfill it. Given time, with you operative
in the world, more caretakers may arise. There were so many
of them once. They kept the world of the living more forgiving

of the lands of the dead, and they served a vital purpose in the health of all things."

"So we took care of you by taking care of our charges?"

"Something like that." They kept walking. "We called you here because we have a problem, Mary Dunlavy."

I was getting a little tired of hearing my full name. "What kind of a problem is that?"

"The Covenant should never have been allowed to flourish as they did. Had we been in our proper place, I would have stopped them long before they could come to such dominance." The anima mundi looked, briefly, tired. "The part of us that is human rejoices to see our children rising to such heights of power and influence. The rest of us is appalled. Parts of us are missing, spaces that were once filled with voices and ideals, unique and glorious, now silenced forever. This cannot be permitted to endure."

"Hey, I discorporated myself hauling explosives across the world to make them stop, and my reward was six months of non-existence and you putting a hard cap on how much power I can draw from you at one time. That was my big attack. I don't really have a better rock to throw at the Covenant, so if you were going to say that what you need me to do is wipe them out, well, you're pretty much out of luck there."

The anima mundi stopped walking and gave me a hard look. "We are the living spirit of this world," they said. "The afterlife to which you cling is the shadow we cast. Your gods are the fragments of our will made manifest. You should be overjoyed to have us asking anything at all of you."

I put my hands up, palms toward the anima mundi. "I'm not trying to be a negative Nancy here, I swear. I just know my limits. Or rather, I know what my limits *were,* and I know they're more extensive now than they were before Penton Hall. If you're going to threaten to discorporate me again if I refuse to do whatever it is you want me to do, then I guess I'm going to double-die after all. Please just remember that Annie is the reason you get to exist again, and let me go back long enough to say goodbye. My family deserves that much."

The anima mundi gave me a withering look, then paused and sighed. "You are correct, Mary Dunlavy. We shouldn't even seem to threaten you; it's not fair, and you've done nothing to earn such treatment from us. But we do need to ask for your help with the Covenant."

"Okay," I said. "What help?"

"The blow you helped to deliver hurt them direly, but it didn't stop them. If anything, it drove them to fight harder, and to find more innovative means of striking back. They aren't as bold as they were, but they continue to chip away at the parts of me they disapprove of, and it hurts, most dearly and direly."

"Yeah. We didn't think it would destroy the Covenant." Logically, what we'd done—setting up a bomb in the basement of their largest training facility—couldn't have wiped out a global organization. They were too widespread for that. What we'd been hoping for was slowing them down and breaking some of their pipelines. Penton Hall was where they trained their new recruits, and where they kept the majority of their recordings. Depending on how much of it had been destroyed, we could have set them back years. Not forever.

"They know you were there." The anima mundi sounded sad about that, almost resigned. "They have sensors and detectors you didn't anticipate in your scouting, and that may explain some of the weariness which dogged your steps between transits. They know they were the victims of an active haunting."

I bristled a little. It stung to think of the Covenant as victims of anything. We'd been fighting back, not opening hostilities. "And?"

"And they have been fighting things they consider 'unnatural' for centuries. They know how to capture and destroy ghosts."

I blinked, trying to understand what this would mean for me. Finally, after a long pause punctuated only by the rustling of the grain, I asked, "Do they have a method of summoning ghosts they want to destroy?"

"Yes," said the anima mundi. "You're in no danger. The channels they would use to summon you are stopped up by your family, but ties that strong to the living are less common now than once they were, and they can reach so very many of your peers. The Covenant is slaughtering the ghosts they call, the unliving, silent memory of the world. This needs to stop."

"And how am I supposed to stop it, if you can't?"

The anima mundi sighed. "We don't know. But you're quite innovative, Mary Dunlavy, you and that family of yours. We understand that you once used the spirit of a dead serpent to kill a woman who had wronged you. That shows both inventiveness and a certain core of essential cruelty. We believe you can do this."

"I can barely decide whether or not to stay solid right now!"

"We are aware."

"If you want me to work for you, I need to be less limited." I glared at them. "I need to be able to move between my family members without being called, and I need to do it with the sort of precision that I had before the crossroads went away. And I need to be solid when I want to be, and intangible when I want to be."

"Would you also like to be restored to the world of the living?"

"Given that everything I just asked you for falls under the umbrella of 'wacky ghost powers,' no, I would not like to be restored the world of the living," I said. "I've been dead so much longer than I was alive that at this point, I'm a lot more comfortable this way. Can you give me what I'm asking for or not?"

"Will you stop the Covenant from killing our ghosts?"

I paused. "I thought you said hauntings were expensive. The older a ghost is, the more predictable they tend to be, and the easier they'd be to hunt down. Those should also be the costliest ghosts to maintain. Isn't the Covenant doing you a favor?"

"If only it were that simple," said the anima mundi. "How nice it would be, for things to be simple for once in a long, long lifetime. But no. They do hunt and destroy the oldest ghosts, finding them easier to catch and more powerful on average, which means their goal of preventing another Penton Hall seems better served. And those old ghosts are more expensive, so removing them frees up our power for other things."

"Isn't that a good thing?"

"It would be, if we had decided to dismiss those ghosts of our own accord and in our own time. We didn't. Without them, that power is feeding back into all the other ghosts nearby, unpredictably and without proper controls."

I blinked, processing this. "Meaning they're juicing up a bunch of immature ghosts without any warning, and leaving those ghosts on the loose."

"Yes."

That would just make it easier for the Covenant to create a situation where they could dramatically unveil the existence of ghosts to the world in some irrefutable way, and get funding and support for eradication efforts. For every person who'd be overjoyed at the idea that they might be able to see Grandma again, there would be two people who wanted the foul phantoms exorcised. The first time an amateur ghost hunter managed to suck a domesticate into a jar, we'd get to see war break out across the human race. Sure, to you, it's just a ghost dog, but to the kid who was walking beside it, it's Bruno, most beloved creature the world has ever known.

"This is bad," I said.

"Yes," agreed the anima mundi, blandly.

"This is really, really bad." I turned away. "We need to stop this. Do you know where these ghost hunters are?"

"Most of them seem to be operating on the East Coast."

"New York again?"

"No. That nest was well and truly eliminated. These are further up the coast, in Boston and in Portland."

"Want a good haunting, aim for New England, I guess," I said grimly. "All right, that makes a certain amount of sense. Lots of old hauntings in that area, and not that many of my kids. What do you want me to do about it?"

"We want you to find the Covenant killers who are behind this, and eliminate them," said the anima mundi. "We don't care particularly how you achieve it. None of them will linger in our afterlife. The twilight is closed to them."

That was grim. Most people don't linger after death—it's not a super fun state to find yourself in, unless you have such strong ties to the world that you don't have any other choice, and even those of us who have jobs waiting for us don't tend to enjoy it. Happy ghosts are rare ghosts. Even so, most of the dead people I've met have been happy to know that they had a choice. They could linger, like I had, or they could move straight into the next stage of existence, but they got to decide, to some degree.

Even the ones who linger aren't cut and dried. Most dead folks don't have the strength to stick around for more than a few days if they don't fall easily and immediately into some sort of defined haunting, like the drag racers who die and become Phantom Riders, or the kids who die and become ever-lasters, eternally returning to the classrooms where they studied in life, never reaching graduation.

There are a lot of sad stories in the afterlife. I mean, it's where the dead people live, with a few terrifying exceptions, and death is pretty sad for most living things. Even if you linger, you're not the same. See also "the anima mundi can set the rules of my existence without giving me a vote" and "that same anima mundi can apparently just decide that no one from the Covenant is going to become a ghost." There's no discussion, no negotiation. There's just the anima mundi, and whatever they decide.

"I can go wherever my kids are," I said slowly. "That was your rule, right?"

"Our rule was that you could go wherever they *called* you," said the anima mundi. "For now, at your request, we will widen that to allow you to move between them according to your whim. You may have what you've requested. But this enhancement of your restrictions cannot last forever."

"But for now, it's like old times, and I can go wherever my kids are."

The anima mundi nodded, looking intensely put-upon.

"I can work with that," I said. Already, the outline of a plan was starting to form. "What resources can we have?"

"Excuse us?"

"You heard me. We're going ghost hunter–hunting for you, we're going to need some resources. Some sort of fancy map or something."

"Oh, for . . ." The anima mundi pinched the bridge of their nose, then waved their hands in the air like they were protesting the entire conversation. Which, I'll note, they started. "Before the Great Disruption, ghosts feared us properly. We're the living spirit of this world, and your individual existence after death is purely upon our sufferance! You should be bowing down before us, not making insolent demands!"

"I'm pretty sure this is why gods are supposed to keep their distance," I said. "You get a pantheon where the gods never show up at the village meetings, you get respect and mystery. Start showing up to discuss local politics and you get the Greeks in pretty short order."

"Meaning?"

"Meaning familiarity breeds contempt, or at least comfort, which starts with the same letter for a good reason. I can't bow down and quake in fear. If I did that, I wouldn't be able to look you in the eye and ask you what you need. You want me to go to Boston and figure out who's killing your ghosts? Fine, I can do that. I even know how I'm going to do it. But it's going to take me a little while to get there, because I can't do it alone."

The anima mundi frowned. "Then you agree?"

"I agree," I said. "For now, though, can you put me back where you found me? I need to talk to my family."

The anima mundi nodded. "It is done," they said, and it was, and I was gone. Again.

Four

"Everyone has their part to play in the story of the world. Some of those parts are tragedies. I wish it didn't have to be that way, but mine is not the hand that holds the pen."

—Juniper Campbell

The kitchen of the Old Parrish Place,
a crumbling farmhouse that (probably)
isn't haunted by evil spirits

THE ANIMA MUNDI WAS AS good as their word: they put me back exactly where they'd found me, in the kitchen of the Old Parrish Place. They didn't put me back exactly *when* they'd found me; I don't know if even they had that sort of power. I appeared, and the sky outside the windows was dark. There was a casserole dish of something layered and tomato-based on the stove, several large portions already missing, and the whole kitchen smelled of meat and cheese.

It was a scene I'd seen play out hundreds of times, in multiple different households. This could have been the Healy family home on the other side of the tree line, with Fran or Enid building the layers of their lasagna one lovingly placed noodle at a time. Or it could have been Evie in Portland, or Jane, although her lasagna had always used ground turkey and half the recommended quantity of cheese. There had even been lasagna nights in this house, before Thomas vanished, and knowing that they were happening again was restorative in a way I had never considered.

There was a basket of bread on the counter, already sliced and smelling strongly of garlic and butter. I picked it up, tucking it under my arm, and started for the dining room.

The Old Parrish Place was originally built by a farmer who truly believed he was going to make his fortune on the edge of the Galway Wood, raising a large family and harvesting the riches of the land. He designed his home accordingly. It was one of the first houses in Buckley with a formal dining room, or as formal as you could get in rural Michigan. It had door-ways to the kitchen *and* the family room. While I'd seen the family room itself undergo various transformations throughout the years, the dining room had always remained essentially the same, dominated by a massive oak table that pre-dated Thomas's ownership of the house.

Sometimes papers and books would creep in to threaten the table's dominion, but not tonight: tonight, the table had been cleared of everything except for dinner. Lasagna, a full bowl of salad, and large tumbler glasses of what looked like iced tea for Sally, milk for Alice and Thomas, and tomato juice for Sarah. A smaller table, sized for a dollhouse, had been set up where a centerpiece would normally go, with dollhouse-sized platters and serving dishes on it, each holding a portion of the night's meal.

It was an impressive spread, especially for only four people. Thomas sat at the head of the table, with Alice at his right and Sally at his left, while Sarah sat at Alice's right. Sarah was the first to notice me. She perked up as I stepped into the room, her expression brightening, but she didn't turn my way.

There was probably a reason for that, and so I didn't say any-thing as I finished walking over to the table and put the bread down in front of Alice. "You forgot this," I said. "Also, you're slowing down. You should have thrown a knife through my head before I cleared the doorway."

"Sarah's here," said Alice serenely, taking a piece of bread and passing the basket to Thomas. She ripped the bread in half and leaned over to place part of it next to the tiny table. "If you were something hostile, she'd have picked up your thoughts and alerted us."

"And if she couldn't read my mind?"

"She'd still have been able to see you, and seeing you when she couldn't read your mind would *definitely* have led to her alerting us." Alice finally turned in my direction, smiling so widely and warmly that I felt suddenly terrible for having been called away, even though I knew it wasn't even a little bit my fault. "Welcome back. How was the anima mundi?"

"Obfuscatory and confusing, as always. I was just telling them they can't keep talking to me and expect me, or probably any member of my family, to address them with deference and respect. Hard to respect things you know too well."

"The mice manage it," said Sally.

I fixed her with a look. "The mice have a religious rite centered around Alice's conception. They used to celebrate it in the kitchen, until Enid told them mice who insisted on recreating her son's idea of foreplay where she'd have to see it were making her reconsider her decision not to get a cat. I'm not seeing a lot of respect there."

"They respect. They just don't have a lot of illusions," said Sarah, taking a piece of bread as Sally passed her the basket. She smiled serenely at me, then dipped her bread into her tomato juice.

"You're going to get crumbs in your glass," I said automatically.

"I know," said Sarah. "It's like having bonus oatmeal if you do it enough."

Sally stared at her. "That's disgusting."

"Everyone's here now," said Thomas. "We can alert the congregation."

Which meant they'd invoked one of the various "bribery for a moment's peace" rituals that could be used to keep the mice out from underfoot. I circled the table to settle quickly at Sally's right, and Alice nodded, tilting her head back so that she was addressing the ceiling.

In her best "I spent my summers as a carnival barker" voice, she shouted, "For lo, did not the Patient Priestess say, It Is Lasagna Night, and You Had Better Get Your Butt to the Table Before It Gets Cold?" She managed to pronounce every single capital letter, a skill she'd picked up from the mice when she was still a child. She'd been adorable back then, this tiny girl with fluffy blonde curls making nonsensical religious commandments with all the fervor of a fire-and-brimstone preacher.

There's nothing like a colony of talking mice for taking the gravity out of organized religion. Fortunately for me, my father had been dead by the time the Healys trusted me enough to let me meet the mice, or Sunday mornings at church would have become infinitely more awkward. The first time I yelled "HAIL!" at the end of a sermon, I would have been in serious trouble.

Summoned by Alice's declaration, mice began to pour out of holes cut into the baseboards, flooding the floor and running up the legs of the table. The holes they emerged from were small enough that they'd been able to blend in to the general darkness of the hardwood floor and navy-blue wallpaper. It was semi-intentional camouflage; while not many people outside the family were allowed into the house, it was occasionally necessary to allow allies inside, and the dining room was usually the location for any important strategy meetings that needed to happen. Keeping people from realizing just how thoroughly infested the place was by rodents was a good idea.

The Aeslin mice swarming onto the table ran first for the smaller version of the meal that had been set up for them, then stopped one by one as they noticed me. It was pretty funny, especially because it didn't happen all at the same time. One mouse would stop, another mouse would run into them, and then both mice would stare at me, becoming a rock for the rest of the wave to break against.

In the end, not a mouse reached the lasagna, and not a sound was made. It was unnerving, having so many little rodent eyes fixed on me, not a one of them blinking, all of them shining with a brilliance that had nothing to do with the overhead lights.

Thomas sipped his iced tea. "This one's your problem, Mary. I've already done my version of the presentation."

"Yeah, but I didn't go missing for fifty years," I protested.

The mice kept staring.

I suppose it would have been too much to ask for the family to wait and be sure I was *actually* dead before they told the mice about it. Even if they'd wanted to, Annie had gone to Penton Hall with the stated intention of rescuing the colony of Aeslin mice living there, the descendants of the splinter colony that accompanied Charles and Ava when they chose not to go with their parents into exile. (If that doesn't make any sense, don't worry about it. I've been with this family for something like seventy years now, and sometimes I still get confused. Feed the children, comfort the babies, and love them, and it all works out in the end.)

Aeslin mice are capable of many things. They can even keep secrets when they have good reason. But there's no force in this world that will compel them to keep secrets from family, or from another clergy when that clergy is impacted by the secrets in question. The mice who'd seen me lost would have gone straight to my congregation and told them everything they knew. Not out of malice: out of mercy.

When your gods can be destroyed, there's good reason to stay committed to knowing exactly where they are and what they're doing. When your gods have absolutely no sense of self-preservation—when your gods are Price-Healys, in other words—there's not just good reason, there's an obligation. Some of these mice were no doubt mine, having chosen the path of the Phantom Priestess when they grew old enough in mouse terms to pledge themselves to a specific liturgical branch of their church. I'd been dead before they pledged themselves to me, but there's dead and then there's gone, and I'd never been gone.

"Um, hi," I said, offering the mice a little wave. "Reports of my destruction have been greatly exaggerated."

"HAIL!" shouted one of the mice, whiskers pushed forward in ecstasy. "HAIL THE RETURN OF THE PHANTOM PRIESTESS!"

Slowly at first, but with growing enthusiasm, the rest of the congregation picked up the chant, all of them shouting and swaying and staring at me. I grimaced.

"I'm sure glad I don't eat anymore," I said. "This would be enough to make me lose my appetite."

"We're used to it," said Sarah, dipping her bread in her tomato juice again.

Sally snickered.

Alice glanced at me, smiled, and took pity. Pushing her chair back, she stood and clapped her hands together. The mice quieted and focused on her, absolutely attentive. They used to respond to Enid that way, paying absolute attendance to the oldest priestess in the room.

Thoughts of Enid still ached a little, as they probably always would. She'd died badly, and for a while I'd hoped that meant she might stick around for a while, even if it was as one of the types of ghost who never manifested in the lands of the living. I could have kept her a secret if it had meant she was *there* for me to lean on and turn to.

But she didn't linger after she died. In my experience, Healy women never did. I'd buried two of them now—three if we counted Jane—and none of them chose to stay.

"Rejoice, rejoice, for the Phantom Priestess is returned to us, having defeated death a second time to come home to her family and her faithful," she said. The mice cheered, but cut themselves off quickly, recognizing that Alice wasn't done.

"She will tell you the story of her absence, that it might be added to the liturgy—*later*. Now is the time of feasting, and did not the Violent Priestess say Lasagna Is Essentially Cake, For It Has Noodles Made of Dough and Layers of Cheese? Eat and be glad that she has been returned, no longer to fade into the silence that awaits for the divine once they walk no more among us."

The mice cheered again, and this time they swarmed the tiny table, picking it clean in a matter of seconds. Thomas responded by shoving a full-sized plate substantially more laden-down with food in their direction, and Alice tossed half the basket of garlic bread into the middle of the teeming mass of mice.

With much cheering and chatter, the mice ran down the table legs, now clutching their offerings. They would carry them back to the central colony—located in the attic in Portland and at the Healy house, located in the disused sun room here at the Old Parrish Place—and share them with the rest of the mice, making sure children and elders were able to eat even if they weren't physically suited to scavenging for their food. It was a tidy system, and one they'd been practicing for so long that it ran without a hitch in the present day. In a matter of seconds, the only sign that the mice had ever been there was the perfectly cleaned tiny table, which didn't look like it had been used for anything.

Sally took a drink of her iced tea.

I turned to eye Alice. "You set me up," I accused. "You knew the mice would be happy to see me, and you waited to call them for dinner until they could all come and stare at me."

"Never met a bandage I didn't think would be better served by pulling it off," said Alice cheerfully. "They were going to find out sooner or later, and this way it happened all at once, with a promise that you'll tell them what happened, which puts in on your own time, rather than sending a constant stream of mice to sniff around looking for the missing scripture."

It was difficult to argue with her logic. No one had more experience with the mice than Alice did, and if she said something was the right way to handle them, she was probably right. That didn't make it any less annoying.

"They do *not* need an excuse for another liturgical scavenger hunt," said Sally, putting more lasagna on her plate. "When we got back from New York, they spent a solid week following the boss around the house and stealing his toenail clippings."

"You still call Thomas 'boss'?" I asked, halfway amused.

She shrugged. "What? You'd prefer 'Daddy'?"

Alice wrinkled her nose. Sarah snorted with amusement, then resumed dipping her bread in her juice. Thomas just kept placidly eating, like a man who'd figured out when it was in his best interests to keep his mouth shut.

I turned my focus on Sarah. "So where are you living right now, kiddo?"

She shrugged, looking down at her plate. "The variable changes," she said. "It shifts with needs."

"You came to me pretty late," I said. "Not as late as Sally and James, maybe, but still, you were seven before I babysat you for the first time. So maybe you don't realize this, but pretending you don't understand what I'm asking enough to answer using your words instead of math terms isn't going to work with me. I don't want to pressure you, but you can't deflect me either."

Sarah glanced up again, focusing on my face for a moment. I always wondered what she saw when she did that. Her species is fully face-blind: telepathy means never needing to say "who are you?" when you're talking to somebody unfamiliar. She still sees expressions, but most people don't register with her as individuals, and she doesn't pick up on a lot of nuance. The world must be fascinating through her eyes.

"I meant what I said, even if I said it that way to be confusing," she said. "Where am I living? Around. Sometimes I'm here, with Grandma and Grandpa. Greg likes the woods, and there's enough room out there for him to exhibit a lot of natural behaviors that he can't get away with when he's in less-rural places."

"And the woods don't mind that?" I asked delicately, shooting a glance at Alice.

The Galway Woods are alive. Oh, all forest biomes are *alive*—they wouldn't be biomes if they weren't alive—but the Galway is special. Whatever it is, I don't know, but something about that forest is alive, aware, and capable of having opinions. And it loves Alice. It's loved her since she was a child, and it loved her mother before her. Maybe it's a Kairos thing; it's probably easier to arrange the world to coincidentally go your way when the local ecosystem is actively in love with you. But I don't really know. No one does. Except for hybrids like Alice and her side of the family, there aren't any Kairos left.

Alice shrugged. "They're not *thrilled*, but they've been dealing with a population explosion among the deer for the last few years, and having something that likes to snack on them is good for the whole ecology."

"And there's only one of him," added Sarah. "I think the woods would probably be a lot less friendly about it if we had a whole bunch of him. Sometimes I think about trying to figure out the math to put him back where I found him, or to go over myself and find him a girlfriend. But I don't actually know what their home groups are like, and if he's from a species where the female eats the male after mating, I'd be really upset."

Her voice started to shake toward the end there. To my surprise, it was Sally who leaned over to pat Sarah gently on the wrist. "It's cool, bird-girl," she said. "No one's going to take your horrifying giant emotional support spider away. You can unclench."

Sarah offered her a weak smile. "Sorry," she said.

"Eat your tomato pudding," said Sally, gesturing toward Sarah's sodden garlic bread. "You'll feel better."

Sarah did as she was told. I caught my breath, refocusing on Alice and Thomas.

Greg was Sarah's emotional support animal, and having him around really did help to keep her stable. Poor kid, she'd been through a lot in the past few years, but then, we all had. And it wasn't Greg's fault that he was a jumping spider the size of a Clydesdale horse. He just limited the places where Sarah could easily spend her time, since he needed an immense amount of space to hunt, and no one really wanted to find out what would happen if somebody spotted him. Nothing good, that was for sure.

"It's good to see you both, but I can't stick around," I said.

"We didn't assume you'd be able to, really," said Thomas. "Not with the anima mundi calling you away almost as soon as you got here. That's new, isn't it?"

"We're currently renegotiating the terms of my haunting," I said. "Things are still up in the air with the crossroads gone, and I need to figure out how I fit into this new spiritual ecosystem. The anima mundi is helping me with that." Putting things into conservationist terms would make them easier for my family to understand, even if they weren't exactly accurate.

"What does that mean?" asked Alice.

"It means that a long time ago, caretakers—which you may have heard referred to as 'nanny ghosts'—were common, but they fell out of favor as infant mortality dropped and people got more diligent about making sure their babysitters weren't dead," I said. "I guess they had less bandwidth to worry about the babysitter's health when they were spending all their time worrying about the baby's. Anyway, when there were a lot of them, they had well-defined rules and restrictions for their hauntings. And since most of the caretakers are gone, and that's the closest category of ghost I can fit into, the anima mundi is having to try to adjust the terms of the haunting I had with the crossroads to keep me from being too much of a power sink. It's not like they can compare me to all the other caretakers when there just aren't many left. And it turns out the crossroads weren't very interested in clarity or restraint when it came to defining their ghosts."

"Aren't there any other former crossroads ghosts you could talk to?" asked Alice.

I paused. "There's one," I said, after a momentary pause. "I don't like her very much, and she's sort of an asshole, but she still exists, and I could probably seek her out and talk to her. She didn't have the same hybrid haunt that I did, though—she was alive, and then she was a crossroads ghost, no frills or fussing about, and now she's a reaper."

"How do you make *that* transition?" asked Thomas.

Sally shot him the look I had come to recognize as "what the actual hell is going on please explain," and he smiled. I wondered if he understood how fondly he looked at her. I suspected he did. You don't court Alice Healy without being *very* aware of your own emotions, because that woman has never met a feeling she couldn't ignore for as long as humanly possible.

"A reaper is a type of ghost responsible for shepherding the souls of the recently dead into the next level of the afterlife, assuming they're not going to hang about and become permanent residents like Miss Mary here," he said. "We don't know much about them, because they're entirely disinterested in interacting with the living, or at least that's what I understand." He glanced at me.

"Reapers aren't chatty, no," I said. "Bethany probably fits right in." That wasn't fair. She'd been totally chatty when I'd met her. Unpleasant and unnecessarily catty, but conversational. I just liked the idea of her trying to deal with an eternity where she had no one to talk to. Call me petty, but I don't like it when people try to hurt me, or my friends.

"And she's the only one?" asked Alice.

"As far as I know," I said. "All the other crossroads ghosts faded away when the crossroads were destroyed. I'm not sure the older ones really noticed what was happening to them. They had a tendency to lose their humanity over time, like rocks losing their sharp edges after years in running water."

"But you held on to yours," said Sally, clearly trying to keep up with conversation. "How?"

"Her." I gestured toward Alice. "Taking care of this little hellion kept me tied to what I originally was, and I didn't fade into something eldritch and uncaring like the rest of them. I got bitter and sarcastic instead."

"I like you bitter and sarcastic," said Sarah shyly.

I smiled at her. "That's because it's all you've ever known. I promise, I can be bracing to adults who meet me for the first time."

"You talk like the boss," said Sally. "I was honestly a lot more disconcerted by the whole 'dead and still standing here talking to us' thing than I was by the sarcasm. The sarcasm was comforting. It meant I was back in a world where people had the energy and the luxury to *be* sarcastic. Not a lot of space for sarcasm in the barren wasteland."

"You really were in hell," I said, looking straight at Thomas, who laughed.

"We were," he agreed. "But it was worth it, in the end."

I suppose it had been. So much had happened while he was gone—he'd missed the entire childhoods of his children, and almost the entirety of Jane's life. He hadn't even known her well enough to truly mourn her; he was missing the faint air of melancholy that I'd picked up around almost every member of the family I'd seen so far. Even Alice, whose relationship with Jane had been fraught at best, looked quietly heartbroken when she wasn't focusing on something else.

And yet, for Thomas, he'd come back to a world where his

family was flourishing, his wife was miraculously not only still alive but by his side, the crossroads were gone, and the healing of the anima mundi meant that sorcerers might return to the world. The Covenant was lashing out in desperation, and best of all, everyone who'd ever tried to hurt him was dead, meaning that for the first time in his life, he didn't have to spend every waking hour looking over his shoulder. He was close to free. For him, all the losses really had been worth it.

I didn't want to think of losing Jane as having been worth anything at all. I returned my attention to Alice. "The anima mundi needs to curtail the amount of energy I pull from the pneuma just to stay on this plane of existence," I said. "That means the rules I operate by are going to be changing. They already are. Right now, I'm pretty flexible, but going forward, assume you'll only see me if you call for me."

"What does that mean?" she asked.

"Before, I could come to you whether you called for me or not. All you had to do was need me, and I could be there, assuming the crossroads didn't have me off doing something horrible. Now, you'll need to actively call for me. I can probably negotiate something less constrictive with the preverbal kids, because they can't possibly call my name, but I won't be able to just pop in and out the way I could before."

Alice frowned, a line appearing between her eyebrows. It made her look so much like Fran that it would have taken my breath away, if I'd had any breath left to take. "That doesn't sound so bad."

"It is and it isn't," I said. "I'll just be restricted like a living babysitter would be. The kids will be able to get into trouble when I'm not looking. Think back. Remember how I used to appear when you didn't want me to? When you were absolutely sure you were on top of things? Maybe it's better this way. I'd be tempted to hover now that the crossroads aren't keeping me occupied all the time, and the new generation would never have the opportunity to make messes. You needed those messes if you were going to grow up ready to deal with the world the way you were supposed to."

"That's not enough of a limitation to explain the look on your face," said Alice. "What else?"

"I can't decide to adopt new family members anymore," I said. Sally looked momentarily alarmed, and I shook my head. "No, honey, not you. Not Sarah either. Both of you were brought into the family by somebody else. But when that asshole from the Covenant snatched Annie's friend Megan, we were able to find her by convincing her mother to hire me as her babysitter. As soon as I took the job, I could 'hear' Megan the way I can hear any of you, and that let me go to her. I can't do that anymore. So I guess it's less that I can't adopt new family members, and more that I can't take on more clients." I could still "hear" Megan if I concentrated. That was going to be interesting. Was my position as her babysitter going to be hereditary the way it was with the Price-Healys? Did her already being a client mean she was grand-fathered in somehow?

Well, if it did, that was fine, I'd just have to learn the proper techniques for taking care of baby gorgons. I could probably start earlier than I did with human babies, assuming they hatched from eggs the same way snakes did—a big assumption, and yet not too far out of line for some of the things I'd seen.

"All right," said Alice. "That's not too bad. Was that all the anima mundi needed?"

"No. The Covenant's still in North America."

"We knew that," said Thomas. "They took grave losses at Penton Hall. Most of their trainers, and a huge portion of their archives. But they weren't eliminated, and the ones who are behind this invasion can't give up and back down. If they did, they'd be telling the rest of the Covenant that they're weak, and open themselves to infighting."

"I don't like these people," I said.

"None of us do," said Alice.

"Well, the Covenant that's here in North America is getting on the anima mundi's nerves. They've started hunting ghosts. Someone saw me, and told the rest of the Covenant that you'd been able to attack them the way you did because you had a ghost with them."

"That's technically true," said Sarah. "Without your assistance, we would have been unable to transport the explosive devices we used to demolish the building."

"I have faith in Annie's ability to make things explode," I said. "You would have figured out another way. You're creative people." I even managed to sound like I meant what I was saying, which was possibly the most difficult part of what I was saying.

"Regardless," said Sarah, and sipped her tomato juice.

"Because the Covenant thinks I was key to the attack plan, they've been harassing the dead. They're posted up somewhere near Boston, where they can find the greatest density of older ghosts who might be powerful enough to help with something like the attack. I don't know if they're trying to catch them and mount a counterassault, or whether they're just destroying them, but either way, the anima mundi doesn't like it. Removing the ghosts releases all the energy that was being fed into their haunt-ings and sends it lashing around, messing with things."

"That sounds . . . bad," said Alice.

"The anima mundi sure seems to think so. The energy has to go *somewhere*, and apparently it can cause newer ghosts to get too strong and become problematic. I'm not entirely clear on how it works. All this metaphysical stuff goes right over my head most of the time. Just because I *am* this metaphysical stuff, that doesn't make it one of my strong points. Anyway, they want me to head up there and stop all this nonsense. How, not really sure about that either. I told them I had a plan, because the best way to find a plan is to get moving and figure it out on the way."

"How are you planning to accomplish this?" asked Thomas.

"Well, I figured I'd start by heading for New York," I said. "I don't expect Verity can be much help right now, between mourning for Dominic and being eight months pregnant."

"She's very angry," said Sarah, eyes on her lasagna as she spoke. "She wants to hurt the Covenant more than she's ever wanted just about anything, even to dance. Please don't tell her about your mission. If you do, she'll try to go with you. She'll want to help. And she could get hurt, or the baby could get hurt, and I don't think she could live with that once she recovered."

"I won't tell her, I promise," I said.

Sarah glanced in my direction and mustered a very slight smile. I wasn't sure she could actually, physically see me. Her eyes were unfocused and glowing very faintly. "Thank you," she said. "How are you going to explain showing up there?"

"I'll just tell her I wanted to check on her and the baby, and make sure she knows I'm back in the land of the living, even if it's on a temporary visa." I sighed. "I do need to pick up some physically manifest help, though, or I'm never going to pull this off."

"What about Rose?" asked Alice.

"Also dead," I said. "The anima mundi would have sent her if they wanted a two-ghost tag team to take on whatever the hell the Covenant is doing. I'm assuming they want to keep from losing two of their favorite toys in the same mission."

She exchanged a look with Thomas, who grimaced but nodded. "We could help," she said. "We'll come back to New York with you, if you want us to."

I paused to consider her offer. Thomas was an experienced, powerful sorcerer, and Alice was a nightmare in combat. Sally was no slouch herself. The three of them could be a great asset, and it was with extreme reluctance that I shook my head.

"No," I said. "Even apart from the fact that I'm not sure I could bring you anywhere near your pregnant granddaughter without you deciding you needed to stay and help her, and deal with the ghost issue later—and that would be completely valid of you to do, 'family first' is the rule for a reason—any Covenant we ran into would stand too high a chance of recognizing you. The only one I'd feel halfway safe taking into the field is Sally, and neither of you is going to let me run off with her."

"I'm supposed to fly to the West Coast next week to see James, anyway," said Sally. "We didn't really get a lot of time to catch up before, and we need it."

James was Sally's best friend, and had been since long before either one of them was involved with our carnival sideshow of a family. They grew up in the same small town in Maine, and she'd made the crossroads bargain that eventually threw her into Thomas's path in order to set James free. They needed the time together more than I needed Sally in specific to help me.

"I can't," said Sarah. "When I'm around Covenant people, I do bad things."

I nodded. "I know, sweetheart. I wasn't going to ask you. And I can't go to Ohio—Shelby and Alex are busy with Charlotte and Isaac, and I'm really trying not to orphan anybody if I can help it. We've dealt with enough parental abandonment in this family to last us a dozen lifetimes. I figure I'll pop back to Portland and see if anyone there wants to go on a road trip. It's only, what, a week to drive from Portland to New York? Less if we can flag down a passing routewitch and convince them to bend the distance for us."

Sarah blinked at me, looking suddenly alarmed.

"Artie isn't— You can't ask— He might say yes just because he feels like he would have said yes before everything that happened, and then you'd have an unstable incubus in the field with you, and he could get hurt."

"Sweetie, any of us can get hurt any time we're in the field," I said, patiently. "Even me, as Penton Hall so brutally reminded us. There's no safety outside a controlled environment, and I'm not going to pretend he's not still a member of this family just because he's a little scrambled right now. But he doesn't have the kind of experience I'm looking for. I'll see whether Kevin's up for a road trip, or maybe Annie and Sam. They're pretty good at this sort of thing." As if they had ever dealt with this sort of thing before.

As if this were a sort of thing *any* of us had ever had to deal with. We were striding quickly into uncharted territory, and I didn't have much time to figure out how we were going to emerge from the other side. I looked to Alice. "How much trouble are you going to be in with the mice if I don't stick around to tell them what happened to me right this second? I promise I'll come back as soon as I can take the time."

"I've heard that one before," she said, with a slight roll of her eyes. Then she nodded. "It's all right, Mary. If you need to go, you can go. I'll placate the mice, and while they're not going to forget that you owe them a liturgical recounting for their records, they're usually easy to bribe with a chocolate layer cake, especially if I'm willing to put frosting roses on it. But you need to keep your promises. I buried my daughter and my son-in-law, but I couldn't bury you."

"Your mother did that a long time ago," I murmured. "She took care of everything."

They'd found my body in the ditch where it had been thrown by the truck that hit me, swallowed by roots and hidden by corn-stalks, and they'd dug it up and carried it back to the old Healy place to bury in the back field, where I could be at rest in the presence of people who cared about me. Maybe that was part of why I'd been so easy to tie to the family, even with the crossroads pulling on me the way they had been. The crossroads may have owned my soul, but the rest of me was buried on Healy land.

"Yeah, well, I still thought I'd lost you, and having a dead babysitter means I'm never supposed to lose you. That's the way this works. So be careful this time, and come back to us."

Thomas shot her a sharp but distinctly fond look. "Are *you* telling someone else that they should be careful?" he asked. "Has one or more of the hells frozen over?"

"Quiet, you," said Alice, and cuffed him in the shoulder.

Seeing them like this—comfortable and domestic, not running for their lives or struggling to claw what fragments of joy they could out of a world where the clock was rapidly running out on them—healed something in my heart that I hadn't known was still wounded. I smiled.

"I promise," I said, and blew Alice a kiss, and was gone.

Five

"I sometimes wonder what it's like for the ordinary dead. One minute they're part of the world as everybody knows it, and the next they're trapped on the outside, learning how much of everything they ever knew was a lie. It's got to be an enormous shock to the system. I still wish they'd leave me alone, though."

—Laura Campbell

Once again in Oregon,
this time appearing in the kitchen
of a small house in the city proper

JANE HAD ALWAYS HAD A complicated relationship with food. As one of the only members of her family not to choose fieldwork as a primary occupation, she'd been worried about gaining weight and not being able to handle the rare trips she actually *did* make into the field, resulting in a life spent counting calories and looking for low-fat substitutions in her meals. I'll give her this much: she never intentionally forced her flirtations with toxic diet culture on her children. While they might not have been able to find potato chips and candy in the pantry on a regular basis, she didn't scold them when they brought those things home, or try to convince them to eat the same way she did.

Her complicated relationship with food had extended to her kitchen, which was basically always spotless. A dish would barely have time to hit the sink before it was washed, dried, and put back in the cabinet where it belonged. As I appeared in what had previously been Jane's kitchen, the absolute proof of her death struck me even harder than the funeral pictures.

The sink was mounded with dishes, piled high enough that the threat of a cascade was impossible to ignore. A few pieces of flatware had already fallen on the floor, and I paused to pick them up and place them gently on the unnervingly sticky counter before taking a closer look around.

The trash can and recycling bin were both in a state similar to the sink, so full they threatened to overflow, while the compost bin was empty, devoid of the fruit cores and vegetable scraps I would have expected. The lights were off and the air was oddly stale, like no one had been lingering here for longer than it took to run in, grab something, and run away again for quite some time. Open boxes of sugared cereal and Pop-Tarts sat on the counter, next to a full flat of Coke cans. The message couldn't have been clearer if it had actually been written on the whiteboard on the fridge: Jane didn't live here anymore. Jane's rules were no longer in effect.

I would have to rethink my normal "if there are no children in the house, always appear in the kitchen" approach to visiting the house after this. I shook my head and left the room, heading for the living room.

The house in Portland that Jane had shared with her husband and children was smaller than the compound outside the city, but so were some chain grocery stores. It was still respectably sized, large enough for both kids to have their own rooms while they were growing up, while Ted and Jane each had an office for their own use. Artie had moved downstairs to the basement as soon as he turned eighteen, preferring the isolation of his own level of the house to the comfort of a bedroom that didn't also contain the washer and dryer. Elsie and Jane had promptly split his original bedroom down the middle, using it for Elsie's art studio and Jane's overflow document storage.

Because the house was smaller, it had always had a more re- liably lived-in feel to it, rather than feeling vaguely like a large hotel complex that was only half in use at any given time. That feeling wasn't here anymore.

The hall was dark, the air thick enough with dust that I started to get annoyed on Jane's behalf. She deserved better than to in- herit the old cliché of "the woman does all the housework," and while she'd been alive, that had never particularly struck me as the case. She and Ted both kept the house tidy, and as the chil- dren got older, I'd helped in teaching them how to clean up after themselves. Artie had been doing his own laundry since he was nine, and hadn't even allowed me to help him fold it and put it away in years. And Elsie didn't let anyone into her room for any reason short of "the world is actively on fire and you have the only extinguisher."

Not that she'd ever been able to keep me out. Being able to walk through walls has its perks.

Frowning, I followed the hall to the living room, finding it empty, and turned to head upstairs to the second floor. That was usually where Ted could be found, if he was home. He and Jane had both worked out of their offices, her as a cryptid social worker—not a position that paid in any formal or legal sense, but which kept her more than busy enough to justify making it a full-time career—and him as a human social worker, which was an amusing inversion, given that she was (mostly) human, and he was a full-blooded Lilu. Somehow, it worked for them, like being a step removed from the species they were trying to support made it easier for them to see the answers.

The door to Jane's office was securely closed when I reached the top of the stairs, and I hesitated for a moment before I walked through it, into the controlled chaos of her workspace.

She had always done her best to keep things tidy in there, and she had never once succeeded; see also "taking half the spare room for her file boxes." Papers have a tendency to cascade, even when they're not being stored in a house also occupied by a colony of sapient talking rodents. And indeed, one of the shelves above her desk was dedicated to a small village of dollhouses, wood and plastic and surrounded by tiny picket fences, creating an idyllic mouse vacation destination. A hole in the wall behind the largest of the houses showed how they were able to stay so clean. The majority of the mice were in the attic, living their ordinary, messy lives out of the way. I walked over to the shelf, stopped, and cleared my throat.

"And lo, did the Violent Priestess not say, Listen to the Babysitter, For She Is Trying To Keep Everyone Safe? And was it not the commandment, from that day on, that the Babysitter Should Be Heeded at All Costs? Well, hi. I'm the babysitter, and I need to talk to someone. *Without* a bunch of shouting or rejoicing. So if somebody could come and check in with me, I'd very much appreciate it. Thanks."

Any sense of silliness I had about directly addressing unseen rodents had long since been beaten out of me by the reality of life among the Healys. I folded my hands behind my back and leaned back on my heels to wait.

Some ghosts can change size, squeezing themselves into a tiny bottle or the hollow of a tree, or passing seamlessly through a keyhole. Most of the types of ghost who can manage that sort of thing can't turn fully intangible the way I can—they traded one set of useful skills for another, and if I'm being quite honest, I like my set of useful skills better. Being able to squeeze through a keyhole is never going to top walking through the closed, locked door of the petulant teenager you're trying to keep in one piece. Still, sometimes, I wish I could make myself small enough to stroll into the network of tunnels and passages that the Aeslin use to get around, meeting with the mice on equal footing.

I had time to contemplate all the reasons that would be convenient before there was a rustling inside the largest dollhouse, a palatial manor that had originally been intended to house Calico Critters dolls and had been gutted and rebuilt for the comfort of the mice. The door opened, and an elderly mouse wearing the raiment of Jane's priesthood stepped out, leaning heavily on a carved bone staff.

I couldn't tell what animal the staff had belonged to when it was alive. That was something of a relief. The mice weren't picky about the bones they used, and would take them from roadkill as readily as they would steal them from the garbage. I know I'm dead and shouldn't be so sensitive, but it's hard to have a civil conversation with someone who's using a piece of a dead cat as a mobility aid.

The priest moved toward the fence around the house, and I amended my impression of its age: this mouse wasn't just elderly, it was *ancient,* possibly the oldest mouse I had ever seen still moving under its own power. It stopped at the fence line and bowed to me, whiskers pressed tightly back along the sides of its white-furred, wizened muzzle.

"Greetings to you, o Phantom Priestess, she who walks the Dark Paths of Death in her Divinity," it squeaked. "You are Welcome Here, in the Protectorate of the Silent Priestess. What brings you forth?"

Was it possible that Ted and the kids had somehow managed to cut the household colony off from the rest of the family mice so completely that they didn't know why Jane wasn't coming home? The thought was ludicrous, and yet. So was the concept of a mouse whose divinity had died still being here this long after the funeral. I frowned. "You speak of the Silent Priestess as if she were still here," I said. "Why do you do that?"

"Because all that is Divine lingers always among the faithful," said the mouse.

That was a new wrinkle on Aeslin cosmology. I blinked. "You know she's dead."

"So are you, Priestess. So is the God of Chosen Isolation. But you have both returned to us, in your ways, and we worship you still, despite all the strangenesses of your presence."

Great. Had my continued refusal to move on to my final reward finally broken the mice of their ability to understand death?

The mouse leaned back, more toward the ecstatic position I was used to them taking when they got to speak directly with their gods, and said, "Most of the Silent Priestess's congregation could not solve the Riddle that had been set by her Passing, and followed her into the Silence that was her Domain," it squeaked. "But some of us were Wiser than that, and understood the Grand Mystery which we had been Presented. We have seen the Truth, and we will Worship Her even unto the very End of Days."

Oh, no. I hadn't broken all the mice. But Jane's death had broken some of them. That was heartbreakingly unsurprising. Aeslin mice who lost their divinity didn't tend to last for very long. Every time a member of the family died, there was a spike in rodent mortality as the elder members of their priesthood either faded from grief or took matters more actively into their own paws, ending their lives rather than continue to exist in a world which no longer contained their living gods.

It was brutal. It was awful. It was the natural consequence of belonging to a species whose survival strategy had evolved to center upon a core of hyper-religiosity that would have been considered a mental illness in any other sapient species. For the mice, it wasn't an illness or an aberration. It was just the way things were, always and from the beginning of everything, and all the way into the end.

Aeslin mice don't leave ghosts, ever. They die and they move on to their final destination immediately, no hesitation, no fussing around with unfinished business or unanswered questions. On my good days, I think that's why the various Healys I've buried haven't chosen to linger. They're on their way to mouse heaven, off to be reunited with their congregations and spend eternity being worshipped by all the mice that have ever been.

Exhausting but fulfilling, as afterlives go.

"May I speak to a representative of the faith of the Polychromatic Priestess?" I asked, carefully. Elsie was still alive. Maybe her congregation would be less unnerving, or at least less dedicated to the worship of a dead woman.

Maybe it was hypocritical of me not to want to talk to Jane's priesthood when she was gone, but I didn't. My priesthood had been formed after I was dead, and had always accepted that fact. Jane's priesthood had been formed to worship her as a living entity, and I really didn't want the Aeslin to transition into a death cult while no one was looking. That sort of thing never ends the way you want it to.

The mouse bristled its whiskers and flattened its ears, displeased by my request. "Must you?" it squeaked. "This is the sacred space of the Silent Priestess, and should be Preserved as such."

"I must," I said. "If they won't come here to meet me, I'll go into the office of the God of Careful Chances and petition them there, and when they come, I'll tell them you refused me. That out of respect for your dead priestess, you refused the request of another dead priestess, one whose seniority within the family is provably greater. I'm guessing you're already having trouble defending your faith before the collected priests. Do you really want to add disrespect to the challenges set against you?"

The mouse shot me what I could only describe as a frustrated look, which was a fascinating expression to read on a rodent face. "Please, Priestess, wait here," it squeaked, and scurried back into the house, slamming the door as it went inside. I didn't even know a dollhouse door *could* slam.

A few seconds passed, and the door opened again, allowing another mouse to emerge. This one was younger than the first, with naturally white fur that had been dyed in a variety of colorful streaks, making it look like something that had crawled out of a Lisa Frank painting and into the real world. It was wearing a crown of construction paper and brightly colored feathers, and a patch-work cloak made from a dozen different tiny scraps of stitched-together fabric. It left optical echoes when it moved, like it was too complicated of a pattern to exist in the real world. Like the first priest, it scampered up to the edge of the fence and stopped there, bowing its tiny head and folding its paw in front of its chest.

This displayed its impeccable manicure to flawless effect, and I spared a momentary thought for whether Elsie had taught her mice to do their claws, or whether she did it with them with the world's tiniest nail-polish brush.

"Greetings to the Phantom Priestess," it squeaked. "We had heard Rumor that you were Removed from this World and sent eternally into the Great Reward to join the Gods and Priestesses of generations lost."

"I did get blown into the afterlife for a little while, but since I was sort of turned into ghost glitter all across the twilight, I didn't actually go to any sort of reward, and I came back together in the end," I said. "Sorry, still don't know what comes next."

"What comes Next for you may not be what comes Next for us," said the mouse, diplomatically. "Your congregation will be overjoyed to hear that the rumors of your destruction had been Wildly Exaggerated. They have been Holding to Hope, but in light of the Unclarity which has gripped the congregation of the Silent Priestess in recent days, they were beginning to Waver in their Faith."

"That makes sense," I said, as noncommittally as I could. I didn't want to get involved in an Aeslin religious dispute if I had any choice in the matter.

"How May this Unworthy Follower of the Polychromatic Priestess best Assist You?" asked the mouse.

"I wanted to get somebody to tell me, honestly, what's been going on around here since Jane died," I said. "I knew the place would be different, but this is like walking into a tomb."

The mouse stood a little taller. "Do you request Plain Text Accounting?" it asked.

I blinked. "What's that?"

"For did not the God of Chosen Isolation issue a Commandment, that we should be willing to Give Account of things he had not seen in as simple of terms as possible, that he might remain Current on Family Gossip without needing a dictionary and an hour of theological debate?" The mouse sounded proud as it finished its declaration, looking at me expectantly.

I blinked again. "Wait. You mean Arthur just *asked* you to talk like normal people, and you said yeah, sure, okay?"

"Yeah," said the mouse.

This was staggering. I took a step backward, halfway through the desk. "Oh, man, that's huge," I said. "Yeah, plain text would be great. I have a lot to cover, and not infinite time. What's the situation?"

"Well, Ted's a widower, and he's depressed as hell about it," said the mouse.

There are no words to express how strange it was to hear that sentence coming out of a mouse's mouth. I stepped out of the desk and turned solid again, so that I could lean back against it, resting my butt on the very edge and my weight on my hands. "Most people get depressed when their spouses die," I said.

"Most people aren't social workers," said the mouse. "He's having trouble controlling his pheromones, so he's been working remotely as much as possible, and he doesn't bathe as much as he probably should. He's mostly been eating Pop-Tarts and whatever he can order off of DoorDash, and occasionally scrambling eggs so he feels like he's still a functional person. He cries a lot. We always knew he'd miss the hell out of her, but this is just sad."

"Right," I said, still trying to adjust to the strangeness of a mouse speaking colloquially. "And what about the kids?"

"Elsie's pissed as *fuck*," said the mouse, and the fact that it was talking about its own divinity made the words almost blasphemous, even though that had never been my faith. "She's just angry all the time, at pretty much everybody, because she can't decide where all that anger belongs. She'll figure out where she wants to point it sooner or later, and then a lot of shit is going to be on fire. Metaphorically. Actual fire is Antimony's job."

"Are there specific people she's more mad at than others?"

"Sarah," said the mouse, without hesitation. "For what she did to Artie, and for not saving her mother. Alice, for not being here most of her life, and for not saving her mother. You, for not bringing her mother back from the afterlife. Kind of everybody."

"I see."

"And Artie . . . whew." The mouse grabbed its tail, wringing it between its paws. "He's not well. He's not mad, because he doesn't know how to be. He's not grieving, either, which just makes Elsie angrier, which makes her feel terrible, because she doesn't want to be mad at him for things he can't control. Whatever Sarah did to rebuild him as a person, it wasn't good enough, and it's coming apart at the seams. If she was willing to come here and perform continuous maintenance, that might have been enough, but she's not, and he's unraveling. He knows less about who he's supposed to be every day. His clergy is discussing a liturgical renaming."

"Really?"

Formal liturgical renamings happened when a god or priestess had drifted so far from their original title that it no longer fit at all, or when they died. Some gods would have multiple lesser titles, but one would always be the "correct" method of referring to them, the specific title that defined them in Aeslin theology. As far as I knew, only two full liturgical renamings of the living had been performed since the mice started worshipping the family: Alice, who got a new name when she began her quest for Thomas and could no longer be considered the woman she'd been before that, and the man who'd been married to Beth Evans, who was known to the mice as the Kindly Priestess. Presumably, he'd had a proper title before he decided to hit her so hard that she died from her injuries, but after that, the mice had renamed him to "the Cruelest God," and intentionally forgotten his name, as well as any other titles he might have borne.

For them to rename someone was for them to effectively declare the person they'd been before dead and gone. Alice's clergy was still split on whether she could return to her original title now that her long quest was finished: it seemed likely that she would always have two distinct liturgical lines going forward.

"Really," confirmed the mouse.

"Poor kiddo. Either one of them home?"

The mouse nodded. "Yes—is that enough Plain Text Accounting?"

"Yes," I said.

"Thank you, Priestess," said the mouse, with evident relief. "The Polychromatic Priestess is not presently in Residence. She has gone to attend the Derby of Rolling, and to Drown her Sorrows in the eyes of pretty girls. The God of Chosen Isolation is Isolated in his Chambers. He last ventured forth at the hour of dinner three days gone, and has not been Seen since."

"That sounds like a job for a babysitter," I said, pushing away from the desk. I nodded to the mouse. "Thank you. You've been very helpful."

It fanned its whiskers at me. "I am Honored by your Conversation."

"Glad you think so," I said, and dropped through the floor. I've never been sure how to end a conversation with the mice when I'm not bribing them to go away and leave me alone; getting the hell out of whatever room they're in works as well as anything else.

Besides, dropping through floors is fun. You see all sorts of interesting things. Mostly pipes and electrical wires and dead beetles, but those are interesting if you look at them the right way.

I passed cleanly through the stairway to the ground floor, rolled my shoulders, and kept going.

◆ ◆ ◆

Dropping through that much empty space wasn't difficult or painful, but it was disorienting. Being a physical haunting means spending most of my time behaving as if I still have a body, as if I need to interact with the physical world in more than a super-ficial way, and living people don't usually fall through floors, and when they do, they tend to plummet. I didn't plummet from the second floor to the first—it was more like I drifted down, light as a feather, moving at the pace of the air.

Then I passed through the floor of the first story, and into the transformed confines of Artie's basement.

Like the rooms of all "my" kids, the basement was a familiar space. I had watched its evolution from a barren storage space to the more comfortable, well-appointed space that he had turned it into after he was given permission to relocate. And indeed, parts of the room were the way I expected them to be. The carpet, for example, hadn't changed, and neither had the bed. But the rest of the space was unnervingly divergent from my memory.

The walls were blank, posters, sketches, and pictures taken down to reveal the cold concrete beneath. The shelves were empty, books and comics and action figures gone. A pile of card-board boxes against the wall next to the washing machine told me where at least some of them had gone. The desk was still in its customary place, computer turned on and quietly humming away to itself, but Artie was on his back on the bed, hands folded behind his head, staring unblinking at the ceiling.

Somehow, he didn't appear to have noticed me. That, or he was so busy counting the cracks in the ceiling that he couldn't spare a glance my way. It didn't really matter. I walked in his direction, giving him ample time to realize I was there before I cleared my throat and said, "Hey, Art." He'd been going by "Arthur" the last time I'd seen him, but the mice were calling him Artie. I wasn't sure what he preferred right now.

"Arthur," he said, eyes still on the ceiling.

"Come again?"

"My *name* is Arthur. Not Art, and not Artie. Artie was someone else. I don't want to use his name. I don't like it when people call me that. It makes me sad and angry and I wish people would stop. I keep asking and asking them to stop, and they do it anyway, and it's not *fair*." He finally turned in my direction, eyes burning with quietly focused anger. "Hello, Mary. I thought you were dead. Again."

"Not quite," I said. "I took a hard-enough hit that it scattered me across the afterlife, but I've reconstituted."

Too late, I realized that was a lot like what had happened to him, although my situation had come with a happier ending—I was still myself, at least as far as I could tell, and not an amalgam of other people's ideas about me.

Artie—Arthur—scowled. "How nice for you," he said, and sat up. "Why are you here?"

"You remember the anima mundi?"

"Living spirit of the earth, took the place of the crossroads after Annie went and made it so they never existed."

"Well, it turns out they're basically the boss of all the ghosts in the world. Most of them, they leave to go about their business, because they're locked in to the rules of straightforward, defined hauntings, which means they aren't running around, getting into trouble. I, on the other hand, was defined by a haunting that no longer exists, and managed to sort of wedge my way into a different sort of haunt by coming at it sideways. So right now, I don't have well-defined rules or a job that I'm expected to be doing."

"Meaning?"

"Meaning they—the anima mundi—decided that if they have a job that needs doing and a ghost without a proper job, they may as well combine the two, and they want me to go to the East Coast to make the Covenant stop dicking with the ghosts there."

"The anima mundi is sending a ghost to stop ghost hunters."

"Yup. Who better to figure out what's going on?"

"I don't know. Anyone the Covenant can't stuff into a spirit jar as soon as they realize you're there to stop them?"

That was a pretty good point that I hadn't really taken the time to consider, preoccupied as I'd been with charging full steam ahead. "That's why I'm here," I said. "I wanted to get some living people who were willing to come with me and be my hands while we figured this out. Where better to start than with my family? At least you're all halfway trained for this sort of thing."

Arthur's mouth twisted in an uncomfortable way. "Trained, sure. Does it count when you weren't the one who got the training, you just halfway remember it happening?"

"I think so," I said. "It's not like anyone has field experience in this sort of thing."

"But you didn't come here to talk to me," he said. "No one comes here to talk to me. I make them too uncomfortable."

"You don't make me uncomfortable," I lied. I'm a babysitter. I have a lot of experience at telling necessary lies to my charges.

Arthur shook his head. "I do," he said. "I wish I didn't, but I do. It's all right, Mary. You can admit how I make you feel."

"You make me sad, not uncomfortable," I said. "I hate seeing you suffer."

"Then maybe you shouldn't be looking at me." He lay back down and rolled over, so that his back was to me.

It would have been hard for a dismissal to be much clearer. I sighed. "Okay, Arthur," I said. "But I'll check in before I leave, and I really do want you to feel better."

"I'll feel better when I'm dead, and then we'll have something in common," he said, not looking back toward me. "We'll both have died twice."

I shook my head and moved to climb the stairs—the normal, substantial way this time—to the basement door.

I hadn't really been expecting Artie—or Arthur—to help me. He'd never been a fan of fieldwork, and he was clearly dealing with a lot on a psychological level, which made a lot of sense. If not for the mouse mentioning him, I might have come and gone without seeing him at all. I felt a little bad about that, and kept feeling bad as I continued up the stairs to the second floor and down the hallway to Elsie's closed bedroom door.

The mice said she was off watching roller derby practice, but my vague sense of her location didn't agree. It told me she was here in this house for me to find, and when push comes to shove, I'll still choose my own instincts over the word of a religious rodent.

Elsie's door was painted a pleasant shade of Barbie pink that didn't go with the rest of the hallway, and patterned with cotton candy clouds that I remembered her painting in her junior year of high school, sitting there and patiently dabbing them on, one brushstroke at a time. Jane hated it so much. She hated that Elsie had a pink door, she hated that it clashed with everything else, and she hated that her daughter couldn't be placated with a nice eggshell that would still have stood out, but not quite as boldly.

I paused with my hand raised to knock, blinking back tears that didn't actually exist but still stung my eyes. If I let them fall, they would get my cheeks and blouse wet, just like real tears, but they'd vanish as soon as they tried to fall to the floor. There are limits to my interaction with the world of the living. I am a discrete creature, and all I can leave behind are footprints.

Finally, I knocked.

"Go *away*, Arthur!" yelled Elsie. "I'm not in the mood."

"It's not Arthur," I called back. "It's me. May I come in?"

There was a long pause before Elsie's voice, now closer to the door, said, "I know you're not really Mary, because Mary's gone. Whatever you are, you do an excellent Mary impression. Now go away."

"Elsinore, come on. I'm not in the mood," I said, peevishly, and stuck my head through the door.

Elsie's room was as cluttered and pink as it had always been, with the bed drowning in a pile of pillows and plush toys that she'd been collecting and refining since preschool. Elsie herself was also as cluttered and pink as she'd ever been, standing off to the side of the door with a machete in her hand. When she saw my head appear through the door, she screamed and brought it down across my neck in a hard arc.

The world glitched, going gray for a moment, and Elsie screamed again as my head fell off and hit the floor.

Six

"Life is a tragedy and death is a comedy, and the reverse is also true."

—Apple Tanaka

The bedroom of Elsinore Harrington-Price,
trying to deal with the fact that
I've just been decapitated

I BLINKED AS I WATCHED my body pitch forward, landing on the bedroom floor in a heap. At least it wasn't doing that cliched "grope around, looking for your own severed head" routine. That was funny in like, one zombie movie, all the way back in the 1970s. Fifty years later it's just tired, and I would have been ashamed to be a part of it.

I couldn't move. I couldn't even roll, which made sense: most of the muscles the head uses to move around are located in the neck, and Elsie's machete had caught me right at the base of the skull, leaving me neatly decapitated and without enough musculature to do more than lay where I was and stare at my own fallen body.

Elsie wasn't screaming anymore. That was a good start toward opening a reasonable discussion—I hoped. "Hey, Elsie," I said, my voice coming out a little strained and barely recognizable, due to my lack of vocal cords. Still, I could force air through my remaining esophagus and out my mouth, which still shaped words the way it always had. Accent is a surprising amount of vocal familiarity. "New way of saying hello, huh?"

She looked at me and screamed again. Then her eyes rolled back in her head and she hit the floor with a thump, dropping her machete in the process. Luckily for both of us, it fell harmlessly to one side rather than impaling her.

"Elsie?" I said. "Elsie? You all right over there?"

She didn't respond, not even to groan. Right. I'd never been decapitated before, and was a little surprised that it had worked, given that I'd only been semi-tangible when I was leaning through the door, but it was neither the worst nor the weirdest thing that had ever happened to me. I tried to think of what might solve the problem, beyond Elsie and a big roll of duct tape, closed my eyes, and dropped myself down into the twilight.

As always, the twilight was the manifestation of the most-loved and treasured aspects of the living area it mirrored. For this part of Portland, that meant it was largely a forest, with a few buildings dotted here and there among the towering trees. There were more buildings in the downtown area, where most of the local ghosts "lived" for lack of a better word: they spent their time and did their business there. It was a large-enough metro area, as cities in the twilight went, to have attracted a Dullahan: Declan Mark, a practicing doctor and dissector of corpses.

Dullahan are strange. They're not dead, because they were never alive. They arise from somewhere deeper than the twilight. Most people think they're from the starlight, since they're nonhuman intelligences. I think they're from all the way down in the midnight, arising from the level that gives birth to so many human nightmares. I've never been friendly enough with one of them to get away with asking.

As I had hoped, I appeared in the twilight back in one piece, although I was now flat on my stomach in the ghost of the loam that had existed here before the house's foundations were poured.

I pushed myself back to my feet and dusted the debris off my stomach before reaching up to cautiously feel my throat. There was no seam in my flesh or other sign that I had just done my best Anne Boleyn impression, which was a pleasant thing to have confirmed. Having never been decapitated before, I hadn't been sure.

I crossed my arms and firmly nodded my head in my best impression of the titular character from *I Dream of Jeannie*, a sitcom almost as old as I am but substantially more dated, and the twilight fell away, leaving me once more standing in Elsie's bedroom. Where Elsie was still flat on the floor in a dead faint. I checked her pulse. She had one, and she was breathing; both of those were good things, given the alternatives.

Signs of life verified, I picked up her machete and put it gently on the bed, where she wouldn't flail around and hurt herself as she woke up. With this accomplished, I sat down cross-legged on the floor to wait for her to open her eyes.

It took a while. I had time to mentally review the events of the day, then the events at Penton Hall, and then a full circuit of "Rattlin' Bog," from the tree in the bog all the way to the submolecular parallel dimension contained in the mote of dust on the feather on a little bird's wing. I was getting ready to loop the song back in on itself when Elsie groaned and began to stir.

I stopped my silent recitation and held perfectly still, giving her the time to finish waking and sit up. When she did, I raised one hand in a small wave. "Hi," I said.

Elsie screamed again.

"Catch a bubble, please," I said, in my most authoritative voice. I was quietly gratified when she promptly snapped her mouth shut, cutting off the scream, and just stared at me. Somehow, despite multiple screams, neither her father nor her brother had come rushing to see what was going on. That was oddly less surprising than the absence of the mice. I would have expected at least part of Elsie's congregation to come charging in by now.

"It's time to be calm, friend, and stop yelling," I said. "Can you do that for me?"

Eyes still wide and glossy with shock, Elsie nodded. I smiled.

"Good girl," I said. "You can pop your bubble now."

Elsie exhaled, then asked, quickly, before I could tell her to be quiet again, "Are you really Mary? If you're not Mary, you need to tell me."

"I don't think that's a rule a hostile spirit is going to listen to, Elsie," I said patiently. "But yes, I'm really Mary. I'm sorry I was gone for so long. I didn't mean to be."

Her mouth dropped open as she stared at me. "I thought you were . . . Antimony and Sarah took you away, and then they came back without you, and I thought . . . Don't you *ever* do that again, do you understand me? You're not allowed to scare me like that!"

"I didn't mean to scare anyone," I said. "I was doing what I could to help the family. We needed to stop the Covenant."

"We still need to stop the Covenant," she said, grimly. "They're still out there hurting people. The man who killed my mother is still out there. Blowing up Penton Hall didn't stop him."

"No, it wouldn't have," I said, quietly. "Elsie, I never told you how sorry I was about what happened."

"Did you see her at all? After she died? You said she wasn't coming back, but did you see her, or did you just guess that she was gone when you couldn't find her?"

"I saw her," I said, keeping my voice soft. "She didn't have any unfinished business."

"She had *me*," said Elsie stridently. "She had her *daughter*. Or was I not important enough to stick around for?"

"We've talked about the rules that govern ghosts enough that you know that isn't how any of this works, Elsie," I said. "If children were enough to bind unquiet spirits to the world, no parents would ever move on to whatever comes next. She didn't have the kind of unfinished business that would define a haunting, and so she chose to go, rather than staying and fading into a whisper on the wind and a cold patch in the hall."

"But I wasn't ready for her to leave me."

"No one ever is, baby. I'm dead, and I wasn't ready for her to leave me, either."

Elsie sniffled, and the first tears rolled down her cheeks, fat and round and obviously too long in coming. "I hate this. I hate it so much. Why do *I* have to lose my mother? I already lost my brother, and Dad may as well not be here with Mom gone. He's just . . . It's like he's gone inside himself and slammed the door."

"He's Lilu, and she was a remarkable woman," I said. "I don't think he ever had to question whether or not she was with him because of his pheromones. You know how rare that is."

"I do," Elsie admitted, sniffling. "I wish I didn't, but I do. Sometimes I wish she hadn't been willing to marry an incubus."

"But if she hadn't, I wouldn't have you, and I'd be so much poorer for your absence," I said.

Elsie mustered a wan smile. "You have to say that. You're my babysitter."

"Your babysitter who you *decapitated*," I said. "Since when are you in the habit of assaulting anyone who knocks?"

"Since my mother died and my brother started unraveling like a badly programmed chatbot, and my babysitter—the dead woman, who was supposed to be indestructible and never, ever leave me for any reason, ever—went and got herself blown up on a mission with the same woman who broke my brother," said Elsie. "I felt like I needed to get a little more aggressive about self-defense, and I still haven't seen anything to indicate that I was wrong. I'm sorry about the whole head thing. You startled me."

"And I guess if you thought I was gone, no one would be sticking their head through your door on a regular basis," I allowed. "Rose maybe."

"Not so much. Since she's gone and gotten herself promoted

to Fury, she doesn't have as much time to just drop by and bother us. Even if she did, she's solid by default a lot more when she's interacting with the land of the living, and she tries not to be an asshole. Pretending to be you when she knows I'm grieving your loss would qualify."

"You knew I wasn't Rose because acting like me would have made her an asshole, and she isn't an asshole, got it," I said.

Elsie shrugged. "So Rose isn't going to be imitating your voice and coming into my room without an invitation."

"In that case, you can stop apologizing," I said. "Just please don't cut my head off again. That was very startling, and I didn't like it."

"Deal." Elsie looked at me, eyes wide and bright with unshed tears. "Are you really here?"

"Really-really," I said. I shifted position to kneel rather than sitting flat on the floor, and opened my arms, inviting her in for a hug. "I was injured about as badly as a ghost can be injured, but not so badly that the anima mundi couldn't put me together again, and now I'm back, and I'm not leaving my family any time soon."

Elsie all but threw herself into my embrace, wrapping her arms tightly around me. I was suddenly, painfully grateful that the anima mundi had returned my control over my solidity. I could tell from the way she shook as she clung to me just how desperately she had needed this hug, and I was glad to be able to oblige.

When she finally let me go, her eyes were still bright, but her cheeks were wet, the tears she'd been threatening having finally managed to fall. She wiped her face with one hand as she sat back, and laughed unsteadily. "Sorry," she said. "Not very cool of me."

"Who told you I cared if you were 'cool'?" I asked. "I don't need you to be 'cool.' Never have, never will."

"But . . ." She caught herself, stopping.

"But what?" I asked.

"Antimony's cool."

"Annie's more than moderately terrifying," I said. "She's prob-ably the culmination of all the traits the Covenant was breeding for when they introduced your grandmother's grandparents." That was easier than trying to get the number of "greats" correct, and it got my point across all the same.

Elsie laughed, but I wasn't kidding. The Covenant of St. George has many appalling qualities, and one of them is the tendency to treat their members like show dogs, pairing them according to a vast and complicated breeding program that's supposed to eventually get them the best possible field operatives. Annie was smart, ruthless, physically skilled, and a sorcerer—all things that made her absolutely deadly in the field, and would have made her an incredible asset for the other side if she hadn't been so dedi-cated to the family cause. And then she'd gone and fallen in love with a cryptid, a therianthropic shapeshifter who spent as little time passing for human as he could get away with.

The Covenant was never going to lure her away from us now, not with Sam in the picture, and I'd be lying if I said I wasn't grateful for that.

"She's still cool," said Elsie stubbornly.

"And this matters why?"

"You spent so much more time with her than you did with me when we were kids." She shrugged. "I always just figured you liked her better because she was cool, and if I could be cool, you'd choose me instead."

I blinked. "Oh, sweetheart, no. It was never about her being cooler than you. It was always down to age. I'm the babysitter. I focus on the youngest children because they need me more. That's the only reason."

"But you stayed focused on her even after she was as grown up as the rest of us."

"Because reaching adulthood didn't change the fact that she was the youngest in your generation, and I needed to keep babysitting if I didn't want the crossroads to start pulling me away even more than they already did. Besides, I thought you liked it when I gave you space. Weren't you the one who was always trying to chase me away when I tried to babysit?"

"Yeah, but I didn't, I didn't *mean* it!" she said, almost in a wail.

"Oh, *Elsie*," I said. "I'm so sorry, sweetheart. I'm here now."

"But there are babies who need you now, and that means you're just going to leave me again. You always, always leave me again."

"I guess that's true," I allowed. "I *do* need to focus on raising the new generation of chaos generators, as soon as I'm done with this little job the anima mundi assigned to me."

Elsie perked up. "Little job? What do you need to do?"

"I'm supposed to head for the East Coast and make the Covenant stop hunting ghosts."

Elsie's smile was neither gentle nor kind. "That sounds like my sort of party. You looking for backup?"

I paused. "I came here to see if I could find someone who'd drive with me. I could ghost-blip myself over there like that, but I wouldn't be able to carry any equipment or do any prep. You have a car, right?"

"I sure do," affirmed Elsie. "I'm a pretty good driver, too. No accidents since I got my license. You really want me, not Annie or Uncle Kevin or something?"

"I want the Ghostbusters, but I don't think they really exist, and real-life ghost hunters aren't usually inclined to work with my sort of person," I said. "I wasn't expecting you to volunteer. I'd be happy to have you. You have to do me two favors, though."

"What?"

"You have to tell your father, and you have to tell your brother."

Elsie frowned. "Why are those separate favors?"

"Because I don't think you're going to be able to get them into the same room."

Elsie considered this for a moment, and then nodded. "All

right," she said, bouncing back to her feet. "Dad's up in his room. I'll go tell him now."

Then she was off, bustling out of the room. I waited until she was gone, then cocked my head and vanished in turn, off to update my current employer.

✦ ✦ ✦

The anima mundi wasn't in the grain for once. I looked around, finally spotting a low farmhouse in the distance. A porch wrapped around the outside, unscreened and open to the twilit air. There, in a rough-hewn rocking chair, was the anima mundi.

I flickered out and reappeared next to them on the porch. "Nice evening," I said.

"They always are, when they're not too hot," they replied. "We're guessing you're here to give us an update on what you've been doing with yourself?"

"Something like that," I agreed. "Elsie's going to go to Boston with me. She's Antimony's cousin. You haven't met her yet."

"And you think she can help?"

"She's field-trained like any other member of the family, she's half-Lilu, and she's one of the better social butterflies I know," I said. "She can manage this. Her mother died recently, and she has a lot of aggression to work out."

"Excellent. We look forward to hearing of your progress."

"About that . . ." I looked up at the sky rather than directly at the anima mundi. "It's going to take about a week for Elsie to drive from Portland to the East Coast, and longer after that for us to get wherever we're supposed to be. Is there any chance you could send us a routewitch to make things go a little faster, maybe?"

"Are you too good to cross our distances at a normal rate?"

"Not at all. You just seemed to want this done quickly, and a week of driving before we can even get started isn't 'quickly.'"

"Can you not ask a family member closer to your destination?"

I paused to think about the family members who could fit that description. "No," I said, after a moment's contemplation. "I couldn't. Verity's not available for right now, and Alice and Thomas need to stay uninvolved in case she needs them. Sally isn't doing fieldwork yet. And Alex and Shelby are taking care of two children under five. There's really not anyone closer."

The anima mundi gave me a measuring, narrow-eyed look. "I feel you might have allies you're choosing not to call upon."

"I might," I agreed. "But they're not family the way Elsie and the others are, which makes it harder for me to just go to where they are. Unless you want to broaden that restriction?"

"No," they said, without hesitation. "You need to be restricted, Mary Dunlavy, and you need to adjust to the idea that you always will be, from this point forward. Begin your journey with the girl you say will aid you. We will send someone to assist you, when the time is right."

That seemed to be as good as I was going to get right now. I nodded quickly, and blipped back to Elsie's room—or tried to, anyway. Nothing happened.

I turned back to the anima mundi, hoping the look on my face would be sufficient to communicate my confusion. They looked calmly back at me.

"You cannot keep coming to us asking for favors, Mary Dunlavy," they said. "We have extended you the greatest favor we are capable of granting, by allowing you to resume your frivolous ways. You are an expense we do not need, going forward, and you would do well to remember that."

"I do," I said, as sincerely as I could manage. "I know I'm not something vital to keeping the world turning. But I'm something vital to my family, and I hope you'll remember that, while you're making decisions about what to do with me."

"We would say that the needs of a single family are insufficiently strong to stay our hand, were it not for the one who saved us," said the anima mundi gravely. "If you see Antimony, be sure to give her our regards, and remember, it is only out of our debt to her that we are willing to fund your ongoing existence."

I was abruptly back in Elsie's room, which was still oddly devoid of mice. I frowned and went snooping while Elsie was off notifying her father of our plan.

The mouseholes behind the bed had been stopped up with plaster and caulk. It was an inexpert repair, but it was sufficient to make the barrier obvious. At some point in the past six months, she'd decided to hang the "keep out" signs on her private space. That was unsettling. In all my time dealing with the Prices, I had never known one of them to shut the mice out so completely. Get frustrated by them, yes. Exile them, no. Never in a million years.

I tapped the plaster. It made a dull *thunk* sound, clearly thick enough that the mice weren't going to break through by mistake. The fact that they hadn't broken through already meant she must have negotiated some sort of temporary restriction on their presence. That, too, was unprecedented, and I didn't entirely like it.

I sat down on the edge of the bed, then flopped over backward, folding my hands behind my head. This wasn't the outcome I'd been expecting when I popped over to Portland—if anything, I'd come by the house as a courtesy, so Elsie and Artie could honestly say that they'd been invited and chosen to stay home before I went and got some of the more action-oriented cousins. I hadn't anticipated that Elsie would be this eager to get payback for her mother, or how much having her come along would complicate things.

I couldn't invite Annie to join us—not when she'd been there to witness Jane's death without being able to stop it, and not when Elsie so clearly resented her for it. This wasn't going to be easier if my backup was fighting the whole time, and depending on how much of the drive we had to make according to normal physics, there might be a long time for things to be harder than I wanted them to be.

The door banged open and Elsie came bounding back into the room, hauling a mid-sized suitcase with her. "He's not thrilled, but he's not going to try to stop me," she announced, tossing the suitcase onto the bed. She flipped it open and bounced across the room to start yanking out dresser drawers and throwing fistfuls of clothing, toiletries, and weapons into the open case. It was a ridiculous jumble. I sat up to watch her.

"How many knives do you think you're going to *need*?"

"Either one more than I have, or all of them," she said. "I'm aiming for the option where I'm not caught under-armed in the middle of a fight." She produced a handgun from the bottom of the drawer and placed it in the suitcase, then moved to unlock the safe in the wall next to it and start pulling out boxes of bullets. "Are we going to be fighting any ghosts?"

"I hope not, but right now, I can't say for sure what we're going to be up against," I said. "Covenant operatives, definitely. What else, I have no real idea."

"Check," she said, and tossed what looked like a spirit jar into the suitcase.

"Elsie."

"Yeah?"

"Why do you have a spirit jar?"

She must have caught the unhappiness in my tone, because she paused and looked at me. "You said the Covenant's been hunting these ghosts on the East Coast."

"Yes."

"And could these ghosts have had friends?"

"I don't know. Maybe." If I was being completely honest, I'd never spent all that much time with more-ordinary hauntings. They didn't tend to like crossroads ghosts very much for some reason—probably related to the fact that "can you let me talk to my dead relative of choice" was one of the more common requests the crossroads asked me to arbitrate, which could result in *more* hauntings as the person who'd made the bargain withered and died or committed suicide—and when I was doing my other job, I didn't have a lot of time for a social death. Maybe stationary haunts had friends and communities, and maybe they didn't. Her guess was as good as mine.

"If they did, they might not be too happy right now, which means I want to be at least minimally armed against grumpy ghosts who have no good reason to like the living very much, if that's cool by you." She added a pair of brass knuckles and a skin care kit that looked to have been modified to include a tiny hammer to her suitcase, then started stuffing things down and adjusting them to guarantee that it would zip. "Don't worry, I'm not going to bottle you up for later consumption."

"Ha ha," I said, still uncomfortable. "See how chill you are when I start painting sigils to contain succubi on everything."

"We both know those don't work."

"Yeah, but spirit jars *do.* And don't think I didn't notice how you danced around telling me why you had the thing to begin with." This seemed like as good a time as any. "Hey, Elsie—why are the mice locked out of your room? And why did they think you were at roller derby practice when you were in your room?"

It was her turn to look deeply, profoundly uncomfortable. "Can we not talk about that right now?" She hoisted her suitcase, then moved toward the door. "It's bad enough that there were a couple in Dad's room, so they know I'm leaving."

"Elsie, did something happen with the mice?"

"No." She paused with her hand on the bedroom door. "Yes.

I don't know. They're just being the mice, I guess, and I can't be too mad at them for that—they are the way they are, always have been, and it's silly of me to expect them to change."

"This is about them not letting your mother's theology go into the archives, isn't it?"

Elsie nodded, not looking at me. "She's dead. She's gone. If I can't have her back, they sure as hell can't keep her, and I wish they'd just let her go. Does that make sense?"

"It does, sweetheart," I said. "You want to grieve, and they keep acting like she's still alive."

"That's exactly it. How am I supposed to start moving on when they keep acting like she's going to come home tomorrow and tell them all the things they've missed? It sucks. I don't want them coming around me telling me what my mother would want me to do. She was *my* mother, not theirs. They need to get over themselves and let us all have a little peace."

"Sounds like getting out of here will be good for you."

She laughed, bitterly. "Honestly, you have no idea."

She left the room then, and I followed her downstairs and through the kitchen to the garage, where she popped the trunk of her car and loaded her suitcase inside, one-handed. Elsie had always been good about doing her upper-body workouts. Something about how all the girls she found attractive appreciated a well-toned bicep.

Then she walked around to the driver's side door, opened it, and froze.

"No," she said, in a voice that had gone suddenly stony and cold. "You were not invited. Get out."

"I was invited," said Artie—sorry, Arthur—from the back seat. He sounded utterly reasonable, like he'd been working on this argument for a while. "Mary came to see me first, and told me she had to go to the East Coast to fight the Covenant. I'm a Price, too. I should get to fight the Covenant before I come apart at the seams."

Elsie shot me a pleading look. "And see, he *says* shit like this, like, all the time," she said. "It's almost as bad as the damn mice."

"Arthur." I bent down and stuck my head inside the car. "What do you think you're doing? This is a serious mission, buddy."

"And I'm serious about coming with you." He looked at me placidly. "I'm not a child, you know. I'm a legal adult. And this is something the mice told me Artie never did. He didn't like field-work. He never went voluntarily. The only time he did anything remotely dangerous was when he was trying to save Sarah." His voice cracked on her name, longing and anger intermixed.

"We're not saving Sarah this trip," said Elsie. "We're not going anywhere near her, so if this is some messed-up way of getting a look at her, it's not going to work."

"*No,*" snapped Arthur. "I'm coming with you because I'm a Price, and this is my heritage. And because I can feel myself crumbling away, a little bit more every day. I wasn't built to last. I want to *do* something before there isn't anything left of me."

"Where do you think you're going, buddy?" I asked, gently.

"I'm not *going* anywhere. I'm just . . . dissolving, like cotton candy in water. It's the weirdest sensation. I don't dream any-more." Arthur looked at me and shrugged. "I'm hoping if I go and do something I don't share with Artie, that he doesn't taint for me, it'll give me something I can hold onto. A memory I know for sure belongs to *me,* and wasn't originally a memory of him."

"You'd need clothes," said Elsie. I could tell from her tone that it was a pro forma objection, one last attempt to keep him off of our road trip.

Arthur responded by hoisting the duffel bag he'd placed on the seat beside himself, and flashing her a wide, toothy grin. "Way ahead of you," he said.

Elsie sighed and slid into the car, getting herself situated in the driver's seat. "You better not make me regret this," she said sternly.

"I'll do my best," said Arthur.

I vanished, reappearing in the passenger seat, where I fastened my seatbelt and leaned back. "Time to hit the road," I said.

Elsie started the car and we were off.

Seven

"If life is a highway, I'm not paying a single toll until somebody gets down here and fixes all these damn potholes. This is shitty road maintenance."

—Rose Marshall

Pulling into Columbus, Ohio
Two days later

Two days in a car with the Harrington-Price siblings was a lot less annoying than I'd expected it to be, probably because all my ideas of how the trip would go were based off riding with Elsie and Artie, and I was riding with Elsie and *Arthur*. Almost but not entirely different. Elsie still fell back on some old habits when it came to dealing with her brother, even though he could make a legitimate argument for being a completely different person now than he'd been on their younger road trips.

So she argued when he wasn't doing anything, just to keep herself awake during the night drives. She refused to let him take a turn behind the wheel. She kept control of the radio like she might die if she heard a single note of whatever he was into these days. And Arthur just took it.

If there'd been any question in my mind as to whether he was exaggerating how bad it was inside his head, it was answered by the end of the first day, when he hadn't pushed back against her once. The Artie I knew wasn't particularly argumentative, but he had opinions, and he would have been making them heard, not just riding passively along in the back seat, trusting his sister to get us wherever we were supposed to be going.

Weirdly enough, Arthur was only the second strangest thing about the trip so far. The absolute strangest was the total lack of mice. Elsie was fighting with them, and Arthur had intentionally not invited any, wanting to enjoy this trip on his own terms and without anyone telling him what he had or hadn't supposedly said in the past. So it was just the three of us riding along until we reached Ohio and angled toward Columbus, where the prospect of a hot shower, a decent meal, and one of the only uncomplicated family reunions we had available to us awaited.

Ted had been calling daily to make sure his kids were still alive, but he hadn't sounded nearly as interested in the answer as I would have expected him to be, given that we hadn't informed him before taking off with Arthur. Both his kids were gone, and he was still just flat, vocally and emotionally. It was sort of terrifying.

Losing Jane had broken more than a few hearts, and we were going to be seeing the damage echo through our family for a long time to come. I guess every death is like that. No matter how much warning you have, how much time you have to prepare, death changes things, and even if the dead linger, it's never going to be the same. It never could be.

Elsie turned down an ordinary, almost generic-looking suburban street, driving deeper into the heart of the city. Houses passed us on all sides, painted the same six HOA-approved shades of blue, gray, and beige. Lawns still gleamed green, spattered here and there with jeweled dustings of fallen leaves. Ohio was so much better at a dramatic autumn than Oregon was. They really understood how to do fall and frost there.

Of course, nothing would ever beat Michigan, where I'd been alive and young and free to run through the fallen leaves, letting them crunch underfoot, unaware of just how sharp and temporary my senses were. There's nothing in this world like being alive. It's why even knowing ghosts endure after death isn't a good enough reason to give up on living.

"Everything here looks like it came out of a 3-D printer owned by a model train enthusiast," complained Elsie.

"That's very specific," I said. "A for effort, even as you're edging closer to coastal smugness than I like. If you say the words 'flyover state' in any sort of tone that implies you mean it, I will wash your mouth out with soap."

"Yes, ma'am," said Elsie.

"What's a flyover state?" asked Arthur.

I gave his reflection in the rearview mirror a hard look, and found nothing there to indicate that he was kidding. "It's a nasty thing people on the coasts say about people in the middle of the country," I said. "Like 'oh, that place doesn't matter, it's just a fly-over state.' Meaning a state you fly over in order to get somewhere important. It's a mean, shitty thing to say, and I like to think I helped to raise you both better than to think like that."

"I don't know whether you raised me at all," said Arthur. "But I feel like you're right, and that's not something you should say about the places where people live."

"I didn't," said Elsie, sounding chastened. "I just said it looked 3-D-printed. That's not the same thing as saying anything bad about Ohio. I don't like cookie-cutter suburbs. We have them in Oregon, too."

"All right," I said, and indicated a house up ahead of us on the right. "That's them. We're here."

Elsie pulled up to the curb and stopped the car, getting out faster than I would have thought possible. She stretched lan-guidly, linking her hands above her head, before slamming her door and shoving the car keys into her pocket. Arthur got out more slowly, moving with the cautious slowness I had come to recognize as his way of approaching entirely new situations.

"Have I been here before?" he asked, voice low.

"A few times, when you were much younger," I said. "Sarah lived here for most of the year until she graduated high school, and you used to come out and visit during the summer." Not that Sarah had attended an in-person high school. Virtual and home schooling had been safer for her and everyone else involved. It had allowed her to get an education without accidentally rewriting the histories of the people around her to make herself the most popular girl on campus—not a position she would have enjoyed very much to begin with.

Since Sarah hadn't been able to socialize much with her peers, Angela and Martin had been overjoyed to have her cousins over during the summers, giving her people roughly her own age to spend time with. And when it hadn't been possible for the cousins to come to Ohio, they'd gladly sent Sarah to Oregon, keeping her in touch with her social group.

"Ah," said Arthur, sounding disappointed. "Is Sarah here now?"

"No. She's in Michigan with Alice and Thomas."

His disappointment grew, becoming visible. "Oh. I hoped she'd be here so I could see her."

"Well, I'm glad she's not," said Elsie. "I might not be able to resist smacking her for what she did to you, and I don't think that would end well for me."

"No, probably not," I said. "You both ready?"

They nodded, and I started toward the house, letting them follow along at their own pace.

I was halfway up the walk when the door banged open and a tan blonde woman with an almost-funereal expression stepped out onto the porch, a cherubic-looking little girl propped against her hip. Charlotte was six years old, and in the middle of that growth stage where she became all arms and legs and huge blue eyes, gangly as a colt. She was wearing a West Columbus Zoo sweatshirt with a ring-tailed lemur on the front, and staring at me like she'd just seen, well, a ghost.

Shelby's expression wasn't much different. Like mother, like daughter. "Mary?" she said, Australian accent flattening the syllables of my name like a butterfly pressed between two sheets of glass. "Is that really you?"

"It's really me," I said.

"Can't be," she said, setting Charlotte on her feet. "Mary didn't come back from England. If something had changed, surely you would have called and told us. Alex was in bits."

"I mean, technically, I was the one in bits," I said. "But yeah, it's really me." Elsie and Arthur were getting closer, coming up the walkway with slow, careful steps. "Can we come in?"

"Aunt Mary?" asked Charlotte. Her voice was high and piping, with just a trace of her mother's accent mixed in with the Midwestern tones she was learning from everything around her. It was oddly charming as a combination.

"Yes, sweetie," I said, and flickered myself, vanishing from where I stood and reappearing right behind her.

Like any good girl who'd been babysat by a ghost since she was born, she squealed and whipped around to hug my upper legs. I ruffled her hair with one hand.

"Did you get like a foot taller in the last six months?" I asked.

"She's growing like it's her job," said Shelby. She was taller than most of the Healy women I'd known, which made sense, since she was a Tanner. As far as I knew, she had yet to marry into the family, although Charlotte was probably a lot more binding than a wedding ring. "You going to tell me how you're here?"

"Not until we have everyone together," I said. "I don't really feel like going over the whole story eight more times."

"You'd top out at four," she said, amiably, and turned her attention to Elsie and Arthur. "Oi! You two look like hammered shit. What have you been doing?"

"Driving, mostly," said Elsie. "We just got in from Portland."

"And you drove?" Shelby raised an eyebrow. "That's a bit of an undertaking. Someone trying to murder you?"

"No, but we're on a job," said Arthur, trying to sound professional and serene, and not like he was talking to someone he couldn't remember ever meeting before. "Mary needed help dealing with a Covenant outpost in Boston."

"That's simplified," I said quickly. "We're looking into some Covenant ghost hunters operating somewhere between Boston and the *other* Portland. We'll have to find them before we can 'deal with them.'"

"Hoping the ghosts they didn't hunt yet will lend you a hand?" asked Shelby.

I nodded, finally letting go of Charlotte and straightening up. Charlotte responded by squeezing my leg like a boa constrictor trying to keep hold of dinner. "Hey, sweetie, can you let go before you cut off circulation?" I didn't actually have circulation anymore, but encouraging her to hug me hard enough to hurt would only mean she'd have trouble hugging other people later in life. We learned that lesson with Kevin, the hard way. It took him years to stop hurting people when he was just trying to show affection.

Charlotte replied by shaking her head and burying it against my side, covering her face. I looked to Shelby. "Still not talking much, is she?"

"Not really. She and Isaac have everything they need without using their outside voices more than absolutely necessary, so why should they bother? We've been working on Lottie, trying to get her to understand that she'll eventually want to talk to people outside the house, but we haven't quite managed to get her there yet." Shelby sighed, looking put-upon. "Since Isaac won't be old enough for kindergarten until next fall, we've decided to hold her back and send them together. It's not perfect, and it doesn't help to get her over her dependence on him, but it means they're more likely to go without tantrums, and doesn't leave us with a preadolescent telepath having a fit because we've taken his sister away."

"Poor buddy," I said.

Shelby rolled her eyes. "Poor all of us. You lot want to come inside? Alex is at the zoo, but he'll be back in an hour or so."

"Don't take this the wrong way, but I would legitimately give you a kidney in exchange for the use of your shower," said Elsie.

"Oh? Whose?" asked Shelby.

"Dealer's choice," said Elsie.

Shelby laughed and stepped to the side, letting the rest of us get to the door. Not that I could exactly walk with Charlotte still latched on to my leg the way she was. I looked mournfully down at her as Elsie and Arthur walked inside.

"Hey, kiddo," I said. "I know I was gone a long while, and that wasn't very fair of me. I didn't mean to be gone for so long, I swear. And now that I'm back, I'm going to be doing my very best never to be gone that long again."

Charlotte pulled her face away long enough to give me a mistrustful look.

"I'll still have to go sometimes," I said. "Olivia's younger than you and Isaac are, and her mommy is expecting a new baby soon; she's going to need my help. But I'll still be here when you need me, and when your parents want to have a night out to themselves. I'm not going to go away the way I did before."

Charlotte frowned, deeply. "Six *months*," she said.

For her, that was a speech. "Yes," I agreed. "I was gone for six months, but I'm not going to be gone for six months again, and your cousins are here. Don't you want to go in the house and see Arthur and Elsie while they're visiting? I bet your mommy is a lot like their mommy, and brings out the specialest treats when there's company, especially *family* company."

"I'm six years old."

I stopped to blink at her, trying to figure out why this was the message important enough to deliver out loud. "Yes, sweetie, you are."

But Charlotte wasn't finished: "You were gone one month for *every year.*"

This was apparently the greatest offense the world had ever known. "I'm so sorry, and it won't happen again," I said. It wasn't really a surprise that a child growing up surrounded by cuckoos would fixate on the numbers. Johrlac are the greatest mathematicians in all reality. Math comes as easily to them as breathing.

I crouched to put myself on eye level with Charlotte, and looked at her gravely. "I wasn't gone six months because I wanted to be," I said. "I didn't have a choice. I got hurt in a special, bad way that only ghosts can be hurt, and it took six months for me to heal enough that I could come back to you. I'm not going to do the thing that hurt me again, so you don't have to be afraid I'll go away for so long."

Charlotte seemed to consider this for a long, solemn moment. Then she nodded, blonde curls flying, and turned to run back into the house, presumably in search of either her mother or the special treats I had essentially promised her.

The anger of a child is rarely strong enough to hold up to the lure of cookies, and thank Persephone for that. I straightened, tugging my shirt back into position, and vanished, reappearing in the kitchen, where Elsie and Arthur were seated at the breakfast table while Shelby set a platter of cookies and large mugs of coffee in front of them. Half the table was covered in paperwork, probably from Angela's accounting business, while the other half was cluttered with sippy cups and plastic cutlery. Shelby glanced over as I reappeared, attention attracted by the flicker of motion, and smiled.

"Time for a change of clothes, eh?" she asked.

I blinked and looked down at myself. My former outfit had been replaced by purple leggings and a *Goblin Market* sweatshirt, which caused me to look back up at Shelby. "Really, still?" I asked. "I thought she'd be all about *Frozen* by now."

"No longer the unifying passion of the preschool set, and Isaac picked up on how much Sarah loved the Lowry stuff, and passed it on to Lottie," she said, matter-of-factly.

If Charlotte hadn't been Alex Price's daughter and thus part Kairos, giving her a degree of natural resistance to cuckoo telepathic influence, I would have worried about Isaac overwriting her preferences with his own. As it was, I knew she was just a kid choosing to enjoy things she could share with her brother and best friend.

Charlotte came thundering down the hall into the kitchen. "Mom! Mary said—" She stopped as she saw the cookies, eyes going very wide and bright. "CanIhaveacookie?" It was all one word, which was more than reasonably impressive.

"It's a special occasion, so yes, you can have a cookie," said Shelby magnanimously.

I suppose I should have anticipated what happened next.

Charlotte rocketed to the table and grabbed the largest cookie she could reach, shoving it into her mouth. She made a happy humming sound as she bit down, and Shelby turned back to me.

"You need to visit more often," she said. "She never talks this much."

"I have that effect on kids," I said, mildly.

Which was when the screaming started.

It came from upstairs, high and breathless, the sound of a child waking from a terrible nightmare. I blinked out without even thinking about it, reappearing in Isaac's room a beat later. There was only one bed; at some point in the past six months, Alex and Shelby had managed to convince the children they should have their own rooms. The walls were the usual mix of educational posters, family pictures, and brightly colored cartoon characters, some of which I recognized, while others were new to me.

Sitting up in the bed, clutching the covers to his chest like a debutante in a horror movie, was Isaac. Like all cuckoos, he was so pale as to seem almost unhealthy, the living definition of "porcelain skin," with jet-black hair and crystalline blue eyes. It was a beautiful combination, if you could get past the part where it belonged to a giant telepathic wasp that just happened to look like a human being. Evolution is a harsh mistress. She knows the shapes she likes making, and she makes them over and over and over again.

On a terrestrial level, that means crabs, beetles, and weasels. On a pan-dimensional level, it means those things, plus snakes and bipeds. Evolution really, really seems to like making things that are almost, if not completely, indistinguishable from humans.

Isaac was a things, in this context. So were Elsie and Arthur, being a mixture of human, Lilu, and Kairos. God forbid any member of this family should ever try to use one of those DNA ancestry sites. They'd cause the whole database to corrupt itself.

Isaac wasn't just wailing. He was weeping, huge, crystalline tears running down his cheeks and dripping off his chin. His eyes and nose weren't getting red from all the crying, which was just another sign of his biological origins: he didn't have blood in the way mammals do. Instead, he had a form of hemolymph, clear and thick and a perfect biological antiseptic. Cuckoo blood is one of the best tools a field medic can possibly have in their kit.

He turned toward me as I appeared, letting go of the blankets and reaching for me with both hands. "Hey, buddy," I said, walking over to sit down on the edge of the bed and let him come closer if he wanted to. "What's the matter?"

Isaac wailed again and burrowed against me. He reminded me of a much younger child when he did that, and I wondered—not for the first time—whether we'd done him a disservice by placing him in a home with another child his own age who was naturally inclined to accept his telepathy. He and Charlotte had set up a feedback loop almost as soon as they'd been introduced, and while both of them were thriving in areas like reading, writing, and being able to do simple math problems, they had also been slow to speak, and even slower to associate with other children. Even adults could have trouble breaking into their closed-circuit relationship.

"I'm not Lottie, sweetheart," I said. "I need you to use your words."

Isaac sniffled again, and finally said, in a small, clear voice, "There's a monster."

"Aw, buddy, monsters are so scary when you don't know them, aren't they? But we can make friends with a lot of monsters, and find out what their real names are, so they won't be so scary anymore. Remember your Uncle Drew? A lot of people think he's a monster, just because he's a bogeyman and they don't know how nice bogeymen can be. Is this monster under the bed? Or in the closet?"

Not for a moment did I think he could be talking about an actual monster in his room. A lot of cryptids are called monsters by people who don't know any better. So are a lot of types of ghost. I'm sure a few people have called me a monster in their day. But this house had excellent security, and the chances of something dangerous sneaking past Shelby were very slim.

"No," he said, and tilted his head back so that he could look at me, tears still rolling down his cheeks, eyes very grave. "The monster's downstairs in the kitchen, with Char. I don't want it there. I don't want it to hurt Char. I don't *want* it."

I blinked. There hadn't been any monsters in the kitchen when I'd been there. "What kind of monster, Zachy?"

"A bad monster. It's all cracks, like the time I dropped an egg and it broke everywhere. But someone put the egg back together with tape or something, and now it's all leaking out through the cracks in the shell."

If Charlotte's increased vocabulary had been a surprise, this was a stunning speech, possibly worthy of an Oscar. And I was dreadfully afraid I knew what it meant. I smoothed Isaac's hair back from his forehead. "It's not a monster, sweetheart. It's a member of your family. His name's Arthur, and you're not wrong about what happened to him. He got dropped like an egg, sort of, and when that happened, Sarah had to put him back together as best she could. But what she used was a lot more fragile than tape, and it's not perfect."

Isaac brightened immediately. "Sarah?" he asked. "Is Sarah here?"

"No, and don't go calling for her, either." I didn't know what the range on his telepathy was like, but I knew hers could cross incredibly large distances when she exerted herself, and we were only about five hundred miles from New York at this point. If Isaac started mentally yelling for her, she might show up. And with Elsie in the house, that could only end badly.

Isaac looked at me, lower lip wobbling in a way that promised more tears in the near future. I looked impassively back. Tears I can handle. The nuclear meltdown if Elsie was suddenly faced with Sarah on what was closer to Sarah's home turf than hers . . . that, I wasn't so sure about.

Isaac must have seen my immunity to tears in my expression, because his lip stopped wobbling and his expression turned cold in that way that only very self-possessed children can ever quite manage. It was less arrogant than it was aspiring to arrogance, like it might be really cutting if the child who wore it was just given a decade or so to practice looking witheringly displeased. I've had a lot of practice not laughing at that sort of look, and to my delight, I managed it once again as I swallowed my initial reaction.

"Did you wake up because Lottie had a cookie?"

A nod, expression thawing by a few degrees.

"Would *you* like to have a cookie? I know the one she ate was chocolate, but I bet there's some oatmeal walnut with sun-dried tomato cookies in the jar."

Cuckoos have weird taste buds—it's not just Sarah, no matter how tempting it might be to think that her passion for tomato in everything is a personal choice, rather than a function of the way her species processes Earth flavors. For Isaac, sun-dried tomato chunks baked into an oatmeal cookie were probably about the most appealing thing I could have offered.

He held his arms out, silently asking me to lift him out of the bed. I leaned over and scooped him up, noting how much bigger he was than the last time I'd seen him. With a kid on my hip, I couldn't just relocate myself to the kitchen, and so I left the room the normal, living way, one step at a time, child balanced against me with his arms around my neck and his head against my shoulder.

His grip tightened as I went down the stairs, until I felt obligated to stop and say, "It's not polite to choke people, Isaac."

He relaxed his hold on my neck, allowing me the air I didn't need.

"Thank you."

We reached the kitchen to find Elsie gone and Charlotte sitting on a puzzled-looking Arthur's lap. That was apparently the last straw for Isaac, who had been trying to hold himself together. He saw his beloved sister sitting in the lap of the monster he'd detected from his bed, and he pushed himself away from me, jumping to the ground before he rushed over to yank Charlotte down from her perch and put himself firmly between her and Arthur, glaring at Arthur with every ounce of menace he could summon into his little cuckoo face. One of the advantages of letting him bond so closely to Charlotte was finally fully apparent: he had a much more expressive face than most of the cuckoos I'd known. He was learning facial expressions from her, and he clearly understood how to put them to good use.

"*No!*" he shouted, balling his hands into fists. "You don't touch my *sister!*"

"Isaac!" said Shelby, hurrying to his side and trying to turn him away from his cousin. "That's not how we talk to our guests!"

"He's not a guests! He's a monster all up inside, where he isn't supposed to be!" Isaac allowed himself to be turned and looked at Shelby with wide, injured eyes. "Make him go away!"

"I'm so sorry, Arthur, he's not normally like this," said Shelby, holding Isaac by the shoulders as she turned to look at Arthur. Charlotte, clearly confused but not wanting to be left out, sniffled and started to cry.

That was the last straw for Arthur. He shoved his chair back as he stood, lurching away from the table like the monster we were all insisting he wasn't. "Thank you for your hospitality, Shelby," he said, and looked to me. "Tell Elsie I'll be in the car."

"Art—" began Shelby, only to cut herself off at his bitterly unhappy expression. He didn't say another word, to any of us, just pushed out of the kitchen and stormed down the hall. Isaac relaxed. Charlotte stopped crying.

The front door slammed.

"That went well," I said. "I should go after him. Shelby, when Elsie gets out of the shower, can you let her know we're outside?"

Charlotte blinked, and then started wailing again, this time while lunging at me. She grabbed hold of my thigh again, even tighter than before. We were definitely going to have a talk about circulation for normal people. "No!" she shouted. "No go!"

"Sentences, please, sweetie," I said. "How about 'I don't want you to go'?"

"No," she repeated, at a lower volume, but with the same vehemence. "Mary *stay*."

I looked at Shelby. She sighed, taking her hands off of Isaac's shoulders. He responded by mirroring Charlotte, spinning around and wrapping his arms around Shelby's hips like she was all that was tethering him to the world. "We've been working on talking to people so they can understand her," she said. "It's hard going. Isaac doesn't make it any easier, and because of the way he is, we can't even think too hard about most possible solutions."

Meaning she couldn't consider separating the pair so Charlotte couldn't rely on Isaac's telepathy anymore. That might be the only way to help Charlotte with her verbal language skills—although from the little I'd seen, the skills were perfectly present. It was just a matter of convincing her she needed to use them. "I'll see if I can come up with some answers while I'm not here," I said, then turned my attention back to Charlotte. "Your cousin Arthur had a bad accident when he was doing something really important with Sarah," I said. "He got hurt, really a lot, and the scars are where Isaac can see them."

Charlotte looked puzzled. "Grandpa is all over scars," she said. "Is Arthur like Grandpa?"

Martin Baker—her paternal great-grandfather—was a Revenant, a reanimated corpse made up of multiple formerly dead people assembled into a unified whole by a scientist with a flexible relationship to things like "scientific ethics" and "physical reality." We didn't know much about Martin's creator. He'd never been something Martin wanted to talk about. But the reanimation process left its scars, some more visible than others.

It wasn't the worst comparison, not least because Arthur as we presently knew him was also a sort of revenant. In her desperation to save the man she loved, Sarah had reassembled his mind using the memories of everyone close enough for her to reach out and touch. He was a patchwork man, and none of his thoughts or memories were originally his own. Unlike Martin, however, he wasn't content with this, and had been trying to fit back into the space he'd occupied before his accident for as long as I'd known him.

It probably didn't help that Martin had died, been reanimated, and gone off to start a whole new life, with people who'd never known him as a living man—not any part of him—while Arthur was still surrounded by his original family, many of whom were hoping, as quietly as they could manage, that he was somehow miraculously going to fix himself and turn back into the Artie we all knew and loved. More and more, it was clear that wasn't going to happen, but we'd suffered so many losses lately, it was hard not to hope.

"Arthur is a little bit like Grandpa," I said. "They have some things in common. But he's also not like Grandpa at all, and he's very sad and very sorry and very tired of people telling him that he's broken. I understand why Isaac looked at him and saw a monster, and I understand why he wouldn't want Arthur touching you, but you need to remember that Arthur isn't a monster. He's your cousin and he loves you."

Isaac, still clinging to Shelby, hiccupped and looked faintly ashamed. I glanced at Charlotte. She was wearing the exact same expression. I frowned. Was Isaac looking ashamed, or had he just managed to copy Charlotte's face when he thought it was necessary? It was impossible to say.

I stepped away from Charlotte, turning intangible so that her clutching arms passed right through my thigh, leaving me free to make my exit. She stumbled and nearly fell at the loss of my support, then looked at me, her huge blue eyes brimming over with tears.

"He's your cousin, and that means he's my responsibility," I said. "I have to make sure Arthur is all right, and that he's not so sad that it's hurting him. We can't stay any longer, not with him so sad. When Elsie finishes her shower, we'll leave for what we're on our way to do, and I'll come back when it's all finished."

"Promise?" whispered Charlotte.

"I promise," I said. Isaac was still holding on to Shelby; he started crying again as he looked at me, probably picking up on how disappointed in him I was. I'm not a Price-Healy by birth, and I don't have their resistance to cuckoo telepathy. It helps that all the cuckoos I spend time with actually *are* members of my family—they don't need to nest-parasite their way into my memories. As a ghost, my thoughts are a little fuzzy and distant for cuckoo purposes, but not being partially immune to their influence makes me easier to read. And I can't hide my disapproval.

I understood why Isaac had reacted so badly to the close sight of Arthur's mind. That didn't mean I wasn't disappointed, or that I hadn't been expecting better from him. Then again, I couldn't see what he had seen. Maybe the inside of Arthur's head was a genuine nightmare. The only adult cuckoo I could have reasonably asked was also the only person I *couldn't* ask.

Sarah would be able to tell me what Arthur looked like on the inside, but she would never voluntarily look.

I gave Charlotte one last, hopefully reassuring look and disappeared.

Eight

"We don't get to choose our beginnings or our ends. All
we get to decide on is what we do in between. And baby,
I hope you shine."

—Eloise Dunlavy

The driveway of a small home
in Columbus, Ohio

I REAPPEARED ON THE EDGE of the lawn, where the shadow
of the house would keep me from being too obvious. Not that I
was particularly concerned: there were no ghost hunters in this
area, and if the Covenant had been sniffing around again, Shelby
would have said something. Most people, when they see someone
appear out of thin air, assume there's something wrong with their
eyes before they jump to "ghosts are real."

Sometimes human stubbornness works in my favor, is what
I'm saying here. I looked around. My precautions had been for
nothing, because there was no one watching me, only Arthur
sitting miserably in the back seat of the car with his shoulders
hunched and his head bowed. Even he didn't seem to have seen
me arrive. I trotted in his direction, testing the passenger-side
door and finding it mercifully unlocked.

A locked door won't keep me out, but a locked door frequently
means the person on the other side is looking for privacy, and
I try not to be that particular flavor of asshole when I have a

choice in the matter. I opened the door and slid into the front seat, kneeling with my back to the windshield and my elbows resting on the back of the seat.

"Hey," I said.

Arthur didn't lift his head. I winced. This wasn't great.

"Hey," I tried again. This time he glanced up, just enough to meet my eyes, before looking back down again.

"Hey," he agreed, in a monotone.

"You okay, buddy?"

"I'm not your buddy," he said. "You barely know me. You remember babysitting this body, I guess, since some of the memories I'm made from tell me that you used to be in charge of me, but you don't know *me*. Don't act like you do."

"I'm sorry, Arthur. I don't mean to make you uncomfortable. And I wasn't trying to act like you're the same person you used to be. But it's hard, sometimes, not to act that way. You were built from memories of him, and as you said, I used to take care of the body you live in."

Arthur turned his face away.

"You just want Artie back," he said.

I paused. I didn't want to tell him he was right, and I didn't want to lie to him, either. But he *was* right. Artie was the kid I had helped to raise, the boy I knew and understood, the man I had been so proud to watch growing up and growing into himself. He was the one I knew, and loved, and treasured, and even though it would have meant this man disappeared forever, I would have brought Artie home in an instant. Not just for me, either. He and Sarah spent so many years dancing around each other that losing him, and losing him due to Sarah, no less, felt less like a natural ending and more like a cruel cheat inflicted by an uncaring universe.

"Arthur . . ." I said.

"You can't even lie about it, can you? You want him back, the same as everyone does, and you hate that I'm here."

"I don't," I said, carefully. "Hate that you're here, I mean. Everything changes. People come and go. I do worry sometimes that you being here means that Artie doesn't get to move on—that because you're using the same body, you're also functionally using the same soul. If that's the case, it's not fair to either of you. I do want him back, but I'd be perfectly happy to have him back and keep you around at the same time, if that were possible. But what I want doesn't matter. He's not coming back. He was erased, and you're here now, and we both need to be okay with that. I *like* you, Arthur. I like the ways you're like Artie, and I like the ways you're not like him, too. I like watching you figure out who you are."

He turned back to me, expression utterly miserable. "It doesn't really matter what I figure out. Pieces of me keep breaking off and dropping into the void, and once they're gone, they're gone forever. I know that sounds weird, but when something falls, it's not like I forgot it. It's just not there anymore. It's *gone.*"

"I don't understand."

"When you try to think about your life, you know how you don't remember every single little detail, but it feels like there's *something* in the spaces you don't remember all the way? Like going for a long walk through a familiar neighborhood, and maybe you won't see every little detail, but what you do see will be coherent enough to fill in the gaps? I don't have that anymore. I just have emptiness." He sighed, visibly frustrated. "No wonder that kid thought I was a monster. The inside of my head must look like a slaughterhouse."

"That kid is your cousin Isaac," I said.

"I've never met him before, or if I have, it happened in one of the spaces that isn't there anymore, and it's gone," he said. "But I know a cuckoo when I see one. That's something I never have to question anymore. Whether or not I see a cuckoo."

"Arthur—"

"I still love her, you know that?" His frustration faded, just a bit, replaced by miserable longing. "I love her with every part of me, because all the memories she used to make me came from people who knew her and knew Artie and knew how much they loved each other. I've talked to Annie and James, and I think I know more about growing up with Sarah than they do, because she deleted their memories of her when we crossed dimensions. She took Artie's, too, but she didn't build me from *his* memories. He was already gone when she made me. So I'm built from all the people who knew how much she loved me, and how much I loved her, and I can't outrun the love, no matter how hard I try. But she can't even stand to be around me. And when I say I love her, she says it's not real, it's just what cuckoos do to their victims, making them think they're in love when it's all just another lie." He paused then, looking at me gravely. "If the love's a lie, then everything about me is a lie, and all of me should be deleted. If I'm real, so's the way I love her, because I'm made of the same memories."

"I'm sorry, Arthur," I said softly. "This has to have been so hard on you. On all of you."

"She didn't know what she was doing when she made me," he said. "She just wanted to save someone she cared about, and she didn't know that it was too late to save him. I just wish she'd stop running away from me."

"Have you tried writing her a letter and telling her what's going on with you? She might want to know, even if she can't be in a room with you right now."

Arthur blinked at me. "Writing her a letter?"

"I'm older than your grandmother, remember? We didn't have email when I was your age—hell, I was *dead* when I was your age—and you couldn't always trust the phones. So people wrote each other letters. It's words on paper. There's nothing in them but what you put there, and no one reads anyone else's mind without meaning to. It might be a way for you to communicate with her without all that other stuff getting in the middle."

"Where would I even send it?"

"Anywhere," I said. "Here, Michigan, even to Verity in New York. As long as it's a family address, she'll get it eventually. Just don't focus too hard on needing an answer immediately and it'll work."

"I may try that," he said thoughtfully.

Outside the car, a door slammed. I twisted around to look out the windshield, and saw Elsie storming across the lawn toward us, hair wet and spiky, clearly furious. She jerked the car door open and swung in behind the wheel, slamming the door again before fastening her seatbelt. I blinked.

"Elsie?"

"Call *my* brother a monster," she muttered. "Say *my* brother doesn't belong. What the fuck ever happened to 'family before all else'?"

I flipped myself around and settled, pulling my own seatbelt on. "It's not Isaac's fault," I said. "He's just a kid."

"We were all kids once," said Elsie. "I didn't go around accusing people of being monsters."

"I know," I said soothingly.

"You okay, Art?" asked Elsie.

"I'm fine," said Arthur.

"You don't sound fine."

"I'm not fine," he admitted. "But can we get moving?"

"Sure. I've had a shower, so I'm good for another eight hours. We stopping in New York or not?"

We'd been trying to decide that almost since leaving Portland. Stopping in New York would mean dealing with a pregnant, hormonal Verity who might decide she needed to come with us. Potentially, it could also mean dealing with Sarah, and we needed to give Arthur time before we tried to force that again.

"I think straight to Boston," I said. "The anima mundi didn't say anything about the people in New York knowing anything

about the ghost hunts, and I feel like we need to get this done."
Not least because we needed to get Arthur home before he fell
apart further, and I didn't like leaving Ted alone like this.

"Got it," said Elsie, and pulled out of the driveway with a
squeal of tires that would have woken the children if they'd been
in bed, and would definitely guarantee that Shelby understood
how unhappy she was.

And once again, we were off.

✦　✦　✦

Driving with Elsie was an experience I would probably have enjoyed a lot less if I'd been alive. She drove like she wanted to get
into an argument with the very concept of traffic laws, shifting
lanes any time she felt like there was a sliver of speed to be stolen
from the world, hitting the gas like slowing down was a personal
affront. Arthur didn't seem to realize how incredibly dangerous
all this could become; he rode quietly and contentedly, humming
to himself as she assaulted the American highway system like she
resented it for not allowing her to become a routewitch.

Routewitches aren't made, they're born. It's boring determin-
istic bullshit, but that's the way the world works. No amount of
wanting to be a routewitch will make you one if you're not, and
no amount of wanting *not* to be a routewitch will save you from
the Ocean Lady if she thinks you're one of hers.

Elsie always wanted to be chosen for something. Not just a
member of her family, but something big and important that she
wouldn't have to work to become, that she could just *be*. But you
don't get to choose whether or not you're chosen, and as time
went on, she'd been forced to admit she was going to need to figure out what she wanted to do with her life. Predestination wasn't
going to give her all the answers.

After we'd been driving for about five hours, Arthur cleared his throat and said, "I want to eat food. Can we stop and eat food, please?"

Elsie glanced at the rearview mirror. "Do you know what food you want to eat?" she asked. The question had the vague air of a test.

Arthur apparently thought so too, because his gaze skittered from her over to me, anxious and afraid of giving the wrong answer. "Er . . ." he said.

"How about something fast and easy?" I suggested. "I think there's a truck stop up ahead. We can probably find something there."

I usually try to avoid truck stops. They're road ghost territory, the protectorate of phantoms like Rose and other spirits of the highway. And the ghosts who hold and haunt them don't always look kindly on intruders. Still, as Arthur looked at my reflection with grateful relief, I couldn't regret anything about agreeing to stop there.

"Sure," said Elsie, with a shrug. She hit the gas harder, and the car rewarded us with a sudden surge forward, pressing us all back into our seats. "Hold on to your butts," she said.

"Yes, ma'am," said Arthur, and I laughed, and everything was going to be all right, no matter how far we had to drive to get there.

I was right about the truck stop: we started passing signs for it in under a mile, and reached the exit in roughly three, pulling off via an offramp barely large enough to be worthy of the name, and from there onto a gravel frontage road that ran straight into the embrace of one of those ridiculously overbuilt and overblown fortresses of travel that only really seem to crop up on the American East Coast, where the threat of blizzard is even more pronounced than the need for greasy burgers and cheap coffee. Multiple gas stations and convenience stores warred for territory in the body of a single interconnected stop, along with an indoor food court

INSTALLMENT IMMORTALITY ✦ 135

packed with fast food franchises, a literal diner, and a small motel that promised hourly rentals and showers.

Add on the sheer amount of neon and chrome on display, and the place looked like an advertisement for the power of capitalism, or at least the power of the road itself. I leaned a little closer to Elsie as we drove, watching the stop grow closer, trying to decide whether I'd made the wrong call.

"What do you think, Arthur?" asked Elsie. "McDonald's or the diner?"

"Diner," said Arthur.

I mustered a sickly smile. This was on my head, no matter what came next. Whether I pissed off the Ocean Lady or got off scot-free, this was on my head.

Elsie pulled up outside the diner, and we all got out, heading inside as a group. The sign at the hostess stand said to seat ourselves, but when we moved to do precisely that, a waitress stopped, tray in hand, snapped her gum, and said loudly, "Wrong way, honey. Your table's already waiting for you."

I didn't like that at all. From her expression, neither did Elsie. Arthur turned eagerly in the direction the waitress had indicated, bouncing onto his toes and waving. I turned more slowly, trying to put off the moment when I'd need to face whatever had decided to complicate our journey.

There, sitting in a corner booth, was a Japanese American teenager in an outdated white peasant blouse with apple blossoms stitched around the cuffs and apples embroidered at the neckline. She was sipping on a milkshake, and there were already three burgers waiting on the table, perfect and glistening with grease and melted cheese. They looked like the sort of burgers you'd see in a catalog advertising the ideal all-American diner, and they weren't made more realistic by the piles of golden potatoes nearby.

The three of us walked toward her, Elsie warily, Arthur naïvely, and me with clear resignation. She gestured for us to sit, and we sat. Arthur wound up to her right, and as soon as she indicated his burger, he picked it up and tore into it, eating like he hadn't seen a solid meal in years and was afraid he might never see one ever again. Elsie scooted in to her left, and I sat next to Elsie, at the outside of the booth, waiting for the other shoe to drop.

"Who *are* you?" asked Elsie, still wary.

"I'm a lot of people," said the girl. "I'm royalty. I'm a runaway. I'm one of the eternal children of the American road—I stopped getting older a long damn time ago, and I'm not going to start again until I decide it's time for me to go, or someone better for my people comes along. My parents called me Tanaka Asuna, although that's not how people know me now. Your friend knows who I am." She shifted her focus to me, then blinked and frowned. "Mary? What happened to your eyes?"

"I died," I said, with a small shrug. "Again, I mean. I got blown to ghost dust and the anima mundi pulled me back together. I'm assuming they're the reason you're here."

"What, I can't want to see an old friend?" she asked.

"You can, you just don't," I said. "I'm guessing this truck stop isn't really here, either."

"Too obvious? Or not obvious enough?" She craned her head to look out the window. "I considered putting a carnival in the west parking lot—thought it might make your traveling companions more comfortable—but then I couldn't decide whether that would be overkill or just the right amount of kill. What do you think?"

"I think introductions are in order," I said, mildly. "Elsie, this is Apple, current Queen of the North American Routewitches. Apple, this is Elsinore Harrington-Price, one of the kids I babysit for, and her brother, Arthur Harrington-Price. They're both under my protection."

"Did you think I managed this many decades as queen by messing with a caretaker's charges?" Apple picked up her milkshake and took a pointed sip, never taking her eyes off of me. "Routewitches walk the border between the living and the dead, Mary. You know this. I've always known what you were, and I've never challenged your authority over the ones within your care. I would no more threaten one of your kids than I would set aside my crown."

"Your predecessor did."

"Threaten, or abdicate?"

"Abdicate."

"Too bad for him, because I like the job more than he ever did, and I'm not following in his footsteps while I have any choice in the matter." Apple shrugged, setting her milkshake off to the side and focusing on Elsie. "Is she always this suspicious?"

"When it's about our safety, yeah," said Elsie. She looked at the cheeseburger in front of her, and then to her brother, who was already halfway through his, barely pausing to breathe or chew. "Mary, I'm guessing from what you said about the truck stop that wherever we are isn't really real. Is this like eating food in a fairy tale? Am I going to wind up sworn to the service of a weird teenager for seven years if I eat this burger?"

"Not if she knows what's good for her," I said, casting a sharp-eyed glance at Apple.

She laughed. Actually laughed, like the situation was genuinely hilarious. Leaning back in her seat, she said, "I am not the Queen of Faerie, and I wouldn't mess with Mary's kids if I were. You can eat. I'll be more annoyed if the food goes to waste than I will be if you eat it."

That was all the permission Elsie needed. She picked up her cheeseburger and took a quick bite, eyes going wide as she chewed and swallowed. Then she ripped in to the rest of the burger like someone was going to take it away from her, eating with the same enthusiasm as Arthur.

I gave Apple a hard look. She laughed, holding up her hands.

"It's just diner food, I swear. Platonically perfect diner food, but diner food all the same. It can't hurt them, although it may be a while before they can eat another cheeseburger. Once you've tasted perfection, it's hard to accept anything less."

"And I suppose that's why you keep the crown," I said.

Apple looked surprised. "No. I keep the crown because the Ocean Lady still loves me, and as long as she loves me, I belong with her. One day she'll find someone she likes better, and I'll fade into obscurity like the kings and queens before me. But for now, I'm comfortable in my reign, and I'm not in any hurry to get myself unseated."

I frowned but said nothing.

"I guess you're wondering why I came to meet you."

"No, I figured you'd show up eventually, after I asked the anima mundi to find me a routewitch," I said. "You do take a personal interest where I'm concerned."

"You were there when my predecessor lost his position," she said. "Makes this personal."

"That's not exactly how it happened—"

"But yes, the anima mundi approached my lady and told her you might need one or more of my subjects to help you get where you were going. I declined to help."

"What? Why?"

"You were getting there just fine the ordinary way, and look at it from my perspective—you people are starting to use *my* people as a glorified taxi service, and that's not what we are. We're a culture and a community in our own right, and we don't exist solely to make it easier on you assholes." Apple took a sip from her milkshake. "Anima mundi did make one good point, though. Those Covenant fucks are killing innocent ghosts, and more than that, they're capturing them."

"Capturing them?"

She nodded. "Sealing them in spirit jars full of mercury, salt, and iron nails, then shaking them until the ghosts inside can't stay out of contact with those components. That's a quick and easy way to drive a bunch of spirits insane."

"It's a quick and easy way to do much worse than that," I said, staring at her. Locking a ghost in a jar is bad. Locking them in a jar filled with things that hurt them and rip bits of their substance away is torture. Mercury shatters the substance of ghosts. Salt seals it away. And iron shreds their thoughts and memories, melting them, for lack of a better term, turning them into something viscous and thick that doesn't want to go back to being a person.

The living have sometimes believed that subjecting a ghost to iron will drive them insane. We know better now. Insanity is a normal, natural thing. It can be harmful to the people it wraps around, but it isn't infectious, and it isn't so easily spread. A ghost who's been shredded by iron hasn't been maddened: they've been reduced to their component parts. What's left after a few days of being shaken in a spirit jar full of iron isn't even a beast—it's a rabid beast, incapable of rational thought, made of nothing but hatred and hurting.

Apple nodded slowly. "True enough. The ghosts they capture are ticking time bombs, and there's no telling who the Covenant might set them against, or where they might release them."

Routewitches—Apple's people—are the only living souls who can move semi-freely through the twilight. They use it as passage and pathway, and it's part of how they can pull off such incredible feats of distance. A mile in the twilight might be twenty miles in the lands of the living.

But using the twilight as a shortcut means putting yourself in the path of ghosts, both friendly and less so. If the Covenant was jarring and weaponizing ghosts, they were in a position to start attacking the routewitches in a way they never had before, where there wouldn't be a lot of defenses. It was a terrifying notion.

From the grim expression on Apple's face, I wasn't coming up with anything new but joining her in a moment of terror already in progress. She'd been given the time to come to these conclusions already, and she didn't like them any more than I did.

"So you're here to help us reach the Covenant, then," I guessed.

"Nope," said Apple.

"But you just said . . ."

"The Covenant capturing ghosts is incredibly dangerous for me and my routewitches, especially since they're here on the East Coast. If they were on the West Coast, they could get to the Rainbow Road, but she's not a goddess yet: she's a demigoddess at best, an avatar. The Ocean Lady is a goddess, and she's a non-human intelligence, which means the Covenant wants to see her destroyed. I have to assume their jarred ghosts are going to be unleashed on her to do damage. And I can't let that happen."

"What do you mean, you can't *let* it?"

"I mean that I am the Queen of the North American Route-witches, and that isn't just a pretty title. It's not just power and position. It's a responsibility, to my people and to my lady. The Ocean Lady wants her routewitches to be safe. We want *her* to be safe. She protects us in little ways every single day. Once in a while, we have to protect her in return. When a ruler of the roads fails in our duty to protect the Ocean Lady, she forsakes us, and we have to move along. I don't want to move along. I can't let the Ocean Lady be harmed by my insufficiency."

"And you're not going to help us reach the Covenant."

"Nope."

"So you're going to do—what?"

"I'm going to show you where to *find* the Covenant, which could take you weeks or more without me, and I'm going to make sure you know where to start your search once you get there."

Apple produced a folded roadmap, the sort of thing I recognized from the decades I'd moved through before the cellphone came along, back when it had been possible to spend a week traveling without anyone knowing where you were or how to find you. Elsie gave it a curious, confused look but didn't reach for it as Apple slid it across the table to me.

I picked it up. It had been folded over and over again until it was the size of a deck of cards. I picked at one corner, folding it upward to reveal a small slice of roads and boundary lines. Apple leaned across the table, putting her hand over mine.

"Don't," she said. "As long as you don't open it, you're still looking at the potential of the trip, and nothing's set in stone. When you unfold it, it will be accurate to where the Covenant can be found. They can move after that, and you won't know."

I blinked. "So it's an unfinished map?"

"No, it's finished. It's just changing until someone looks at it and fixes it as it is."

That was the sort of illogical logic the routewitches specialized in. I tucked the map into my pocket. "Thank you," I said.

"Don't thank me yet. I have an additional task for you."

Why was I not surprised to hear that? I frowned, leaning back in my seat, and gestured for her to continue. Apple took a deep breath.

"According to the Ocean Lady, the anima mundi asked you to find and stop the Covenant operatives who are behind all the current trouble."

"Yes," I said.

"Well, I want that too. None of us wants a Covenant team wandering around the area, making trouble, and even if you could make them stop without hurting them, they'd still be a problem. I want them gone, you want them gone, we're going to get rid of them. Bing, bam, boom. But once that's done—once they aren't a threat anymore—I need you to deal with the ghosts they've captured."

"The ones they've turned into weapons."

"Yes." Apple looked at me solemnly, not blinking, and something about the way she held herself was so much older than she looked that it made me want to disappear and run. I guess it takes one eternal teenager to be terrified of another. She looked like she was just about my age. She was still older and more terrifying than I was, and I wanted to grab my kids and get the hell away from her as quickly as I possibly could. "The ones they've turned into weapons."

"I don't know how to do that."

"I don't think anybody does." She shrugged. "You'll figure it out. Or you won't. You're not one of mine, so it doesn't entirely matter to me one way or the other how this goes down, as long as those ghosts aren't a threat by the end of it."

I paused for a moment and just stared at her, then shifted my attention over to Arthur and Elsie. To my surprise and satisfaction, they were also staring at her, Arthur with a French fry lifted halfway to his mouth, Elsie with her hands resting against the edge of the table. Both of them looked utterly stunned. Elsie turned to me.

"Do we have to sit here and listen to this?"

"Nope," I said, and slid out of the booth, the hard outline of the folded map pressing against my hip. I turned back to Apple. "Thank you for your help, even if it's coming only because you don't see any other choice. I have never been a friend to the Ocean Lady, and I know that means I've never been a friend to you, but I still appreciate it. And because I appreciate it, I'm going to give you a warning."

"Give me a warning?" she asked, sounding politely amused.

"Yes. If any harm comes to my kids because of what you've asked me to do, what you're sending us off to do without any backup, without any support, if they suffer so much as a broken fingernail, it's going to be you versus me. The anima mundi versus the Ocean Lady, avatar against avatar, and you've been a queen for a long time, Apple. You've been comfortable and cosseted and cared for, while I was doing the bidding of the nastiest eldritch force this world has ever known. The twilight taught you to be merciful. The crossroads taught me to cheat, to lie, and to never surrender an advantage. So that's the warning. If they suffer because you don't want to put yourself out, I will come for you, Apple Tanaka of the Ocean Lady, and I will *end* you."

For just a moment, I saw fear flash in her eyes. Then her expression clamped down, turning cold and regal. The face of a queen. "So noted," she said, and snapped her fingers.

She didn't disappear so much as she had abruptly never been there in the first place. Neither had the diner. I was standing in the middle of one of those cracked-concrete-and-weeds empty lots that crop up alongside major highways, flowering when fortunes are low and being replaced by new construction and money-makers when fortunes are high. The car wasn't very far away, and beyond it I could see the highway itself, black and raw and gleaming with broken glass and glints of light off passing cars.

Elsie, who had been halfway to her feet when the diner disappeared, straightened. Arthur had still been seated, and he yelped as his butt hit the glass-speckled concrete. I glanced over at him.

"You okay, buddy?"

"Yeah," he said, pushing himself carefully to his feet. He rubbed his rump with one hand, checking it carefully when he was done, and looked relieved when his fingers came away bloodless. "Are all your friends like that?"

"Okay, first, Apple's not really my friend. She's more like a business acquaintance. Second, yeah, pretty much. The crossroads really weren't into letting me go out and meet people. I never made more than a handful of friends."

Elsie blinked at me. "What about Grandpa Thomas? You say he's your friend."

"He was never one of my charges," I said. "I met him when he moved to Buckley. That was when I was still taking care of your grandmother—not that I've really ever stopped all the way. Anyway, she liked him, and so she introduced us."

"Am I allowed to introduce you to my friends?" asked Arthur.

"If they're ex-Covenant and you're planning to keep them, you are," I said. "Tommy was—is—probably my best friend, because he *was* my friend. Not my work colleague, not one of my kids, my friend. And I betrayed him, because the crossroads didn't give me a choice."

They both blinked at me.

"Just hold on to that, all right? Apple is working for something just as big and just as alien as the crossroads, and she has to do what her master tells her to do, even if she'd rather not."

"She didn't look coerced to me," said Elsie, sullenly.

"No, and maybe she wasn't, but I'm going to give her the benefit of the doubt until all this is finished," I said. "You ready to go?"

"I'm not hungry anymore," said Arthur.

"The cheeseburger was there before I pissed her off, and she knows better than to open by messing with a caretaker's charges," I said. "I'm sure the lunch she had set out for you was fine."

"I feel better hearing that," said Elsie.

"Good, I'm glad," I said. "Let's get the hell out of here."

Nine

"Don't grow up to be your father. Don't grow up to be me.
Grow up to be yourself. You're going to be amazing, I'm
sure of it."

—Jane Harrington-Price

On the highway, heading for Boston

Food definitely seemed to have improved Elsie's driving.
She kept her hands on the wheel and her eyes on the road, trusting
me to tune the radio to a local classic rock station while Arthur
leaned over the seat and commented quizzically on lyrics she and
I had heard thousands of times, but which apparently hadn't been
bundled with his new memories. It was a pleasant hour or so of
travel before I realized the map in my pocket was getting hot.

Not warm—*hot*, like it had been replaced with a burning coal.
"I think it's time we start following the map," I said, pulling it
out.

"You sure?" Elsie asked.

"Pretty sure," I said, trying to unfold the little rectangle without burning my fingers. Normally, while I can feel pain under
a remarkably large assortment of conditions, I can't actually
be *hurt*, what with me being dead and all. When the pain was
coming from an enchanted item given to me by the queen of the
routewitches and empowered by the Ocean Lady, I had to assume
that it could do me actual harm.

I finally managed to peel back an edge of the map and shook it out, unfolding it into a massive sheet of highways, byways, and roughly outlined cities. That part was perfectly ordinary. Less ordinary was the route traced out in ink that gleamed red and gold like a raging fire, showing us exactly where we were supposed to go.

"That's new," said Arthur.

"That's what Apple promised us," I said, and tapped the map with the tip of my finger. "Looks like we're heading for Worcester."

"Worcester?" asked Elsie. She stumbled over the syllables, mangling the name of the town.

"*Woost*-er," I said, purposefully exaggerating the syllables. "That's not what it says on the street signs, but pronounce it any other way and the locals are likely to eat you alive. It's not quite as big and old as Boston, but it's close. Second-largest city in the state. It makes good sense as a place for the Covenant to post up and start hunting, and they'll be able to get just about anywhere else they need to go from there."

"Like Boston?" asked Arthur.

"Or Portland, or New York," I said. "Or any of the little haunted farms in the area. Lots of people died hard in this area. Lots of spirits still hanging around being pissed off about it. You want to go ghost harvesting, this is the place to do it."

"That's . . . charming," said Arthur. "I don't like you being here."

"That's fine," I said. "I don't like me being here either. I don't like any of us being here. But the anima mundi said I had to do it, and you both volunteered, which means this is where we need to be."

Grumbling, he sank back into his seat and folded his arms. I moved the map to where Elsie could see it, and we drove on.

Before long, we were passing the Worcester city limits, and driving into the sort of beautifully bucolic New England city that has launched a thousand horror franchises, some more capable of independent flight than others. It wasn't a small town by any means—the buildings were plentiful and tall, if not quite tip-ping over into skyscraper territory, and made of the red brick that spoke to me of my childhood, rather than the flexible wood and siding I had grown accustomed to in Portland.

It's amazing how "normal" can shift with time. Elsie eyed the brick as we drove, looking dubious as only a child of earthquake territory can.

The map continued to gleam and glow, leading us deeper into the city, until we finally turned off into a residential neighbor-hood where every house was a mirror image of the homes around it, most with two cars in the driveway and several with sporting equipment scattered around the lawns. It looked like an area that could use a babysitter. It just wasn't going to be me.

The line ended at a small house with white paint on the wooden portion of the walls and a wraparound porch that went all the way around the house. We stopped in front of the house across the street to get a closer look, Arthur leaning forward to peer out the window like he expected the Covenant to just present themselves. Given the map that led us here, maybe he wasn't wrong to do so. I eyed the house at the end of the map with suspicion.

Someone knocked on my window.

I yelped and jumped, but managed not to vanish as I whipped around to see who was knocking. The redhaired young woman on the sidewalk outside the car answered with a little wave, beaming at me. I motioned for Elsie to turn the car back on, then rolled down the window, looking suspiciously out.

"Can we help you?" I asked.

"Thought I might should be asking you the same thing," said the woman amiably. "Seeing as how you're parked outside my house and not moving around too much, and that usually means stalker or police stakeout. Now, I'm cute, but I'm not *that* cute—never have been—and I haven't done anything illegal enough to garner that sort of attention from the constabulary."

She had a rolling Irish accent, which managed to sound both out of place and perfectly reasonable for this random suburban street. It was a neat trick.

"We just got a little lost coming off the interstate," said Elsie, leaning forward and grinning at the woman. "I'm Elsie. What's your name?"

"Ophelia, but my friends call me Phee," said the woman.

Elsie kept smiling at her, eyes very nearly managing to turn heart-shaped. Her voice dropped about half an octave as she continued, and I wasn't sure she knew she was doing it. "Well, Phee, I hope we can be friends."

"I don't know. I've not had much luck with Lilu, or with dead people," said Phee. "Begging your pardon, ghost miss. I'm sure you're a lovely haunting, and it's probably not your fault that you're dead. The ones who aren't raving and trying to possess people usually didn't die because of anything they did particularly wrong."

You could have heard a pin drop in the car. But only for a moment, because Arthur breathed in sharply and started choking on his own spit. I vanished from the front seat—no point in pretending when she already knew that I wasn't exactly a breath-and-heartbeat kind of a girl—and reappeared behind him, rubbing his back in what I hoped would be a comforting circular motion.

After a few more seconds fighting for air, Arthur calmed down and started inhaling and exhaling normally, shooting me a grateful look.

"Sorry, Mary," he said.

"S'okay," I said. "I remember coughing. Coughing was the worst."

I vanished again, this time reappearing in my original seat. Phee looked at me, clearly amused.

"Guess I don't need to ask whether you're a friendly ghost," she said. "Unfriendly ghosts usually aren't that quick to help someone who's choking."

"My form of haunting is usually considered morally neutral," I said. "We're not good and we're not bad. We're just loyal, and if you're not one of the people we're loyal to, things can go either way."

"Whoa, whoa, hold up," said Phee, holding her hands out toward me, palms first. "I'm not trying to start trouble. It's just that when a carload of nonhumans comes this close to my house, I've got questions. Question one: are you here to do me harm. Question two: are you looking for a pot of gold, because I have to tell you, no matter how many of you people show up here, I'm not going to suddenly turn into a leprechaun. I wasn't one yesterday, I won't be one tomorrow, and if I were, the dragon Nest over in Boston would already have robbed me for everything I have."

Elsie frowned and leaned forward, eyeing Phee carefully. "You're talking like someone who isn't human either," she said.

"Takes one to know one," said Phee brightly. "Not human, never have been, popped out of my mam not human, planning to eventually go to the great rainbow in the sky not human. So are you here to hurt me or nah?"

"Nah," said Arthur, looking faintly dazed. "We have better things to worry about. How'd you know we were Lilu?"

"The smell," said Phee. "Lilu reek like everything you might ever want to fall into bed with. Trouble is, I don't want to fall into bed with anything. It's never been what you might refer to as an interest of mine."

"You're asexual," said Elsie, sounding almost excited.

"Sure, if that's the label you want to put on it. I always liked 'otherwise engaged,' but yours works too. Anyway, Lilu don't mess with my head, but I can still smell them. It's the scent of absence for me, empty rooms and hallways where the dust has time to really settle. Between the two of you, I bet you can get anyone who's into the pleasures of the flesh to go along with whatever you want them to do—and who decided *sex* was what got the title 'pleasures of the flesh,' anyway? I find a nice cup of tea, a warm fire, a roller coaster, all pretty pleasurable, and all very much engaging of the flesh. I think you lot are being selfish."

"It's not like we got to pick our species off of a character creation table," said Arthur. "And we're not pure Lilu, anyway."

"Hey, hey." I held up my hands. "This is a lot of species-specific shouting in a public place, when we still don't know what our . . ." I faltered for a moment, then settled on, ". . . new friend is. Ophelia? Identify yourself please?"

"Clurichaun," she said, with visible satisfaction. "Not a leprechaun, and it's a grand insult to call one of us by that name. Tragically, we're related, and near enough that people do go getting us confused—once."

She grinned, and for a moment, her mouth was full of small, sharp teeth, serrated like a ghoul's, close-fitting as an otter's or a seal's. Then she dropped it, and when she spoke again, her teeth were flat as any human being's. It was a nice bit of camouflage, and it left me unsure which version of her dentition was the real one. Kevin might have been able to tell me more about what to expect from a clurichaun, or Thomas, but neither of them was here, and I was on my own for figuring out my next move.

I sighed and blipped out of the car, reappearing next to Phee on the sidewalk outside. She looked at me with mild amusement, eyebrows lifted in silent question. I folded my arms.

"We're here because we know the Covenant of St. George has been active in this city, and the map that was supposed to lead us to them appears to have led us to your house, instead," I said. "Unless you're sheltering the Covenant for some reason. If you are, you should know, they're going to kill you when they're done with whatever it is they're doing. They don't forgive nonhumans for existing, even after they've been useful. Don't get confused about that."

"You done?" asked Phee.

"I'm done," I said.

"All right, then I'll give you this bit for free: I'm not working with the Covenant. I'm not that bog-stupid. A leprechaun might be, but I told you, that isn't what I am. And you, my dead friend, just told me exactly who you are."

I looked at her flatly.

"Dead girl traveling with two Lilu, getting snippy and protective when I look at them the wrong way? You're the Price family babysitter, Betty or Veronica or whatever your damn name is. Never thought I'd see the day. Cryptozoologist royalty on my doorstep." She bowed exaggeratedly to Elsie and Arthur.

I bristled.

"The name's *Mary*," I said. "And if you know who we are, I'm sure you want to help us."

"Knowing who you are makes me want to ask how much money it would take to get you out of my city before anyone else knows you're here," she said. "Barring that, yeah, I'll help you. That's my place." She indicated the house across the street. "I know boardinghouses are old-fashioned and out of style in this brave new world of Airbnbs and the like, but some of us still need a place that doesn't come with electronic records and a paper trail. So I rent out rooms as people need them, and I have two open right now, if that suits Her Majesty."

According to Apple's map, this was where we needed to be. And while I might not be particularly happy with Apple herself, I trusted her not to actively screw with us. She had too much to lose to think that was a good idea.

At this point, we all did.

I glanced to Elsie and Arthur, waiting for the confirming nods before I returned my attention to Phee and said, "Yeah, that suits us just fine."

"Wonderful. Fifty dollars a night for the three of you—as a

group, not each. If that seems ridiculously cheap to you, be aware that when humans try to rent from me, their rates start at two hundred a night."

"I was human when I died," I said.

"You want to pay more?"

"I'm dead. I don't have any money."

"No, but you're the kind of dead who sometimes turns solid just because she thinks it's funny, and that means you could rob a bank if you wanted to. Don't make me force you to rob a bank."

If it came to that, I'd just pop myself back to Portland and snatch some money out of the petty cash that Kevin maintained, or go to Michigan and do the same with Thomas's stash. I had options, even if I wasn't particularly inclined to use them when I didn't have to. I turned to Arthur and Elsie, gesturing for them to get out of the car.

Arthur was the first one out. "Are we really staying here tonight?" he asked.

"And probably the next several days, until we find out where the Covenant is and what they're doing," I said. "So let's be nice to our host, because she's giving us a place to stay that isn't either the back seat of the car or the nearest Holiday Inn. The house of a random clurichaun that we met on the street seems marginally less likely to give us bedbugs."

Elsie made a sour face. "I *hate* bedbugs."

"Hatred of bedbugs is the unifying factor of all sapient life," said Phee airily. "I'd get your things, if I were you. We're a safe-enough city, but safe and 'immune to theft' are two different sentences. You want to be sure you keep having things when you're done here, bring them inside."

"Yes, ma'am," said Arthur. He leaned back into the car and retrieved his duffle bag.

Elsie, meanwhile, walked around the car and opened the

trunk, extracting her suitcases and giving Phee a perplexed look. Phee smiled sunnily and waved the fingers of one hand in a wave.

"Got a ghost carpet bag, ghost nanny?" she asked.

I shook my head. "I travel light," I said.

"Grand. We'll move along," she said, and turned to cross the street to her house. The rest of us followed her.

The porch was even whiter up close, painted with a meticulous care that spoke of either loving maintenance or a low level of obsession. There were several hanging swings and one egg-shaped hanging chair, which was occupied by a brown tabby cat that looked old enough to have witnessed the Nixon administration. Phee stopped to caress its ears, and it made a weary creaking sound, then rolled over without opening its eyes.

"Mary," said Arthur. "Mary, that cat has two tails. Two tails, Mary."

"That's Maron; he's a bakeneko," said Phee. "He's about three hundred years old, and he's a lazy old bum who spends most of his time asleep."

Maron made the creaking sound again, this time opening one eye and flicking one ear flat against his head. He didn't otherwise acknowledge our presence. I offered him a little wave.

"Nice to meet you," I said. Bakeneko are originally from Japan, and I've never been entirely sure how intelligent they are. I don't spend a lot of time around four-legged cryptids.

"No, it's not," said Phee. She opened the door and strode inside, leaving the rest of us to follow her.

Elsie and Arthur followed her through the door. I took another look at Maron and followed her through the wall, stepping into a pleasant, perfectly ordinary living room, complete with worn brown couch, hanging spider plants, and television that was two sizes too large for the space. I stopped there, turning to take a look at the full space.

It looked lived-in. That wasn't an insult: rooms *should* look lived-in, or what's the point of having them? There was no organization to the bookshelves against the walls, and there were piles of mail and junk magazines on the coffee table. A dark blue cat tree sat in front of the window, presumably for Maron's benefit.

"This way," said Phee perfunctorily, and gestured for us to come with her down the hall. We passed several closed doors. She gestured to one of them. "Bathroom," she said. "Please take cold showers, so you don't get your pheromones all over everything. I'm immune, not everyone in the house is. If you can't tolerate cold showers, you can do hot sponge baths or rent a room at the Best Western down the road. Kitchen's behind us, first door off the living room. Anything unlabeled is fair game, but I ask that you play *The Price is Right* and replace a roughly equal value in groceries."

"You don't want us to hand you money?" asked Elsie.

"More fun this way," said Phee. "How else would we get experiences like 'that time everyone replaced everything they ate with cheese' or 'why do we have seventeen bottles of olive oil?' You can track the sales by what appears in the fridge. Makes meal planning interesting. Which reminds me. Breakfast is included in the cost of your rooms, but only if you fetch up between seven and nine. After nine, it's all hands for themselves, and usual rules apply. I set hours so no one else will try to cook then, and you get what you get. Usually boxty, apple cake, and oatmeal are on offer. Other things come and go as they do. You can complain if you like, but it won't do you any good." She had stopped between two doors. Beaming, she opened them both and pushed them open.

The rooms on the other side were small, square, and perfectly genericized, with white walls, beige carpet, and medium brown curtains. There was a twin bed, and a basic IKEA dresser under the single window. Both rooms were identical, if mirrored.

"Here's the two of you," said Phee cheerfully. "Ghost can sleep wherever she likes. Do ghosts sleep?"

"Not the way you're thinking," I said. "I'll probably spend the night trying to find the Covenant and find out how much damage they're doing."

"Just don't lead them back to my door," said Phee.

"I won't," I said. "I'm better at my job than that."

Another door banged open farther down the hall, and a woman emerged. She was tall, solidly built as a professional wrestler, and wearing a pink-and-orange tie-dyed bathrobe. She was also heading straight for us.

"Urk," said Elsie, eyes going wide, round, and shiny. Unlike her brother and his unending devotion to one woman, she had always been ready to fall in love with the next pretty face to come down the sidewalk, and it looked like love had just managed to strike her again, right where she least expected it.

"Afternoon, Phee," said the newcomer, with a Boston accent so thick I could almost taste it, butter and maple syrup on the tongue. She paused to eye the three of us suspiciously. "New kids?"

"They'll be staying with us for a little while," said Phee. "They're on a bit of a road trip."

"Huh. They got names?" She turned on Elsie, perhaps recognizing her as the weak spot in this current conversational tree. "You got a name, sweetheart?"

I thought Elsie was going to swoon at being called "sweetheart." She managed not to, although her cheeks flushed pink with either delight or arousal—I couldn't really tell which. "Elsinore," she said.

"What, like the castle from *Hamlet*?" asked the newcomer.

Elsie nodded, and the woman nudged Phee with her elbow.

"Better watch your back, if Elsinore Castle's coming to you," she said.

Elsie laughed like this was the funniest thing she'd ever heard.

"Anyway, I'm Amelia, and I live here at this little boardinghouse of horrors. I'm a bit bouncer and a bit keeper of the chore chart, and Ophelia'd be lost without me, wouldn't you, Phee? Say you would, you know you would."

"Get off, you great lump," said Phee, with obvious fondness. "Amelia was one of my first tenants, and she's never left. People stay anywhere from a night to, apparently, forever."

"We'll be somewhere in the middle of all that," I said. I gave Amelia a harder look, trying to find any sign that she wasn't human. Amelia obliged me by meeting my eyes, smiling wickedly, and blinking both sets of eyelids at once.

I blinked. Only once. Humans don't have a nictating membrane. It's a definite design flaw, but it's something evolution decided we didn't really need, and so didn't bother to equip. A variety of the homo-form cryptids *do* have nictitating membranes, either due to an aquatic or nocturnal lifestyle, or just because evolution made some different choices when it was putting them together.

Amelia laughed. "Thought that's what you were looking for. You're dead, aren't you?"

I was getting a little tired of being pegged for a ghost on sight. "Caretaker ghost," I said, curtly. "These two are my responsibility."

Elsie looked like she wanted to sink into the floor and disappear forever, which meant I was doing my job as her babysitter, even if she was a grown adult who could generally be allowed to flirt without supervision. Still, sometimes it was good to remind people of my role in this little family unit.

"Hockomock Swamp Beastie," said Amelia, with a toothy smile. "I'm nobody's responsibility but my own."

These days, it's relatively rare for me to encounter an intelligent species I've never heard of before. Even apart from all the time I've spent with various Prices, when I was working for the crossroads, they were happy to prey on anyone who fell for their brand of bullshit. Humanity didn't really matter to them. There's nothing so special about a human that they should get the attention of an entire eldritch entity to themselves.

(Of course, we humans do have one thing going for us: numbers. We've managed to outbreed everyone else on the planet to the point where we've been given ownership of a whole layer of the afterlife, just so we'll leave the other kids alone and let them rest in peace. There are people who genuinely resent the fact that former servants of the crossroads, like me, are still rooted in the starlight, rather than packing our ectoplasmic bags and getting the hell out of there before they have to force the issue.)

"What's a Hockomock Swamp Beastie?" asked Arthur, before I finished gathering my thoughts enough to form the question.

Amelia gave him an indulgent look. "It's not nice to ask for details before you've told me your name, hon."

"Oh. Um, Arthur. Elsie's my sister."

"Which explains how a couple of Lilu can travel together and not cause all sorts of issues for each other," said Phee. She turned her attention back to me. "Around here, since I've already told you everyone in the house isn't human, it's polite to identify your species, just so everyone can feel at ease. When we do have humans here, I put them up on the second floor, and I warn everyone to make sure they won't run into unexpected humans in the halls and maybe have an issue that requires tarps and bleach to resolve."

"Uh-huh," I said.

"Lilu, huh?" asked Amelia. "Fascinating. Anyway, as I said, I'm a Hockomock Swamp Beastie. We have our own name for ourselves, but we're rare enough that I find it easier to just use what the local humans do. Means there's half a chance in hell you'll have heard of us."

"We're from Oregon," said Elsie.

"All right, substantially less than half a chance. Anyway. We're related to the Jersey Devils, but try telling *them* that. They have just as narrow a habitat as we do, but they got better press when they were discovered, so they think they're super important."

"Huh," I said. Jersey Devils looked less human than this

woman did, but their inhuman attributes were almost all defensive or survival-based: they could hold their breath for hours, and had nictitating membranes in their eyes, as well as the ability to stop off their nostrils and prevent themselves from breathing water.

Amelia nodded like she could see my whirling thoughts. "Anything you're laying on my cousins, we can do that too. I'm also immune to most poisons, resistant to the ones I'm not immune to, and I never get bit by mosquitoes. Also, my skin doesn't absorb water the way a human's does—it's more like a dolphin's or a hippo's—and that means I can lurk in the swamp as long as I need to without worrying about my skin sloughing off or rotting."

"It looks like normal skin to me," said Elsie.

Amelia winked at her. "Camouflage."

"Did you need something, Mia?" asked Phee, sounding exasperated.

"Ah, yes!" said Amelia. "Just about to go the grocery run, need your credit card. Unless you'd rather I shop according to *my* list, instead of yours."

Phee wrinkled her nose and pulled a card out of her pocket, passing it to Amelia, who made it disappear.

"Cheers," she said, and winked again at Elsie, then continued down the hall, off to her errands.

I turned to Elsie and Arthur. "All right," I said. "You two get your stuff settled, and I'll hang around here until dinnertime. After that, you go to bed, and I'll go looking for the Covenant."

"We're not children anymore," said Elsie. "We don't have to go to bed when you tell us to."

"That's true enough," I said. "But you're not coming out to find the Covenant with me—I need to know where they are, and be ready to come up with a plan, before I'm willing to trust you to the field."

"You said you needed help," she said. "I drove all the way here.

I'm not sitting on the sidelines while you go after the people who killed my mother."

"And I don't want you to," I said. "But scouting is important, and we need intelligence."

"Everyone remembers Artie as being so amazing with computers, while I've barely touched them," said Arthur. "Maybe that means I *am* amazing with computers, and I can start finding information if you just set me in front of a keyboard and wait to see what happens. It can't hurt anything."

"And if that doesn't work, he can email Uncle Drew and get help that way," said Elsie.

"Great. It sounds like you have a plan that involves staying here and not spiking my blood pressure through the roof for funsies," I said. I turned to Ophelia. "I know they're adults and you're just our temporary landlady, but if you could please not let them leave the house tonight, that would be absolutely amazing."

"I'll keep them safe as houses," she said.

"Great." I looked back to Elsie. "You leave anything in the car?"

She nodded, and I disappeared to go and get it.

Ten

"When the curtain goes up and the lights go down, you don't worry about what might be waiting in the wings. Stage is yours. Showtime."

—Frances Brown

Worcester, Massachusetts,
waiting for the sun to set

W<small>E'D MANAGED TO PULL INTO</small> Worcester about two hours ahead of dinner, which was going to be spaghetti and garlic bread. Plentiful, easy to expand if more people showed up at the table, and, as long as we didn't have any gluten or allium allergies, relatively inoffensive. Somehow, I wound up in the kitchen with Ophelia, helping her chop things, while Elsie got a shower and Arthur charged his laptop. For some reason, this didn't mean just plugging it in and walking away; it meant sitting in the room and staring at it while it powered up. Whatever worked for him, I guess.

I suspected it was at least partially an attempt to reduce outside stimulation while he dug deep into memories that were only technically his own, looking for the moments where people had witnessed Artie doing something spectacular with a computer. This had all been a lot harder on him than he was letting on. Not the erasure and reconstruction—we knew that was difficult. No, the sheer overwhelming stimulation of being out in the world, forming his own memories of things Artie had never seen or done. It was stretching his brain in ways that would either be amazingly good for him or accelerate the speed with which pieces of his identity dropped off into the void.

There was no way of knowing. But no one had forced him to come along with us on this trip: he'd volunteered, and he was still an adult. Whatever happened next, he'd be the one to deal with the brunt of it.

Ophelia passed me a handful of green onions to be diced into the pot, and fixed me with a stern look. "I wanted to get you alone, ghostie," she said.

"Um?" I responded, with utmost cleverness.

"What are you really doing here?"

"Really, we're hunting for the Covenant operatives who've moved into your city," I said. "They're hunting ghosts, and some of the forces that dwell in the twilight don't like that very much. They'd like it to stop. I owe some of them some pretty big favors, and so they've asked me to deal with it as best I can."

"And the Lilu?"

"Two of the kids I babysat, all grown up and ready for adventures," I said. "I needed backup who could carry things and not get sucked into spirit jars if they missed a step, and they were the first ones to volunteer. They're not here looking for territory or intending to mess with anyone who isn't already messing with us."

"Seems to me you just got to town, no one's had a chance to mess with you yet."

"Like I said, some of the forces in the twilight don't like what the Covenant's been doing. I work for those forces, and that means the Covenant is already messing with me."

"Technicalities," said Phee, waving a hand like she could brush my argument away. "That, and a big heaping helping of 'family sticks together,' which is why I wanted to talk to you. No one in this house is a combatant. We're all peaceful people who are lucky enough to pass for human when we need to—which is most of the time, sadly—and we don't want any trouble following you back here. We're not suddenly going to agree to take up arms and fight alongside you. If you're expecting that, you're going to be very, very disappointed."

"We're not," I said. "I'm going to accomplish as much of this on my own as I can. For the parts that need a living hand, Elsie's pretty solid in the field. Arthur's more of a guy-in-the-chair type, but he's good at that, and I've been doing this ghost thing for a long time now. We shouldn't need any help."

"That's encouraging," said Phee. She began smashing cloves of garlic with the flat of her knife, dicing the resulting mess and tossing it into the pot. "We were all shocked when the Covenant started sniffing around here, and even more shocked when they ignored all signs of us to focus on the ghost population. Do you know what happened?"

"I have a question, first: how did you know who we were?"

"Come now, this is Massachusetts. We're the ghost-story capital of the United States. If we have a haunting, we know the true story behind it, or close enough to the true story that we don't sound like total bogans when we try to explain what happened. This is where urban legends are born. You really think I wouldn't know the last of the caretakers if she turned visible in front of me? Mary Dunham died trying to protect her charges from Bobby Cross, right after he'd made his deal with the crossroads, and she still takes care of their descendants. Meaning the Price family, where a lovely Lilu lad name of Theodore married in a few generations back. Meaning that when I saw a caretaker ghost with two Lilu, I took an educated guess."

"How did you know I was a caretaker?" I didn't correct her about my last name. She hadn't proven yet that she deserved that kind of trust.

She shrugged. "The hair."

Suddenly self-conscious, I reached up to touch the crown of my head. "What do you mean, the hair?"

"Caretakers aren't always old, but they always look at least a little old by the standards of their time. Usually that means gray or white hair, no matter what color it was in life. I'm surprised you didn't wizen up just a bit for good measure. According to the old records, that happens about three-quarters of the time. How are you one of the lucky ones?"

"I don't know," I said, gathering my hair over one shoulder and staring at it where it lay, white and frozen, across my fingers. "I . . . I guess it's because the family that first employed me had a live-in grandmother and a relatively young mother. I fit in better if I was a teenager than I would have as another old lady."

More realistically, I had never seen anyone older than around thirty working for the crossroads. If it helped caretakers to seem older than they were, it helped the crossroads if all their interlocutors seemed to be young, naïve, and easily exploited. The two sides of my nature had been in conflict from the very beginning, and for a long time the crossroads had been dominant.

Was I going to start aging now that I was free of the crossroads, or would the fact that my family knew what I was "supposed" to look like keep my clock stopped where it was, where it had been for the last handful of decades? Only time would tell. I found that I wasn't upset with the idea. Whether I started aging or not, I'd still be a ghostly babysitter, and I'd still have children to care for.

"Why do you call me the last of the caretakers?"

"Because there hasn't been one since you manifested, and there won't be another any time soon," said Phee. "The time of the caretaking ghost is over. Today's parents like *living* caretakers for their children, and you only ever manifested among the humans. I'm not sure why."

Species-specific ghosts have always existed. Caretakers aren't among them. I frowned. "That's not right," I said. "Wadjet have caretakers. So do bogeymen."

"You're letting facts get in the way of a good story, and if you knew more about clurichaun, you'd know we don't tolerate that sort of thing," she said primly. "But it's true that there hasn't been another since you on the human side of things, at least not that I've heard anything about. And I would have heard. Nothing happens on this coast that I don't hear about, and very little happens anywhere else that I miss."

"But apparently you missed what's got the Covenant on ghost patrol," I said, deadpan. "Just like you missed my surname and why I don't exactly fit the template for a standard caretaker."

"Really?" Phee turned toward me, suddenly interested. "What's your last name, Mary? What's your real last name?"

"I like 'Dunham' well enough. I could roll with that one."

"No. No, if it's not the one on your gravestone, I don't want it."

"I don't have a gravestone," I said. "I was a hit-and-run. I died before Bobby Cross went to the crossroads—long before he went to the crossroads. And I wasn't a caretaker when I was alive. I babysat for random neighborhood kids because I needed to help my father pay for groceries. I wasn't particularly attached to any of them until I was already dead."

"Wait. That's not how that works. Caretakers happen when someone with a strong protective connection to a child or vulnerable person dies and doesn't give up their duties. If you died with no one to take care of, you should have moved on to what comes next, immediately."

"I had my father," I said, but that was a lie. He'd been alive, and I'd been trying to be a dutiful daughter, to keep him healthy and as happy as he could be in a world without my mother, but I had resented it on some level, hating the fact that I was trapped in our house and our town and a pale parody of the life I'd had when I was alive too. I'd wasted every minute I had among the living trying to make someone else happy, and it had never, ever worked.

It wasn't until I was already dead and Frances Healy handed Alice to me that I'd finally come to understand what it was to care about someone else without hating them for it, without feeling like they should have been taking care of me instead of me taking care of them. I'd been a child who was never allowed to be a kid, forced to parent my own parents long before I was old enough to understand how wrong it was, and then I'd been a ghost who belonged, utterly, to an eldritch force dedicated solely to causing as much pain as possible. By taking care of the Healys, I'd finally been able to take care of myself.

"And that was enough?" asked Phee.

"No," I answered. "My father was an angry, bitter man who drank too much because he was more interested in killing himself than he was in staying with the teenage daughter who needed him. I died before he did, and I got hired by Frances Healy to take care of her toddler a little while after my accident. So I guess I did it in the wrong order."

"But you can't have done it in the wrong order. It's not possible."

"Oh, did you miss the fact that I had two employers? The Healy family hired me to take care of their children after I was already dead, but the crossroads hired me to broker deals for them while I was dying." I smiled at Phee, lips drawn tight against glossy teeth, and felt my cheeks hollowing out as my appearance slipped from schoolgirl to sepulcher. "I was bleeding out, and the voice of the void spoke to me and offered me a way to stay. I wanted to go. I was ready to go. But my father needed me, and I'd been taught that the best thing I could be was a dutiful daughter, so I stayed. I let the void convince me that it was worth it, that I would do anything that was asked of me."

Phee stared, speechless for once.

"So I served the crossroads. I did as they asked. I brokered deals, and I helped people sell their souls; I ruined lives. So many lives. I don't like to talk about it with the people I care for, because none of them realize how much damage I really did when I had the opportunity. They think I'm a good person. I'm not a good person."

"You're not Mary Dunham," said Phee, sounding horrified. "You're Mary *Dunlavy.*"

"So you have heard of me."

"That can't be right. Mary Dunlavy serves the crossroads. She's a demon, a monster, the worst collaborator the world has ever known. No one would allow her near children. Mary Dunham is the caretaker."

"Mary Dunham doesn't exist," I said blandly. "I'm real, she's not, I'm sorry you got your story confused. I died, the crossroads caught me, the Healys hired me while I was still solidifying, I became a hybrid caretaker–crossroads guardian, and I stayed that way until the destruction of the crossroads set me free. So now I guess I'm just the babysitter, and it's my job to keep my kids safe, whatever that means." I leaned over and took an onion from the pile on the counter, beginning to chop it into small, even pieces. "It's a good thing I like kids, I guess."

"Are you the reason the Covenant is so interested in ghosts all of a sudden?"

"Good guess," I said. "They brought the fight to us. North America was supposed to be off-limits for those assholes and their bullshit. Neutral territory if they absolutely refused to stay away. But they decided they needed to start shit and get hit. They hurt two members of my family. Technically, they hurt my entire family, but they killed two. And once they did that, all bets were off. We came up with a plan to take the fight to them, to Penton Hall, where they trained their people. It was only possible because

I was able to help. We filled their basement with explosives and set it off before they realized we were there. And somehow they figured out that a ghost was involved, that a ghost was helping their enemies, and they decided that was never going to happen again. They couldn't find me. They didn't know who I was. And so they've expanded their target profile to cover all the ghosts in North America, even the ones who couldn't possibly have been responsible for what happened to their training facility."

"Wow, girl, you really did decide to start shoveling the shit, didn't you?" asked Phee, dumping a colander of mushrooms into the saucepot. "First you help the crossroads ruin lives for however long, and then when they went away—which, maybe they'll come back one day, we don't know—and now you've gone and pissed the Covenant off at all the ghosts who didn't do anything wrong. You just like making enemies, don't you?"

"The crossroads aren't coming back," I said. "Promise."

Phee raised an eyebrow. "You trying to tell me that you know what happened to the crossroads?"

"You said stories were your 'thing,'" I said. "I'm not giving you another story for free. Keep my kids safe while I'm out hunting for the Covenant tonight, and I'll tell you what happened before we move along."

"Deal," she said. "But if the Covenant finds their way back here, deal's off, and I'll sell you out in a heartbeat."

"No problem," I said.

The front door banged open. I turned to look in that direction, resisting the urge to turn invisible. It's the ghost skill I use the least, in part because it only works when I'm not holding anything that isn't also made of ghost stuff, whatever that means. I've never been entirely sure. Ectoplasm or whatever. My shoes, the contents of my pockets, things I pick up in the starlight, those are all made of the same intangible material as my body, solid when I'm touching them, otherwise not. But the knife I was holding, and the half onion still in my hand, those were living things, made of the same solid material as the rest of the universe.

There was no "real" or "unreal" in this distinction: a knife I stole from the starlight would cut in my hands, and could absolutely be used to dice an onion. But if I turned invisible while I was holding a knife from the lands of the living, it would just become a floating knife, and that wouldn't exactly be inconspicuous.

Amelia, who had just come in with her arms full of grocery bags, marched across the living room and into the kitchen, where she dropped her bags on the counter. "Mission accomplished," she announced. She looked at me, nodding a quick acknowledgment, then turned back to Phee. "Where are the new kids?" she asked.

"Why? You going to try to pick up the new girl?" Phee replied. "She was already undressing you with her eyes. I bet you could see the underside of her sheets by the end of the week if you really wanted to give it a go—and if it doesn't offend Miss Babysitter over here."

"Ha ha," I said, waving my knife carelessly in front of me. "Once they hit legal age, I don't care what they do behind closed doors. It's not my business. I'll prevent teen pregnancies, solely because their parents expect it of me, but beyond that, I don't tell my charges who to get busy with."

"Nah, I was thinking of the new boy," said Amelia. "He gives off that shy-but-sexy vibe I like."

I nearly dropped the knife.

Amelia laughed. "So much for little Miss I Don't Care. I knew you cared. You have that look about you. I'm not sure when the last time you didn't care about something was. You're a serial carer."

"Guilty," I said. "Look, if you're going to flirt with Arthur, there's something you should—"

"Nah," said Amelia. "I was kidding. The girl's more my speed. I like a lady with fluffy technicolor hair."

"And we're back to me not caring," I said, putting down the knife. I glanced at the window, where the sun was more than halfway down in the sky. "Close enough to dark that I can get started, and there's no reason for me to stay for dinner, what with the whole 'I don't need to eat' aspect of my existence."

"I'll feed your Lilu," said Phee, waving a ladle before she started stirring the sauce. "You have fun with your genocidal maniacs."

"I always do," I said, and disappeared.

✦ ✦ ✦

When all else fails, find a haunting.

All ghosts can locate other ghosts, if we're given sufficient time and good-enough reason to deal with one another. Most hauntings are fairly territorial. The reason we haven't lost Baltimore or some other major metropolitan area to a massive ghost vortex is because we can't stand each other for long periods, or sometimes at all.

Road ghosts are more social than the rest of us. I guess when your haunting is a mobile one, you sort of have to be able to tolerate the presence of other ghosts every once in a while.

I've never been as bothered by other ghosts as some of my kind are, maybe because caretakers are another type of mobile haunting. We don't stay with a place: we stay with the people who make it relevant to us. That makes me unusually suited to dealing with other hauntings, and I tried to hold that firmly in mind as I appeared on the outskirts of a city park, green grass around my ankles and half-lit buildings all around. I was deep enough into the city's commercial district that most of the things around me were closed; the living had all gone home for the night, leaving this place to the inhuman residents of the city. Including the dead ones.

Everything in me was screaming that there was a ghost near here. I turned in a slow circle, breathing in the night, trying to feel for the spirit I could halfway sense. When I didn't find any- thing more precise than "nearby," I started walking into the park, crossing the grass with long, careful strides.

Something whistled behind me, sounding almost but not quite like the wind. I turned. Behind me, lit from below by spotlights, was the great white box of City Hall, recognizable as a major civic building even before I saw the signs. I turned back the way I'd been facing. In front of me, beyond the grass and in the middle of a brick courtyard, was a pink marble basin topped by a bronze statue of a young boy standing behind a sea turtle.

"Public art is *so* weird," I said, and kept walking.

As I got closer to the statue, I heard the whistling sound again. I stopped to look behind me, trying to find its source. There was nothing. Still, there was nothing.

The night and the noises were beginning to make the back of my neck itch, which was a fascinating reminder of the fact that no matter how dead I got, my spirit still remembered what it was to have had a body. Sometimes the autonomic reactions I no longer really had would kick in and make things weird, muscle cramps and sneezes and itches and other things that dead girls shouldn't need to worry about. I turned steadfastly back toward the statue and resumed walking faster, heading for the boy and the turtle like they had been my destination all along.

The statue got stranger and stranger-looking as I drew closer, making me question who would have sculpted such a thing, much less installed it in a public park. Then I was right up on top of it, and stopped, squinting at the placard that identified it as the Burnside Fountain. There was no water.

"Go looking for ghosts, find weird-ass statue," I said, eyeing the boy with the turtle. This close, it was difficult to find an innocent explanation for the pose they had been sculpted in, with the boy behind the turtle, holding it by the sides of the shell and pulling it back against his groin. The turtle looked startled and unhappy. The boy looked pleased with all his life choices up until this point. "Massachusetts is officially freak central."

"Why would you come here, then?" asked a voice, from directly behind me. The hair on the back of my neck stood on end, and I turned to find myself facing a boy about the same age as the one in the statue, maybe twelve, maybe thirteen. He was faintly transparent, with dark, messy hair and bare feet, wearing a nightshirt in a style that had been outdated and forgotten before I was a child. There was something distinctly old-fashioned about his face, although I couldn't have identified it exactly if you'd been offering to pay me.

"I'm pretty freaky myself," I said, mind racing. Child ghosts aren't as rare as I'd like them to be, and they mostly sort into one of two categories: the majority are ever-lasters, the ghosts of kids who haunt schools, trying to finish their trek to the strange, distant country of adulthood before they move along to their rewards. They're the only ghosts that naturally age, getting older as they learn. It can take them centuries, but they *will* grow up if you give them enough time.

The rest of the child ghosts fall into a big bucket I like to call "trouble." They died too young, and they're pissed about it. They tend to become poltergeists and hostile hauntings, the sort who wind up with opportunistic filmmakers making horror movies about them.

This kid didn't look like an ever-laster.

As if he'd read my mind—which was impossible; I've never heard of a telepathic ghost, much less met one—he looked me up and down, then smirked. "You look like you'd get freaky."

I folded my arms. "Don't tell me you're one of those kids who's been dead for so long that you think you get to be gross about things you didn't live long enough to properly understand," I said. "It's not funny, it's not cute, and it's not going to change anything."

He looked faintly disappointed. "You're no fun."

"I'm lots of fun. I'm just age-appropriate fun, and it's late. You should probably be in bed."

"I can't be in bed," he said sourly. "I'm dead."

"That's never stopped me." Not entirely true, but good enough for this encounter. At least I'd managed to find a local ghost. "So are you haunting this park, or this weird-ass fountain?"

"Neither," he said morosely. "I haunt City Hall, most of the time, but there's been ghost hunters around the area for the last few months, and it's not safe for me there."

I turned to look speculatively at the city hall. It was a solid-looking building, and it felt old, but it didn't feel old enough to have been used as any sort of schoolhouse or hospital wing. Those are the places most likely to be occupied by the ghosts of children—well, those, along with orphanages and mental asylums. But the ghosts you find in orphanages and old asylums don't tend to be very friendly, and they definitely don't try to weasel their way into tame sex comedies.

"City Hall? Really?"

"I didn't die there, if that's what you're trying to get at," said the kid. "My family home used to stand there, and then they knocked it down to build the new city hall because we were all dead and they didn't think anyone would care about it. Well, I cared. I cared a *lot.* So I moved into their stupid civic building, and I haunted their fancy new halls, and I've been haunting them ever since then. Only now it's all stupid ghost hunters, and I'd be in a jar with Martha and Agnes if I went back there."

"Do you have a name?" I tried to keep the question as light as I could. Older ghosts don't always know who they were. Older ghosts who've been traumatized somehow—say by having their traditional haunting disrupted by a bunch of ghost-hunting assholes—are even more forgetful.

"Jonah," he said, and looked at me flatly. "Same question, fun police."

"Mary," I said.

To my surprise, he laughed. "Oh, thank the good Lord, you have a *name*. The last umbramancer who came through here, she called herself 'Sunbeam,' like that wasn't something you'd call a good draft horse. Who names their daughter 'Sunbeam'? Who thinks the inanimate exists to be mined for nomenclature?"

"Lots of people," I said. "One of my closest friends is named 'Rose,' and she's from the 1930s. I also know a girl called 'Apple,' and she was born in the 1920s, although 'Apple' isn't her given name. We've always used nature names for babies. There's just an arbitrary list we think of as 'normal,' and then everything else gets filed under 'weird.' I don't know anyone named 'Sunbeam,' and you got one part wrong."

"Only one, lecture lady?"

I decided to ignore that. Decades spent with a sarcastic, verbose family—they get some of it from me, and some of it from the mice, and regardless, they think mid-conversation lectures are perfectly normal—has left me inclined to lecture when the opportunity arises. I'm not proud of it. That doesn't make it less true. "I'm not an umbramancer."

Jonah looked at me disbelievingly. "You can see me, you're out here at night, and you must have followed the screams the ghost hunters ignore. What else could you be?"

"Dead."

"Nuh-uh."

I flickered, reappearing in a dated skirt and blouse I could have worn to school once upon a time. The outfit wasn't comfortable anymore, not the way it would have been when this was clothing rather than a costume. Time changes everything, even me, in its own terrible ways.

Jonah stared. I crossed my arms.

"Believe me now?"

"You *can't* be dead," he said. "You're too solid. I can't see through you at all. Your hair is moving with the wind. My hair doesn't do that, not even when a really big storm rolls in. The grass is bent where you're standing."

I lifted an eyebrow. "You're observant."

He shrugged. "I get bored a lot. Watching stuff's about the only thing I can do where it doesn't matter that I'm dead and can't touch anything. I'm really, really good at birdwatching and I don't have to tell you any of this, because you're alive and playing a trick on me."

This was fun, but I needed him to take me seriously and answer my questions, not keep trying to dismiss me as an unwanted representative of the living world. "Could a living person do *this*?" I demanded, and lunged forward, grabbing his wrist with one hand, before dropping down into the twilight.

He had time for a single startled squawking sound, and then we were standing on the same brick courtyard, next to the same fountain, under a sky the color of a child's watercolor painting of the sunset, complete with vacantly smiling sun. I do mean "smiling"—the sun had human features sketched across its gaseous surface and looked like it had been hitting the "special brownies" pretty damn hard, since it was staring off into the distance with unfocused eyes, unblinking. But then, I don't know how often a sun is supposed to blink.

There were other figures around, in this modified version of Worcester, people walking on sidewalks in the distance, or floating serenely through the sky. One small family was having a picnic on the grass, two adults and two children. One of the children had tentacles in place of arms, long, fleshy things that curled and uncurled as she chased the other child in circles. The adults watched her indulgently.

"She's going to be a fascinating haunting when she finishes settling," I said, letting go of Jonah. He sputtered and stumbled backward, away from me. I turned to focus on him, blinking. "What? You never seen the twilight before? This is where you're supposed to go when you're not haunting the halls."

"I— You— *How?*" He stopped sputtering as he turned and stared at me, betrayal in his eyes. He looked suddenly even paler than he'd been in the lands of the living, washed out and reduced to a sketch on paper.

I blinked, and everything fell into place. "You haven't been here since they tore your house down, have you?" I asked, making my voice as gentle as I could. He was a scared child, and I was a babysitter; softening my response was easier than I would have expected it to be.

Jonah shook his head. I winced.

"Shit. I should have realized, but all that stuff about moving, like it was voluntary, well, it threw me. They used part of your old house when they built the city hall, didn't they?"

"No sense in wasting the brick," he said, voice high and quavering. "So they gathered it up when the wrecking was done, and they built it into the new foundations. They didn't want to use too much where people could see—it wasn't the right color—so some of it's in the courtyard around the fountain, too. That's why I can go so far."

"Oh, kiddo, I'm sorry."

Jonah wasn't a house haunting, however strange and misplaced. He was a homestead that had been stopped from fully forming. "For what?" he demanded, lower lip jutting.

"They didn't just tear your childhood home down because they wanted the land, did they?" He looked away. I pushed on. "They tore it down because it was a ruin."

"There was a fever," he said, going paler still, red spots beginning to appear livid on his cheeks and temples. The pox crusted over almost immediately, seeming to almost glow against his skin. "It ran through the whole house, and everybody died. Mother was first, and then my sisters, and then the baby, and then Father and me. I was the last to go." He shot me a hard, challenging look. "I didn't want to go."

"Most people don't," I said. "When you died, were any of them waiting for you? You mentioned Martha and Agnes—were they your sisters?"

"No," he said, almost sullenly. "They came later. Mother's ghost was still in the house when I died, trying to wake up the baby, but the baby wouldn't wake up. The baby was like a doll made of rotten dough."

"I'm sorry." That happened sometimes, with dead parents who were immediately predeceased by infants, or to people who died in childbirth. The babies didn't have enough connection to the world to leave any sort of unfinished business, and they didn't linger, but their parents couldn't let them go. So they conjured false babies for themselves out of ectoplasm and need, and they never woke up, and they never cried or fussed or needed anything again.

There *are* infant ghosts, but they're rare and specialized, and almost never happen when there are loving parents anywhere nearby, living or dead.

"For a little while, we were all right," said Jonah. "Mother missed the girls, but I liked having her attention almost all to myself. And then one day, she tripped—she was a ghost, I don't understand how she could trip—and she dropped the baby. And when it hit the ground, it burst, like a rotten egg. What came out wasn't blood or meat or even maggots. It was just slime and stinking. Mother looked at it, and said, 'Is that how it is,' and then she was gone, and I was alone. The house fell apart all around me for years, until the day the men came with their hammers and pulled it down for pieces."

I nodded. "I think I understand now."

"That's great," he said, in a flat tone. "How about you explain for me?"

"You know how there are different kinds of ghost?" I asked.

He nodded vigorously. "Yes. I'm just a ghost, no special kind. I haunted my house and now I haunt the city hall, and that's all I need or want to do, ever."

"Well, buddy, you're not just a ghost. You're what we call a homestead. You may have heard the term 'caddis fly' used for what you are. You're the ghost of a person *and* a place. Normally a homestead happens when there's a fire, or a flood, or something else that destroys a house without giving the occupants time to escape. For you, because you were so young and your whole family died of a sickness circulating inside the house, you took longer to form than most would."

"So?"

"So if you'd been all the way formed when the living tore down your house, it would have appeared here with you, in the twilight, and you would have been bound here, not in the land of the living. You should never have been stranded there for so long. That isn't how this is supposed to work."

There must have been some sort of system once, older ghosts telling new ones what they were becoming and what their existences were going to be going forward. I thought back to when I'd been newly dead and trying to figure things out. A few of the other crossroads ghosts had made excuses and opportunities to come and speak with me under the watchful eyes of our mutual owner, explaining how things were going to work for me as best as they could. They'd been mostly correct in the beginning, until Fran hired me to sit for Alice and things started to get weird. Fresh ghosts are malleable, as Jonah was demonstrating.

He glowered at me. "What are you trying to say?"

"That half of your haunting is missing. You should have had the time to carry your house down into the twilight with you, and you didn't, and I'm sorry. But also we're getting away from the point here, and I'm definitely dead." I flickered again, returning to my modern clothing. "I came to the city hall area looking for ghosts who hadn't been caught by the ghost hunters yet. I'm here to stop them."

"Why didn't you say so to begin with?" asked Jonah. "I can take you to the others. Come on."

He offered me his hand. After a moment of hesitation, I took it.

We disappeared.

Eleven

"Original sin isn't real. There's only so much time you have to spend apologizing for the crimes of people you never knew. At the end of the day, you're only really responsible for yourself."

—Enid Healy

Worcester, Massachusetts,
in what looks like a basement,
because that's not uncomfortable after
what happened in England or anything

WE REAPPEARED IN THE DAYLIGHT, into a dimness that made that label seem more ill-fitting than ever. We were standing in a small, cluttered basement, surrounded by cardboard boxes and the omnipresent scent of something gently molding in the corners of the room. A single overhead bulb cast stark white light throughout the room, its brilliance coaxing sharp-edged shadows out of everything it touched.

And everywhere I looked, there were ghosts.

There were at least a dozen of them sitting on the boxes, all different types of haunt, ghosts that should never have coexisted. Jonah let go of my hand and waved to the room, motioning for the ones who had started to stand and tense to calm themselves.

"It's all right everyone, she's with me," he said. "Everyone, this is Mary. Mary, this is everyone."

"Uh, hi," I said, raising one hand in a brief wave.

A stunningly beautiful dark-skinned Latina woman in what looked like her early twenties shoved her way through the crowd toward us. She was wearing a halter top that looked like it had been sewn from pure liquid gold and a pair of denim jeans so tight that I wouldn't have been surprised if she'd died from cutting off the circulation to her entire lower body. She muttered something in Portuguese, tossing her long, auburn-brown hair and glaring at me as she hurried to put her arms around Jonah and pull him away.

"Hi," I tried again. "You are?"

"Benedita," she snapped, eyeing me like I was the most dangerous thing she'd ever seen. "You can go, you Mary you. Whatever you are, you stink of the living, and new ghosts don't just appear in an area that's dealing with an active hunting."

I had never really considered how much "hunting" sounded like "haunting." I swallowed. "You're right," I said. "I *do* stink of the living, and I'm not here by coincidence. I'm pretty sure the current hunt is at least partially my fault, and I want to stop it. I *have* to stop it." If I didn't, I wasn't sure what the anima mundi would wind up doing to me. Dealing with gods and godlike entities was still new, and I was increasingly sure that I didn't like it one little bit.

"Why do you stink?" asked Benedita, lip curled. "You been haunting the wrong halls, prissy girl?"

"You're a midnight beauty, aren't you?" I countered, the pieces falling together in my head: her appearance, her accent, the almost-envy in her voice as she talked about me reeking of the living world. Midnight beauties—more properly "bela da meia-noite"—are party girls, pretty much always female, spending their nights in clubs and exclusive parties, shaking their groove things and reminding themselves what they're missing after they die. The only other crossroads ghost I know of who survived the destruction of our boss, Bethany, was offered the chance to become a midnight beauty.

She passed, which was probably for the best. She was never much of a party girl when she was still working for the crossroads. She's a reaper now, and I have to assume that's going better for her than an endless Carnival would have. At the very least, if she's had any complaints, she hasn't felt the need to deliver them to me.

Benedita narrowed her eyes. "What do you know of midnight beauties, skinny girl?" she demanded.

"I know that the only one I've seen in a while seems bound and determined to be pissed off at me, which isn't helping my mood much." I crossed my arms. "You all hiding here from the ghost hunters?"

Various voices shouted confirmations from around the room. To anyone alive, it would just have sounded like wind whistling through a keyhole, but I could hear them clearly. As her companions shouted their agreements, Benedita continued watching me warily.

Right. Well, Phee had known who I was from little more than the sight of Elsie and Art. Maybe I could be equally notorious here. "My name is Mary Dunlavy," I said. "I'm the last of the caretakers. And six months ago, I traveled to the United Kingdom with some of my charges, where we attacked the Covenant stronghold responsible for recent crimes against the cryptid population of the East Coast. People died, and in response, the Covenant has started hunting ghosts."

Benedita glared at me, eyes taking on an eerie glow and hair beginning to writhe like it possessed a life of its own. "This is *your* fault?" she demanded.

"We didn't anticipate this being the Covenant response," I said. "They attacked us first; we just responded in kind. And then they responded to us responding to them, but going for the ghosts is such a diagonal move that we didn't see it coming. I'm not sure what we'd have done if we had. We didn't really have another avenue of attack open to us, but they're attacking the dead because they somehow figured out that I was there before the bombs went off."

Benedita scowled and began to open her mouth for another accusation when another ghost drifted forward, cutting her off.

"Mary Dunlavy," said the ghost. This one was male, and had the sturdy, windblown look I tended to associate with field hauntings. Sometimes they were farmers, sometimes they were park rangers or naturalists or people who'd done roadwork before they died, but what they all had in common was that they'd been outdoor laborers in life, of one kind or another. Seeing one under a roof was jarring, like I was witnessing something that should have been entirely impossible. "You're the crossroads' girl, aren't you?"

"I was, when they still existed," I said. "They're gone now, and I'm nobody's girl but my own."

But that wasn't true, was it? I belonged to my family, and to the anima mundi. I couldn't think of a time when I'd belonged entirely to myself, not even when I was still alive.

"How can you still be here, with them gone?"

"Like I said, I'm the last of the caretakers. My family provide enough of a tether to keep me in the twilight." I turned my attention back to Benedita. "Jonah didn't seem to know much about the hunters, although he mentioned two companions who'd apparently been caught. How long ago were they taken?"

"Martha, a week ago, Agnes, yesterday," said Benedita. "Agnes got cocky. She thought they wouldn't do another sweep of the city hall after they'd already managed to nab Martha, and she forgot that she glows to the eyes of the living."

"She's a white lady," said Jonah. "She glows in the dark. It makes her really bad at hide and seek."

White ladies are incredibly dangerous. They're one of the rare migratory types of ghost who aren't tied to the road, being defined by things other than their tendency to move around. Most of them are set on revenge, trying to get payback for whatever killed them. I shot Benedita a concerned look.

She laughed, shaking her head. "Agnes *is* a white lady, and she's also a pacifist," she said. "She was technically murdered, but when she tracked down the man who'd killed her, he was able to prove it had been an accident well enough that she believed him, and she spent the rest of his life with him, haunting his house and helping him come to terms with what he'd done to her. By the time he died, he didn't have any unfinished business, and he moved right on along to whatever's next. Agnes didn't want to leave her garden in the middle of the season, so she stayed to tend it. She still has flares of vengeance when people mess around with things she considers her own, but she's not really in a hurry to fade away."

Ghosts who manage to linger past their purpose and change fascinated me. Gosh, I wonder why. This Agnes might be someone I could really get along with, if not for the fact that . . . "And the ghost hunters caught her?"

"Yeah," said Benedita. "Aoi saw it happen. They put her right into a jar, just like she was a bunch of preserves in need of canning. I don't know what they're doing with the ghosts they catch. None of us do."

"Martha isn't a white lady," said Jonah, more subdued. "She's a house ghost, just like any house ghost, only she's the ghost of a maid who died at City Hall. She belongs there. It's her only and always home. But they took her out of it like she was nothing at all, and it wasn't fair of them, and she never hurt *anybody*. She used to vanish for *days* if she even startled somebody who was still alive, she got so flustered! It's not right!"

A murmur of agreement swept through the other ghosts in the room, distant and unnerving as the creaking of rusty hinges in an old mausoleum. I shivered. They didn't seem to notice, not even Benedita; they were too absorbed by their own anger over the treatment of one of their own.

"Have any of you seen these ghost hunters?" I asked. "If you can give me descriptions, I can start trying to track them down."

"Oh, we can do better than that," said Benedita. "Remember, I said Aoi saw Agnes caught. Aoi, can you come over here?"

Another of the ghosts separated from the group and started toward us. They were slim and a little shorter than I was, with long dark hair and a well-tailored blazer over jeans and a white shirt. They would have looked perfectly normal and possibly even alive if not for one small issue.

They didn't have a face. Or rather, they had a face, because everything with a head has a face, but it didn't have any of the features a face should have. Where their features should have been there was nothing but an expanse of smooth, evenly tanned skin, unbroken. There weren't even divots to imply the presence of eyes or mouth or other such anatomical standards. I still got the feeling they were looking at me when they turned in my direction, head tilting first up and then down as they took my measure.

"Hey," they said. They didn't have a mouth, and speaking didn't change that, but the sound still seemed to come from where their mouth should have been. "I'm Aoi."

I stared. Impolite, sure. Understandable, also sure.

The figure's featureless face rippled and became a mirror of my own, even down to the little scar on my left cheek where I'd run into the corner of the kitchen table at the age of four. I'd bled all over the kitchen floor, and Daddy had laughed himself silly at all the fuss, and Mama had yelled at him for being insensitive, saying a scar on my face might make it harder for me to find a good husband, and I'd grown up with a weirdly mixed feeling about it, especially since it was barely visible most of the time.

But there it was, on the face of a stranger, attached to features I recognized and had no desire to share. The mirrored eyelashes and eyebrows were as white as my own, while the figure's own hair remained black. They smiled at me with my own lips.

"Hello, caretaker," they said. Their voice was a curious mix of the one they'd used before, with its bland Mid-Atlantic accent, and my own, still Michigan to the core. "You look surprised to see me. Am I scaring you?"

"No," I said, recovering my composure as best as I could. "I just didn't anticipate this multicultural a group of haunts in a New England town, that's all."

"We're right next to Boston, sweetheart," said Benedita, dryly. "We're as diverse as it gets. You want a good international haunting, you come to Worcester."

"Cool," I said. "Still, noppera-bō aren't even common in Japan. You can forgive me for being a little thrown when I see one in Massachusetts."

The stranger used my face to look disappointed. "Aw. I wanted to shock you. It's only fun when I can shock you."

"Sorry." I shrugged. "As we've already established, I spent a long time serving the crossroads. That means they could send me all over the world, and they loved sending me to places where I didn't speak the local language. It meant they could show off the fact that within their boundaries, all languages were the same language, and that language was the language of demanding. They called me to answer the needs of their petitioners, and I went. A few of the people I helped negotiate for became noppera-bō after they died." In the seventies, asking for beauty had been very common. Noppera-bō most frequently rose when they had felt invisible in life, or when they'd been unusually passionately focused on their appearances. I couldn't tell which one Aoi had been, and honestly, it didn't much matter either way. They were dead no matter how you sliced it.

Aoi sulked, which remained eerie when done with my own face. Benedita kicked them in the ankle.

"Stop messing her about and show her the hunters," she said. "She wants to see them, and maybe she can find them. From there, she either gets rid of them or they waste some time taking care of someone we don't care about. Either way, we win."

Aoi scoffed and rolled my eyes before their face began to melt and morph again, leaving mine mercifully behind. First, it settled into the face of a sharp-boned man, pointed chin, long nose, and wide-set, rounded eyes. Color bled into their eyebrows and lashes, turning them a sandy, nondescript brown, and the change flowed further down their throat, producing an Adam's apple where none had been before.

"We call this one 'the boss,'" they said, voice once again becoming a blend of their own and the face they were wearing. Unsurprisingly, their accent morphed with it, turning British, even if diluted by the mixture.

"Right," I said. Their current face wasn't one I'd seen before, and despite the resemblance, wasn't the Covenant team lead I'd met when we were all in New Gravesend, Maine: Leonard Cunningham either wasn't hanging around here or wasn't in charge of this group after all the failure. Honestly, if his legacy in the Covenant was failure after failure, I wouldn't be upset about that. It couldn't happen to a nicer guy.

Aoi's face shifted again, this time turning feminine but retaining the same basic coloration. They looked enough like the prior face for the two to have been siblings, and both of them looked enough like Leonard that if I hadn't seen him before, I could have believed they *were* him.

The third face was male, darker-skinned, with brows and lashes a few shades darker than Benedita's hair. Benedita made an unhappy sound and looked away.

"Someone you know?" I asked.

"Drop it, crossroads bitch," she replied.

That felt like a sore spot I shouldn't palpate until I was willing to deal with the consequences. I looked back to Aoi, whose face was morphing again, remaining masculine but scrawny and pale, with dark brown lashes and brows. They shook their head, and the changes faded, their natural featureless state reasserting itself.

"That's all I've seen," they said, voice back to its default state. "I didn't hang around when they started bottling my friends."

"Understandably," I said. "Thank you for what you've been able to show me. It's going to be a huge help." Annie's report on her time in the Covenant had included every name she could dredge out of the depths of her memory. She'd mentioned Leonard, but also his two siblings, Chloe and Nathaniel. I was pretty sure those were the first two faces Aoi had shown me. The other two were unfamiliar, but I'd know them soon enough. That was the whole point of my coming to town, after all.

I straightened. "Where can I find them?"

"This time of night, probably near the city hall," Aoi said. "They know they've missed at least one ghost, and they're not going to rest until they catch him. Do you know why they're doing this?"

"Like I said, revenge. Are you aware of the Ocean Lady?"

Aoi shook their head. For not having a face, they were remarkably easy to read, having learned to compensate for their lack of expression with body language and positioning. "Never heard the name."

"It's an old term for the Old Atlantic Highway, which used to be the longest continuous road in North America," I said. "When the road was broken up and functionally killed, it relocated to the twilight, where it became self-aware, took on female pronouns, and ascended to the rank of goddess. That is the super short, condensed version, and no, I can't really unpack it much further than that, but the Ocean Lady is part of why I'm here. She's the patron and residence of the current Queen of the Routewitches, Apple, who asked me to come and see what was going on around here."

"Okay," said Benedita. "Your point?"

"My point is that Apple, through the Ocean Lady, knows some of what these Covenant fucks are doing with the ghosts they capture," I said. "They're stuffing them into spirit jars filled with salt and iron and other spirit-shredding devices, and they're torturing the dead to turn them into weapons. And the more ghosts the Covenant removes, the stronger all the remaining ghosts get, until every one of us becomes a ticking time bomb."

The room fell silent, the sort of deep, palpable silence that's only really possible when there's no one living around. In a room full of live people, there will be breath, and shuffling, and even the distant, dampened sound of heartbeats keeping things from going too quiet. But we were all dead. We had no sounds to offer to the void.

Then Jonah shouted, "We have to go get them! We have to *save* them! It was bad enough when they were just taking them like, like souvenirs, but if they're *torturing* them—"

"No," said Benedita, harshly. "We don't have any proof this crossroads bitch is telling us the truth about what they're doing. Maybe they just want to collect ghosts and save them for later. Maybe they think they're laying us to rest. It doesn't matter. We're not running off and putting ourselves in harm's way on her say-so."

"I think she's right about the rest of us getting stronger," said Aoi hesitantly. "I can't normally cycle through this many faces, this quickly, but right now, it feels like I could be a one-ghost improv troupe."

Jonah glared at Benedita. She glared back.

"You found us this place, and we're grateful," she said. "You made sure we had a safe hole to cluster up in, and we appreciate you. But you're still a *child*. You don't get to tell us to risk ourselves."

I blinked, slowly. Jonah was a caddis fly who'd never quite

finished forming, and his childhood home had been torn down, probably because it was considered a plague pit, then used to build new structures, like the city hall. I took another look around at the brick walls of the basement where we were hiding.

"Jonah, is part of your house here?" I asked.

He nodded, still glaring at Benedita. "They used my bricks all over the city when they pulled my house down," he said.

"How *much* of the city would you say has pieces of your house worked into its walls?"

"I don't know. Everything they were building that year. The city hall, and the courtyard outside the fountain, and some old stores, like this one—it used to be a general store, and now it's part of a strip mall. A bunch of houses. The library."

"And you can go to any of those places?"

He nodded.

"Can you tell what's happening inside the places you're connected to?"

I had never heard of anything like this, a caddis being broken up and patchworked across a city, but if I could exist, so could Jonah. He frowned, face screwing up in concentration for several seconds before his eyes went wide and bright with sudden revelation. "Oh!" he said. "Oh, I can *hear* them."

"Hear who?" asked Benedita.

"All the people who live in buildings my house is a part of. There are so many. They're having dinner, and putting kids to bed, and watching television programs, and I could join any one of them if I wanted to—"

"Focus, Jonah," I said. "What about City Hall? What's going on there?"

He frowned again, this time in irritation rather than confusion. "There's a broken window, cold air over glass, and there are people who aren't supposed to be there inside."

"Where?"

"Basement."

"Great. Can you take me to the lobby?"

Jonah looked surprised. "Why would you want to go—"

"I don't know your city hall well enough to aim for somewhere specific without help, and I want to talk to these people before they realize I'm dead," I said. I flickered, replacing my clothes with a generic security uniform, buttoned white blouse and tan slacks and a heavy black belt around my waist. My name tag said I was Eloise and that I worked for the city. Mom wouldn't mind me borrowing her name for something this important. My hair was shoved up under a police cap that felt like a good affectation for the role.

White hair would have been a major tip-off twenty years ago, or even ten, but now, with fashionable hair colors on the rise and dye available in every corner store, it would just make me look too young for the job I was pretending to have, naïve and easy to manipulate. That was all part of the plan.

I offered Jonah one hand, pulling the flashlight from my belt with the other. "Come on, kiddo," I said. "You can get me there."

He took my hand, glancing anxiously at Benedita. She turned her face resentfully away, refusing to acknowledge us, and then she couldn't acknowledge us, because we were gone.

Twelve

"Sometimes thinking about your life gives me a headache
so big I think it's going to split my skull in two."

—Juniper Campbell

*Worcester, Massachusetts,
in the lobby of City Hall, preparing to play
bait for a bunch of Covenant ghost hunters*

We APPEARED IN THE DARK lobby of the city hall, Jonah's hand
tight on mine, his face pale and pinched in the light coming in
through the windows. I looked down at him, relieved to see that
he wasn't measurably glowing. Homesteaders don't, usually, but
again, he'd already done things his type of ghost wasn't meant to
do. A broken caddis could be capable of just about anything, and I
wouldn't necessarily know about it. It was a complication I didn't
need, with ghost hunters lurking around every corner and two—
two—divinities watching over me.

The lobby looked like the lobby of every other city hall I'd seen
in the last decade. Modern design sensibilities had a way of pressing things into the same mold, homogenizing them one curved
desk and brass seal at a time. Even the air had the cool, dry, dusty
smell that I associated with government buildings, perfectly generic, perfectly neutral.

Jonah released me. "This is where they took Martha," he said.
"I have to go."

"Will you go back to the others?" I asked. "I can find that place now, since I've been there. I'll come when I'm finished here."

"You promise?" There was a world of mistrust and damage in his eyes as he looked at me.

I nodded. "I promise," I said, and he was gone, leaving me alone in City Hall.

Clicking my flashlight on, I started for the hall that would take me deeper into the building. I needed to find these people.

Once out of the lobby, I could hear the distant sounds of motion, of living people trying to navigate in the dark. I nodded to myself and started toward them, flashlight high. The longer I could keep them from getting a clear look at my face, the better my chances would be. I walked, and tried to figure out whether I was being clever or foolish. I was walking straight into danger, but that was the only way I was going to know what that danger really looked like.

Elsie and Arthur were with me so I'd have backup, but they weren't immortal, and I wasn't making ghosts out of any more of my charges. I might have, if I'd known they would linger; I'm not too proud or too ethical to admit that the temptation was occasionally there. A lifetime ago, when Alice was wounded in the Galway Woods, I tried to convince Thomas to back out of his bargain with my employers and let Alice slip into the afterlife, with me. I'd been trying to save him, yes, but I'd also been thinking of myself, of binding Alice to the crossroads so she could never leave me.

I'm not Peter Pan, but I'm the Wendy Darling who never left Neverland, who never stopped playing mother for children who would inevitably outgrow her and slip away. Sometimes I get lonely. Sometimes I wish they'd die young enough to keep needing me forever. And every time that thought pops up again, I push those shameful pieces of myself down as hard as I can, burying them under obligation and understanding that dead is very rarely better. It's not their fault they still have lives to lead, while mine is incontrovertibly over. So I was going to risk my own unlife before I asked my kids to come and risk the only real lives they were ever going to have.

Besides, they were probably eating dinner by now, Elsie possibly flirting with Amelia, Amelia possibly flirting with Arthur, everyone laughing and a little bit uncomfortable at the same time as they tried to work out how serious everyone else was being. Phee seemed like the sort who'd set a warm and welcoming table, the kind of place where everyone felt comfortable and no one walked away hungry. It was better this way. Let me do the legwork; let them enjoy being young and alive and together for just a little longer.

I turned a corner, and there they were, three living people in a place that should have been left to the ghosts at this hour, the taller of the two men positioned in front of the single woman, a flashlight of his own in his hands. She was carrying a large mason jar, the lid already removed, the interior painted with sigils in silver paste of some sort. Crushed rosemary filled the bottom inch or so. I could feel it calling to me, pulling at me across the distance between us. A second man lurked a bit farther back, this one the dark-haired man who'd made Benedita scowl so, and his hands were empty, which meant he was the most dangerous of the three, or would have been, if I'd been a living opponent. He was ready to go for a weapon.

Weapons are bad. For me, in the moment, the open spirit jar was worse. "Hello?" I said, trying to make it more of a demand than a simple question. You *will* answer me, you *will* tell me what I want to know. You won't turn and run away, even though it would be the sensible thing to do. "You can't be here."

That seemed like a very security-guard thing to say, and I was momentarily proud of myself before the man in the lead replied, in what sounded like the same British accent I'd heard from Aoi, now stripped of its Boston undertones: "Oh, no, miss, we have permission from the mayor."

"No one told me about any permission." True, if incomplete. No one associated with the city was likely to be telling me anything. "Why do you have permission from the mayor? To do what? And if you're allowed to be here, why are you creeping around with the lights out? That's creepy-cakes territory, and I don't like it."

"We're ghostbusters," said the woman with the jar, keeping her voice light, bright, and measured, like she thought she was auditioning for a children's television show about creeping around municipal buildings in the dark. I couldn't imagine it was going to get particularly good ratings, although I've been wrong about that sort of thing before. "We're taking care of that pesky haunting you've been dealing with." Her accent matched the first man's perfectly.

"We've caught two of the ghosts so far," said the man. "Tell us, do you know where the little boy normally manifests?"

If he was smart, in the courtyard by the fountain, or the strip-mall basement where his friends were. But the two Covenant operatives who'd spoken were looking at me with too-bright eyes and artificial smiles, while the third watched the hall behind them, keeping an eye out for ghosts who might want to sneak up and get a little revenge.

Not that I'd blame any ghost who wanted to kick these people in the throat for what they'd been doing, but it would a wasted effort for most phantoms. Very few of us are capable of interacting concretely with the material world, and touching actual, living humans was beyond even most ghosts who *could* float a rock or slam a door when they wanted to. He was keeping an eye out for nothing.

"Ghosts don't exist," I said, crossing my arms. "Did Davey put you up to this? Nerd. Just because I got freaked out at *The Blair Witch Project* one time, he thinks he can prank me with *Scooby-Doo* stories any time he wants to." I pitched my voice louder, not quite shouting. "Not funny, Davey, you hear me? You're not funny, and I'm *not* going to prom with you, no matter how many times you try to scare me into saying yes."

The nonexistent Davey didn't reply. The three Covenant operatives flinched, moving a little closer together, while the man at the front turned his flashlight on my face, shining it directly into my eyes.

I was suddenly, fiercely glad that the anima mundi had stolen the graveyard from my eyes. You can bluff even trained killers like these Covenant operatives, if you do it the right way and with absolute confidence. But I didn't think there was a bluff in this world that would stand up to them looking into my eyes and seeing the impossible.

"I assure you, miss, ah, Eloise, ghosts are very real," said the man smoothly. "We've been moving up and down the coast hunting for them, and we've managed to collect quite an assortment. When we heard that your city hall was home to not one but three spirits, we knew we had to intervene."

"So where's the TV cameras?" I asked. "If you're saying actual real ghosts exist, and you can actually for reals catch them, you should be filming it and making, like, *all* the money."

"We're doing this for our own reasons," said the woman. "We don't want to be famous."

"Oh yeah? What reasons are those?" I didn't actually like how long this conversation had been going on. The longer we talked, the more chance there was that they'd realize something was wrong with me, or that an actual security guard would come along. No matter how smooth they were about claiming to have permission to be here, I didn't buy it. They were getting nervous, although they were covering it as well as they could.

Not for the first time, since I'd been in New York when things were just starting to get bad, I was struck by how *young* all of these operatives were. So far, I had yet to encounter a Covenant agent who was older than my kids, and sure, my kids were reaching the age where they settled down and had kids of their own, but still. I never saw any Covenant elders, none of the people who supposedly ran the show. Were they all in hiding, or were they all dead?

If the Covenant was putting on a good show of still having a coherent leadership in place when they were really just a bunch of kids trying to keep the monsters away from their doors, this all might come to a much easier end than we were afraid of. I would like that. My kids would like that. And we probably weren't going to get it, because nothing is ever that easy, not really.

"A ghost—a very dangerous ghost—damaged our family home," said the woman, earning herself a sharp look from the man who was probably her brother. "We don't know exactly how. Poltergeists aren't supposed to be that powerful. But the ghost managed to cave half the building in on top of itself, and our mother was killed."

"Oh, no," I said, and I meant it. "I'm so sorry."

We knew when we set off the bombs that people were going to be hurt. We'd been hoping for it, even—what was the point of an attack that didn't hurt anybody? We wanted the Covenant to go away and leave us alone, and that meant making a point they couldn't ignore. But there was an abstract "people might get hurt," and then there was someone right in front of me with hollow, grief-struck eyes, telling me that I had helped to kill her mother.

I spent decades working for the crossroads. I killed a lot of people's mothers, either because they came to us with a petition and the price destroyed them, or because they'd been collateral damage to someone else's bargain. I killed a lot of people, period. And none of that made it any easier to face this girl who looked a few years younger than Antimony and know, completely, that I had put her mother in the ground.

"So we're going to hunt down every ghost in the world and

make sure they can't hurt anyone else," she continued, as if that were a perfectly reasonable, proportionate response. My brief spark of sympathy flared and died.

"Ah," I said.

"My mother is alive and well," said the darker-skinned man, accent South American and sweet. "She's back home in Brazil, waiting for me to return and tell her that my sister's soul is finally at rest."

"Your sister?" I asked, dreadfully afraid I already knew the answer he was going to give me.

"She was a foolish girl. She ran afoul of a silbón in the club where she spent her nights, and she danced with him until dawn. She returned the next night to do it again, and again the night after that, and every night until he had drained the life from her body and she collapsed in the street, old beyond her years, with a heart as worn and tattered as tissue paper. We buried her in holy ground and thought to grieve her in peace, only for people to see her at the club the night after her funeral. She had risen as a midnight beauty, compelled to return from beyond the grave by her cruel lover. I will find her, and I will bring her home to our family, where she can rest at last."

That explained Benedita's reaction when Aoi had put on the man's face. He was her brother. All these people had been victimized by the dead, one way or another, and all of them were good arguments for why the twilight and the daylight needed to stay separate.

And I couldn't feel too bad for them, because their response to that victimization was to turn around and hurt people who didn't have anything to do with their fight. It didn't matter that the people they were hurting were already dead: we were still here, we had feelings and dreams and reasons to keep existing, and as far as I could tell, Agnes and Martha had never hurt anyone. These people were lashing out in all the wrong directions.

I unfolded my arms. "Gosh, those are some sad stories," I said. "Guess I could understand why you wouldn't want to go on television and tell the whole world how the ghosts hurt you."

"Thank you," said the first man. "Now if you could just—"

"But I didn't hear anything about you being allowed in the building after we locked up for the night, and I really need this job. So if you want to wait here for a minute, I'll go back to the lobby and call the mayor's nighttime office. They can tell me if he gave you a pass to come in while we're closed."

His face fell, then slammed shut, all geniality gone in an instant and replaced by a hard, cold shell of businesslike efficiency. "I don't think you want to do that," he said. His free hand dipped into the pocket of his jacket, and produced a Taser.

I blinked at him, trying to maintain the aura of guileless, somewhat bumbling security guard that I'd been projecting thus far. "Gosh, mister," I said, aware even as I spoke that I was on the cusp of laying it on too thickly. But then, none of these folks were from around here. Maybe they'd assume all American teenagers talked like me. Sorry, American teens. "I didn't know you could hurt ghosts with a Taser."

"You can't."

"So why are you carrying one?" I let my eyes go wide and round. "Unless you're going to hurt something that's not a ghost."

"I don't want to," he said, and he sounded almost sincere; I could almost believe him. "If you just turn around and walk away, and promise not to call anyone about us being here, I won't have to."

"If you really believe that, then you're as tactically inexperienced as you look, and you have no business being in the field," I said.

"What?" he asked, looking genuinely startled. So did his sister. Benedita's brother was a bit older, or just a little more jaded, because he looked less surprised than he did resigned, moving closer to his companions with a small frown on his face.

"You can't let me walk away," I said, shining *my* flashlight full in *his* face for a change. "Even if I promise not to call anyone, I'll have seen your faces. I'll be able to identify you on the street. And I know you're creeping around government buildings at night with a Taser in your hand, which isn't the sort of thing a security guard is supposed to just let go. It would be worth my job."

"Is your job worth letting yourself be shocked into unconsciousness?" asked the girl, sounding genuinely concerned.

"In this economy it might be, if this were my job," I said.

"What do you mean?" asked the man, warily.

I measured the distance between me and the girl with her so-threatening jar. Sure, it was open, and sure, it was technically magic, but it wasn't a vacuum cleaner. She'd need to be much closer to threaten me properly.

I grinned, a little manically. "Dead people don't normally have jobs," I said.

To my surprise, the man with the Taser laughed, lowering it. "Is that so?" he asked. "Anything else you want to tell us about how ghosts work?"

I blinked. "Not really," I said. "There's being a good neighbor, and then there's giving information to the enemy, and I prefer to stay on the side of the equation where I don't wind up in a jar."

The woman was the first to get my meaning. Her eyes widened incrementally, and she began trying to ease her way forward, past the man with the Taser. He didn't move out of her way. He was too busy staring at me like I had suddenly become a puzzle very much in need of solving. I raised my free hand—the one that wasn't holding the flashlight—and wiggled my fingers in a mocking wave. If I timed this right, it would be the wave that he remembered, the feeling of dismissal that it carried. It would haunt him when he tried to sleep.

"Boo," I said, and vanished.

I remanifested on the other side of the room, behind the trio, remaining invisible. No sense in making this easy on them.

"Shit!" said the man in the lead. "Shit, shit, *shit!*"

"You kiss our mother with that mouth, Nathaniel?" asked the woman. "Oh, no, wait, you don't, because *ghosts* like the one you just let get away from us killed her. Well, swear away! I suppose that's all you're good for."

"That ghost was taunting us," said the man at the rear of the group. "The locals must have called for backup."

"Can ghosts *do* that?" demanded the woman, voice going shrill. "Can they just phone up other ghosts and ask them to come help them haunt innocent people?"

They both looked toward Nathaniel, who had apparently been elected "guy who knows things about ghosts and how they work," whether or not he wanted the position. Based on his expression, the answer was very much "not."

"Some ghosts can," said Nathaniel, flicking his flashlight's beam quickly around the edges of the room, clearly looking for me. I spared a momentary thought for appearing when he reached the corner where I stood, giving him one nice, cinematic jump scare, but decided against it.

They were armed and anxious and already looking for ghosts. Playing with them wasn't going to help at all.

"Why in the formerly living fuck are ghosts like Pokémon?" demanded the woman. "We don't need all these fucking flavors! We could have done perfectly well with the ones who haunt houses and the ones who haunt highways, full stop, close the book and walk away! Ghosts should be easy and predictable."

"Shut *up*, Chloe," said Nathaniel. "Ghosts are as diverse as people. It makes sense that they'd have different capabilities."

"It makes sense," repeated Chloe, in a mocking tone. "God, there's a *reason* you were never supposed to be out in the field. Heitor, have I reminded you recently that my brother is going to get us all killed?"

"You're not helping," said Benedita's brother, who I now presumed was named Heitor. "Strong emotions make for stronger ghosts. Are you hoping to return and haunt us from beyond the grave?"

"Of course not," said Chloe, sounding offended. "But my brother just decided to have a long chat with a ghost instead of getting rid of it, and that means there's one more haunt out there for us to deal with."

"We knew there was a third ghost tied to this location," said Nathaniel.

"Yes, a ghost that appears as a prepubescent *boy*," snapped Chloe. "Even if we want to say that we can't guess ghost genders—not that they matter, they're dead, they don't need genders anymore—that ghost was *definitely* postpubescent."

Still bickering about ghosts, the trio moved on. I watched them until they were out of the room, then turned visible again with a silent sigh of relief. Invisibility isn't easy. My "body's" first impulse, when I tell it not to be seen, is to drop down into the twilight, where there's no chance the living will spot me. Useful as an escape strategy, not too great for hiding.

On the positive side of things, holding invisibility is no harder than holding my breath or tensing a muscle was when I was alive. It even seems to use the same part of my brain—not that I have one of those anymore, either. I was sure our three intrepid ghost hunters would be thrilled to shift their argument to ghost anatomy—why do human ghosts tend to look like people, anyway? Why do we behave as if we still possess the bodies we lost when we died?

(And looking like people isn't voluntary for most of us. There are ghosts like Aoi, who can change their faces, and there are ghosts that can turn themselves into fireflies or change their apparent age, but for the most part, what you see is what you get. A ghost like a coachman, who's bonded with their vehicle, will always be bonded with that vehicle. They don't get to turn themselves back into an independent biped just because they're tired of it. The spirit endures after death, and it endures as itself. There's probably something profound about that. If so, it's not something I've ever seen clearly. I just work here.)

With Jonah safely out of the building, the ghost hunters could search until dawn and not find anything. It didn't feel like there were any other ghosts in the vicinity, and so I vanished again, this time reappearing outside, in an alcove against the side of the building.

If City Hall had CCTV, someone might see the flicker of my appearance, but I doubted that any of the building's security was currently connected or staffed. The Covenant ghost hunters wouldn't have been strolling around so casually if there'd been a chance they'd be caught on tape, and I didn't believe they had permission to be here. Maybe in a different world, or if they'd hired some mooks to follow them around pretending to film a reality television program, but in this world, without their own cameras? They were skulking about where they weren't supposed to be, and I was perfectly willing to exploit that.

Safely outside, I looked down to see what I was wearing, and decided the Sabrina-from-*Archie*-esque black-skirt-and-sweater ensemble with thick blue tights was acceptably neutral to be believable as something a teenage girl might wear while taking an ill-advised midnight walk. There was a strange pressure at my scalp. I reached up and verified that the outfit came with a headband.

I am the universe's Barbie doll some days, and I'm pretty much okay with that.

Stepping away from the wall, I began circling the grounds of City Hall. Halfway around the building, I found my target: a plain blue-gray van parked at the curb, next to an unfed off-hours parking meter. The engine wasn't idling, but there were no windows beyond the bare minimum legally required for them to remain road-legal. I walked closer, then did a quick circuit around the van before knocking on the rear door.

There was a scuffling sound from inside. Several seconds ticked by. I knocked again. The door swung open, and a pale, scrawny man with dark hair and the beginnings of a mustache on his upper lip stuck his head out. His had been the fourth face Aoi showed me, but the way he wore it looked so much like a stereotypical Hollywood nerd that I almost wanted to blip myself back inside and scold the Covenant team for playing in to expectations. Instead, I folded my hands behind my back and smiled at him with all the innocent teenage guilelessness that I could muster.

The longer I've been sixteen, the funnier it's been to me that most people over the age of twenty—living or dead after that age—will accept anything I say as true, as long as I say it with a smile. It's like they've forgotten what it was to be young, and innocent, and heartless.

"Hi," I said, cheerfully. "This is a no-parking zone. Are you okay, mister?"

"I have a permit," he said, moving as if to close the van door.

"No, you don't," I said, before he could.

He stopped, blinking like a member of an improv troupe whose "yes, and" had suddenly transformed into a "no, why" without warning. "What?" He had a generic American accent, and I silently cursed Hollywood for making it so much easier for people to sound like they came from nowhere, everywhere, and Toronto all at the same time.

"My uncle's in charge of parking for this area, and I know he didn't issue any parking permits for the no-parking zones around City Hall," I said. "He always tells me, because I like to TP the cars that aren't supposed to be here. Makes it easier for the traffic cops to find them the next day."

He blinked again, before alarm blossomed in his face like a strange, terrible flower. "You do *what?*"

"Toilet paper," I said. "Eggs, too, to help it stick to the cars. They damage the paint sometimes, so I'm not supposed to let anybody see me, but it's a civic service and I have a lot of fun doing it. So again, are you okay, mister? Because vans are big, and it'll take a lot of toilet paper to really mess yours up. I'd rather not, if you don't mind moving along before I absolutely have to."

He looked over his shoulder and back into the van. That was long enough for me to flicker out, and when he looked back, I was standing exactly where he expected me to be, still smiling angelically.

I promptly pegged him in the chest with a roll of toilet paper. He yelped, and I tried not to scowl.

You'd think after raising three generations of Price-Healys to adulthood that I'd have the aim of a Greek goddess, and yeah, I hit the guy. But I'd been aiming for his face, not his chest, and I was annoyed by my own inaccuracy.

"Hey!" he said, straightening up and looking wounded. "What was that for?"

"Just proving that I'm serious, mister," I said, and grinned. It was easy to grin at the expression on his face.

"You shouldn't throw things at people," he said.

"And you shouldn't be parking here," I replied. I'd already confirmed one thing beyond all question: they weren't somehow sneaking around City Hall on a permit from the mayor. If they were, this guy would be bragging about it. He looked like the sort of jerk who liked to brag to teenage girls about how cool he was.

". . . fair enough," he said, and stepped out of the van, closing it behind himself before I could get more than a glimpse of blinking lights and static-filled monitors. There was no sign of anyone else. I didn't think he was working alone, not with that trio inside, but I suspected he was the only one they'd left to watch their backs.

Amateurs.

"My friends and I are doing a very important, sort of extracurricular project, and I don't have a parking permit because there wasn't any way for me to ask for one, but please don't TP my van, I can't really afford to get it detailed right now," he said, all in a rush.

I raised an eyebrow. "What, your friends won't help you after they left you out here to be their van guy? What could be so important that you're willing to sit alone in a van like a giant creep in the middle of the night? Oh, are you trying to kidnap local kids? Should I be worried?"

"I'm pretty sure anyone who kidnapped you would put you right back where they found you," said the man.

"That's not very nice!"

"Neither is hitting people with toilet paper, and yet here we are."

"Rude," I said, biting my lip the way Elsie did when she wanted someone to think they might have a chance. Either he would find it incredibly off-putting, due to my age, or he would find it incredibly appealing for the same reason. If it was the first, I could back off and try something else—maybe bringing Elsie for a chat with him, maybe abandoning this angle completely. If it was the second, then he was the kind of skeeze who thought teenage girls walking alone at night were reasonable dating prospects, and I wouldn't have to feel bad about anything we decided to do to him.

Not that I was going to feel bad one way or the other: he was working with the Covenant, if he wasn't a full member—and having an American accent didn't exempt him from membership. They might not have been very active in North America for the last few decades, but Americans had a tendency to travel, and vulnerable people can be recruited anywhere.

Ask me how I know.

To my vague disappointment, he stood up a little straighter, looking like he wanted to straighten the tie he wasn't wearing. A cute girl was paying attention to him. He wanted to look his best. Gross much?

"If your uncle's in charge of parking, I'm sure you've heard the old city hall is haunted," he said, sounding suddenly self-important.

I shrugged, like that was the least impressive thing I'd ever heard. "Yeah, three ghosts, big spooky, much scare, wow. What about it?"

He blinked and frowned, looking suddenly less inflated and more wary. "Well, they've been here forever," he said. "My friends are ghostbusters. Real ones, like in the movies. And they gave me a list of things to watch for when I'm trying to keep an eye out for ghosts. Things like outdated clothes and slang. Did you know that doge fell out of favor on the internet more than a decade ago?"

Since it had been more than a decade since I had a teenager to take care of, no, I hadn't been aware of that. I tried to cover my surprise by looking down at my outfit. "This isn't outdated," I protested. "These are my creeping-around-in-the-dark clothes, and black is timeless. Besides, I wasn't aware that saying 'far out, man' was an offense worth calling someone a phantom over."

"I didn't call you anything. I just implied."

"Yeah, well, when guys like you imply things about girls like me, we're somehow always the ones who wind up with our reputations in tatters, while you get to keep hanging out in your creepy vans like nothing happened."

He frowned. "Okay, that's a little extreme, and my van is not creepy."

"If I were a ghost, could I have thrown that toilet paper roll at you? You should give it back, by the way. The stuff's expensive." It was still on the pavement where it had fallen after it bounced off of his chest, and Alice wouldn't want it back after it had absorbed all that grease and oil from the street—I just wanted him to touch it and confirm that it was real, not some ghostly trick.

I mean, it *was* a ghostly trick. The trick was just that I had blipped myself to Michigan and swiped the paper from the bathroom, then come back again before he could see that I was gone. Alice hadn't changed where she kept anything since she moved into that house, and I'd been banking on that still being the case.

"Sorry," he said, a little sullenly, and bent to pick up the toilet paper, grimacing at the wet, sticky feel of the side that had been against the pavement. "You sure you want this? It's pretty nasty."

"Give it here," I said, holding up my hands.

My ability to catch is better than my ability to throw, and I'd been assuming he could at least toss a gentle underhand. I was braced. Instead, he threw that roll of gross paper like it was the football at the big game, and it bounced off my arm with a nasty squelching sound.

That was almost better than me catching it. I yelped—half a beat too slow, but he was so busy looking horrified that I was pretty sure he didn't notice—and pulled my arm to my chest, glaring at him.

"*Look* at my sweater!" I said, turning to show him the mucky, oily stain now spreading through the fabric. "Do you feel better now, dick?"

"I—I'm sorry," he said. "I guess I just got sort of freaked out sitting here in the van all by myself, and then you came along, and you ticked off so many of the 'might be dead' boxes, and I . . . I'm sorry." He opened the van door. "Come inside, I'll help you clean that up."

I looked at him mistrustfully. A real teenage girl would have to have been a fool to get in that van with a strange man. I, however, wasn't real in the "can be hurt" sense, not anymore. I was a dead teenage girl, and the rules were different for me than they were for anyone with a pulse. After taking what I hoped would read as a long enough pause to consider, I shrugged, said, "Why the hell not?" and walked over to step past him into the van.

Two things immediately jumped out at me. First, in addition to the wall of monitors and blinking electric equipment, there was a wall of metal shelves bolted into place and loaded down with glass mason jars in a variety of sizes. They contained a wide assortment of objects, nails and railway spikes and bits of broken mirror. That was the unimportant part, because they also held ghosts. Every single one of them was occupied, phantoms beating intangible fists against the glass, mouths open in silent, endless screams.

When you don't need to breathe, you can keep screaming for a long, long time. Like forever.

The second thing was more subtle, but more alarming. Someone had etched a Mesmer cage into the van's frame, making the whole thing one big, mobile, ghost-containment unit. Which I was now standing inside.

Fuck.

Thirteen

"Life isn't all there is. Everything wants to keep existing, even things that have never been alive. Sometimes you just have to let them."

—**Apple Tanaka**

Worcester, Massachusetts,
in the back of an unmarked van with a man
who doesn't seem to realize how upsetting this is

SEE ANYTHING?" ASKED THE MAN. He moved to sit in front of the bank of monitors, looking far more relaxed now that we were inside the van. As well he should. He could leave.

And I couldn't.

Mesmer cages were invented by the spiritualist of the same name, and quickly became popular with umbramancers, who saw them as a way to ward off and contain intrusive spirits. Ghosts are drawn to umbramancers like moths to flame, sometimes with the same self-immolating ends. I remembered how much the general spirit population had harassed Laura before her disappearance, and I couldn't really blame her for putting up walls to try and buy herself a little peace.

Umbramancers aren't common. The majority commit suicide before the age of thirty, choosing to pass on into nothingness rather than remain a target for an army of ghosts. But they don't have a monopoly on Mesmer cages, sadly. And I do mean that "sadly": this man, this boy, was no umbramancer. He was watching me with the earnest smugness of someone who thought he'd just done something really impressive in front of a cute girl, and I realized he thought I was fixated on the rack of bottled ghosts, not frozen with horror.

Well, that was useful, at the very least.

The Mesmer cage made sense: they contain ghosts. At the end of the day, that's their primary purpose. And with all those ghosts under glass in here, he had good reason to want to know that they'd be contained if something happened, if there was an accident or an earthquake or whatever. Some of the ghosts barely looked human anymore. They were just agonized, howling faces ringed by the dust kicked up by their panic. That, too, was a bad sign. Ghosts settle shortly after death, taking on whatever form they're going to inhabit for the length of their afterlife. Not many ghosts settle as poltergeists. These ghosts were demonstrating poltergeist abilities by making the dust hang in the air, and they didn't even necessarily know that they were doing it.

No wonder the anima mundi had wanted me to get involved. This was horrifying no matter how you looked at it.

"What's in the jars?" I asked, trying to sound nonchalant, like I wasn't watching human spirits being tortured while I stood inside something that was essentially just a larger jar. I've heard stories of ghosts escaping from Mesmer cages by mimicking the living so well that the symbols making up the pattern can't detect the difference, but I've never needed to mimic the living that well. I had no idea whether I'd be able to exit without help, and if I tried and failed, the man who'd invited me inside would realize that he had something more than just a midnight prankster.

"Can't you see them?" he asked, sounding honestly curious. "I couldn't at first. Not until Nathaniel started adding iron filings to all the jars. He says it encourages them toward solidity, which doesn't make sense to me, but then, none of this has made any sense to me, not since the very beginning. You should be able to see *something*."

I frowned and moved closer to the rack of jars, straining like I was trying to see something that wouldn't quite come in focus.

One of the jarred ghosts abruptly rushed the glass, mouth hanging open in an agonized howl, bits of salt and iron and broken mirror swirling around it like they were caught in a localized wind storm. I didn't have to feign my yelp, and I jumped backward. The man from the van was there to catch and steady me, placing one hand on my waist and leaving it there.

"Easy, easy," he said, like he was trying to soothe a frightened horse. "They can't hurt you. I told you my friends were ghost-busters. Well, this is where they put the ghosts they catch."

"I can see them now," I said, blinking rapidly, as if the shock had suddenly brought all the other spirits into focus. Not all of them were screaming. Some were crying, or huddled on one side of the jar, doing their best to avoid the offending items. The truly agitated ones seemed to have incorporated all those bits and pieces into themselves, becoming the things that hurt them.

Even if I could somehow get them all out of here, they might well be past saving.

That was a problem for later, when I knew how I was getting *myself* out of here—something I'd need to do soon, since the Covenant stooges inside the city hall were going to figure out eventually that Jonah wasn't there, and they were chasing a hollow haunting. They might recognize me. They might not. Either way, I didn't want to deal with them right now. I wanted to get back to Phee's boardinghouse and tell Elsie and Artie that we were definitely in the right place. I wanted to go to Oregon and ask Annie whether any of these people sounded familiar.

I wanted to go to the King Spa in Palisades Park and spend a few hours scrubbing myself, until I felt like the filth of this whole encounter had been removed from my spectral skin. They're used to ghosts at the King Spa. As long as we pay our way and don't bother the other customers, they don't make too much of a fuss about the fact that we're there. I appreciate people who can show the dead that much respect.

"Impressive, aren't they?" His hand was still on my waist, holding me in place, barely shy of possessive.

I glanced back at him, trying to figure out how I wanted to play this. I never had a lot of practice flirting. When I was alive, I was trying to keep my father above water, and once I'd been dead, I'd also been busy. Somehow, sorting out the confusing mess of human sexuality had never seemed to matter half as much as keeping the crossroads from swallowing my chosen family whole. I was pretty sure I didn't like his hand on me, didn't have any interest in the half-formed thoughts I could see coming together in his eyes; you don't need to be a telepath to read certain intentions.

My choices were this man, the door I might not be able to get through on my own, or the rack of screaming, desperate spirits. I took a half-step back, so that the back of my thigh was pressed against the side of his, and let my voice get high and anxious as I asked, "*What* are they? Those can't be real ghosts, not really. Ghosts aren't real. I don't like them. I don't like the way they're looking at me."

"Maybe ghosts aren't real. I don't think they're the spirits of dead humans. But whatever they are, they're what we've always referred to as 'ghosts,' and they exist. My friends have been catching them all along the coast. We go to old places, or places like this city hall that were built with materials taken from old places, and we catch what we find there. I'm new to the organization, so I don't get to help with the hunting, but I handle the research." A certain pride crept into his voice there. "I look things up, I find the places with stories we might be able to chase down, and I track construction records to find out where all the stained glass from that demolished church that supposedly had a holy spirit wound up going."

"But . . . but if they're ghosts following the pieces of their homes around, and not hurting anyone, isn't it wrong to bottle them up like this? Isn't it like—like torturing people?"

"They're not people anymore. They gave up the label of 'people' when they died."

"How is that fair? What makes a ghost, anyway? Not everyone can become a ghost, or there would be so many of them that there wouldn't be any room left for the living." I stepped away from him, breaking the connections between thighs and waists and hands, and turned to give him my best, time-honed glower. "We have laws against desecrating graves and bodies because those things still represent people, even if they're not people anymore. Why would we protect ghosts any less, if we knew for sure that ghosts existed? Most people don't *choose* to die. So you're saying that because something happened to them, all these ghosts don't count as people anymore, and don't deserve the protection of basic human decency?"

"Not when they might hurt the living," he replied.

"Oh, come *on*. There must be thirty jars here! If thirty ghosts were hurting the living every year, we'd know for sure that ghosts are real. There wouldn't be any question. You know all these ghosts haven't been hurting anyone."

I turned again, this time toward the van doors. As I did, I pulled as much solidity into myself as I could, mimicking humanity the way I would when I needed to take the kids to a public park, the sort of place where we'd run into human parents who could see through every weakness.

I don't borrow life from the living the way a hitcher does. I take my substance from the world itself—from the pneuma, probably, which meant this was probably one of the expensive things the anima mundi complained about me doing. In the moment, I didn't care. I needed to know whether I could be solid and real and *alive* enough to trick a Mesmer cage.

I grasped the handle on the van door. I said a silent prayer to whichever of the various deities I knew might be listening. I opened the door.

I stepped outside.

There were no sparks or flashes of light, or anything else that might indicate I'd beaten the Mesmer cage. There was just the Covenant's data man, looking at me with disappointment but without surprise. Then I closed the door, shutting him inside, and even that was gone.

I vanished, leaving the van at the curb and the roll of toilet paper in the street.

✦ ✦ ✦

One nice thing about doing fieldwork on the East Coast: for once, the time zones were in my favor. I vanished in Massachusetts, and I reappeared in Oregon. Specifically, I reappeared in Antimony's bedroom, where I promptly shouted and threw one arm up to cover my eyes.

Annie and Sam were even faster. Sam scrambled away from her, hauling most of the bedding with him, and wrapped it securely around his waist and torso, creating a makeshift toga of sorts. He didn't bother shifting back toward human. He remained visibly Fūri, with faintly simian features, ears that were slightly larger than the norm, and a sinuous tail as long as he was tall, which he was using to hold part of the toga in place.

Annie tugged her nightshirt back down over her hips and gave me a sullen, baleful look, pulling the remaining sheet around herself and settling back into her pillows, of which there were at least six. She's always liked her pillows, that girl, and it was a good sign that there were so many of them. When her flames first started manifesting and she started setting the bedding on fire, she'd removed most of the pillows from her bed in the interests of keeping them unburnt. If she had this many, she wasn't setting things on fire in her sleep.

Of course, from the way she was glaring at me, she was currently contemplating how flammable ghosts might be. Sadly for her, the answer was "not very." If she tried to burn me to death (killing me for the second time? Or would that be third? I never thought "How many times have I actually died?" was going to be something I needed to keep track of) we were both going to have a very bad night.

"Mary," she said, voice so cold that it could almost have extinguished the flames she was so close to calling. "There's this thing called 'privacy,' if you've heard of it? I'm an adult now. I'm allowed to have some."

"Sorry," I said, lowering my arm. "I didn't see anything I haven't seen before, if that helps?"

"You changed my diapers. It does *not* help."

"She, uh, didn't change mine," said Sam. "And the one time she popped in on me while I was in the shower, she was very careful not to see my junk. So I think I'm going to take 'no new landmarks' as a win. Hi, Mary. What's going on?"

"Your dick is not a landmark," said Annie.

"That's not what you said last night."

She hit him with a pillow. He stood there and took it like a man who was already committed to marrying into the family, and understood that dodging every missile just meant more flung objects in the future. Sometimes the people I've raised are predictable in ways that make me question what I've done to them.

Raised them all to be adults Frances Healy, the Flower of Arizona, would recognize and adore, that's what. They're happy, and that's what really matters as far as I'm concerned.

"I am a grown, mature ghost, and I am not going to join this conversation in any meaningful way," I said. "I'm here because I need to ask Annie some questions about her time with the Covenant, and I popped into the bedroom because I don't really want to *answer* any questions just now. Which you know your parents will probably have for me."

"You came back from the double-dead, kidnapped my cousins, and fucked off to who-knows-where," said Annie, sitting up straighter against the pillows. "Yeah, I'll say we have questions."

"I didn't kidnap anyone," I said. "I needed someone solid, who had hands and could do things I couldn't always, and Elsie volunteered."

Annie blinked, then scowled.

"This whole situation involves the Covenant, and you're burned," I said. "Timpani having been a member means that Antimony can't exactly go into the field with me without raising the kind of questions that could end with me on the wrong end of an exorcism."

"She has a point, babe," said Sam, tail snaking around her ankle and gripping it loosely, like he needed the reassurance that she was still solid. After the number of times she'd slipped away from him, I couldn't really fault the impulse. Sometimes, watching them together reminded me of Johnny and Fran more than anything, one of them always running for the dangerous horizon, the other perpetually trying to pull them back to land.

Alice and Thomas weren't quite the same dynamic. With them, it had only ever been a race to see which one was going to fall off the edge of the world first. Sam wasn't human, but he'd have been utterly content to stay where he was, patiently watching things go wrong all around him, until he didn't have a choice about whether or not to get involved.

"As for Arthur, he was a stowaway," I continued. "Just got in the car without permission, and when we tried to put him out, he argued until we let him stay. He made some really good points. He's a Price, too, and he has every right to go out into the field."

Annie frowned, looking profoundly uncomfortable. "I'm not sure that's true," she said.

"Which part?"

"Both of them." She shrugged. "He's not Artie anymore, Aunt Mary. He's . . . someone else. A patchwork person."

"Your grandfather is a patchwork person," I said. No one's sure how many people went into Martin's construction, just that it was several, collected lovingly by the scientist who originally assembled him. They say time heals all wounds, but sometimes lightning will do in a pinch if you don't have a lot of time before the angry mob arrives.

"I know," said Annie. "And Grandpa's always been very clear about the fact that he *isn't* any of those people anymore. He's someone new, and so is Arthur. Sarah made him from the memories and ideas and opinions of everyone she could reach. He's *not* Artie. He can't even focus long enough to get through a full D&D session, and he's the reason we don't allow phones at the table. He wanted us all to be properly immersed. Well, now, his phone is glued to his hand, and he's not keeping track of things like he should."

"I don't think you can eject him from the family because he doesn't enjoy Dungeons & Dragons the way he used to."

"It's not the game, it's what the game represents. It's the time and the teamwork and everything else. If he's such a different person that D&D doesn't make him happy, is he even Artie at all?"

"No, he's Arthur," I said. "That's what he's asked me to call him, and if you're that worried about him, is there any place safer for him to be than with his babysitter?"

Annie frowned, still looking uncomfortable, but finally nodded. "All right, I guess I can understand where you're coming from," she said. "What did you need from me?"

"When you were at Penton Hall, who seemed to be in charge?"

"The Cunninghams, of course. They're the ones running the

place. Reginald Cunningham is technically the head of the Covenant, or was the last time I had any intel on the matter. He's the big boss. Leonard, who you've met, is his eldest grandson."

"Eldest? How many does he have?"

"Two, that I know of. Leonard and Nathaniel. And then there's Chloe, his granddaughter. I was her roommate for a little while. She snores like a rhino. That girl needs a sleep study and an assessment for apnea, or she's going to choke to death trying to breathe in the middle of the night."

"Well, I think I met the two non-Leonard pieces of that family pie," I said. "The names are correct, anyway, and they both sounded like they were from England."

"They're here?" asked Annie, leaning forward. "Where?"

"Massachusetts, for the moment." That was nonspecific enough that I wasn't worried about her tracking me down. Annie's sorcery is impressive but destructive: it doesn't come with any sort of teleportation or dimensional distortion. The routewitches were unlikely to bring Annie and Sam to join us—not when they knew Apple was already annoyed. And Sarah wouldn't bring her anywhere near Arthur. Sarah's desire never to see him if she could help it was well established and reliable.

"Why?"

"Assignment from the anima mundi." I shrugged. "The Covenant knows I was with you in Penton Hall. They've started ghost-hunting."

Annie looked down at her hands and grimaced. "I guess that makes sense," she said. "Not them knowing you were there—I have no idea how they managed that."

"The anima mundi says they had some sort of ghost detector on the grounds, or else my being destroyed on their property set off some sort of monitoring system. I don't know exactly what method they used," I said.

"Yeah. But once they *did* know, going after the ghosts makes sense. The Covenant is big into an eye for an eye. Ghosts don't tend to have any sort of centralized communications, and so many of them are bound to their houses that they'd be sitting ducks if someone wanted to come along and attack them. Are they hurting the road ghosts? Is Rose okay?"

"They've been going after road ghosts when it was convenient, but not focusing on them, and I saw Apple earlier; I think she would have mentioned if Rose had been a target. Sadly, I think the Covenant is marginally smarter than that. No one who enjoys continued survival messes with a Fury." I shook my head to hide my shudder. "Regardless, they're here, they're hunting, and they're having a horrifying degree of success. They've been jarring the ghosts they capture, and torturing them to make spirit bombs."

"Wait, what?" said Sam. "How do you torture a ghost? *Why* do you torture a ghost? What good is that supposed to do?"

Sometimes it was easy to forget how new Sam was to a lot of this stuff, sometimes surprisingly so, considering he was half-human and had been raised by a traveling carnival with a reputation for sheltering cryptids capable of coexistence with humans. But he'd been safe and relatively sheltered there, spared the greater complexity of our world. It had taken Annie to break him out of all that, and I still wasn't entirely sure that had been a blessing for him.

"You torture a ghost by trapping them in a spirit jar—which is just a normal glass jar that's been treated to make it ghost-proof, so we can't get out once you suck us in—that's been outfitted with things that can harm ghosts. Iron shavings, bits of mirror, rosemary, candle wax, pine splinters. And salt, of course."

"Of course," echoed Sam, sounding almost stunned.

"If you *really* want to torture them, you shake the jar once you have the ghost secured. Force all that nasty stuff through their body, disrupt and unsettle them."

Sam frowned. "I'd be pretty unsettled if you kept pelting me with anti-Fūri junk."

"What would you consider 'anti-Fūri'?" I asked, unable to help myself.

"I dunno. Bananas and human shoes?"

"You are a very understandable man, Samuel Taylor," I said. "But no, that's not what 'unsettled' means when you're talking about a ghost. Most of the ghosts you find haunting human houses were human before they died."

"Makes sense."

"For human ghosts, they die, and they appear in the twilight as essentially the same sort of haunting—sort of the larval form of whatever kind of spirit they're going to become. That's what we call the 'settling' phase. During settling, all ghosts are functionally the same. They won't develop the talents or physical distinctions of their type of spirit until a few days have passed. That's when ghosts are at their most vulnerable."

"To what?"

"All sorts of things." I looked at him grimly, noting that Annie was also paying close attention. For most of her life, I'd been bound by the crossroads, unable to answer even simple questions, much less explain complicated systems like settling. "If something interferes with an unsettled ghost, they can influence what that ghost will eventually settle as. That's part of how we get haints."

"What are—?" began Sam.

"A haint is a faded spirit. They don't really remember who they were when they were alive. Memory is one of the first things an unsettled ghost starts to lose. They forget everything they cared about in life, they forget themselves, and they become, essentially, half-aware cobwebs fluttering through the twilight. But they can hunt and hurt the living if they're summoned into the daylight world, and they can still manifest under the right conditions. They're weak, but they move in packs, and it's hard to fight a ghost that has nothing left to care about. Nothing to care about means nothing to lose."

"Oh," said Sam, sounding horrified.

"Haunts are a kind of ghost in their own right. I tend to use 'haunt' interchangeably with 'spirit,' and I really shouldn't. The vocabulary is just so *limited* when you're talking about the dead."

"This isn't *Just a Minute*," said Antimony. "You're not being graded on hesitation, deviation, or repetition. Keep going."

"Right. So ghosts settle, and if they're stopped from settling, they can develop into haints, which is bad. No one wants an infestation of haints."

"And the Covenant is *un*settling ghosts," said Annie, slowly. "Mary, this is not good."

"No, it's not," I agreed. "Better: if a ghost is going to develop poltergeist abilities, it happens during settling. I saw some of the captive ghosts back in Massachusetts. I'd say about a third of them have started to become poltergeists."

Annie winced. "That's way too many to be normal."

"Yeah," I said grimly. "The Covenant is hunting down ordinary ghosts, catching them, and torturing them until they turn into poltergeists, which makes them ten times more dangerous than they would have been otherwise."

"And you're here instead of protecting Elsie and Artie because . . . ?"

"Because you're the only one of us who's seen this current generation of Covenant operatives. What do you know about Nathaniel and Chloe Cunningham?"

"They're loyal, and they're ambitious," she said. "They know they won't inherit, or they did when I was there—that was before Leonard lost me, twice. There's a chance Reginald is reconsidering who holds the position of 'favorite grandson.'"

"So Nathaniel may be hungry to move up; got it," I said. "Isn't it a little sexist to dismiss Chloe like that?"

"Yeah, but it's also accurate to how Reggie's going to look at things," she said. "He'd never hand the Covenant off to a girl, even if he liked her best of all. It's just not an option."

"Asshole," said Sam reflexively.

Annie leaned over until she was resting halfway against his hip, snuggling up within the limits of propriety while I was in the room. "Yup," she said. "He really is. Were they alone?"

"Half of a four-person team. One guy, American, was in the van outside, and seemed content to stay there. He said he was doing a lot of the research."

"New recruit, then," said Annie with confidence. "They'll have picked him up to provide a local view on things. Can't hunt ghosts if you don't know where to look."

"That matches with what I was assuming," I said. "He's about your age, a little socially awkward, a little too willing to be flirted with by a sixteen-year-old girl who says she's there to toilet-paper his van."

"You *didn't*," said Annie, suddenly grinning.

"Hey, it was an excuse that worked when *you* were a teenager, and I never had the opportunity to get up to that much mischief," I said. "It worked. It got me into his van, which is where I saw all the ghosts in jars. They're not in good shape, Annie. Some of them are too far gone to ever be themselves again."

She swallowed hard, smile fading as she nodded.

"The fourth man is Brazilian, and I don't know whether he's a recruit of convenience or a longtime member who got unlucky; I met his sister before I met him, and she's a midnight beauty. Whether he believes in this hunt or not, he's in it to find his sister."

"I guess you'll know where his loyalties lie when it comes time to put her in a jar," said Annie, harshly. "Are you going back?"

"I have to. The ghosts need me, and so do your cousins." I thought of Elsie and Arthur. It was late in Massachusetts, late enough that they were probably done with dinner and snug in their rooms, either sleeping or waiting for me to come back and report on my evening. Either way, I needed to get back to them. "Thanks, Annie. This is really helpful."

"Well, it's mutual, because it helps me to know where you are," she said. "Knock next time, okay?"

"If I have the time, I will," I promised, and disappeared, throwing myself back across the continent to where my charges were hopefully still waiting for me.

Fourteen

"I try not to mess with the divine when I can help it. I'm the ghost of a high school student from Michigan. The divinities people like me have access to are the ghosts of *gods.*"

—**Rose Marshall**

Worcester, Massachusetts,
in the hallway of a cryptid boardinghouse

Remembering how distressed Annie had been by my sudden appearance, I tilted my return toward the hallway of Phee's boardinghouse, appearing outside the room assigned to Arthur. I looked around to be sure I hadn't just scared the life out of a boarder, then leaned to the side and looked at the bottom of the door. A thin line of light greeted me there: Arthur was still awake, or had fallen asleep with the lights on. I raised my hand and knocked lightly.

A few seconds later, Arthur called, almost timidly, "Come . . . in?"

I walked through the door.

Arthur's suitcase was open on the bed, still packed, and his backpack was open on the floor next to the chair where he was seated, body half-turned toward the desk where he'd set up his laptop. Nosiness is a hard habit to break when it comes to the people in my care: I took a quick look at the screen before he could catch on and close the lid, and blinked at the sight of a familiar forum page. Cryptid teens need peers as much as human ones, and some of them get really good at network security, really early on. They have their own secure websites and forums, and if they're a little more early 2000s internet than the modern stuff, well, I don't hear any of them complaining.

I wasn't as subtle as I thought I was. Arthur saw me looking and sighed, cringing a little as he turned back toward the laptop.

"I know I shouldn't, but I can't help myself," he said.

I moved closer, taking his position and failure to shut the lid as a tacit invitation. The user name at the top of the screen was an unfamiliar one, but the thread he had open had been started by a user named "MidwichGirl." I frowned, giving him a hard, sidelong look.

"Are you *stalking* Sarah?" I asked.

"I don't think I am," he said. "I know her user name because she gave it to me, and this forum doesn't require disclosure of real name, age, or species. If she thinks I'm a bogeyman from Iowa, that's her business."

"Honey, you know that's not the way."

"Do I?" he asked, with a sudden spike of swift anger that wasn't Artie, wasn't Artie at all. That boy had always been sweet and steady, trying his best, never losing control when he could help it, even a little. Artie had been my helper on so many occasions, the child it was easiest to buy off with gold stars and extra peanut butter cookies. This anger, though: I knew this anger. I recognized it. It belonged to his mother, who never stopped *wanting*, not even when she fell. It belonged to his sister, who wouldn't thank me for calling her the best parts of Jane. It belonged to so much of his family, but it had never been his, and it hurt, hearing it from his lips, even if I knew someone else was speaking.

He wasn't done. "I don't think I *know* anything, except how much I miss her. She took herself away because she decided I couldn't make my own choices, and now I'm trying to hold on, but I have those blank places crumbling all through my mind, and if I want to spend some of the time I still have keeping track of the woman I was made to love, I think that's allowed."

"Would Sarah agree?"

He didn't answer. Just stuck his chin out at me and glowered, waiting for me to offer a response.

"How was dinner?"

"Good, except that it was all tomato-based, and that made me think of Sarah, and that's why I'm on the forums again. I keep promising myself I won't go back, because you're right—it's a little creepy that I know who she is and what she's doing when she doesn't know it's me. But I keep logging in, every time I can't stop thinking about her."

"I'm sorry." I meant it, too. Arthur didn't deserve any of the things that were happening to him.

"Yeah, well. Watching Elsie flirt with that swamp-beastie lady the whole time didn't help. She makes fun of *me* for getting tongue-tied, and I swear she could barely talk for half the meal."

"I hope Amelia was flirting back?"

"She was," said Arthur sullenly. "Big fun, being the third wheel at a table full of strangers. Did you find the Covenant team?"

"I did." I sat down on the edge of the bed. "There are four of them that I know of so far, two from Penton Hall, one a local recruit, one semi-wild card. He's got a Brazilian accent, and I know they've been able to get their claws into South America, so he could be a loyalist. He could also be a casual ghost hunter who got swept up in their mission. It's hard to say. I don't know how much institutional support they have for what they're doing." What I'd seen so far felt more like one of the family's field missions than a proper strike team. But without knowing how much damage we'd done to the organization as a whole, I couldn't say what that meant.

"Do you know anything about the ones from England?"

"Their older brother, Leonard, is the one who shot your mother," I said. "He's not here, or I'd be in Elsie's room, begging her not to go on a suicide run."

He looked thoughtful. "Maybe they can tell us where to find him. I look forward to asking."

"They've been catching and torturing ghosts. They have at least two dozen of them currently captive. It's not safe to go anywhere near them until we know how to neutralize all those spirits." I shook my head. "They're keeping them in a mobile Mesmer cage right now, which means they're mobile, but also means they're contained."

"I guess that's good." Arthur frowned, looking at me. "You shouldn't go out alone. If they caught you, we'd have no way of knowing it had happened. I look enough like Dad that I don't think I'm much of a security risk, and Elsie doesn't look like anyone except for Elsie. Never has."

"I wasn't planning to go out alone again unless I have to," I said, trying to reassure as best I could. "I just wanted to see how many of them we were dealing with, and vaguely where they were. Now that we know, we can get started with the real work. Did Elsie's flirting reach the point of anyone inviting anyone else back to their room?"

"Not quite."

"Great. I'll be right back." I stood, walking toward the wall his room shared with his sister's.

I was almost there before he called, "Mary?"

I stopped and looked back to him. "Yes?"

"You're not going to get hurt again, are you?"

This was something we were all going to need to work on. I'd been dead long before any of these people were born, and it had led to a certain understandable tendency to think of me as indestructible, the one person none of us would ever need to worry about. Annie had been disabused of that impression when the crossroads had decided to punish me for helping her, a nasty, withering decay that still sometimes ached in the spaces where my soul believed I had bones. The rest of them had lost that soft self-deception in a blast in the basement of Penton Hall, when their beloved, immortal babysitter had been blown to bits for six long months of nothingness. He was just learning how to worry about me, while I had a lifetime of practice worrying about him.

So I looked over my shoulder and I did what babysitters have been doing for centuries, when their charges asked questions they didn't know how to safely answer. I lied, with a smile on my lips and a bright twinkle in my eyes.

"Of course not, silly. These are amateurs. There's no way they're going to catch me in a box I don't want to be in. We're going to catch them, free the ghosts, and stop the hunt, and then we're going to go home and make things right again. Now wait here. I'm going to get your sister."

Before he could ask me anything else, I walked through the wall.

Elsie was in her room. No one else was, which was a pleasant surprise, even after Arthur's reassurances. Not that I would have judged if she'd been having a little frisky fun time with a cute Hockomock Swamp Beastie—everyone has their own needs— but it might have startled Amelia enough to make this next part difficult.

Instead, Elsie was on her side on the bed, scrolling through her phone with practiced swipes of her thumb, liking pictures so quickly that it seemed impossible she could have fully registered what she was looking at.

Since she was mostly looking at adorable kittens and half-naked women, I guessed she knew enough not to need the details anymore. I circled around behind her, watching the endless scroll of soft, pretty things, and waited until she hit an ad before I said, "I'm back."

Elsie didn't jump. She did tense, shoulders going tight as she took more time to identify my voice than she had with any of the bikini models or white-faced Ragdoll cats. After several seconds, she lowered her phone and rolled over, focusing on me. "Mary," she said, voice cool.

"What? Are you mad at me for not knocking? Because the last time I knocked, it didn't go very well."

"No. I'm mad at you for existing, and for going away, and for coming back." She sat up, pushing her hair away from her face with one hand. "It's too much, and it's all stupid, and I just want to be alone and angry for a while. This is more time than I've spent with anyone since my mother died. I flirted with Amelia at dinner. *Flirted*, like my mother wasn't rotting in the ground. Like I deserved to flirt. Like I deserve to do anything at all other than atone for letting her die when I wasn't there."

"Elsie, where is this coming from?" I moved to sit on the edge of the bed. She pulled her legs in, away from me, as she scooted herself into a more-upright position. That hurt, just a little, like she was moving away from me on purpose and not because it made conversation more convenient.

"My mother *died*," she said, like I didn't know. "She went out into the field, without me, and she *died*. Someone shot her in the chest, and she *died*."

"Not 'someone,'" I said. "Leonard Cunningham, heir apparent to the Covenant of St. George. He's not here, but his brother and sister are. Their mother died too."

Elsie paused, blinking. "What?"

"Their mother? She died when we set off the bombs in the basement of Penton Hall. Does that make this feel any better? Does it make it easier to breathe?"

"How do you know how this—?"

"I wasn't always dead and rootless," I said. "Once upon a time, I was a teenage girl from Buckley Township, just the same as your grandmother. Well, not *just* the same. I raised her, but I don't think we'd have been friends if we'd been alive at the same time. She was too busy for me. She never liked to sit still. I was very good at sitting still. It was one of my best skills. And I wasn't big on playing with dead stuff, unlike Alice, no matter how cool or interesting or whatever it looked. I was just a girl. I went to class, I did my homework and my chores, and I loved my mother very much."

"I never thought . . ."

"Why would you? She died decades ago. Cancer. I sat with her in the hospital almost every day, and I prayed and I prayed and nobody answered me. She didn't get a miracle. She got a headstone, and my father withered into nothing without her. I buried him, too. Technically I died before he did, but since no one noticed, I don't really know how to measure that specific tragedy. But I was alive when my mother died, and it took all the air out of the room. Every room I walked into, for months, the air would just whisk away, like it had never been there to begin with. Naughty little girls with dead mothers don't deserve to breathe."

Elsie nodded, expression telling me that she understood exactly what I was saying.

"I blamed myself right up until I died. If I'd just prayed a little harder, or believed a little more, or hadn't been late getting to the hospital so many times. If I hadn't resented her for getting sick when I was trying to have a social life. If I'd agreed to go out with that boy she tried to hook me up with." I didn't even remember his name anymore. Somewhere in the gulf between my mother's death and the moment, so many things had fallen away. "And then I died, and she wasn't there to welcome me to the afterlife. I learned the rules of being a ghost, and more, I learned that spirits linger when they have unfinished business. When they want something so badly that death isn't enough to make them stop reaching for it. So what did it say that my mother died and couldn't even stay for me? How much was I worth if I was so easy to walk away from?"

Elsie didn't move or speak, but her eyes were too bright, and I knew that she was listening.

"And then, after I'd been dead a while—it wasn't overnight; I think Alice was your age when it happened—I realized that moving on hadn't been about me. It was about her. She was at peace, she knew she'd done everything she needed to do, and she didn't want to make my life about her death. She didn't linger because it wouldn't have fixed anything. It would just have meant *I* never got the chance to move on. She would have become my unfinished business by holding on too tightly to her own."

Elsie sniffled, tears starting to roll down her cheeks.

"My mom lived a good life, and it ended too soon, and she never got to see me grow up. I never got the chance to disappoint her, and I guess that means she never got the chance to show me she wasn't perfect. But she moved on rather than burden me with everything that might have been and didn't get the chance to be, and that *was* perfect of her." I turned my focus more fully on Elsie. "Your mom wasn't perfect. She was petty and mean and she held a grudge like she was going to win a cash prize for keeping it the longest. She was also smart and quick and funny—fuck, she was so funny that sometimes she made me grateful I didn't need to breathe. I loved her from the day she was born until the day she died, and I know she didn't stick around because she didn't have any unfinished business, and she didn't want to burden you with all the things her death was going to mean. She moved on so you could be free, just like she was going to be. She loved you so, so much, Elsie. Watching her fight not to hurt you the way her mother hurt her was hard and painful and inspiring. She made me believe we could be better than our upbringings. It's okay to mourn her. She was your *mom*. I grieved mine for decades. But you can't stop living while you do it. You have to breathe and plan and eat and flirt and fuck around and fuck up and get on with things. That's the way you show her she was right to trust you to carry on while she was gone. You live. That's all you need to do."

"I don't know *how*," said Elsie, voice gone thick with snot and tears and grief. "She never told me how I was supposed to live in a world without her. She just told me how much she'd always hated living in a world without her own mother, and she didn't want me to even *think* about doing it. So I don't know how."

"One day at a time," I said. "One hour, one minute, one second at a time. You keep moving forward, because standing still isn't even for the dead. You go to parties and laugh until beer comes out of your nose. You meet someone who makes your heart beat faster and you kiss them until your lips hurt. You dance and you sing and you scream and you keep moving. And then one day, something wonderful will happen, and your first thought won't be about how you should call her. And you'll probably feel guilty when that happens, and that's okay, because you'll keep moving forward. You live. That's all you have to do."

Elsie wiped her cheeks with the back of her hand, phone forgotten on the bed. "You were always there. No matter what happened, you were always there. So I guess I just assumed that if any of us died, it would be the same. And it isn't. It isn't the same at all."

"I'm sorry."

"I lost my mother and my brother and I hate everything about this. I'm supposed to have them forever. They're not supposed to leave me." She looked at me defiantly. "I don't want anyone else to leave me."

"Then you're going to be disappointed," I said. "People in this family may come back sometimes, one way or another, but people will always leave you. That's what it means to be a person."

"Don't you mean 'to be alive'?"

"No," I said. "Don't be vitalist. I'm not alive, and people leave me all the time."

Elsie mustered a chuckle.

"Now, can we get back to the less-depressing reason I came in here? I told you I found the Covenant team. Two of them are siblings of the man who killed your mother. They're here because their mother died in the collapse at Penton Hall, they know a ghost was involved, and they're taking out their aggressions on the entire phantom population of the East Coast."

A sick idea was starting to grow in my mind, telling me what they might be doing here. Every enraged, unsettled phantom they had jarred up was essentially the equivalent of a small bomb, getting steadily stronger and less controlled. Take as many as they had in that moving Mesmer cage, and you were looking at a spiritual explosive easily the size of the one we'd set off in their basement. Enough of those ghosts had poltergeist powers manifesting that I had no doubt they could—and would—tear a building down around themselves, and even if they didn't do that, they could possess and confuse, they could scream their dead misery into the ears of the living and cause riots, or worse. They had so many potential targets that it was almost dizzying.

This wasn't just about saving the dead from the living. It was also about saving the living from the dead, and always had been.

"Mary?" Elsie snapped her fingers in front of my face.

I blinked, snapping back into the moment. "Sorry. Just . . . thinking."

"Cool. Did you know that when you're thinking about something *really* unpleasant, the graveyard comes back to your eyes? They went all unfocused, and then they started getting gray and spooky like they used to be."

"I did not know that."

"These Covenant jerks. You said their last name was Cunningham. Did you get a first name at all?"

"Nathaniel and Chloe. Why?"

Elsie grabbed her phone, beginning to type. "How old would you say they are?"

"Your age. Maybe a little older, for him, and a little younger, for her."

"Cool." All her focus was on the screen now. She stopped typing and began to scroll again.

"Elsie, maybe this isn't a great time for—"

"Got her." She turned the phone toward me, looking smug. "Artie's not the only one who understands how technology works. I was always better at social media. Mom made me show her every new thing that came along, so she could monitor where the cryptid communities were moving. It's pretty interesting stuff, and you can tell when a platform's going to break big by when the bogeymen start setting up there. Anyway, most people aren't as good at it as I am, so they're not prepared to hide their tracks."

She shoved the phone closer to me. I looked at the screen, and there was a picture of Chloe Cunningham flashing a cheery V in front of the turtle fountain, the sun bright behind her, a wide grin on her face. The caption read: *Spicy statuary here in the States! Love and kisses (not from the turtle). #adventures #tourism #massachusetts*

"We already know she's in town," I said. "I saw her."

"Yeah, but now we know she didn't think to lock her Insta, and I can keep an eye on her. Learn more about her. Scroll back and see what kind of person she is."

"Careful," I cautioned. "She's the kind of person who carries a spirit jar in hopes of catching the ghost of a child. Anything else is incidental."

"Still, know thine enemy, right?"

"Right," I said. "Arthur's next door, if you want to come and plan next steps with us."

"I think I can handle that," she said, sliding off the bed.

Since I was walking with someone who wasn't dead, I followed her to the door and let her open it before stepping into the hall. We left the room—

—and nearly ran right into Amelia, who was standing outside, looking like she was preparing herself to knock. She blinked and took a step back, clearly confused.

"Hi," said Elsie, shutting the door behind us. "Did you need something?"

"Just your number," said Amelia. "How am I supposed to send you suggestive text messages if I don't have your number?"

"You're not," said Elsie. "I'm sorry if I gave you the wrong idea at dinner, but I'm not looking for anything serious."

"Did I say *I* was?" asked Amelia. "A few teasing texts do not a relationship make."

"I know," said Elsie. "I really am sorry. I need to go and talk to my brother."

She ducked her head as she pushed between us, heading to Arthur's room. I refocused on Amelia.

"We didn't really get to talk much before," I said. "Elsie's a grownup, but she knows what she wants and what she has the time for, and if she says no, she means no. I appreciate you picking up on how awesome she is, though."

"If she thinks this is about her pheromones, you can tell her she's wrong—*please* tell her she's wrong," said Amelia. "I had a cold all last week, I've got so much Vicks VapoRub on my chest and sternum that I won't be able to smell anything else for the rest of the year. It's all menthol and regret. So she doesn't need to worry about influencing me."

"I don't think that's her concern, but I'll pass it along," I said.

"I really appreciate it."

"Okay, two things before I go. First, you realize I'm her babysitter, right? I'm not her sister or her friend, I'm her dead babysitter who tries to keep her from getting into the kind of trouble people don't get out of while they're still alive."

"I know that." Amelia frowned. "You think I don't know a ghost when I see one? Please. Hockomock Swamp Beasties aren't as big on lines between the living and the dead as humans tend to be. One of my uncles has been married to his current wife for twenty years, and she died nineteen years ago. They just figured it was a bump in the road and kept on going about their business. It works for them."

"Huh." Mixed marriages like that aren't unheard-of, but they don't tend to work out in the long run. Something about one partner remaining exactly the same while the other ages and grows tends to put a damper on true intimacy.

"What was the second thing?"

"The— Oh." I shrugged. "We're here for a reason, and the job has to come first, for all three of us. If Elsie thinks she doesn't have the time for something meaningful right now, she's probably right, and it's less about her pheromones than it is trying to be fair to you. If you really want to get to know her better, wait until we've done what we came here to do."

"What are you here to do?"

I shrugged. "Save the world," I said, and walked through the wall into Arthur's room, leaving her behind.

Fifteen

"Don't put that in your mouth, young lady. You have no idea where it's been."

—Eloise Dunlavy

*Worcester, Massachusetts,
in a rented room at a cryptid boardinghouse*

ELSIE WAS GOOD AT SOCIAL media. Artie had always been our computer guy, basically from the time that he could reach a keyboard, and so when Sarah had rebuilt him, she'd done it with the memories of a dozen or more people, human, mouse, and other, who believed he was a fantastic computer wizard, capable of doing almost anything.

Trouble was, none of the people who'd been contributing those memories had been computer wizards. So Arthur *thought* he was great with computers, when in actuality, he didn't know much more than I did. And because he thought he knew everything already, he was remarkably resistant to picking up a book and learning.

Meaning we effectively didn't have a tech guy. After ten minutes of watching him fumblingly try to match his sister's trick, he threw up his hands and slumped in his seat. "I give up," he said. "It's impossible."

"She has her brother's profile friended, but he's set to private," said Elsie mulishly. "Do you think we have time to catfish him for access?"

"We don't even know whether he's straight, and coming at him with multiple profiles at the same time would probably tip him off that something was going on," I said. "No catfishing."

"But—"

"No."

Elsie made an exaggeratedly put-upon face, and I knew we were going to be okay. Whether it was because I'd gotten through to her or because she'd just decided it wasn't worth her time to be mad at me didn't matter. All that mattered was moving forward.

Arthur had spun around in his chair to put the computer to his back, folding his arms. "Couldn't we just orchestrate a meeting, if we know where they are? Bump into them at a coffee shop or something? Once we see which one of us she looks at like we're a chocolate cake with thumbs, we'll know who should be hitting on her online."

"Okay, one, gross, and two, that would be exploiting your pheromones, which is not okay," I said. "You know that. Consent matters, and when you go all incubus at someone, they don't get to consent properly."

Arthur looked briefly shamefaced—although not as much as Artie would have. I was starting to recognize the differences in their expressions, and some of them were pretty striking. They were like twin brothers, similar but never quite the same.

"These people are capturing and torturing ghosts," he said. "As long as I don't actually take advantage of them getting infatuated with me, I'm not sure I count it as an equal atrocity."

There was an ethics-measuring contest I never wanted to get involved with. I shook my head. "No catfishing," I said again. "All right: we know there are four of them, minimum, two fully trained and from Penton Hall, two more local and maybe not fully equipped for the field. I'm not sure the guy I met in the van has any training at all, beyond the technical side of things. Heitor . . . I get the feeling he's here mostly for his sister."

"So he won't fight with them?"

"Oh, assume he will. Just also assume he won't be quite *as* sophisticated, tactically." I rubbed my eyes with the palm of my hand. "This is such a mess. I don't even know if they have more team members in town."

"You can find things, right?" asked Arthur abruptly. "Mostly people, but stuff too."

"If the stuff is important enough, yes, at least currently," I said. "The anima mundi gave me some extra freedom while we're dealing with this. Why do you ask?"

"I think a van full of scared ghosts is pretty important. You could try going to the van, and then look to see if it's parked where they're all staying. I know you can't take a phone with you, but you could pop back over here and we'll be ready to go."

I blinked at him. I had been focusing so hard on not splitting the party again unless I absolutely had to that I hadn't considered my own ability to move freely. "That could work."

"This would be easier if we had Sarah to keep us all in contact with each other, and to bring us to you once you figure out where we're supposed to go, but we can make it work," he said, clearly trying not to look pleased with himself. He wasn't doing the best job. He didn't need to be.

"We need a plan beyond 'find them, hit them, go home,'" I said.

"All right," said Elsie. "Most ghost hunting happens at night, right?"

"That's when normal ghosts tend to be the most active." Neither Rose nor I were good examples of "normal ghosts." We were active when we needed to be—which for Rose meant daytime, since it was easier to get people to pick up hitchhikers when they could see them clearly, and for me meant whenever the kids I was taking care of were awake. I was nocturnal during their infancy, and then rolled slowly back to a more diurnal schedule.

Whatever the ghosts in those jars had been before they were captured, they were unlikely to have been hitchers or caretakers. Ghosts with jobs are harder to trap that way.

"Okay. Do you think they'll be done at City Hall by now?"

I paused to consider. "The only ghost that's still haunting City Hall wasn't there tonight," I said finally. "I assume he'll have to go back around dawn. The people who built the place used the remains of his house in the foundations. It's why he's haunting the place. When you have a tethered haunting, it's hard to stay away past a certain point. But since the Covenant can't exactly go creeping around the place playing junior ghostbuster in the middle of the day, he should be safe until sundown."

"And do you think they'll be going *back* to City Hall?"

"They know there's at least one ghost still there."

Arthur, who was still new enough that he listened to every word spoken by the people around him, rather than assuming he could understand from half-statements and things he'd heard before, frowned. "What do you mean, 'at least'?"

"What?"

"You said 'at least one ghost.' What do you mean?"

Well, crap. I shrugged. "I showed myself to them, to distract them and try to get a better idea of what they were doing there. I had a hat on, it was dark, and everyone was shining flashlights on everybody else. I doubt they'd recognize me by daylight."

Arthur and Elsie both stared at me. "Mary, these are *Covenant people*," said Arthur. "They're trained to remember faces, and they've been looking for us for decades."

"That's where you're wrong," I said. "I know you think of me as part of the family, and I am, where it counts, but I'm as much an adoptee as James or Sarah. I don't look like anyone the Covenant knows to be looking for. Even if I had in the beginning, the crossroads bleached me out so much that I don't think they'd make the connection."

Elsie stared at me for a long moment, eyes hard, before she sighed and looked away. "All right, fine," she said. "They don't know to look for you. That doesn't mean we have to like you taking risks."

"Fair enough," I agreed.

"But we have the start of a plan," she said. "We get some sleep, because no one likes going into a fight exhausted, and then in the morning, Mary goes looking for the van. I'll keep an eye on Chloe's social media, see if I can figure out anything about their movement, and whether they have anyone else with them. A team of four, we can take. A team of eight might get difficult."

"Do you think you can sleep?" I asked. "That goes for both of you—I want you rested if we're going into a potentially dangerous situation."

"I do," said Elsie.

"I can try," said Arthur.

"Well, I don't sleep," I said. "But I can go explore the local twilight a bit, or go to the kids if any of them need me. Three children under ten, someone should want a glass of water in the middle of the night, right?"

It had been so long since I had three kids that young to take care of, I wasn't sure I fully remembered how chaotic things could get. I cocked my head to the side, "listening" with the part of me that had nothing to do with sound. There was nothing. All three kids were sleeping soundly, as were most of the adults. Verity felt like a vast, distant bruise, all sorrow and stillness, which was so out of character for her that it made me want to drop everything and rush to New York.

I couldn't do that. I was needed here. So I dug deep and mustered a smile for Elsie. "Sounds like we have a plan," I said. "I'll see you both in the morning."

Then I disappeared, removing myself so they could actually get some sleep.

♦ ♦ ♦

I reappeared in the living room. I didn't have a room of my own to go to, and I wasn't sure how much I wanted to explore the local twilight. I'd already met enough of the ghosts in the area; I could find them again if I needed to. As long as I didn't really have anything to tell them—beyond "your brother is here to hurt you" and "all the missing ghosts are being tortured"—there was no point in rushing.

Of course, both of those were things Benedita would probably want to know, and that was part of what made me hesitate. The last thing I needed to do was trigger a mass haunting of a group of ghost hunters. These people were prepared for spirits in a way that normal living humans weren't, and they might respond to any action with violence.

The dead *can* die. I didn't want to be responsible for that.

With none of my kids calling for me, I had a few minutes to myself, and I didn't know what to do with them. I walked toward the kitchen. Being dead, I don't need to eat or drink; being solid enough to serve as a good babysitter, I sometimes enjoy it, and there's something to be said for a hot cup of tea in the small hours of the morning. We were renting two rooms. Surely Phee wouldn't begrudge me a little hot water.

There was a proper kettle on the stove, a lot like the one my mother used to use. I stood up a little straighter at the thought, feeling haunted. Everything I'd said to Elsie was the truth, and I'd had decades to get past the worst of my sorrow, but grief never truly goes away. It's not a wound that can be healed. It's more like a small, biting animal that lives in your ribcage, ripping and tearing at everything around it, made of teeth and claws and misery. So many parts of me had died in a field in Buckley, but the core of me survived, and the grief was a part of that.

I sniffled, then filled the kettle and placed it on one of the burners, turning it on to heat while I went digging for mugs and teabags. To my delight, Phee had plenty of both, and I was shortly settled at the table to wait for my water to be ready.

"Making yourself right at home, I see," said Phee. I turned to find her standing behind me in the doorway to the hall, wearing a green robe so bright that it hurt my eyes. "That's rightly grand. I'd hate for you to go back to all the other ghosts and tell them I'd been a poorly host when you were washed up on my doorstep. Will you be wanting honey, sugar, or milk?"

"None of those," I said, politely. "They're all nice things to put in your tea, but they won't change the flavor much for me at all, and I don't see the point in pretending that they might."

"Fair enough." She pushed away from the doorframe and strolled into the kitchen, smirking and amused. The kettle began to squeal and she took it off the burner, seeming to weigh it in her hand for a moment before she said, "Enough water for two cups. Someone taught you manners, miss ghost."

"My mother liked her tea."

"Did she, now? My mam was fair fond of it as well, so you see, we've something in common after all." She turned to take down two mugs from the cabinet full of them, one a novelty Ireland design with a cartoon leprechaun on the side that felt stereotypical and offensive to me, but she would know better than I did if that sort of thing was a problem. The other was an advertisement for a local haunted house, complete with leering red-eyed ghosts in the classic "sheets with holes in" design. I eyed it and snorted lightly. Talk about stereotypical representations.

Phee dropped a teabag into each mug, added hot water to both, and followed it up with honey and a generous splash of whiskey in her own. This done, she set the undoctored mug in front of me and stepped back.

"There. Now the bare minimum is managed, in terms of hospitality, and my mam shan't rise from the grave to swat me about the head and shoulders with her ladle."

"That doesn't sound likely even if you hadn't fixed my tea." I wrapped my hands around the mug, letting the heat travel through the ceramic and into my palms.

"How do you know? Have you ever dealt with clurichaun ghosts?"

"Most nonhuman ghosts spend their time on a different level of the afterlife than I do," I said. "Picture it as sort of like a multi-level apartment building, all stacked together. I can be on the second floor directly above you, and we'll never see each other. Only it's more like papier-mâché, where every layer is built on top of the one beneath it, so they get gradually bigger as you go along. And if you look at it that way, clurichaun ghosts would be at least two layers down from where human ghosts tend to be."

"Interesting." She sipped her tea. "You saying human ghosts inhabit the highest position in the afterlife?"

"Not like that, no. There's more of us than anyone else, so we have the outer layer, I guess, where there's the most room. And honestly, it's good for us to be separated. Keeps us from running roughshod over everyone else."

Phee nodded gravely. "I can drink to that. You find your Covenant coveys?"

"I found the strike team, yeah. They've definitely been catching and confining ghosts—and not just here, unless Worcester is the most haunted city in the world. A lot of local towns are going to be missing their resident hauntings. I'm hoping some of them will be able to go back once we release them."

"Why only some?"

"Because the Covenant's been torturing them, and some of the ghosts they have are already past saving."

Phee sipped her tea again. "Then why are you sitting here having a cuppa, and not off saving your people?"

"My people are the two Lilu asleep in your guest rooms. Not every ghost is my responsibility."

"Ah, but you feel *some* responsibility, or you wouldn't be doing this. So why aren't you out there playing hero?"

I frowned. "You have some sort of problem with me? Because this doesn't feel like a very friendly cup of tea."

"You served the crossroads for decades, Mary Dunlavy, and no one has your whole story, but bits of it have been circulating for years, and I know enough to know that I don't trust you around *my* people. You've done a lot of damage in your master's name. You've cut a lot of stories short. Now you show up here with two scions of a turncoat family and you call yourself redeemed. I don't know that I care to buy what you've been selling. It seems a trifle too convenient to be worth the cost."

She sipped her tea again, giving no sign that she was bothered by either the heat or the fact that it was half alcohol by volume. She just sipped, swallowed, and looked at me steadily, waiting for my response.

I sighed, putting my own mug aside. "Right. I guess we're doing this. Yes, I served the crossroads. They recruited me as soon as I died, and they didn't tell me what I was choosing when I agreed to work for them. While I'm sorry I served them for as long as I did, I can't regret taking their original offer. Them grabbing me was what kept me from settling properly long enough that I could become a caretaker ghost for the Price family, and now I've been raising them for generations."

"Oh, so it's your fault they're like this."

"Sure, if that's the way you want to look at it. It's all my fault. That's a blame I'm *glad* to carry. Because they're good people.

They help people who can't help themselves, they set things right whenever they can, and they deserve a chance to grow up safe and healthy. I can give them that. I take care of them."

"What makes them so special, that they deserve that sort of loyalty?"

I paused. "Nothing," I said. "They were in the right place at the right time, that's all. Sometimes the world can be kind even when you don't 'deserve' anything. I take care of them because they're mine, and they're mine because when I needed something to hold on to, they were offered to me, in the form of one little girl who needed a sitter."

"And now you're here, in my space, getting ready to bring the Covenant down on our heads."

"Not if I can help it."

She eyed me mistrustfully. "You'll forgive me if I don't believe you."

"That sounds like an order."

"Maybe it is and maybe it isn't, but I don't believe you either way."

"Fair enough." The thought of drinking more tea brought me no pleasure. I stood. "I guess I'm off to track down the Covenant again, now that I have a better sense of where to begin. We won't be bringing them down on your head. Don't worry about that."

Phee gave me a flatly disbelieving look. "Really. And how can you be so sure of that?"

"I can't. You'll just have to trust me."

And on that note, I disappeared, reaching across the silence of the void for the shape of their van. I didn't normally move around by looking for inanimate objects, but I had some experience. When the kids were little, they'd been forever losing some favored, be-loved toy or other, and being able to find them quickly had been the only way I had of keeping the peace. I could find Alice's taxidermy jackalope or Alex's favorite plush alligator as quickly as I could find the actual children. Faster, sometimes, since the toys didn't tend to keep running off when I was looking for them.

I blinked and Phee's kitchen was gone, replaced by a suburban street a lot like the one outside her place. It was dark, and most of the lights were out in the nearby houses. As far as I could see, I was the only person moving on the sidewalk. That was good. It's hard to be seen when there's no one there to see you.

Just to be sure, I flickered, dropping momentarily into the twilight before pulling myself up again. There was no one watching me there, either. Actually, there was nothing there. No suburban street, no dark houses, no sidewalks. Just primeval forest stretching out as far as the eye could see, the memory of a continent as it had once been, sleeping peacefully in the shadows, waiting for the day it would be called to walk the world of the living once again.

When I returned to the sidewalk, the chill of that forest clung to my skin, seeming to worm its way down toward my bones. I shook it off, trying vainly to warm myself, and turned to scan the street for the van. I didn't find it, which made no sense.

I'd gone looking for the van, and I'd appeared here, which meant logic said that it should have been nearby. I turned again, this time making a full circle, and still saw no sign of it. Frowning, I closed my eyes and tried to move myself toward the van.

When I opened them, I was still in the same place, outside a perfectly normal, boring suburban house. I paused, blinking, and then walked toward the closed garage. I reached out with one hand, cautiously touching the garage door, allowing my fingertips to skate just under the surface of the wood. Nothing tingled or bit at my flesh: there were no traps, at least not as far as I could detect.

I took a deep, unnecessary breath and walked through the door into the garage.

And there was the van, as unremarkable as ever, doors closed and engine off as it idled. I eyed it like I would a dangerous animal, circling it carefully. I could feel the Mesmer cage like static in the air, a containment unit for ghosts whose only crime was being in the wrong place at the wrong time.

The garage was empty except for the van. None of the tools or piled-up boxes of holiday decorations that I would have expected to find. I frowned and started for the house. A single wooden step led up to the door, with no welcome mat or attempt to soften the transition. When I got close, I could smell fresh lumber, like someone had sawed off a plank to make the step.

No one lived here, then. This wasn't even an Airbnb or a boardinghouse like Phee's; it was an empty home, maybe owned by the Covenant, maybe belonging to some unwitting local realtor who had no idea what they were currently playing host to.

I touched the door to inside, testing it with my fingertips to be sure it wasn't trapped, then turned intangible and stepped through it into the hall beyond. I was visible for one dizzying, nauseating second before I managed to will myself otherwise. Only then did I begin making my way quietly deeper into the house.

I found Nathaniel in the first room I checked, sound asleep and looking younger than I'd assumed when I saw him before. He snored, but delicately, like he'd been chastised for it so often that he'd somehow learned to control it, refusing to give up even that much control. I looked at him for a moment, wishing it didn't feel like it was already too late for this to end in any way other than him joining me in death, and then moved on.

Chloe was in the next room. She was snoring substantially louder, passed out on top of her bedcovers with a mason jar clutched in her arms. I moved closer to see what it was, and jumped, almost turning visible, as the ghost inside pressed itself against the glass and screamed silently. I didn't feel nearly as bad about the thought of killing her. Maybe that makes me a bad person. I think it just makes me a person with an eye for harm reduction.

The room after that had two beds, one occupied by the man from the van, the other empty. All three rooms had this in common: they were virtually empty, except for suitcases and, in the case of the third room, computers.

The missing man bothered me, though. I worried over the thought of his location as I left the room and moved deeper still.

I found the fourth member of the team in the living room. Heitor was asleep in an easy chair—or so I thought. I paused to watch him sleep for a moment, then turned away. And as I did, he sighed and said, "I know you're there."

Shit. I froze, still invisible, trying to figure out how that could be possible.

"I always know when ghosts are there," he said. "I knew you were there in City Hall, but you were taunting Nathaniel, and I thought it might do him a little good to be reminded that he doesn't know everything. He's so damn cocky because he's been with the Covenant since he was born, like that matters when he's never been in the field before? Benedita and I were recruited when we were in our teens, and we've been in the field ever since. We were hunting iara and pishtaco when we were sixteen, and we were *good*. Then my sister's head was turned by a haunt, and she let herself be hunted. She let herself be led astray. Now she dances to the midnight tempo, and she'll never come home again."

He sighed, opening his eyes, and looked right at me. "Are you stupid, little ghost, or simply tired of your existence?"

I gasped, dropping back into visibility in my shock. Heitor looked at me as calmly as if this was something that happened every day. And abruptly, it all made sense. Why he was with a European Covenant team on a ghost hunt. Why they knew so much about catching ghosts.

Why they had a Mesmer cage.

"You're an umbramancer," I said, and my voice didn't shake, and I had never been more proud of anything in my life. "Why didn't I see it before?"

"You're an American ghost. You learned your tricks and techniques from other American ghosts. We do things differently in Brazil. You ward off the dead with salt water, for tears and the sea. We do it with freshwater, for survival and the river, which knows us far more closely than your oceans can ever know you." He hooked the chain around his neck upward with his thumb, showing me the small vial of water he had dangling there. It was clear, save for half an inch or so of sediment at the bottom. "The Amazon travels with me, and protects me from the eyes of the dead when I don't want them to perceive me."

"Do the Cunninghams know?"

"Those children?" He scoffed. "They believe all witchery is the same as their loathed witchcraft. They would call for my destruction as soon as they would work alongside me. No, they don't know."

"Then why . . . ?"

"Did we join the Covenant? Money. Boredom. To prove a point. My sister and I loved each other dearly, and our parents were dead, and we needed to protect each other. Then the Covenant came to call, and they told her witches were wicked and evil and deserved to be destroyed. We were afraid, Benedita and I, that these strangers would realize what I was, and we decided the safest place for us was in the shadow of the beast. Their attention turned outward, so we burrowed inward, and we found safety, and we found purpose, and I have never regretted our decisions. Not even here. Not even now."

"I see." I wanted to blame him. Him being an umbramancer explained so much about how they'd been able to find and contain the ghosts they were systematically destroying. He had made all this possible.

And yet, hadn't I done the same thing when I joined the crossroads? Maybe I'd been less aware of what I was doing, since I'd been a dead child at the time, but Heitor had been in the field at sixteen, which implied him having been younger when he was first recruited. He'd put his own survival above the survival of others, and that had been the right choice for him, and for his sister. He wasn't a malicious man. He wasn't even necessarily a bad man. He was just a man who'd chosen himself over the rest of the world.

That didn't mean I could forgive him for the people he'd killed and the ghosts he was killing even now. But it meant I could understand, a little better than I necessarily wanted to.

"Are you going to hurt me?" I asked.

"I should," he said. "I should put you in my pocket to save for later, suck the marrow from your soul a drop at a time and savor it. But no. I'm tired, and you're dead, and if you're stalking us, you must know the other phantoms of this city, so I'm willing to offer you a deal. Bring me my sister and I'll go. Bring me Benedita."

"And the ghosts you've already captured?"

"You must have seen them by now. You know they're past recovery. I would say they were past redemption, but all phantoms are." He leaned back in the chair, looking even more profoundly exhausted than he'd been when I entered the room.

I inched closer, trying to keep my distance and see the vial at the same time. The sediment at the bottle was moving, shifting around like a living thing was burrowed all the way to the bottom of it and still squirming restlessly. It made my stomach churn, another physiological holdover from the days when I'd had a body to harm.

"If you're ready to leave, why—"

"They put out the word that they needed grunts to handle their dirty work—not them, of course, pampered scions of Covenant royalty; I don't think Nate had ever washed a dish before he came here, and Chloe's cooking is better described as the opening stages of chemical warfare—after the destruction of Penton Hall. They're on the verge of destitution, you realize."

I blinked. "What?"

"Didn't you know, with your sniffing around and prodding them for weaknesses? The European branch of the Covenant has been keeping up appearances and living up to their ancestors for generations. They empty the coffers of every field office they open, keeping them running on shoestring budgets, and they lock every penny away behind blood wards. No one can get at their money without a direct bloodline claim. They lost more than lives when their stronghold came down. The whole organization is a year, at most, from total insolvency. They can't afford their hired help, or their equipment, and they're having to risk their precious children in the field. This won't be their last field action, and there will be cells like mine scattered around the world for years, but the head's off the serpent at this part; the body thrashes before it dies."

"*What?*"

"My sister is dead, the people I answered to are dead, and the survivors can't afford to pay me," said Heitor. "My time with this organization is coming to an end, little ghost. Bring me my sister and it ends now. Without me, they'll have the tools to catch and torment the dead, but they won't have the power to *find* them. Protect your own kind by bringing me my kin."

"I . . ." I'd only just met Benedita, and according to Heitor, she'd been a willing member of the Covenant. But she was dead now, no longer a part of the group she'd served in life, and if death couldn't absolve her for what she'd done, we were all doomed.

I took a step back, away from him. "I'll see what I can do," I said.

"Remember, if you do it, this ends." He shrugged. "If you don't, we unspool the haunting of this entire coast, and we leave the barrows empty. It's your decision."

It was too big a decision for me. I turned away from him and vanished at the same moment, leaving their little suburban nest behind.

Sixteen

"We're not our parents. We're ourselves, and if that means we're the sum of our own choices, well, there are worse things we could be."

—Jane Harrington-Price

Worcester, Massachusetts,
the basement of a strip mall of some kind,
I don't know, I haven't seen it
from outside the basement

I REAPPEARED IN THE BASEMENT where Jonah's bricks had been lain, standing in the strange, shadowy space and trying to convince my memory of a body that my chest *didn't* hurt, my heart *wasn't* beating too hard. My heart wasn't beating at all. I'd been prone to mimicking basic functions of the living ever since I'd died, but it had been getting worse since the crossroads were destroyed, like my spirit was remembering all the things it should have finished working through decades ago.

It was honestly annoying, and even if it hadn't been, there was no room in my schedule for having a heart attack. What was it going to do, anyway? Kill me?

The pain subsided. I exhaled and straightened, looking around. There was no one there. I was alone in the basement, which would normally have been a good thing. Normally I was trying to avoid the living. Here, I'd been hoping to catch the local dead, and the fact that they weren't here was a little worrisome.

I looked around to make sure I hadn't somehow missed a cluster of ghosts in my hurry to get away from Heitor, then started for the door on the far wall, heading toward it with the slow, uneasy steps of an ingenue in a horror movie. Whether the ghosts were in hiding from the Covenant or had already been captured, there was nothing good waiting for me on the other side of that door. But there was nothing good waiting for me on this side of it, either, and all I'd do by putting it off was give it more time to get really bad.

The door was locked. That didn't matter. I walked through it, into the dim concrete hallway on the other side. Bare bulbs lit the space, illuminating every crack and cobweb and making it look dauntingly like the backstage area of a carnival haunted house. Multiple metal staircases led down from the floor above me, presumably connecting the various street-level stores in this strip mall. This was the underground passthrough for maintenance and stock transport, and no one was ever going to find me down here. Fun.

It was still the golden period between midnight and morning, when the living were largely asleep in their beds, not thinking of ghosts trying to get around their places of business. There might be cameras, but I could handle those if I needed to. I cautiously approached the first set of stairs, squinting upward.

The problem with the whole "ghosts can generally pick up on the presence of other ghosts" thing is that it doesn't have a very clean proximity cutoff. I knew there were ghosts nearby. That just meant they were probably within a mile of me. Maybe they were upstairs in the shops, and maybe they were down the street haunting the local Denny's equivalent.

Only one way to find out.

I climbed the stair to find myself in a pet store, the independent kind with close-set, overstuffed shelves and the omnipresent smell of sawdust from both rodent bedding and accident cleanups. I paused, then smiled, feeling for the first time like something had broken in my favor.

Modern chain pet stores don't usually stock puppies and kittens, except during the day when they're brought in by reputable rescue organizations and placed in sunlit temporary shelters to serve as the animal equivalent of impulse shopping. Older pet stores, on the other hand, will often have a close relationship with the local backyard breeders, leaving them with cages and cages of puppies and kittens slowly marching toward "no longer cute enough" to sell to every child who comes through the doors.

It's not a good thing. I would never call it a *good* thing. But where there are puppies and kittens, there will be children. I started for the back of the store.

And there was Jonah, kneeling next to the pen of sleeping puppies. They were fluffy golden things, all ears and tail, piled up together like they didn't have a care in the world. And maybe they didn't. They were puppies. They didn't know they were in a shabby, potentially predatory pet store, or that they'd age out of adorableness soon. They just knew they were puppies, and they were together, and they had full bellies and a warm place to sleep.

There's something to be said for being a dog. I walked up behind Jonah. He didn't look at me.

"Hey," I said. "You know where Benedita is?"

"She's all grown up, and people can see her when she's in a nightclub or at a party, so she went to a party as soon as it was late enough for things to start," he said, voice dull and almost monotone. "I didn't think you were going to come back. Why did you come back? Did you find Martha and Agnes?"

"Maybe," I said, hedging. How was I supposed to tell this child that his friends were probably lost forever, driven past their breaking point by petty bastards who thought *we* were the real monsters? "Did the others go with her?"

"Aoi did. They can be visible to the living when they want to. I can't, unless you're standing right near the pieces that used to be my house, and even then, people can generally see right through me. Makes it hard to make friends."

I needed to introduce this kid to the local ever-lasters. There had to be some, unless Heitor had taken the Cunninghams to an elementary school. If he'd done that, I was going to kill him. I might have to do that anyway—a rogue umbramancer is nothing to sneeze at, especially not one who's willing to sell their services to the highest bidder. But if he'd intentionally taken the Covenant to target kids, rather than just stumbling over them while targeting random hauntings, there was no way I could let him live.

"All right," I said. "Is the club one of the places you can go?"

He shook his head, then resumed looking at the puppies. "I wish I could pet them," he said wistfully.

"I'm sorry you can't," I said.

"They die sometimes, and I can't even pet them when that happens. Why?"

"Because they're too young, and they haven't had the chance to be truly loved yet," I said. "Is there a shelter around here that you can go to? A place with lots of grownup dogs and cats?"

Jonah frowned. "I know there *is* one, but it doesn't use any of my bricks. I can't go there."

"Maybe there's a way we can fix that." I looked at him, small and translucent and alone, and I hated the Covenant just a little more. As if I needed the encouragement. "All right. I'm going to go looking for nightclubs now. You can stay here or go back to City Hall; the Covenant team's gone to bed for the night, and I don't think you need to worry about them until tomorrow."

"Okay," he said. Then, with a sigh: "If you can't get Martha and Agnes back, do you think you can show me how to move on?"

I'm not a psychopomp. Never have been. Even the members of my family who've died have moved on without my help, by and large, and I don't know how I'd guide someone to whatever comes next. It's just not part of my skill set. I shook my head. "Sorry, kid. I think moving on is something you have to figure out on your own, not something I can help you with. but if you really want to go when all this is finished, I'll do what I can to help you."

Maybe the anima mundi could help us. They had to understand how ghosts moved from this reality to the next, didn't they? They were in charge of the afterlife as we know it, after all.

I took a step back and vanished, throwing myself into the ether. Now came the hard part. When I'd served the crossroads, I had sometimes been expected to find the greatest local density of living people, because that was where petitioners who'd changed their minds thought they could hide. Sometimes people hid from the crossroads when they realized what their wishes were actually going to cost. When that happened, it had been my job to find them and bring them back again.

I couldn't locate people who weren't family members with the precision I brought to my duties, but I could at least make an effort. So I hung in the emptiness between manifestation and silence, and I reached out across the town, looking for ghosts, looking for celebrations, looking for anything that might get me where I needed to go.

One by one, traces of haunting flared into being behind my eyelids. Some of them felt hollowed-out and ancient, like the ghosts that had occupied them were long since gone; others felt recent and bright, sizzling with afterlife. Only one felt like it contained more than a single ghost, and I pulled myself in that direction, dropping back into the world of the living on the sidewalk outside of a nightclub drenched in neon. Music thudded from inside, heavy with bass and electronic shriek.

A living bouncer, human, looked at me without interest as I pulled myself together. I flinched, preparing to vanish again if he started screaming. I didn't normally appear in front of the living.

Then I saw that his eyes were somehow managing to be bright and empty at the very same time, filled with the swirling shadows that only come from certain pharmaceuticals.

"Hi?" I ventured.

"No cover charge for dames, but there's a dress code," he said. "You're wearing too much clothing."

I looked down at myself. I was back in the black-sweater-and-skirt combination I'd been wearing during my discussion with the still-nameless information tech in the Covenant van. I flickered, and I was in a tarnished silver minidress that gleamed like liquid metal as it ran down my hips to stop barely past the top of my thighs, the neckline so plunging that anyone who looked in my direction could tell that I wasn't wearing a bra. If my ankles had been flesh and bone, I would have worried about breaking them in my towering stiletto heels.

I felt more exposed than I would have if I'd been completely naked, and had to swallow the urge to cover myself with my hands as I lifted my chin and looked challengingly at the bouncer. "Better?" I asked.

"Better," he agreed, and unclipped the rope blocking the front of the club. "You have a nice time, and maybe come see me when I come down from this trip. I wanna know if your hair is really that white."

"You got it," I said, and walked inside. He was still doing his job, even if he was drugged to high heaven, and while he hadn't carded me, he was doing everything else correctly, which was damned impressive however you wanted to look at it.

Thoughts of the bouncer flickered and died as the club reached out and swallowed me, dim, glittering lights and pounding bass brushing my thoughts aside like they were barely more than nothing. Everywhere I looked was a teeming throng of bodies, all dancing to a beat that bore very little resemblance to the music. Verity would have loved this place. She would have taken one look at the crowd and decided that she'd died and gone to heaven, then hit the dance floor already synchronized to the beat.

I had never been a dancer. I was more Sunday school than sock hop when I was alive, and short of toddler dance parties in various living rooms, I'd never seen the point. So I eeled myself awkwardly into the crowd, trying not to bump into people, failing utterly, and replacing the effort with the slightly more successful attempt to not wind up wearing too many random drinks. Sure, they fell through me and landed on the floor shortly after they hit my dress, but I had to stay at least partially solid whenever I was touching someone. I couldn't count on the whole club being drugged to the point of accepting ghosts.

And there, in the middle of the dance floor, I found her: Benedita in a red dress that made mine look conservative, wearing heels so high they seemed unrealistic, dancing with a brown-haired college boy who looked like he couldn't believe he could ever be this lucky. He had his hands around her waist, and she was clearly using them for balance as she flung her head back and pranced and slithered all around his body.

She looked like she was having the time of her life, and so did he, and part of me wanted to leave them alone to dance. She wouldn't hurt him: midnight beauties almost never do. They want to dance and drink and remember what it was like to be alive, not harm their partners. A surprising number of types of ghost are entirely harmless to the living. They just don't tend to get as much attention as their scarier cousins do.

Sadly, leaving them to their dance wasn't an option. I threw myself into the crowd, pushing and sidestepping until I was right beside them, then grabbed hold of Benedita's shoulder as she swung toward me.

"Benny, it's me," I said, trying to sound breathless and a little tipsy. The first was easy. The second, not so much. "Did you forget we have a biochem final tomorrow? Sorry, mister." I turned my attention on the man she was dancing with, who just looked even more wide-eyed at the sudden bonus girl in his orbit. "I know you're having an awesome time—Benny's always an awesome time—but I have to steal her. I promised not to let her fail any classes this semester."

Clearly regretful, he released her waist, and Benedita turned fully toward me. "Oh, hey, Mary," she said, concealing her own flicker of surprise. "I thought you were busy tonight."

"I was. Am. I found what I was looking for, and figured I'd come and check in on you, see how you were doing. Glad I did, since it seems like you forgot all the way about your homework, and that's no way to get a passing grade."

"Are you here to nag me about homework or a test? Get your story straight," she said, a thin line of hostility creeping into her tone.

Midnight beauties aren't just drawn to party: they *have* to party if they want to stay coherent. Keep them away from the dance floor for too long and they start coming undone at the seams, which is great. For Benedita, I was getting in the way of what might have been her first solid meal of the week.

And I couldn't worry too much about that right now, because I needed to get her someplace where we could have a reasonable conversation. That wasn't here.

"Both," I said, and took a step back, tugging her with me. "Come on, you're the one who made me promise."

"Right. Sorry, Chuck. See you tomorrow night?"

"If I'm here, I'm yours," he said, with what sounded like true sincerity.

He seemed like a nice guy. I hoped she wasn't going to break his heart. But if she did, it would be after my kids and I were long gone, and they were what mattered right now, not some frat boy I didn't know, no matter how nice he seemed.

Switching my grip to Benedita's wrist, I pulled her off the

dance floor and through the crowd to the door, where we were able to exit for the street. The dull-eyed bouncer was still on duty. He blinked, looking at the pair of us.

"Hey, it's optical-illusion girl and . . . a friend?" He squinted. "I hope you brought better shoes, lady, or you're going to hurt yourself."

"I'll be fine," said Benedita. Then she frowned, looking closer. "You might not be, though. Do you know what you took?"

The bouncer shrugged.

Benedita stepped closer. "May I?" she asked, reaching out with one hand, like she was about to touch something precious.

The bouncer looked bemused but nodded, and she leaned closer, caressing his cheek. The blurriness cleared from his eyes and he staggered back, catching himself against the wall.

"What the hell just . . . ?"

"Let's go." Benedita turned back to me and then kept walking, motioning for me to follow her down the street. She didn't pause or look back.

I scurried after her. "What was that?"

"What was what?"

"What did you do to that man?"

"Purged his system. What?" She looked amused. "You thought the clubs in Brazil encouraged the midnight beauties because we look cute on the dance floor? We do, but we don't drink, and that means we pull down the club's profit margin. We make up for it by protecting the people we party with from the worst effects of excess. No hangovers, no overdoses. A club haunted by a midnight beauty is a safer place for everyone. And before you ask, no, we don't advertise what we can do for the living, because we don't want to be jarred and sold as panaceas to rich bastards without scruples."

I wanted to tell her that wouldn't happen. I wanted to tell her not enough people believed in ghosts.

I couldn't do that. Since Verity's appearance on *Dance or Die*, and the subsequent disappearance of an entire university in Iowa, people had been paying more attention to the world around them. I'm not saying the supernatural and preternatural aspects of the universe were in danger of full unveiling, but they were definitely under more scrutiny than they'd been not all that long ago. With as much as some humans wanted to live forever without ever facing the consequences of their choices, I could absolutely see a black market in midnight beauties springing up, and the poor, beautiful ghosts finding themselves tethered to new masters, with no way of ever breaking free.

We turned a corner, moving into a dark alley, where Benedita stopped, folding her arms, and looked at me. "Well?"

"Well, what?" I allowed myself to flicker, exchanging my too-short dress for the sweater and skirt I'd been wearing on and off all night. All my clothes were illusions, pieces of the twilight snatched and asked to behave like fabric for a little while, but I felt better with less skin on display.

"Well, why did you come and pull me away from Chuck? He's very young and enthusiastic, and I'm worried he'll get hurt if I leave him to dance with the living." She raised an eyebrow. "Also, did you just change your clothes because you're calling me a skank, or is that a convenient side effect?"

"What? No!" I shook my head in hard negation. "I'm more comfortable like this, that's all. You wear whatever you want. I think your shoes should qualify you for some kind of physics degree, just because you know how to walk in them."

"My shoes?" Benedita glanced down. "I was wearing higher heels than this the night I died."

"How did you die?"

"Oh, it's story time? Fine. I was out clubbing, I met a guy. He was tall and handsome and sweet and about as clever as a brick. Turned out that was because he'd been dead for about a decade. He was a haunt—the classic kind, not the generic term for ghosts. He thought I was beautiful, and he courted me for months before he kissed me, and my heart stopped."

I winced. "Bad luck."

Haunts are sort of a fifty-fifty case when it comes to them interacting with the living. Half the time, they can heal any wound, cure any illness, and bring people back from the very verge of death. It's impressive as hell. The other half, they kill with a kiss, stopping hearts instantly. It's not a gamble most people are really looking to take, and that's pretty reasonable, if you ask me.

"Yeah," she said. "I died, and I rose up three days later in the same club, where the owner—he'd been a friend of mine when I was alive, thank God—hurried to get me off into a private room, so I wouldn't start a riot. He told me I was gone, and that my brother had collected my body and set ghost traps all around the club to catch the haunt that killed me. I wasn't thinking straight. One minute I was fine, the next I was being told my favorite club was a trap for people like I'd suddenly become, and my hot new maybe-boyfriend had been a monster. Only he wasn't a monster. He was a sweet guy who probably hadn't remembered his kiss could kill, and he didn't deserve whatever my brother was going to do to him." She paused, and looked at me levelly. "You've met Heitor, haven't you?"

"I— How could you tell?"

"You're looking at me differently, like I might be dangerous, like I might be something more than another eternal party girl looking for her next dance partner. That means you know who I used to be when I was alive. I thought death was supposed to be the big release for people like us, huh? We die, we get all our sins forgiven, and the twilight makes us over into what we were always meant to be. I'm the life of the party. I'm just dead at the same time."

"I think some things carry over."

Benedita exhaled, half-laughing. "I hope not. Because the way Heitor acted when he saw me, I lost everything as soon as my heart stopped. No brother. No purpose. No place in the Covenant. He looked at me like I was a monster, and he tried to jar me. I got away because I spent so much of my life training with him that I don't think he could get the drop on me if he tried. And he *tried*. Oh, how he tried. I had to run, and I kept running until I got to Orlando, where I thought I'd be safe. But he found me there, and I started running again, following the coast, trying to get far enough away that he'd leave me alone."

I managed, barely, not to groan. "The Covenant's been following *you*, and using your presence as a bellwether for local hauntings. They've been sweeping up the ghosts in your wake."

"I didn't do it on purpose."

"I know. But you did it, and now that it's done, we have to deal with it." I huffed. "Your brother said that if I bring you to him, he'll walk away. He'll stop working with the Covenant. Without an umbramancer, they won't be able to do half as much damage as they're doing right now."

"He'll hurt me."

"They've already hurt so many people, living *and* dead. I can't force you, but I can ask, and I'm asking you to make the right decision. If not for me, for Jonah. That poor kid's on the cusp of losing everything."

"That poor kid lost everything two hundred years ago," said Benedita. "Shouldn't I get a longer afterlife?"

I just looked at her. She glared back, hands flexing like she was thinking about hitting me. That would be an interesting choice on her part. Physical fights between ghosts *can* happen, but all I'd need to do is blink away and she'd be fighting nothing. Not the most productive use of her time.

"Look, I'm not the boss of you; I can't force you to go to your brother," I said. "But I can, and will, tell the other ghosts that you're the reason the Covenant is hunting here instead of somewhere else, and I bet they'll find that fascinating."

"You wouldn't *dare*."

"Wouldn't I? You're putting us all at risk. You're putting *my family* at risk, because you're so busy running away from your own. Your brother is looking for you. I'm not asking you to stop the Covenant. Just to take away one of their tools, and slow them down."

Benedita sighed, looking briefly cowed. "I miss my brother," she said. "Heitor and I were always inseparable, until I went and got myself killed like an amateur. I should have picked up on the signs before I let him kiss me. But it was nice to have someone want me that much, you know? Every club I went to, he was there. Every party. And it wasn't creepy, somehow, it was just— nice."

I didn't say anything. She was convincing herself at this point, working through what she needed to do without involving me. I wasn't going to interrupt, not when there was a chance she could end all this.

"When I was with the Covenant, I had a purpose. I was part of something larger than myself. I think, sometimes, that I miss that even more than I miss Heitor."

"I understand," I said, and I did. There were moments when I missed the steady, selfish presence of the crossroads. There's something nice about having a greater force telling you what to do.

Benedita looked at me, and it was suddenly obvious how young she was, under the phantom makeup that came with her place in the afterlife. She'd lived longer than I had, but only by a few years. "Did Heitor say what he was going to do with me?"

"No," I said. "Just that he missed you. And you've just said that you miss him. Don't you think it's time we brought this to some kind of an ending?"

I held out my hand. After a moment, she took it, and I took her, both of us, into the other side of the twilight.

✦ ✦ ✦

We appeared, not in the living room where I'd left Heitor to wait for me, but in the shadows of an unfamiliar orchard. The trees around us were more like extremely ambitious bushes, reminding me of some blueberry farms I had visited, but instead of dusky blue sprigs of fruit, they had long stalks growing off the branches, each covered in clusters of small, bright red fruits that I didn't recognize.

Benedita clearly did. She blinked, then turned on me and asked, sharply, "What kind of joke is this?"

"It's not a joke," I said. "I just . . . don't know where we are."

"It's a fazenda," said Benedita. "And frankly, I'm insulted that you'd assume I was a farmer just because I'm Brazilian."

"She didn't," said a new voice, familiar only in that it was uniquely unfamiliar, shifting on every syllable, so that it could never be truly recognizable. "We didn't either, to be clear; we brought you to us to find out what you know, but the space selects the shape. Only it's always growing, and always ready for the harvest, because the reaper loves the crop, or what's the point in planting?"

Grateful, I turned, and there was the anima mundi, standing between two of the strange trees with a basket over their arm and a small pair of shears in their hand. The basket was half-full of the little red fruits. Despite their unfamiliar surroundings, the anima mundi was as beautiful as ever. It was impossible to label or define their beauty, which changed constantly, but it was equally impossible to deny it.

"'S'up?" I said, with forced nonchalance.

Benedita blinked, looking between the two of us, before stepping away from me and demanding, stridently, "What the *fuck* is going on?"

"Um," I said. "You know how I used to work for the crossroads?"

She turned to stare at me, then bolted into the trees, running as hard as she could. The anima mundi sighed.

"Mary, that was poorly handled," they said.

"What? I didn't expect to wind up here! I wasn't prepared," I objected. "I've been being very careful about how much energy I use, and I'm really not in the mood for a lecture."

"This isn't a lecture, this is a congratulations," they said. "You've done quite well by finding the midnight beauty and bringing her so neatly to heel. Once this is all concluded, you should be able to return to your family, and not darken my door again any time soon. Unless . . ."

"Unless?"

"Unless you wanted to serve me as you once served the crossroads. I won't force you. A service forced is barely a service at all."

I blinked at them. "I just got free to spend more time with my family—a family, by the way, that's having kids again, which means they're going to need me more than they have in years. Why would I come to work for you when that's going on?"

"Because I could keep your restrictions lightened if you did," they said. "And because you've been very insular for a very long time, Mary. You've served two masters, and spent as little time among the dead as possible, lest they envy or reject you. But the crossroads did no curation of my lost children. Ghosts like the boy are more common than you may care to know. He never got to become what he should have been, and he lingers without place or purpose. You could help him, either to move on or to find ghosts like him, to form a more secure haunting. If you agreed."

That did sound appealing. There were too many ghosts like Jonah, stranded and unable to move on with their afterlives, because there was no one explaining the rules to them, no one making sure they understood what they were supposed to be becoming. "Do I need to answer right away? We're still kind of in the middle of the last job you gave me."

"No," they said. "You can have a bit of time to consider our offer."

"What, exactly, are you offering me?"

"What you have now, in terms of movement and flexibility. What the crossroads offered you once, before me—the freedom to put your family first, to choose them whenever a choice must be made, without censure or blame. And all the afterlife as your playground."

I frowned. That sounded *real* appealing, which meant there was bound to be a catch somewhere that I couldn't see just yet.

Before I could answer them, Benedita came running out of the trees, looking back over her shoulder as she came, which made me suspect that the anima mundi had bent space around her, causing her to run in a loop. She hooked one high-heeled foot over a rock and went sprawling. The anima mundi looked at this and sighed.

"You needn't be afraid, child," they said. "I'm not going to hurt you, and if I were, there would be nothing you could do to stop me. Fear serves no useful purpose, only wearies you when there is no cause."

Benedita scrambled to her feet again, turning to glare at the anima mundi. "You can't trick me," she snapped. "I was trained by the Covenant of St. George. I'm smarter than your games!"

"How did that work out for you?" I asked sharply. "Did you enjoy your time with the monster hunters? Are you enjoying the fruits of your labors?"

"To be honest, it kind of sucked," she said. "I did it because I needed to do *something*, and they said they would pay us. And for a long time, the money was good enough that I didn't really care all that much what they had us doing. But then I died and my own brother said I was a monster, just like all the ones we'd hunted through the years, so I started really *looking* at the monsters. And you know what? Most of them weren't. Most of them were perfectly normal people who just wanted to be left alone so they could get on with their lives. Why were we hunting them? Why were we hurting them? And why was my brother, who said he loved me, why was *he* suddenly hunting *me*? It wasn't right."

"If you came back to life right now, does that mean you wouldn't rejoin the Covenant?" I asked.

Benedita shook her head. "I wouldn't. I swear, I wouldn't."

"Well, then, you've learned something from being dead. Too bad it's not Halloween." Under the right circumstances, ghosts can use Halloween night to come back to life. I know people who've done it. I've never really been tempted. My world faded into history a long time ago, and I don't really feel like becoming a fish out of water for the sake of growing up.

The anima mundi sighed. "I called you here to tell Mary she had done well so far, and was on the verge of discharging her duties to me, and to tell you that you're not at fault for your brother's actions. There was no way you could have predicted how he would handle your death. Umbramancers never leave ghosts behind. Their close kin almost always do. It's like they're such black holes for the dead that they can't conceive of coming back once their time is done, but that same position bathes the people around them in the power they channel. It suffuses them, and when the time comes, they rise. They always, always rise."

"You saying it's my brother's fault I'm like this?" demanded Benedita. "I would have been normal if not for him?"

"Ghosts *are* normal," said the anima mundi. "You're a part of the cycle of sapient life. But yes, if he'd been other than he is, the chances are very good that you would never have risen, for you would have been less tied to the lands of the dead."

"And you brought me to a coffee estate to tell me that?"

"I brought you here because Mary was in transit, and that made it easier for me to redirect her."

Benedita looked bemused. That was fine. I wasn't feeling all that much more sure of what was happening around me, and I'd at least been here before. Although in my defense, it was normally a field of wheat.

"I'll think about your offer," I said, to the anima mundi. "I'm not saying yes or no just yet. I'm also not finished with the job you already assigned to me. I'm willing to discuss new limits on where I can go, as long as you're willing to listen when I tell you what my family needs. Agreed?"

"Agreed," said the anima mundi. They offered me their hand. I took it, and the world turned gray as fog around me. Benedita grabbed for my other hand, holding on tight, and then the coffee farm dropped away, and we were nowhere.

Seventeen

"Always take the win. No matter how strange or subjective it might seem, always take it."

—Frances Brown

Worcester, Massachusetts,
the living room of a house being rented
by the Covenant of St. George, because that's
a great place for a ghost to be

WE POPPED BACK INTO EXISTENCE in the world of the living, in the middle of the living room where I'd last seen Heitor. That was the good part. The bad part was that Heitor was gone. The chair was empty, the cushions having long since returned to their original level of compression. Benedita dropped my hand. "Where is my brother?" she demanded, whirling on me.

"Oh, he's a little busy," said the voice of the man from the van. I turned. He was standing in the doorway to the hall, leaning up against the frame like he had nowhere better in the entire world to be. He smirked a little as he saw the recognition flood my face. "Oh, come off it. I'm the guy in the chair. You think I haven't been over every frame of the security footage from Penton Hall with a fine-toothed comb?"

Well, crap. I crossed my arms, trying to look like his words didn't send every nerve I didn't have into a state of high, jangling alert. "So you looked at some old home movies. Big deal. Why should that worry me?"

"Because your face is in them, clear as day and larger than life. Which is pretty funny, since you're not alive, are you?"

I tamped down the urge to recoil, looking at him calmly. "I don't know. Do I look dead to you?"

"Before these two whacked-out British kids came to me asking about ghost hunts and whether I was any good at reviewing security footage, I would have said no, of course not. Now, though? Now I know 'dead' isn't always as obvious as people want to make like it is. Still haven't seen any vampires, though. I want to, but no matter how hard I look for them, they just don't appear."

"That's because there's no such thing," I said, and I meant it. Sanguivores—creatures that live on blood—exist, and sometimes people call them vampires as a sort of catch-all term for people with a liquid diet, but the classic Bram Stoker vampire isn't real. There's no such thing as a dead person who has a physical body all the time, sleeps during the day, turns into a bat and flies around at night drinking blood. Manananggal and similar creatures exist, but they're not the same, and trying to cram them under the umbrella of a myth is just colonialist thinking applied to biology. It's basically a way of saying "Things like this exist over here, so naturally, Europe must have something bigger, better, and similar."

"You're one to talk," he said with a sneer, and turned his attention to Benedita. "He said you were something called a 'midnight beauty.' You're not that hot. Six out of ten, tops."

Benedita shrugged. "The beauty is individual, and not for you to name. I am what I am, and I do not deny it. She's not *dead*. She's been hunting me on Heitor's behalf, and now that she's managed to find me and bring me here to him, you're concealing him from me."

"I saw you appear," he blustered.

She shrugged again, more fluidly this time, like she was trying to draw attention to the elegant line of her neck, the grace of her arms. "A gift of the dance. I crossed the land of the dead, and I pulled her in my wake, safe as a duckling following its mother."

"Really."

"Really," she agreed.

"Every ghost I've spoken to has said that wasn't possible," he said. "That the lands of the dead are sealed against the living."

Benedita scoffed. "Oh, because the ghosts *you've* spoken with have had such cause to tell you truth over lies. Tell me, do you always assume the terrified and trapped are speaking truly? Is the Covenant teaching you to believe those without hope will forever betray themselves to their own ends?"

"Take me, then." He stepped forward, toward her. "If you can carry people through the lands of the dead, take me."

"They survive only when I wish it," she cautioned. "My brother would survive the experience, for I would wish it. You would not. If you wish to see the lands of the dead, die. I promise you'll see them clearly on that happy day."

He swung his head around to look at me. I spread my hands. "I can't take you anywhere," I said.

"Right. But I know what you are. I know what you *did.* And I know that any moment now, Chloe and Nate will be back, and finished preparing to face you, and you'll finally pay with everything you have to give."

I stiffened, looking around. Heitor was still gone, and the chair where he'd been sitting wasn't stained or damaged; if he'd been attacked, he hadn't been sitting there when it happened. No one else seemed to be moving around. And yet . . .

We had an unaccounted-for umbramancer, and two Covenant operatives with good reason to hate the dead. And there's no reason a Mesmer cage can't cover an entire house.

There's no point in maintaining a masquerade so hard that it gets you caught. I glanced to Benedita. "Where Aoi is," I said, and vanished, hoping she would understand what I was saying.

I reappeared in front of the club a split second later, where the still-sober bouncer only blinked at me. "Change your clothes before I can let you in," he said.

"Sorry," I replied. "No time." I rushed forward, passing through the still-clipped rope and into the club. The dance floor was alive with thrashing bodies and flashing lights, like a headache made manifest. I plunged into it, careful to stay solid, and pushed through the crowd, looking for a slender Japanese dancer of uncertain gender.

I found them toward the far edge, dancing with a pretty girl who had probably been legal for less than a month. Aoi was wearing the face of a handsome young Japanese man, their hair gelled back and their collar popped at a jaunty angle. I grabbed them by the elbow, stopping their gyrations, and they turned to look at me quizzically.

"Yes?" they asked.

"It's me, Mary," I said. "Benedita's in trouble."

"No she's not," they said. "She's been here with me all night."

"Yeah? Point her out to me."

They turned to scan the dance floor while their erstwhile partner looked more and more annoyed at the intrusion, pretty cheeks going red as she crossed her arms and glowered at me. I blinked, then realized what this looked like: I was clearly younger than Aoi, and not dressed for the club at all, interrupting what must have seemed like a singularly pleasant night out.

Aoi finished their scan and turned back to me. "Where is she?" they asked.

"I took her to see her brother. He wasn't there. I think something may have happened to him. The people he's been working with aren't good people."

Aoi blanched. Too literally—the color drained from their

cheeks, which then continued to pale, slipping fast toward a dead, bleached-out white. I elbowed them in the side, and they yelped, jumping as the color came flooding back.

"We need to go," I said. "Jonah can't help. He's just a kid, and they're not in a place his curfew allows."

I paused for Aoi to take my meaning, then added, "I have a couple of people who might be able to lend us a hand. Can you come with me?"

Aoi nodded, turning to make apologies to their dance partner. She rolled her eyes and muttered something I couldn't make out over the music, then turned and stomped off toward the bar, leaving Aoi staring helplessly after her. I grabbed their elbow, pulling them with me as I made for the exit.

Again, I didn't bother to unhook the rope, and again, the bouncer looked at me with a flat lack of surprise.

"How long has this nightclub been haunted?" he asked.

I raised an eyebrow. "You really want us to answer that?"

"Not particularly, no." He shook his head. "They don't pay me enough to care about dead girls breaking dress code."

"Not a girl," said Aoi.

"Not breaking dress code, either."

"Fair enough." Aoi turned to me. "What was all that about?"

"Exactly what it sounded like. Now, I don't know how your kind of ghost moves around the twilight, but I was able to haul Benedita with me by holding her hand. That work for you?"

"Why, Miss Mary, I had no idea you cared," said Aoi, face morphing into my own as they batted their lashes at me.

I rolled my eyes and grabbed their hand, and we were gone, reappearing a moment later in the hallway of Phee's boarding-house.

The doors to Arthur and Elsie's rooms were standing open. Panic flooded through me like bleach, sucking the color and sub-stance out of everything, and I staggered, dropping Aoi's hand as I braced myself against the wall. They couldn't be in danger or distress; they weren't calling for me. I'd hear them if they were calling for me, wouldn't I? They were my family. I was supposed to hear them.

But I couldn't feel them at all when I tried to reach out and locate them. I'd been so busy with everything else that I hadn't noticed the absence. Now that I was feeling for it, though, I couldn't pay attention to anything else. The absence was all. Elsie and Arthur were gone, and there was a hole in the world where they should have been.

"Seeing" that hole made me want, more than anything, to hurry and check on everyone else I cared about, rushing from place to place until I knew that they were all safe. The desire was almost overwhelming. I breathed slowly in and out through my nose, forcing it aside. I would know if they were dead. That was a certainty. They weren't here, they weren't dead, and they weren't currently in active distress. That left very few options, and I wasn't sure what most of them meant.

Aoi turned to give me a puzzled look, clearly not understanding why two open doors would upset me so much. "Are you okay?" they asked.

"No," I managed. "The kids I babysit for are supposed to be here."

Aoi blinked. "And they're not?"

"No."

Something moved farther down the hall. I vanished immediately, reappearing in front of Phee, who had been retreating toward the kitchen. "Going somewhere?" I asked, voice barely above a snarl.

"Hey, we're all friends here," she said, laughing a little as she raised her hands in surrender. "I was just getting a fresh cuppa, since it seemed you'd come back for the nonce. Who's your friend?"

"You don't get to know about my friends," I said. "Where are they?"

"Who? The adults you made sure to stress could take care of themselves? That 'they'? Because it seems to me a bit hypocritical of you to come here looking for them after you told me they'd be fine on their own."

I ground my teeth together, stepping closer, and for a moment, allowed the pleasant masquerade of "virtually alive" to slip from my features. My eyes and cheeks sank inward, my flesh going waxen and slack as my bones strained to show themselves. I don't enjoy looking like a corpse. Sometimes it's the only way to get my point across.

"I'm a caretaker," I said. "I always know where my family is. *Always*. Well, I can't feel them right now. They're gone. But they're not dead, because I would know if they were dead. I last saw them in your house. Where are they?"

I hadn't felt anything like this since Alice was in college and Laura was trying to ward off the spirits that constantly tried to get closer to her. She'd set up wards and runes and Mesmer cages, finally layering them together so tightly that she not only kept out the ghosts, she kept out my awareness of Alice. That had been a deeply unpleasant weekend, until we figured out what was going on and I managed to convince her to loosen her shields enough to let me through.

Heitor was an umbramancer who'd constructed at least one Mesmer cage for his Covenant allies. Could Elsie and Arthur be inside one of those, cut off from me but not dead, just outside my ability to detect?

Oh, I hoped so. I would have said there was no reason I'd ever hope for one of my kids to be taken into Covenant custody, but right now, it seemed like the best thing that could have possibly happened. If the Covenant had them, they were hostages against my eventual surrender, making them stuck but safe. They were just . . . shut away for a little bit, and when I managed to bust the doors open, they'd be there, waiting for me to bring them home.

Phee stared at my withered visage, her own face going pale—although not as pale as Aoi's had been earlier. Nothing living could be that pale. "I don't know," she said. "I swear, I don't know, and I didn't know your ducklings were gone until I came to use the loo and found the doors standing open. I thought they'd decided to sneak out without paying, that you'd judged my hospitality insufficient and stolen them away. I know you wanted them kept safe, and I did nothing to go counter to that. I'm not a combatant. I've been staying out of trouble for too long at this point to go looking for it now."

"Well, you found it," I snapped. "Did you let a couple of humans into your house by any chance? Just open up the door and let them stroll on inside?"

"She didn't," said a voice from the end of the hall. "I did."

Aoi whipped around, looking anxious as a rabbit in a field full of foxes. They didn't disappear, though, which was more than I could have asked of them, under the circumstances.

I shot them a reassuring look as I turned, and there was Amelia, watching me coolly. Despite that, I could see the anxiety in her eyes. I flickered, vanishing from in front of Phee and reappearing in front of Amelia. "You *what*?"

"The habitat of my species is in our name," said Amelia, voice still cool. She looked untroubled by my corpselike appearance. "We don't have a lot of options when it comes to hiding from people who know we exist, and when those Covenant freaks hit town, one of the first things they did was send a message to our village elders. Watch over the local cryptids for them, or they'd come and 'watch over' our entire population."

"You could always start expanding your population," said Phee, moving toward us at a more leisurely pace. Aoi walked with her, mouth shut and eyes wide. "Buy houses near the coast, send your kids to Chicago for college . . ."

"We *can't*," said Amelia. "We get sick if we're away from the swamp for too long, and we can't reproduce, not even using IVF. Nothing we do gets us clear of the Hockomock. We evolved there, and we'll go extinct there. I just wasn't ready for it to be now."

"What did you do?" I demanded.

"Nothing." She looked at me, expression flat and resigned. "I just brought them a bedtime snack. Milk and cookies for the boy, cookies and a nightcap for the girl. Plenty of aconite for both."

I managed, barely, to restrain myself from wrapping my hands around her thick neck and starting to squeeze. "Aconite is *deadly* to Lilu! And it's not very good for humans, either."

"I'm sorry, did I imply that I used pure aconite? My bad. I ground up purple-lined sallows and mixed them into the drinks. They're a species of moth that feeds on aconite plants when they're young, and when they're powdered, they're a classic defense against Lilu. They drug and disorient without killing."

I already knew Elsie and Arthur weren't dead, and that was enough to let her words work their way through the red fog of rage now threatening to overwhelm me. I swallowed hard, letting some of the life come back into my face as I took a half-step back. Aoi put a hand on my shoulder, bolstering me. "So you drugged them. Why? Why now?"

"The woman from the Covenant who's been monitoring me called and said they thought the local ghosts were catching on to them. She asked if I knew of anything that had changed recently, anything that might have stirred up the spirits, and of course I thought of the three of you, the last caretaker and the two Price children. Oh, she was *very* excited to hear about your little friends. Excited to hear about you, too, but I didn't exactly have a way to hand you over, so we had to put a pin in that for right now."

"I am going to see you dead," I said, coldly.

"Are you?" asked Amelia. "I thought you people were all about conservation. Well, there are thirty-eight of us left, and I'm the only girl in my generation with multiple possible sexual partners who *aren't* siblings or first cousins. So if you kill me, you could be responsible for driving a species to extinction. But no big deal, I guess."

"You could have told us years ago that you were having issues keeping your breeding population large enough to be meaning-ful," I snapped.

"Could we? Really? Because I promise you, we're not unique."

I didn't know what to say to that. I only knew that my kids—my *kids,* no matter how old they were—were in trouble, and they needed me to save them before things got even worse. I flickered back down the hall, grabbing Aoi by the elbow, and turned a hard stare on Phee.

"If they die, I'll be hosting a Price family reunion in your living room, and your homeowner's insurance will *not* cover the result," I said, and vanished, dragging Aoi with me. It was time to bring this whole messy affair to an end. Whatever that happened to entail.

Eighteen

"No one here cares whether or not you're dead. You're family, and that's more than good enough for us."

—Enid Healy

Worcester, Massachusetts,
the sidewalk outside a house being rented
by the Covenant of St. George

Aoi wrenched their elbow out of my grasp as soon as we reappeared on the sidewalk, taking a step away and glaring at me with my own eyes.

"You have to *stop* doing that!" they said.

"Can you please take off my face?" I asked, scrubbing at my own version of it with one hand. "I'm tired and I'm upset and my charges are in danger, and I don't like looking in a mirror all the time."

Aoi blinked, and their facial features began melting back into the smooth expanse of nothing that seemed to be their default. "Sorry," they said, voice no longer a blend of mine and their own. "Where are we?"

"This house is where the Covenant is holed up," I said, concealing a shudder as I indicated the modest suburban home in front of us. Watching my own face melt was not a fun experience. "They're apparently just about out of money after what happened to their main stronghold, so they don't have a lot of backup. Beyond, apparently, the people we thought were on our side."

The unfairness of Jane being dead was trying to rise up and overwhelm my concern about her children. She would have been absolutely overjoyed to have both a cryptid social issue to resolve and a traitor to take apart, one shrieking, miserable piece at a time. But Jane was gone, and I was going to save her kids. There was nothing else I could do.

The lights in the living room were on now, when they hadn't been before. It was difficult to say whether that was a good thing. "The Covenant has four people, and they have my two kids," I said. "Benedita was in there when I came to get you, along with several dozen jarred ghosts. I don't know how much support they have that isn't already in the building."

"I'm a *faceless ghost*," said Aoi. "What the hell do you think I'm going to do against the Covenant of St. George and a bunch of ghosts in jars?"

"To be honest, I have no living clue, beyond the fact that the anima mundi says you can access more power than you normally could while those ghosts are cut off from the twilight," I said. "I'm just the babysitter. This is way above my pay grade." Oh, but I hoped. Linger in the twilight as long as I have, you get to see a lot of people achieve more than they think they're capable of. "Now come on. Let's haunt these motherfuckers."

I strode toward the closed garage door, a small part of my hope shifting toward hoping I wasn't about to bounce off of some kind of complicated ghost ward and find myself locked outside. But locking me out of the house wouldn't have served the revenge they'd come here looking for. Maybe they hadn't been expecting the ghost who leveled Penton Hall to come looking for them in return, and maybe they had been; either way, if they wanted to face me, they needed to first let me inside.

I reached the garage door and walked through rather than bouncing off, finding myself in the virtually empty garage. The van was still there. I assumed that was a good sign.

I still couldn't feel Elsie or Arthur. They were just *gone*, excised from the world, the way Annie and the others had been when they went to another dimension. They could have died there—Artie did, in a technical but very real way—and I might never have known. Artie's death, such as it was, never registered with the part of me that knows those things. He just left and sent a stranger back in his place, whatever that meant for his place in the family.

So this was all fairly terrifying, and didn't get any less so as Aoi walked through the garage door behind me, still faceless, turning their head from side to side like they were looking at everything around us with the eyes they didn't have.

"Okay, this is creepy," they said.

"Not going to argue with you there. Don't get too close to the van."

"Why not?"

"There's a Mesmer cage drawn across the inside. I was able to get out earlier because I'm virtually indistinguishable from the living when I want to be. If you're not capable of becoming that level of material and solid, you could get stuck inside."

"Huh." They turned their head toward the van again, and I got the feeling from their posture that they were looking at it with deliberation. "Could your people be inside there, do you think?"

"It's possible, but a Mesmer cage weak enough for me to walk out of it under my own power doesn't feel like it would be enough to cut off the connection between a caretaker and their charges. Wherever they're holding my kids, I expect it to be deeper in." I gestured toward the door to the rest of the house. "This way."

"Got it."

"You don't have to come if you don't want to."

"Oh, now she tells me I'm free to go." Aoi threw their hands up. "Wow, if I had just realized that sooner, I might not be here now." They let their hands fall back to their sides. "Benedita is my friend. You have those, don't you, caretaker?"

I nodded. "I do."

"When I died, my face melted off my head, and I was terrified. She was the one who found me in a nightclub in Miami, haunting the bathrooms and terrifying the janitorial staff, and told me what I was now and how it was going to work moving forward. Without her, I'd still be there, thinking I was never going to be good for anything but scaring people ever again."

"What was your . . . ?"

"My unfinished business? Fucked if I know." Aoi shrugged. "I was murdered, if that helps at all, but if every murdered person turned into a ghost, we'd be up to our armpits in the restless dead, and I just haven't seen any evidence of that. I figure I'll find out eventually, but until that happens, I'm happy to keep clubbing with Benedita, hang out with the kid, and try not to get put into a jar. The jar thing seems to really, really suck."

"It does," I said. "Well, I'm sorry you got killed, and I'm sorry your face melted, and I'm glad you want to help your friend, because I was *not* excited about the idea of doing this alone."

"Somehow, didn't get the feeling you would be."

Together we walked through the door into the house proper, and two things happened at the same time: my vague awareness of Elsie and Arthur as living creatures whose welfare was my responsibility snapped back into place like it had never been disrupted, and the runes that had been painted on the doorframe in dull silver ink flared to life, completing the ghost trap someone had been industriously building. I turned to stare at them in open-mouthed betrayal. Half of them looked like they'd been there for weeks, waiting for the moment when they would be put to use and the whole house would be turned into the slightly more vicious equivalent of a Mesmer cage. The other half were clearly fresh, the paint still gleaming and wet.

"Those *fuckers*," I said.

"Mary?" Aoi moved closer to me.

"They knew the ghosts would follow them home eventually. I found Heitor in the living room, and he said that if I brought him his sister, this would all be over. So I went to convince Benedita to come. I don't know whether he meant it when he said he wanted to quit, or whether that was all part of the trap, but I believed him either way. I thought I could end this. When I brought her here, there was no ghost trap. They must have closed the loop to keep her contained."

I fucked up. I resisted the urge to put my hands over my face and give myself a moment of regret. Instead, I flexed the mental muscle that would allow me to drop down into the twilight, and found the passage was blocked. The ghost trap we'd wandered into might not be the standard design, but it was solid, and it was designed to make sure that anything bodiless that stepped over the threshold wasn't going to be stepping out again.

Mesmer cages fell out of favor in part because any sufficiently incarnate ghost can beat them with a Sharpie. I thought about going to the kitchen and digging through the drawers in search of a get-out-of-jail-free marker, but the thought was too repulsive to pursue. It made my gut twist in a very visceral, living way, like I was going to vomit ectoplasm all over the floor. I pushed the idea aside, and the cramping sensation went with it. They'd constructed a ghost trap designed to preserve itself by punishing ghosts who even thought about destroying it.

Great. I love a good advancement in fucking with the dead technology. This was not good.

"Can I borrow your face again, please?" asked Aoi, a little desperately. "I feel naked without one, and I don't like feeling naked in this house. It's like the opposite of haunted in here. It's uncomfortable."

"Go for it," I said, and started down the hall. I peeked into the bedrooms as I passed them, and while I could still move through the walls, there were no people there to find. That wasn't much of a surprise. Arthur and Elsie were somewhere inside the cage with us, and it didn't extend to cover the garage: that was all I knew, and that was going to have to be enough.

The anima mundi wasn't in the twilight. They were in their own place, part of the afterlife but pinched off somehow, forming a unique realm. They were also technically divine. I wondered if I could pass through the cage to get to them, and dismissed the idea. Even if *I* could go to the anima mundi, there was no guarantee I could take *Aoi* with me, or that I would be able to get back here again. I couldn't leave my kids. Not when they were in Covenant custody and possibly still drugged.

"I found Heitor and one of the other agents in the front room before," I said. "That's where we go."

Aoi, who now looked like my black-haired twin, nodded and kept following me, staying close. I was grateful for the company, however unnerving their appearance might be. I didn't want to be doing this alone.

I felt the next layer of the ghost trap slam shut as we stepped out of the hall and into the front room, passing another set of freshly painted silver runes on the doorframe. I barely paid it any attention.

Heitor was back in the armchair where he'd been initially, head lolling and eyes glassy, throat an open ruin of sliced flesh and severed arteries. The chair was drenched with his blood, as was the front of his shirt. He must have bled out in seconds, too quickly to realize what was happening or pull any tricks of his own. Benedita was on her knees next to the body, hands over her face, weeping hysterically.

There was no sign of his ghost. There never is, with umbra-mancers. When they die, they're gone, and that's the end.

Chloe and Nathaniel were at the end of the room in front of the window. Chloe was holding a mason jar. The man from the van was nowhere to be seen.

"You," said Nathaniel, pure venom in his tone. I looked at him, unsurprised to see the loathing in his voice reflected in his eyes. He hated me. Truly and completely hated me, as I had hated nothing in my life outside of the crossroads.

"Me," I said, agreeably enough. I glanced to Aoi. "Might want to go and borrow Benedita's face while you have the chance. These people don't like me much." I didn't wait to see what they were going to do before I returned my attention to Nathaniel. "Elsie and Arthur don't have anything to do with this. Let them go."

"On the contrary, they're the proof of how far their degenerate family has fallen," he said with a sneer. "My brother thinks to secure his legacy by bringing the youngest Price daughter back into the fold of righteousness, but we have two of her bloodline who bred with monsters. There is no coming back for them. Leonard would found his dynasty on a sister to beasts."

"Okay, wow, wish Antimony were here to have heard you say all that, because I would genuinely enjoy watching her remove your lower jaw as a souvenir of that time she kicked your ass, but she's not, so fuck you, on behalf of the entire Price family," I said, sharply. I looked to Chloe. "You believe this shit?"

"I believe you're a demon summoned up from hell by the forces of darkness," spat Chloe. "You'll burn in hell for all eternity for what you've done."

"What *she's* done?" demanded Benedita, uncovering her face and climbing unsteadily to her feet. "*She'll* burn for what *she's* done? Find a mirror, bitch, because there's blood on your hands, and if there's a hell, it's waiting to welcome you home!"

"Benedita, maybe catch a bubble before you antagonize the lady with the ghost trap," I said, but she wasn't listening. She stalked toward the Cunninghams, stiff-legged and furious.

"Whatever Mary did, she did to save the family you won't just leave alone! What *you* did, though—there was no reason for what *you* did. All we ever were was loyal to you. All we ever did was try to serve and uphold the ideals of the Covenant of St George. But Heitor wasn't willing to choose you over me, and so you killed him, for what? For the satisfaction of wiping his blood off your hands? You're murderers and monsters and worse than any of the things you hunt."

"You said you were loyal and then you rose from the grave as an abomination," said Nathaniel.

"I *was* loyal. I didn't know any better," said Benedita. "I served you well, and I didn't choose to rise when I died. My brother—"

"Was a monster, yes, we knew that," said Chloe dismissively. "He thought he hid it so well, but we've known for years. That's why we called him when we decided it was time to bring the fight to North America. We knew he would answer, and we knew his presence would summon the dead, like luring cats with dead fish."

"You bitch," said Benedita, sounding almost awed.

"Maybe, but at least I have a pulse," said Chloe.

Benedita lunged for her, moving with the speed of someone who'd been training for years for exactly this sort of moment. I recognized the way she braced her legs and jumped; it was the way Verity did the same thing, exploiting the strength of her well-developed lower body to accomplish her goals. She jumped, and Chloe calmly brought her mason jar around, removing the lid as she did.

Howling, Benedita was sucked inside, and Chloe replaced the lid on the jar, screwing it tightly down before giving the whole thing an experimental shake. The items already lining the bottom of the jar clattered and rattled through the dense fog the jar now contained, which whirled frantically in response. For a moment, Benedita's face pressed against the glass, drained of color and substance, now made of insubstantial gray mist. Then it was gone, and only the whirling fog remained.

"She was *one of your own*," I said, staring at Chloe. "She was *Covenant*. Doesn't that matter to you people?"

"Timpani was one of our own too, but she chose your side over ours," said Chloe. "She's on the footage, too. We know she helped you set the charges. We know she helped to kill our mother. She's going to pay for what she's done. You're all going to pay. You filthy little killers are going to be sorry you ever tangled with the Covenant of St. George."

Babysitting small humans means having a lot of experience with people whose grasp of cause and effect is faulty at best. For a small child, them pushing a glass vase on the floor doesn't always mean "I broke the vase." Sometimes it means "the vase broke," and removes them from the equation entirely. I stared at Chloe.

"We attacked Penton Hall because your people were attacking us! You came after us in New York, and you sent assassins after members of my family and you attacked an innocent carnival because you thought they *might* be harboring cryptids!"

"I was there," said Chloe stiffly. "Those people weren't innocent."

"Any animal will bite if it's provoked enough. Isn't that what you're trying to do? Bite the hand that hurt you? I'm sorry you lost your mother. Those two people you took tonight lost their mother too. Your brother shot her before we set the charges at Penton. She died protecting strangers, not seeking them out to do them harm. You're shaming your own mother's memory."

"Don't you talk about my mother," spat Chloe.

"Or what? You've already caught Benedita. Your jar is full, and your brother doesn't have one. I guess he could shoot me, but I'm already dead, and all he'll do is hit the wall. I can't exit your ghost trap, but while I'm inside it, I can still do my best to ruin your plans for me."

"Sure you can," said the man from the van, behind me. I turned. He grinned, taking the lid off his own mason jar. "But we can ruin your afterlife first."

The pull from the open jar was like a vacuum cleaner, yanking me forward harder and harder. I whirled around and grabbed hold of Aoi's hand, trying my best to hold on. She yelped. I held on harder.

My feet left the floor. I didn't let go. She leaned back, grabbing the armchair with her free hand, holding us both in place.

The man from the van moved toward me, holding the jar out in front of him, smirking. Aoi's grip on the chair began to slip, and her copy of my eyes widened, sheer terror flooding her expression.

I'm a caretaker. It's what I do. And I can't adopt everyone—my family has to be finite—but that doesn't mean I want the people who don't belong to me to suffer. I met Aoi's eyes and nodded solemnly, and then I let her go.

The vacuum from the spirit jar grabbed me and jerked me backward, through the open mouth of the physical jar itself. I hit the bottom, hard enough to knock the breath I didn't have out of me, and then the lid was slamming down, and the world narrowed to a field of endless gray, and everything was icy cold and burning at the same time, and I was trapped.

Nineteen

"We owe the dead. We can't live for them, but we can live remembering what they gave for us to exist as we do, to live. If nothing else, we owe them kindness."

—Juniper Campbell

Inside a spirit jar, which is an experience
I had managed to avoid up until now,
and really wish I'd been able to
continue avoiding

THE GRAY WAS ALL-ENCOMPASSING, LIGHTLY scented with salt, and painful against my skin. I couldn't seem to stop myself from breathing, and it felt like every breath scoured the inside of my lungs, bleaching and burning them. A living person could never have been able to fit through the mouth of the jar, but here, inside the glass, it felt like I was more alive than ever. Which didn't exactly jibe with the swirling clouds of diffuse mist I'd seen in other spirit jars. Maybe the experience of being inside one didn't synchronize with the experience of looking into one, a voyeur in someone else's agony?

Speaking of which, I couldn't see the walls of the jar. No matter where I looked, it was just the endless, stinging gray. Experimentally, I tried to disappear and move myself in a random direction, but nothing happened. Living people can't disappear and reappear just by thinking about it. It doesn't work.

I was trying to decide on my next move when the world around began to shake. I spun in place, hunkering down and bending my knees in an effort to keep my balance despite the increasingly vicious shaking of my impossible prison. Inevitably, I failed, and went flying through the air like Dorothy inside the tornado, bits of debris slamming into me from all sides. They stung when they hit, but no worse than the fog.

Until an iron bar as big around as a tree trunk came flying at me, and the wind that held me captive left me no way to dodge out of its path. I braced for impact as best as I could, but wasn't prepared for the moment when it slammed into my chest and kept going, tearing through me like a butcher's knife cleaving through a prime roast.

The pain was inconceivable, sharp and bright and agonizing, and I blacked out for a moment.

I blacked out and I was sitting by my mother's bedside in those long last days, when every minute seemed to last for an hour, and I wished them away as hard and as fast as I could, wanting to be anywhere but there, in that small white room where my mother lay dying, all the miracles of modern medicine unable to do anything but ease her pain. Hospital bills hadn't been as dear in those days. For all our fears and all our clutching, clawing certainty that this was going to be the end of the world, we'd never been worried about losing the house—or if we had been, my father's last great act of mercy had been handling the death of his wife without letting his only child fully understand how bad it had become.

I stood, the book I'd been holding open and unread in my lap tumbling to the floor, and my mother turned her face agonizingly toward me, every motion clearly costing her more than she had left to pay. She looked more dead in that bed than I ever had, so pale that she would have seemed bone white if not for the sheets around her, skin drawn taut across her knobby skeleton. The cancer was a hungry beast. It had swallowed every scrap of her, wearing her down to nothing one grain at a time.

This didn't feel like a memory. I looked around me, and every detail of the hospital room was precisely as it was meant to be, unchanged from the last time I had seen it. So no, this didn't feel like a memory, didn't feel like my mind trying to protect itself from the pain by dredging up something even worse to put it into perspective. This felt like real life.

"Mary?" croaked my mother, and my breath caught in my throat.

How could I have thought this was anything other than reality, that my mother was dead and buried and gone, that I was a ghost? Sure, I'd felt like one for weeks, like I was dwindling alongside her, soon to disappear, but that was just a feeling: that wasn't real. She was here and I was here, and we were both alive, if not well. She was my *mother*. How could I have dreamt her dead?

A daughter who dreams her mother dead might as well be wishing her mother dead, and a daughter who wishes her mother dead is no daughter at all, just a monster walking around all wrapped up in girl-skin. That explained why my weird fantasy had been so focused on the lives and rights of monsters: I'd been trying to forgive myself for the unforgivable, to rewrite the world so that I didn't have to blame myself for what I was so blatantly becoming. How *could* I?

"Mary," croaked my mother again, reaching for me. I reached back, moving closer to the bed, and just before her hand would have closed on mine, I was back in the whirlwind, tornado buffeting me with stinging air and cascades of salt from all sides. I felt suddenly less solid, less anchored in the memory of my own bones than I had been before the iron bar slammed through me. I looked down, and there was no injury.

Of course there wasn't an injury. You can't wound the dead.

The wind kept flinging me around like a rag doll, and then

there was a woody branch flying toward me, one which I recognized as a spring of rosemary the size of a great broken bough. I tried to twist away from it, to no avail, and it caught me in the throat. There was the same terrible tearing sensation, and I was standing at the crossroads, the sunlit physical manifestation of my own employer, the place where they took their penitents to negotiate their terrible bargains.

The hot sun baked down against my exposed neck, and the air was filled with the lazy drone of locusts—only these were no locusts that had ever existed on the Earth. These were the droning wings of something from another reality, ones that had become a terrible intelligence that preyed about the Earth for years without number. And I had been its servant.

No, wait. I was its servant. Any illusions of a world where I didn't belong to the crossroads were just that: illusions. Nothing was ever going to defeat them. Certainly not a descendant of the girl who lay on the ground in front of me, her eyes closed and her breath coming so shallowly that I could almost believe she was already gone.

Not that she could die. Not here, in this time out of time, this place out of place. No one ever died when they stood before the crossroads. That was part of the point. Sometimes the people who came looking for deals really just wanted a place they could stand while they came to terms with the fact that they were already past saving anywhere else but here.

Alice hadn't brought herself here, of course. She wasn't the petitioner. She was the prize.

The man walking slowly toward me through the heat haze of this eternal summer afternoon, he was the one who was coming to sell his soul to the proverbial Devil in exchange for everything he'd ever wanted—a concept which took the form, currently, of a gangly teenage girl with hair the color of a dragon's prized possession, the skin on her leg already softening and breaking down as the venom the bidi-taurabo-haza had pumped into her bloodstream broke her down on a cellular level. She was going to die soon, unless the crossroads intervened.

And the crossroads were *going* to intervene. I could almost taste their eagerness, their panting desire to have Thomas Price for their own. He was one of the last true sorcerers in the world, and if he served them, he couldn't hurt them. They'd be safe from whatever threat a sorcerer was destined to one day offer them. They'd be safe.

He wouldn't be.

I clapped my hands over my mouth. "Thomas, what have you done?"

He was suddenly directly in front of me, not down the road and coming closer. "I'm ready to bargain with you, and with your employers, for the life of Alice Enid Healy. This isn't how she dies. I refuse to allow it," he said, and his voice was heavy with understanding and hobbled with grief. Grief for the girl dying on the ground; grief for the life he had been building for them every night when he slept, when he forgot their happiness was impossible and started turning it into something shining and secure.

His accent was so much thicker in those days, and even then, it was thinner than it had been when he first came to Buckley. He sounded like the children whose mother I would eventually help his grandchildren kill, like the Covenant coming home. He sounded like a future that was never going to be.

"I'm here for the same reason," said a second man, this one behind me. I turned and there was Jonathan. Poor, dear Johnny, who'd never deserved the number of funerals he attended: his son, his wife, and soon, his daughter. He'd been trying to found a legacy, and all he'd done was become a ballad.

"I asked first," said Thomas sharply. "I have prior claim."

I didn't want to have any part in this. I wanted to vanish, to leave them to fight for the fate of a dying girl who I loved more than I loved anything else in this world. But I had a job to do. I was going to do it. "My employers aren't bound by your human ideas of fairness or waiting in line," I said. "Fortunately for you, I am. And as your representative in this negotiation, I get to choose who speaks first. You're dismissed, Johnny." He made a wordless sound of unhappiness. I looked at him, face hard and cold. "You have nothing left to lose worth taking away, and a sorcerer is a better prize by far."

I knew—I *knew*—that this was a memory. This all happened long ago, and there was no taking it back or changing what had happened on that sundrenched road, the sound of locusts hanging heavy in the air. Thomas had traded his freedom and his magic for Alice's life, and she'd lived. Oh, how she'd lived. She'd lived, and she'd found her way back to him, and they'd had two children before the crossroads ripped them apart, and with those two children, they had founded a dynasty. It was still going, and I was going to do what I could to keep it going forever, because those children were my home and my heart and it had all started here. Could it have gone differently? Yes. Should it have?

That was harder to say.

I turned to Thomas, inhaling to speak, and I was back in the whirlwind, being thrown carelessly back and forth, the rosemary bough no longer embedded in my flesh. I felt even less solid, and when I looked at my hands, I could see right through them to the other side. The spirit jar was unmaking me, unraveling me one trauma and trial at a time. The gray fog around me looked like it was getting thicker all the time, and I was willing to bet without proof that its increased thickness was my substance, unraveling but with no place else to go.

The jar shook again. This time, when I saw the jagged piece of broken mirror flying toward me, I didn't even try to dodge. There was no point. I stayed where I was, spreading my arms, and it slashed through me in a white lance of pain and penance.

◆ ◆ ◆

I don't know how long the man from the van kept shaking the jar that held me, mixing and remixing its contents, before he finally stopped. I just know the shaking continued for another half dozen traumatic flashes of my life, things I'd seen and said and done swallowing me alive and digesting me, one layer at a time, until I was stripped bare and defenseless. That had to be how a spirit jar broke you down. It showed you the parts of your life that had hurt the most, and it carried them away, but the pain never stopped. Combine that with the gnawing loss of self, and it was no wonder that ghosts who spent too much time in spirit jars became unsettled and irrational.

I pulled myself back together as best as I could, collapsing to what felt like the bottom of my prison. The gray mist still swirled around me, but it was thinning, settling as the lack of motion allowed it to return to a more neutral state. I felt myself growing more solid, or at least more coherent, and sat up, hugging my knees to my chest.

Being a ghost means always being a disembodied entity trying to trick the universe into treating you like you still exist. I didn't have knees to hug, and so I wasn't hugging them; I didn't have a behind to sit on, and so I wasn't sitting. My whole body was a phantom limb syndrome, and I was just occupying it. I knew that, but the habit of being human is hard to break, and so I felt myself doing the things I thought I was doing, trying desperately to be small and compact and contained.

The mist settled farther, until I could see through it and out the side of the jar, into a distorted world viewed through thick, uneven carnival glass. I was looking at a large room of some sort—probably the attic, based on the slope of the walls and the boxes shoved against them. Large glass jars were stacked on every flat surface, every one of them filled with a familiar swirling mist.

But that was less important than the bodies sprawled on the floor, with the boneless carelessness I associate with small children and the deeply unconscious. Elsie was on her back, face pointed toward the ceiling, while Arthur was on his stomach; they were equally motionless. But I could see that Elsie was breathing, her chest moving in long, slow inhales and exhales. Neither of them had any visible injuries, which was something. I didn't know how long secondhand aconite would knock them out; were the moths poisonous to humans at this stage? Or was it just the Lilu sensitivity that was keeping them under?

I stood, trying to rush for the glass, and got nowhere. The distance inside the jar remained unutterably vast, and no matter how hard I tried, I could never quite get anywhere. In the end, I sat back down, trying to collect myself and think of what I might be able to do next.

Fact: they had dozens of ghosts captive in these jars and were working at turning us all into weapons. I didn't know how many of us might already *be* fully weaponized, but I did know none of the jars could be safely opened in the daylight. Even the twilight might be too close. Ideally, I'd be able to get out of this one, and start grabbing the others and transporting them down to the starlight, where I could find someplace to safely let the ghosts inside them out.

Or maybe I could take them to the anima mundi, who might be able to help them heal.

Or maybe I was just telling myself stories, because I was as trapped as any of the spirits around me, and I was never getting out of here.

Lilu are empaths. Most of the focus gets put on their preternatural attractiveness, which they encourage with their incredibly potent pheromones, but they can also read, manipulate, and amplify emotions. Elsie got a stronger dose of the empathy than Arthur did—his big trick had always been pheromones so strong that sometimes he wasn't willing to leave the house—but they both had it. And maybe that was going to be the answer to getting me the hell out of here.

I settled in to wait, trying not to pick at the raw wounds the fog—which I now knew to be a mixture of water, salt, and iron shavings—had opened in my psyche by dragging me back and forth through the memories of my worst moments. It felt like I'd gone ten rounds with a cheese grater, and the cheese grater had scored a decisive win.

As I watched, Elsie's eyelids began to flutter, until finally, with a groan, she opened her eyes and blinked up at the ceiling. She raised a hand, pressing it hard against her temple like she thought she needed to hold her brain inside despite its desperate attempts to escape.

Groaning louder, she pushed herself into a sitting position and looked around the attic, squinting and blinking, like she was trying to clear a film from in front of her eyes. She paused when she saw Arthur, then scrambled over to shake him with one hand.

"Artie? Art—thur?" she whispered. "Arthur, wake up. We're not in the boardinghouse anymore."

The urgency in her voice was unmistakable, and I was quietly proud of her for remembering to keep her voice down. If she shouted, someone would probably hear her, and she'd have to deal with the armed Covenant assholes downstairs even sooner than she was already going to. Not fun. She and Arthur had been allowed to keep their clothing, but I had little doubt that they'd been searched for weapons.

Too bad for the Cunninghams that every child of the current gener— No. Every child of the *previous* generation had been trained in unarmed combat and improvised weapons as well as the more common forms. Elsie might prefer a couple of knives and a nice garotte, but if you forced her hand, she'd be perfectly at home smashing a chair and stabbing you with a leg.

She kept shaking Arthur until he groaned and started to swat at her hand, trying to push her away. Relief washed over her face and she grabbed him by the shoulders, yanking him into a seated position so she could hug him. He opened his eyes and blinked, pure bemusement in his expression.

"Wha'?" he asked.

"I thought you were *dead*," she said. "I thought I'd lost you *again*."

"You've never lost me before," said Arthur, pushing her away. "How many times do I have to tell you I'm not your brother?"

"But you are my brother. My pheromones don't affect you, and yours don't mess with me. We have the same blood type, and you still have the scar on your collarbone from where I shoved you—or the body you live in—down the stairs when I was seven. I know I used to say I didn't want a baby brother, but I didn't mean it. You *are* my brother. You may not be the same brother I used to have, but you *are* my brother, and I don't want to lose another one."

Arthur frowned, then rubbed his face with one hand. "I guess that's fair," he said. "I didn't really think about it like that. I just thought you were trying to wish Artie back, and I don't know how to give him to you. Sometimes I wish I did."

Elsie nodded then, before she pulled away from him and sat back on her heels, resting her hands on her knees. "I guess it's hard to find yourself living a life where everyone expects you to be somebody else," she said. "I'm sorry I haven't made that easier for you."

"I don't think anyone *could* have made it easier for me," he said. "Sometimes *I'm* mad at me for not being him. I can't imagine what it feels like for everybody else."

Now that they were awake, I started thinking about every

moment of their lives that had ever gotten an emotional rise out of me. I'd been present for Elsie's birth. Not Artie's—when you have a babysitter who can watch the existing child during labor and delivery, you take advantage of it—but Arthur's, the moment when Sarah slammed the last broken pieces of memory into place and the patchwork boy came to life under her unpracticed hands. I thought about my terror when we'd thought that Artie was dead, and my lonely, lost regret when I'd realized he truly was, no matter what the living seemed to think.

I thought about Elsie's first girlfriend, her first kiss, the dress she'd worn to prom and the joy she'd taken in every scrap of it all, like she was the first high school girl in history to fall in love and figure out who she wanted to be when she grew up. I thought about how much she did and didn't look like her mother, all the ways they were similar, all the ways they were different, and how much both the similarities and the differences could hurt. She had Jane's way of biting her pinkie when she was thinking really hard, and Jane had learned that mannerism from Laura, following the woman who'd had most of the job of raising her like a child in a fairy tale following the Pied Piper off the edge of the world.

Laura was still with us in the shape of the children she'd raised, just like I would always be with the Price family, carried in a thousand little gestures and turns of phrase, a generational tendency to mouth off to danger when running away would have been the better choice. Maybe letting people with poor senses of self-preservation breed and then hand those children off to a dead girl for care and feeding had been a bad idea, but we did it, and now we were reaping the rewards.

Arthur started crying, fat tears rolling unchecked down his cheeks. At first, he didn't seem to notice. Then he blinked, swiped a hand across his face, and looked at his wet palm in confusion.

"Is the roof leaking?" he asked.

302 ✦ SEANAN McGUIRE

"What? No," said Elsie. "What's going on?"

"I just felt really sad all of a sudden. Like something bad was about to happen."

Elsie gave him a flat, disbelieving look. "Arthur, we've been drugged and kidnapped, and I can tell even without groping myself that someone's taken the knives out of my ankle sheaths. I'd say something bad already happened." Then she started to giggle, eyes going wide with surprise as she did. She put a hand over her mouth, trying to stifle the sound.

It didn't do any good. The giggles continued as I stared at her, thinking hard about the trip we'd taken to the state fair when she was four, when she'd gone to her first petting zoo and made friends with all the sheep. We had laughed so much that day, just laughter piling on top of laughter, endless and bright, like the world was a kinder place than I had ever known it to be.

"Elsie?" asked Arthur, sounding concerned. "Elsie, what's wrong?"

"I don't know! I can't stop *laughing*!" She turned away from him, looking at the shelves of mist-filled jars surrounding them. "I think I'm picking up on feelings from inside one of these jars."

Oh please, oh please, you can do it, I thought. *You're halfway there already.*

"Mary said they'd been jarring ghosts to turn them into weapons," said Arthur uneasily. "You need to be careful."

And normally I would agree with you, but right now, let's not do that, okay?

"Most of these jars feel like static, like emotional slurry. But one of them is making big, clear feelings, like it's trying to get our attention," said Elsie stubbornly. "It feels like Mary."

"You can tell whose emotions belong to who?"

"Yeah. I've always been better at that than you were, whichever version of 'you' is living in my brother. I'm guessing it's biological.

You got stronger pheromones than I did, I read emotions more clearly."

Arthur made a face. "That doesn't seem entirely fair."

"Seems fine to me."

"You *would* think so. You're the one who got the good part!"

"Try saying that when you're trying out for the spring musical with fifty other teenage sopranos who believe their entire lives will be defined by how successful they are in high school." She pushed herself to her feet and moved toward the nearest assortment of jars, reaching out to touch one. Then she recoiled, sending the jar rocking with the force of her withdrawal. "Augh!"

"Elsie? What's wrong?"

"It felt . . . wrong. Like sticking my arm into a puddle of frozen slush and warm vomit. Both things at the same time. It shouldn't have been possible, but it was, and it *hurt.*" She gave the jar a mistrustful look. "I don't think that's where the feeling was coming from."

"So what do we do, just touch every single jar in this room? There must be dozens."

Carefully, I thought. *If you have to do it this way, do it carefully.*

Elsie and Arthur exchanged a look and nodded, almost in unison. It was the closest to seeing Artie again that I had come since Sarah dragged his hollow husk home from her cross-dimensional adventures.

Together, they rose, and began moving to touch the various jars, shuddering each time, moving away from outcomes that weren't correct but at least weren't upsetting enough to make them knock something over. And I sat in the bottom of my own jar, and tried to think about the things that would make my emotions ring out over the rest of the room, the things that would tell them to come for *me.*

It was tempting to go back to the sore spots the spirit jar had ripped open in my memories, the places where I was unsettled and leaking ectoplasm into the air around me. They were raw, they were agonizing, and they were *right there* to be exploited. But they were all terrible things, moments when I'd been so ground down that I thought I might die, moments where hope had been little more than a lie. All these shattered, shredded spirits were capable of that kind of suffering. I wasn't special.

What I was was still coherent enough to focus my mind where I wanted it, and right now, I wanted to project emotions that would help me stand out from the rest of the unquiet dead. I thought back almost to the beginning of my afterlife, to the moment when my family's phone rang and I'd answered it to find an exhausted Frances Healy on the other end. She'd been looking for someone to take care of her little girl, and I'd agreed on the spot. The town hadn't known that I was dead yet—technically, Buckley never did know, since we'd buried my father while I played at being among the living, and then I'd simply drifted away rather than staging a funeral of my own—and my flyers advertising babysitting services had still been posted at the library.

I didn't know when Fran called that taking the job would mean shifting myself into a whole new kind of haunting. If I had, the crossroads would never have allowed it. But it did, and they did, and now here I was, doing my best to mentally scream the hope and joy that had come from that simple call.

When neither Elsie nor Arthur looked in my direction, I shifted my thoughts forward to the day Alice had called me to the porch of the Old Parrish Place, exhausted and wreathed in bandages like she was trying to emulate a mummy. "Mary," she'd said, "guess Thomas loves me after all, because he says I can stay, and I think I'm going to do it. Can you haunt me here?"

It had been such a little question, and it had carried an entire future on its shoulders. I'd long since given up hope that Alice would fall in love with anyone else, and she wasn't the sort of girl who went out and had children with strangers for the sake of having had them. She'd embraced me on that porch, and I'd held her in return, and I'd known that it was all going to be all right. The world was going to keep moving forward, and I'd be able to move with it, and life would go on. That was all I'd wanted. For life to go on, and let me keep haunting it as it unfolded.

I hopscotched from happy moment to happy moment. Jane's birth, Jane's wedding, and then, bright as a new star, Elsinore, first child of her generation, family to me before she ever drew breath. Alex and Artie and Verity and Annie, and then Sarah, bright bauble fished out of a storm drain, adopted but no less dear for any of that. School plays and school pictures, Alex's first SCA meeting, Annie's first cheerleading practice, Verity leaving us to go on television and dance for the world . . .

Thomas, coming home at last, and Alice promising me that they were finally back to stay.

Elsie stopped where she was, turning her head and looking directly at my jar. Then she started toward me.

Yes, yes, yes! I thought. *Good* girl, *Elsie.*

"What did you pick up on?" asked Arthur.

"Spike of joy from one of these jars over here," she said. "I think I may have found Mary. If not Mary, then a ghost that's still coherent enough to be happy at the prospect of being found, and right now, that's good enough for me."

"If you can't be sure, I don't think that's a good ide—" he began, and stopped as Mary picked up a jar two away from my own and began to loosen the top.

She hadn't finished unscrewing it when the attic door swung open and Nathaniel appeared, a small pistol in his hands and a grim expression on his face. "Put your hands up and put that down," he said, sternly.

Elsie raised her hands in the universal gesture of surrender, letting go of the jar at the same time. Nathaniel realized what was about to happen and shouted, firing a single round before he slammed the attic door.

As moments went, it was so like the moment when his brother shot Jane that the world seemed to stop, everything going gray-scale and slow. The bullet caught Elsie in the shoulder, jerking her back and spinning her halfway around. She grunted. Arthur howled, diving for his sister.

And the jar hit the floor.

It didn't shatter on impact so much as it exploded, shards flying everywhere. A gray mist rose from the broken bits of glass and assorted debris where the jar had been, starting to laugh a horrible, distorted laugh. I stood and rushed for the wall of my own jar, intending to at least attempt to reason with the emerging spirit, but as before, no matter how hard I ran, I didn't get anywhere. I was trapped on a treadmill in my own private hell, with no way to move backward or forward.

The mist rose higher and higher, and then, without any warning of what it was about to do, pulled together into a thin column of smoke-dark air and drove itself at Arthur. Being a smart boy who remembered everything about dealing with ghosts that had been known by anyone in his hospital room when he was constructed, he clamped his mouth shut and turned his face away.

All this happened in a matter of seconds. Elsie was still falling, not yet having made her own impact with the ground. She wasn't covering her mouth. She was still falling, and I'm not sure she could have covered it if she tried.

People always cover their mouths. They forget about their noses, their eyes, all the other points of entry into the human body.

The smoke whipped around Arthur's head, surrounding it like a cartoon cloud, and then, abruptly, it was gone. Arthur turned back to his falling sister, moving to grab her hand even as her ass hit the attic floor.

Gripping her hand firmly in his, he pulled her back to her feet and looked pointedly at her wounded shoulder, which was bleeding freely. "That looks like it hurts," he said, and his accent was wrong, thick Boston instead of relatively neutral Portland. "Think there's a first aid kit up here?"

Elsie clapped her free hand over her shoulder and narrowed her eyes, glaring at him. "Get out of my brother, asshole."

"Don't believe I will, sweetheart, if it's all the same to you," said the man in Arthur's body. "He's barely anchored to this thing as it is. Seriously, no grip strength at all. I could boot him out of here no trouble, and then it'd be *my* body, unless you wanted me to leave it to fall down dead on the attic floor. That your idea of a good time?"

"I said *get out*," said Elsie, all but hissing the words.

"Or what? You'll bleed on me? Sorry, but that's not a great threat. Blood smells kinda funny, though, you might want to get that looked at when we get out of here."

"They took all our weapons. We're not getting out of here."

"Nah. They didn't take them all." He moved nonchalantly away from Elsie, not sparing her a backward look, and began peering into jars. He studied each of their contents for only a few seconds before moving on, and when he reached my jar, he barely glanced at it before he turned his attention to the next jar in the line. "They left us all the weapons we could possibly need."

"What are you talking about?"

"See, we're surrounded by pissed-off ghosts who don't have anything better to do with their time than help us get revenge, and I can tell without even trying that they've warded the house to keep the dead from getting away. So you let me hold onto your brother's body for a few minutes, I let all these not-so-friendly spirits out of their jars, and then they tear the people who hurt us both to pieces. I just gotta find a ghost who'll fit your body."

Elsie blinked. Then, expression hardening, she said, "My

babysitter's in here. I felt her. If you need to put a ghost inside me, I want her."

"Not all ghosts can do the possession thing," said the ghost in Arthur's body. "You can't just break any old jar and expect it to work out the way you expect."

"Mary will figure it out," said Elsie. She paused for a moment, closing her eyes as she clutched at her shoulder. "She always figures it out."

"Right. How long ago was she jarred?"

"I don't know exactly, but it can't have been more than six hours, if she was jarred at all. I don't know for sure that she was."

He turned to give her a disgusted look. Elsie scowled.

"I felt her before your jar got broken. She was somewhere near where I found you. She's here, I swear she is, and that means she's in a jar, because if she *could* appear, she'd have done it already."

"Last few hours, you say?"

"Something like that."

"So she'd still be most of the way intact. Hold, please." He turned to go back to scanning the jars. This time when he reached me, he paused, expression turning contemplative. "What's your Mary look like, anyway?"

"Late teens, white hair, probably wearing something with no sense of style behind it. On the skinny side. Nice tits, though." Elsie paused. "And she's been my babysitter since I was a literal baby, so I probably shouldn't admit that last part, but it's true and if it helps you find her, she can be mad at me about it later."

Oh, honey, like that's the first time one of the kids I've raised has had inappropriate thoughts about the babysitter, I thought. As long as they didn't vocalize them until they were legal adults, and didn't try to do anything about it, I didn't care all that much. People get crushes. People think other people are pretty.

At least that's what I've heard, about the crushes. I know it's true about the pretty people.

The man in Arthur's body picked up my jar, moving it gingerly so as not to set the mist swirling again. He squinted at me through the glass. "You fit the profile, but I hope like hell she's right about you being able to figure things out, or this isn't going to help," he said, and dropped the jar.

There was one last rush of stinging mist, and then the glass was breaking all around me, and I was breaking free. I turned toward Elsie, or attempted to, anyway—no matter how hard I tried, I couldn't force myself to take the bipedal form that had been my default since my death. I was a formless cloud of pale, swirling smoke, hovering in the air above my broken jar.

The man in Arthur didn't look surprised. He also didn't look particularly sympathetic. "Sorry, princess, but even a little time in a spirit jar scrambles everything," he said. "You'll need to resettle, and that's going to take time. So seize what you can get. Take the girl."

I didn't like the way he was talking about Elsie, but if this was going to be how it went for all the ghosts inside those jars, I wasn't going to sit around waiting to settle. I dove for Elsie, and this time, when I tried to move, I moved, arrowing toward her with a speed and accuracy that felt totally alien to me, and totally right at the same time.

She inhaled as I struck her face, and I was pulled inside her, out of the formlessness, out of the cold. Her body enfolded me, warm and solid and alive—and in agony, the wound in her shoulder still bleeding openly. The shock of the pain almost knocked me loose, but I dug in with everything I had, holding tightly to the shape of her skin.

Elsie blinked, and she was me, and I was she, and this was going to be *weird*.

Twenty

"Everything hungers for life. Even when it says it doesn't. It may not know it lies, but it does; everything hungers for life."

—**Apple Tanaka**

Inside Elsie, which is sort of like
being inside a spirit jar, only squishier

*M*ARY?

Elsie? Oh, Elsie, you're still here! Can you hear me?

I can hear you. I'm just glad it is you.

Elsie's words felt like my own thoughts, just delivered in a slightly different tone of mind, like I was talking to myself. I couldn't be sure she was actually there to talk to me, or whether she was actually giving her tacit consent for what I'd done by acknowledging that I was the only ghost she would have wanted to possess her. I still felt emotionally compromised and about as solid as well-used cheesecloth, like even the slightest shock would blow me apart.

And I was inside Elsie's body, which was simultaneously fascinating and deeply, *deeply* unpleasant. It was fleshy and squishy and filled with sensations I barely remembered and might never have felt when I'd been alive. And then there was the gunshot wound, which was *definitely* something I'd never felt before. It hurt. Like nothing I had ever experienced, it hurt.

"Mother*fucker*," I snarled, clapping Elsie's hand over the wound once again. It must have fallen when I invaded her, the effort of keeping her blood inside seeming suddenly secondary to experiencing a spiritual takeover. The blood pumped between her fingers, hot and thick and nasty in a visceral way.

Unlike the kids I helped to raise, I had lived a fairly sheltered life, one that didn't involve a lot of stabbings or gunshots or other opportunities to interact with blood. I didn't like it.

I also didn't like the feeling of Elsie's heartbeat, or the slow shifting of her internal organs. Fun fact I lived my whole life without knowing: there's a part of the human brain whose only purpose is keeping the person it belongs to from feeling their own organs move, something which happens basically all the damn time. Apparently, naughty ghosts who take over other people's bodies don't get to use that piece of brain.

"Hurts, don't it?" asked the man inside Arthur, without a trace of sympathy. "Gunshots will do that. You the one she wanted me to look for?"

I nodded Elsie's head. "I'm Mary. The babysitter. Who are you?"

"They called me 'Banjo' when I was alive, and that works well enough for me now that I'm dead. Would do me some good to hear you call my name, sweet little thing like you."

"Okay, um, ew. The body you're using is this body's *brother*, and I raised both these bodies from infancy, so please don't make any comments like that." I glared at him, unwilling to take Elsie's hand off her shoulder to fold her arms. Managing an open gunshot wound was proving more difficult than I would have expected. "What kind of a name is 'Banjo'?"

"Mine." He looked around, then shrugged out of Arthur's plaid flannel, grabbing it by the collar and ripping it briskly in half. "Come over here, will ya? I know you modern girls have big ideas about boundaries and consent, so I don't want to lay hands on your meat shell without permission, but if we don't stop that bleeding soon, you're going to need a new one."

"Elsie is not just a 'meat shell,' and she's not going to die—Wait. You know how to deal with a gunshot wound?"

"Lady, my name was Banjo DiCola, and if I'd lived a little longer, I would have run the Boston mob. Yeah, I know how to bind a gunshot wound, maybe not as good as a doc would do, but good enough that your pink-haired little princess probably won't drop dead before we get you out of her."

"All right," I said, reluctantly, and walked over to him, letting him guide me to perch on the edge of a nearby steamer trunk. He began to pack and wrap the wound in Elsie's shoulder, which was a whole new variety of pain that I could have gone my entire afterlife without experiencing. But the tighter he pulled the cloth, the more the stabbing agony was reduced to a throbbing ache, and the more the blood slowed. I realized I wasn't breathing, having stopped in the face of the pain, and forced myself to start again. Elsie's body knew what to do, even if I didn't remember how to breathe.

Ow, complained Elsie.

I know, baby, I'm sorry, I replied, while privately glad that she was aware enough of her own body to feel pain when her gunshot wound was dressed. I was wearing her like a coat, and I didn't much care for the sensation—or for how addictive I could see it becoming. It was no wonder most ghosts didn't have the capacity to possess people anymore. It was too effective. Ghosts that *could* do this *would* do it, constantly, and that would result in the living rising against the dead in a whole new, horrible way. Exorcisms as far as the eye could see.

And we shouldn't have been able to do this. The extra strength the anima mundi said was floating free while the area's ghosts were jarred, it was feeding into us, making possession possible. That was good. It meant that when this was all over, I wouldn't need to be afraid it was going to happen again. My people would be safe.

Banjo-in-Arthur pulled the makeshift bandage a little tighter and tied it off. "That's as good as I can do without cutting off circulation completely. You don't want to lose that arm, do you?"

"No, I'm sure Elsie would prefer to keep it," I said, flexing it experimentally. The resulting bolt of pain was unpleasant but manageable, especially compared to what it had been before. I turned to look at him. "Now what?"

"Now we unleash hell," he said, and swept his arm across the nearest shelf, sending jars cascading to the floor, where they broke on impact. Individual plumes of foggy smoke began to fill the air, some hanging where they were, some swirling around us. They varied in shade from white-gray to virtually black. I yelped.

Banjo smirked. "They won't hurt us," he said. "Like knows like, and they can tell we're dead on the inside. But anyone living they find inside this house isn't going to be so lucky."

Several smoky plumes dove for the floor, only to bounce off like birds that had run into a closed window. They swirled fast, managing to look pissed off without facial features or heads. Aoi would be proud of them. Banjo scowled.

"They went and put ghost traps *inside* their ghost trap? What the hell is wrong with these people?"

"Too long at the top of the food chain," I said. I looked toward the attic door. "You any good with locks?"

"Never needed to pick 'em when I could shoot 'em out or kick 'em down, but I know the basic principles."

I can pick a lock, said Elsie.

I paused, frowning. "If we let go of our possessions, the ghosts you've released will attack Elsie and Arthur."

"Yeah, and I ain't letting go."

"What?"

Banjo folded Arthur's arms. "I ain't letting go. Getting a good grip on a living person is hard enough, and doing it a second time is just this side of impossible. I need a living body if I want to get out of this shithole, and I'm holding on to the one I have."

"You'll let him go after we're out of the trap, though."

"That remains to be seen, but for the moment, we'll go with 'yes, of course.'"

"Right." I didn't trust him any farther than I could throw him, and while Elsie was fairly strong, she wasn't "toss your brother like a caber" strong. But that was all a problem for later, when we were out of this attic. "So we can't let go right now. Can we share space?"

"What? Why would you want to do *that*? You get to be alive again, and the first thing you think to do is *share*?"

"I've been a babysitter for a long time." I closed Elsie's eyes, trying to concentrate on loosening my grip without entirely letting go, giving her the space to come forward and share this possession with me. I tried to think of it as teaching her how to ride a bicycle, those days when she'd been gripping the inside of the handlebars, pedaling for all that she was worth, while I'd held on to the outside and focused on running along beside her. Awkward, yes; also effective.

Are you sure? she asked.

Just trust me, baby, I replied, and then she was there, shoving me aside, and I felt the body we shared moving without my telling it to do so. It was . . . odd, like being a passenger in the back seat of a car, with no way to control or influence where we were going. I didn't feel helpless, though, although I might have expected to do so; I could tell from the balance between us that I could seize control back in a moment if I felt I needed it.

But I wouldn't need it, because this was *Elsie's* body. I was just here to make sure we got it safely home. She stooped, picking up a few nails, some needles, and a sprig of pine from the mess on the floor, then moved toward the door, carrying me along with her.

Several swirls of phantom smoke followed us, some brushing against our shared skin. They were cold, and I tried to flinch away from them without giving up any more of my now-tenuous hold on Elsie. If I lost much more, she'd be able to shove me out entirely, and then she'd have no defenses against the dead.

Don't push me out, honey, I thought, fiercely. *You need me in here to keep you safe.*

I know, Mary. I won't. She hunkered down in front of the door, beginning to work on the lock with the items she'd collected from the floor. Banjo crowded in close behind us, casting a proprietary eye over her work.

"You're gonna have to get out of my brother, mister. I don't care if you are some big-time dead gangster," said Elsie calmly.

"Oh yeah? Or what?"

"Or I'll tell my Aunt Rose, and she'll *make* you get out of my brother." There was a click from inside the lock, and she pulled her makeshift tools away. "I don't think you want to deal with Aunt Rose. She's a Fury."

Banjo blanched. The expression wasn't like anything I'd seen Arthur, or Artie, wear. It was a relic of the man now occupying their body like it was a rented Halloween costume. "I'll keep that in mind," he said, and picked up a nearby jar, throwing it as hard as he could into another pile of them.

That seemed to be the signal the dead had been waiting for. They began ripping through the remaining jars, shaking them and knocking them to the floor, until the attic rang with the sound of shattering glass and rattling torture instruments. Elsie squeaked in surprise and bent back over the lock, working even faster than before. There was another click, and the door swung open.

"Thanks, sweetheart," said Banjo, grabbing it and pushing past us to the outside. A torrent of smoke followed him, endless and crackling with a sharp static that made Elsie's skin crawl. She straightened up and staggered back, plastering herself against the wall.

"Mary, I think you're up," she said, and retreated into her own mind, leaving me to push forward and retake control. It took a moment, and when I reasserted my claim over the body, I found Elsie's hands tingling like she'd fallen asleep on top of them, the blood flow struggling to return to normal. I shook them, then stuck them up under her arms, trying to warm her freezing fingers.

Finish this, she thought.

"Yes, dear," I replied, aloud, and followed Banjo out of the attic, into the larger ghost trap of the house.

♦ ♦ ♦

The hall was quiet, Banjo and the spirits already gone. I paused to listen, but I didn't hear anything, not footsteps and not screams. That didn't necessarily mean that he wasn't doing something horrible to Chloe and Nathaniel, just that if he was, it was happening far enough away that I couldn't hear it.

Did I *want* him to be doing something horrible to Chloe and Nathaniel? They had come to America on a mission of revenge, not caring who might get hurt in the process of finding the people who'd killed their mother. That was terrible, truly, but was it so different from what we'd done? We'd gone to England to make the Covenant *stop*, and we hadn't worried enough about the collateral damage of *our* actions. No matter how we tried to assign blame, there was always someone who'd hit someone else, an action triggering a reaction, all the way back to the very beginning.

I'm not a true Price, wasn't born into this endless conflict, but I've spoken to enough of them, and to enough ghosts with an interest in history, and near as I've ever been able to determine, this is what happened: a long, long time ago, dragons were well on their way to becoming the dominant intelligent species on several continents. They were massive, they could breathe fire, they could fly until they reached a certain size, and most importantly of all, they were territorial carnivores. The Covenant of St. George formed to stop the dragons from burning down entire human settlements, as a final effort against extinction. And it worked!

Maybe a little *too* well, as those early Covenant members realized they really liked being the ones who got to decide who lived and who died. Everything that's happened since then has been the continuation of that first fight. So who wins? Who gets to say "okay, we've hit each other enough, it's time to put down the rocks and start treating each other with some basic decency"? Is there an expiration date on striking back?

What Chloe and Nathaniel had done was unforgivable. They were acting as they'd been taught, and lashing out in pain. Heitor had just been trying to find his sister; Benedita had just been trying to survive outside of a spirit jar, unaware that she was leading the Covenant to her fellow dead. Even Amelia, who I desperately wanted to blame for everything that had happened tonight, was just trying to preserve her species. Everyone had a reason for hurting people. And at this point, I was just about ready to say that we were starting over, clean slate, no more revenge, no more graves.

I inched along the hall, finally finding myself at the top of a narrow flight of stairs, and descended to the first floor one step at a time, trying not to get distracted by the sound of Elsie's heartbeat or the feeling of her lungs expanding. I didn't remember those things being so noticeable when I'd been alive. Her legs were getting weak from the blood loss. I caught us against the wall before we could fall down, pausing for a moment while I tried to catch my breath. I just needed to breathe. Why was that so hard?

Because I was using someone else's lungs, in a body that desperately needed medical attention, and that was making things more difficult than they had to be. Naturally. Gripping the bannister firmly, I started down the stairs.

I was halfway down when the screaming started.

I sped up as much as I dared. Any faster and we'd go sprawling. With the injury in her shoulder, Elsie couldn't take too much more. Falling down like that could knock me clean out of her and leave her defenseless against the formerly jarred dead.

Who were nowhere to be seen right now, and were probably off causing the screaming. I reached the bottom of the stairs and tested my balance before letting go of the bannister, continuing to move *toward* the sound of people being horrifically tortured. I reached the living room, and stopped in my tracks.

When I was a kid, before she got sick, my mother liked to do little science experiments with me, saying they would encourage me to have a playful mind and a generous approach to the universe. I think she just liked an excuse to make messes and blame them on the kid. Regardless, one of my favorites was something she called "hurricane in a jar." It was soap, water, and food coloring, and the way the soap and the water pushed against each other would make it swirl and spin like a for-real hurricane. Little me found it endlessly enchanting.

The live-action version that had taken over the front room was somewhat less enthralling. Solid walls of smoke and fog ringed the room, patchworked in all the different shades of spirit, spinning wildly enough that they were generating a for-real wind. The darker patches were the more powerful ones, I realized, the ones who had managed to steal some poltergeist abilities from their pain; they were throwing papers and small objects into the air, where they were buffeted and flung around by the force of the storm. Banjo-in-Arthur was standing just on the other side of the wall, head cocked to the side, looking like he'd never seen anything more fascinating. I moved forward a bit to see what he saw, and promptly gagged.

Living reactions are inconvenient things. I never saw anyone in real danger of dying before I was dead myself, with none of those unfortunate hormones or reflexes to make a corpse more than an abstract complication. Even when I'd found Enid melted on her own kitchen floor, I hadn't thrown up. But now, bile was burning the back of Elsie's throat and her stomach was lurching, literally moving inside me from the force of the muscular contractions caused by her disgust.

The man from the van—whose name I still didn't know—was hanging in the middle of the room easily a foot and a half off the ground, arms out at his sides like he was auditioning for the role of Scarecrow in a very modern production of *The Wizard of Oz*. His toes were pointed straight down at the floor. Not a natural position until you considered that he might not have a choice in the matter. The swirling smoke was thicker around him, the hands of a hundred furious, scrambled ghosts holding him captive.

"I didn't— You can't— Let me go!" he shouted.

"Mmm, no," said Banjo. "The kids are angry. They don't like bein' bottled like so much cheap gin, and they really don't like being stacked up in the attic for later. You shouldn't have gone messing with the dead."

"The world belongs to the *living*," snarled the man, right before the dead who were suspending him ripped his eyes out of his head with a wet sucking sound and threw them to the hurricane. He howled. The eyes bobbed along on the smoky tide, held aloft by the anger of the dead, spraying blood and vitreous humors on the walls.

"Try again?" suggested Banjo.

"Go to *hell*," said the man, somehow still forming words.

"Oh, buddy, you're already there." Banjo snapped Arthur's fingers, and the ghosts— There really isn't a pleasant way to say this, or a non-graphic way to describe it. They *peeled* the man. They began with the skin on his face, grasping his eyelids and the flesh under his eyes, and then they ripped it off with a vast, bloody tearing sound, exposing the raw muscle beneath. He howled.

They kept going. They ripped his clothing away, and then the skin that had been concealed beneath it, flensing him with the sharp little knives of their substance, until there was nothing left but a hanging, rotating side of meat that dripped unspeakable fluids and was still, somehow, managing to gibber and howl.

Banjo smiled. "That's better," he said. "Should have been a little nicer, mister. Wouldn't have saved you, but maybe then we'd have let you die. Now where are those little brats you're working for?"

I blinked, taking my eyes away from the rotating horror long enough to glance around the room. Heitor's corpse was gone. So were Nathaniel and Chloe.

"House isn't that big," I said. "We can find them."

Banjo made a noncommittal sound that I took as assent. I started moving toward the hallway entrance.

"Where do you think you're going?"

"To find them." And to find a phone, if I could. Elsie and Arthur didn't have theirs, and I'd seen nothing to indicate that the house had a landline. People like to talk about the convenience of cellphones, the way they've opened up the world. Reach people when they're on the road! Map your way to your destination! They never mention how much harder they make it to call for help when you're abducted by asshole ghost hunters and can't stop possessing the girl you used to babysit for unless you want her to get skinned alive by pissed-off ghosts who have good reasons to be mad but shouldn't use them as excuses to hurt her.

Banjo turned to watch us go, frowning the whole time. He thought I was up to something, I was sure of it, and to be fair, I was; if I could find a phone, I was going to call Michigan and ask Alice to send Sarah to help us. She couldn't be around Arthur-in-Artie because she built him and it hurt to see him walking around not truly knowing himself, or her. Well, maybe Banjo-in-Arthur would be a different story. We'd just turn him into a nesting doll of one person on top of another, stacking them like bricks until she could stand to be in the same room.

And then, when we were out of this situation, she could go home, and she and Arthur could go back to avoiding each other. Simple. Anything that would let me get Elsie out of this house and to someone who could help her. A normal hospital was out of the question. Lilu blood is even more potent than their pheromones. She'd start a sex riot if we took her to a normal human hospital, and the nearest cryptid hospital I knew of was in New York. With the amount of blood she was losing, there was no way she'd make it there alive.

The bedrooms were empty. I moved onward, finally reaching the garage, and pressed my ear against the door. I heard rustling from the other side. The door wasn't locked. I opened it and stepped through.

My grip on Elsie wavered as we crossed the threshold, but she grabbed hold of me and held me where I was. Interesting. The ward couldn't keep me out, because I wasn't a disembodied spirit, but if she hadn't been willing to help me maintain my possession, I would have *become* a disembodied spirit, and she would have stepped into the garage without me.

It made me wonder what would happen if Banjo tried to come into the garage. Nothing he was going to enjoy, I was sure, but as I wasn't sure how close to the surface Arthur was at this point, I didn't want to risk him trying to step through, coming dislodged, and leaving Arthur's body to drop to the floor, possibly unconscious, definitely defenseless.

This was all too complicated, and I didn't like it.

There was another scuffling sound, coming from behind the van. I walked closer, one hand clamped over the wound in Elsie's shoulder, and called, "Hello? Cunninghams? Don't you think it's about time we finished all of this?"

Whoever had the gun didn't bother looking to see where they were aiming as they stuck their gun around the corner of the van. I ducked. Their shot went over Elsie's head, embedding itself in the wall. Cautiously, I straightened. "I don't mean 'finish it by killing us.' That isn't going to happen today. I'm sorry. But this doesn't have to go on. If you just go back to England and promise not to come to America again, we can let you go. We can let this all be over. Call it equal."

They killed our mother!

And we killed theirs. Now hush. No one's leaving happy—I just want us leaving alive. Or not, as the case might be. I wanted the living to stay alive, and the dead to stay dead. I wanted to put things back the way they were supposed to be.

"Screw you!" shrieked Chloe.

I didn't have time to realize what she was going to do before I heard the back doors of the van slam open, followed by the sound of jars breaking against the concrete floor. I craned Elsie's neck as I looked in that direction, and saw the field of broken glass behind the van. Smoke rose from the shards, mostly dark gray but some almost black, as Chloe kept on smashing. There was a crash that sounded like it came from inside the van, and Chloe screamed. Nathaniel yelled something frantic and climbed after his sister into the now-rocking van.

Elsie's body was increasingly unstable from the blood loss, but I managed to run us to the van. "No!" I yelped. "Stop! Don't do—"

It was too late. There were two more screams from inside the van, both shrill and abruptly cut off, and I came around the end to find an abattoir coating the interior. Chloe and Nathaniel looked more like they had simply popped than anything else, bits of them coating the walls and ceiling in a thin red film.

About a dozen unbroken jars still stood on the shelves.

We were inside a ghost trap of massive proportions, and it was filled to the brim with furiously angry spirits capable of working together to literally explode a living person. The doors and windows could never be opened. We could never let them out of here. We could never leave.

It was easy to convince Elsie's legs to lower us to the garage floor. Sitting was an incredible relief. So was closing her eyes.

Mary? Are we going to be okay?

I don't think so, baby. The air around us was thick with ghosts, poking and probing at the edges of my possession. That was a way they might be able to escape from the trap they were still in: if they could unseat me or Banjo, they could walk Elsie and Arthur through the doors. Or they could all try to pile in at once, which was what I suspected had happened to the Cunninghams. Either way, it wasn't going to end well.

Can't you go and talk to the anima mundi?

I can't take a living person into the twilight, Elsie. You know that.

Is the anima mundi in the twilight? The way Annie talks about it, she went there, when she had to kill the crossroads.

That made me pause. Annie had killed the crossroads by shifting herself physically to the place where they made their bargains, an in-between space that I had been empowered to access, as their representative in the world of the living. And I'd been able to carry her with me, because it hadn't technically been the land of the dead but was a different sort of land of the living. If we could have layers, why couldn't they?

Why couldn't they?

Eyes still closed, I tried to focus on the feeling of shifting that had always accompanied the beginning of a bargain, of making that transition between one place and the next, however dissimilar those places happened to be. I thought about dusty roads and fields of wheat, and when the cold concrete beneath me began to feel like warm asphalt, I exhaled, and opened my eyes.

Twenty-One

"End of the road. Here's where I get out."

—Rose Marshall

The realm of the anima mundi,
which I wasn't sure was actually possible,
but here we are

MY EYES, NOT ELSIE'S. ELSIE'S eyes were still screwed tightly shut. She was sitting beside me on the blacktop, bandaged shoulder covered in blood. That top was beyond all saving. Price women know a hundred ways of getting blood out of fabric, and none of them were going to work here.

The road we were sitting on was as warm as if it were the middle of a summer day, but the sky overhead was bruised with twilight, and a cool wind was blowing through the fields of golden wheat that grew all around us. I pushed myself to my feet, newly aware of the fact that however solid my body felt, it was a dead body: nothing inside it moved or beat or decayed, and that was just fine by me. I was happier in a dead body. That was where I belonged.

"Hey, baby," I said, turning back toward Elsie and leaning down to offer her my hand. She lifted her head and finally opened her eyes, blinking at me.

"Mary?"

"Yeah. We're separate again. No more possession." Nor was it something I was ever intending to try again. I could see why it would become addictive for a ghost who had the capability—and I wasn't sure I would *have* the capability when the damage from my time in the spirit jar finished resolving itself. I still felt unsettled deep in my gut, like the substance of my body had been replaced with frozen slush, sloshing around instead of staying solid and pretending to be part of a normal human being.

That's the afterlife for you. Always coming up with new and exciting ways to make things more complicated than they ought to be. It doesn't help that we're all super-specialists, adjusting our approach to our individual hauntings to suit whatever we need them to be. Time, for example. Most ghosts experience it as a nuisance but don't really feel or experience the passage of time. They don't get bored the way living people do; they don't lose track of things; they don't change. They just live life in the present tense, with nothing mattering more than the moment.

I take care of children, and I've never had the luxury of splitting myself off from the forward progression of time. So I was far too aware that we were here, Elsie was injured, and Arthur's body was still in the possession of a dead man we barely knew.

"Come on, honey, get moving," I said, still holding out my hand. Elsie looked at it dully. I shook it, trying to transmit the urgency of our situation to her without explicitly vocalizing it and running the risk of her getting stubborn the way she used to as a child, digging her heels in and refusing to be budged.

She wasn't a child anymore, and after a few seconds of looking at my hand, she reached out with her uninjured arm and took it, letting me lever her up off the pavement. She staggered a bit, putting her other hand to her temple.

"Woozy," she proclaimed.

"You've lost a lot of blood."

"I didn't lose it," she said. "I know exactly where it is." Then she cackled, and there was a hysterical note I didn't like to the sound, an element of brittleness that hadn't been there before her mother died. But this wasn't the time to dwell on it. I tugged her out of the middle of the road, moving toward the grain, and plunged us both into the gold without hesitation. I couldn't see any sign of the anima mundi's farm or homestead, but they had to know that we were here by this point. I wasn't sure the anima mundi's land *could* be accessed without them knowing someone had crossed their boundaries.

I led Elsie onward, deeper and deeper into the gold, until swaths of short, stubbly stalks began to appear around us, patches where the harvest had already happened. She staggered, yawning, and said, "I'm tired. I think I just want to sit down for a little while. Can't I sit down for a little while, Mary?"

We weren't in the lands of the dead. Elsie was alive, and that meant she could die here. I tugged a little harder, trying to keep her moving with me. She grumbled and groaned, and I felt bad for not allowing her to rest, until finally she just let go of my hand and sat down on the grain with a hard thump.

"No," she said, petulant as the child she'd been when officially in my care. "I don't go any farther than this."

"Okay, baby." I tilted my head back, addressing the air. "You're the living world. She's alive. Can't you help her? Just this once, can't you find it in your heart to help? She wouldn't even be in this situation if not for what you asked from me." I paused. The wind whistled around us, cool and scented green. "Please," I repeated.

"I'm sorry, Mary; I was busy elsewhere," said a familiar voice behind me. I turned, and was facing not the anima mundi but Jane. *My* Jane, mom jeans and loose blouse and all, the way she'd looked in the days before she died. Younger than she thought she was, older than she felt, healthy and vital and breathing and so very *alive* that it made my heart ache to see her so.

"No," I said.

She blinked. "What do you mean, no?"

"I mean Jane chose to move on. She didn't have any unfinished business, and she didn't linger. That means you're the anima mundi wearing her like a Halloween mask for reasons I don't understand, and *no*. I don't want you doing that to Elsie. She deserves better."

The anima mundi—because it was them, it had to be—blinked, and then narrowed their eyes. "So you brought a living girl here and now you think you can give me orders? I think you've fundamentally misunderstood our relationship, Mary Dunlavy. I think it may be time to disabuse you of a few direly incorrect notions."

They snapped Jane's fingers, and we were no longer in the wheat. Instead, we were standing in the middle of a blueberry field, chest-high bushes dripping with fat berries stretching out in all directions. It was less obvious here where the harvest had already happened. Pails of berries sat alongside bushes that looked completely untouched, so full that fruit was tumbling out to land in the grass. Elsie was still sitting on the ground beside me, eyes closed, seemingly unaware of what was happening right in front of her.

Good. Sometimes ignorance really is the best option. "What are you disabusing me of?" I asked.

"You have no say in the faces we wear," said the anima mundi. "For you, we appear as a combination of the women of the world, because it brings you the most comfort. We are not a woman ourself, but we are a mother to this noosphere, as well as a product of its growth. When the living face us, we show them the face that will comfort them the most. When your Antimony came before us, we showed her your face, and she called us 'Mary' until she saw how wrong she was. A dead woman's face to comfort a living one. Why should this child be any different?"

"Because Jane was her *mom*," I said. "Look. Mothers and daughters are complicated. Even when they don't like each other very much—and they don't always like each other very much—

losing your mother is a life-changing event. You don't have to grieve for her to know that you're never going to be the person you were before you lost her. Elsie *just* lost Jane. She's in the process of losing her brother—her second brother, who was built on the bones of her first one. She's grieved enough. Please. I know I don't get to order you around, but don't do this to her. She deserves better."

The anima mundi sighed. "Really? Better than the chance to say farewell?" They looked past me to where Elsie sat. "We think she deserves that opportunity."

I paused. Elsie hadn't been able to say goodbye to Jane. She hadn't been able to say goodbye to Artie, either—he'd gone to save Sarah, moving too fast to think about what he was doing, and then only his empty body had made it home. Arthur was dissolving a little more every day, and there was the chance that she wouldn't be saying goodbye to him, either. The last few years of Elsie's life had been all but defined by not getting that final farewell.

"You said you want to disabuse me of several things," I said. "What else?"

"You don't command us," said the anima mundi. "We aren't your friend, or your servant."

"But you want to be my employer," I said. "That means sometimes I get to need things from you. Even the crossroads understood that I needed things." They'd been sullen and unkind about it, but they'd been able to understand. "And sometimes those things will be a part of doing whatever it is you've asked me for, like this time."

"Oh? The Lilu's well-being is part of answering my request?" They moved toward Elsie, stooping down and helping her off the ground. She unfolded easily, rising with no sign of weariness or weakness, and only swayed a little as the anima mundi stepped back. "She looks less like a fulfillment and more like a favor."

"She is," I said. "She needs medical help or she's not going to make it, but if she opens the door and goes outside, she'll break the wards keeping the ghosts from the spirit jars contained. That house is a phantom nuke in the middle of a populated area. Bringing her here lets us keep the wards intact a little longer, while we figure out how to disarm it."

"I cannot heal the child," said the anima mundi, sounding genuinely sorry. "She's too small. I would heal her into nonexistence, make her into something else, and lose whatever of her it is that you treasure so."

"I didn't expect you to heal her. Just to help me get her out of the house. Please."

The anima mundi didn't answer. Instead, they leaned in and kissed Elsie, ever so gently, on the forehead. She took a shaky breath and opened her eyes.

Then she blinked, rapidly, like she was trying to clear her eyes. "Mom?" she asked, with fragile, burning hopefulness.

"Yes, and no," said the anima mundi in Jane's voice. "I was, but I died and I moved on, and now I'm a part of the great beating heart of the world. I belong to the anima mundi now, the spirit of Earth."

"What?" I breathed.

"What?" asked Elsie.

The anima mundi smiled Jane's smile. "I know, it's a lot to take in. Not every spirit chooses to come back and belong to us, but your mother, when she died and found herself with nothing to bind her to the living world, chose to return to where she had begun. She became a part of us, and we know everything she was, and we know how much she loved you. It was an honor, Elsinore, to be allowed to be your mother. I always knew it wouldn't last forever. I always knew I'd have to go." Then, to my surprise, the anima mundi started to cry. "That's what the mothers in our family do, after all. We leave. I'm so sorry I left you."

In that moment, I began to understand. The anima mundi wasn't trying to make light of Elsie's loss, wasn't pretending to be Jane. The anima mundi *was* Jane, or rather, Jane was the anima mundi. This wasn't just a chance for Elsie to say goodbye.

Elsie's eyes filled almost immediately with tears, and she embraced the anima mundi, pulling them close to her. "Oh, Mom, no, no, you were an amazing mother. You didn't leave me, you were taken away from me. There's a difference. I love you so much. I'm not angry at you because you had to go. It's not like you had a choice in the matter."

"Really?"

"Really."

"Good girl." The anima mundi pulled back. "So can you stop being angry at your brother? Please? He didn't choose to die when he followed Sarah—and you know he'd have followed that girl to the ends of the world and beyond. Hell, he actually *did*."

"Yeah, and that's what it took for him to find out she actually loved him," said Elsie, a bitter chuckle in her tone. "How many years did they spend circling each other like it was nothing, like everybody gets that kind of love just *handed* to them? He still loves her, and she won't even talk to him. It isn't *fair*."

"Life isn't fair, bun," said the anima mundi. "Neither is death. Your brother died, and now the man who's taken his place is dying, and it's awful, and you can't stop it. *I* can't stop it. You have to just love him until it's time to let him go."

"I'll try," said Elsie, voice soft. Then she swayed, catching herself on the anima mundi's arm. "I'm so tired, Mom. I don't feel good. I've lost a lot of blood. Do you think I can rest now? Is it okay if I rest now?"

"Sure, baby," said the anima mundi. "Just close your eyes."

Elsie closed her eyes. The anima mundi raised a hand, and we were inside the little homestead that sat on the edge of the wheat fields, in a bedroom that looked like something out of a frontier living museum. The anima mundi lowered Elsie onto the bed, where she made a bloody splotch against the blue and white log cabin quilt.

They turned to me once she was down. "Do you have a plan?"

"I think so."

"Talk quickly." They pushed their hair back, and they changed with the gesture, abandoning the veil of Jane for their normal shifting mask of aggregate faces. It was soothing to see them the way I thought of them, protein and ever-changing. "She doesn't have a lot of time."

That wasn't encouraging. "I don't think Arthur does, either," I said.

"My ability to interfere directly in the land of the living is limited, or I wouldn't need ghosts as go-betweens," cautioned the anima mundi.

"Yes, but you can pull ghosts into your presence whenever you want to, can't you?"

The anima mundi nodded. "I can."

"Then what I need to ask you to do is reach into the land of the living and pull all the ghosts who are currently trapped in that house through to the farm," I said.

They blinked. "That's . . . an interesting notion."

"They're hurt. They've been tortured. Many of them probably won't be safe to send back for a long, long time. They need a place to heal. Can't you let them have a fallow field or something?"

"Removing them from the lands of the living won't correct the power imbalance created by their removal."

"Neither will them killing a few dozen living people when they get out of that house and go rampaging through suburbia. Can you get them out?"

"We can give them space, yes. Come with me."

They walked out of the room, gesturing for me to follow, and I did, as quickly as I could, although it pained me to leave Elsie behind. She was my charge. I could still feel her, and I would know if she died. In the moment, it was the best I could do.

The anima mundi led me to a door, opening it to reveal a wide, empty field that looked suspiciously like the one between the old Healy house and the Galway Wood. There was even a barn in the distance, run-down and tattered, holes forming in the roof. They stepped onto the porch, raising their hands high. I stayed in the doorway, sensing that this wasn't a situation I wanted to walk into the middle of without taking the time to prepare myself.

When they brought their hands down, the field filled with ghosts. Some of them were pale, see-through outlines of human beings; some of them were nothing more than puffs of skidding smoke. A few—a very, very few—had traces of color and solidity.

Two of the more solid-looking ghosts saw the anima mundi and started toward the porch while the rest were still trying to reorient themselves, looking around with confusion or hanging in motionless patches of wind-defying fog. One of them was a man dressed like he came from my time period, complete with slicked-back hair and unreasonably well-defined facial hair. The other was a woman Elsie's age, who glowed a steady, lambent white that overwhelmed the rest of the color she might have once possessed. She was dressed like my mother used to when I was young, barely a generation ahead of me, prim and proper and perfectly polite.

"Hello, Banjo," I said, once the man was close enough.

He eyed me. "You that Mary girl?"

"I am."

"How'd you know?"

I shrugged. "Lucky guess."

"How'd we get here?"

The anima mundi sniffed, looking at him. "I called the ghosts from the building you were trapped within, and you came."

Banjo shot them a dismissive look. "Nah, see, I was possessing this hollow little guy—he was *perfect*, an unbroken vessel, just waiting for someone more useful to come along and put him to good use. I want to go back."

I stepped forward, eyes blazing. "Excuse me?"

"Aw, yeah, little babysitter. Your boy's got a good body. I can use it. Better still, he's got a lousy grip on the thing. You sure he's not already a possession? Maybe the original got on your nerves? I could live there forever."

"But you won't." I looked to the anima mundi. "Please don't send him back."

"I dislike the dead occupying the living," they said coolly. "I will not enable it."

"Thank you." I turned to look at the white lady. "You are . . . ?"

"Agnes, ma'am," she said, voice polite and deferential. "Have we been called to the great hereafter?"

"Technically you've been in the great hereafter since you died, but you're currently in a new layer of the afterlife," I said. "This is the anima mundi. They're making sure the ghosts damaged by the spirit jars don't have the chance to make things worse."

"Yes, ma'am," said Agnes, sounding confused. "The spirit jar was very unsettling, and I didn't much care for it. If we're here, does that mean we're all moving on, or is there a chance we can go back to our familiar hauntings? You see, I've a garden to tend, and a ward of sorts to care for."

"Jonah, right?" I asked. She nodded. "I want to talk to you about him. I have a few ideas that might help make his afterlife a little more pleasant."

"That would be very nice, ma'am, if it's possible for me to return where I belong."

"Ask the anima mundi."

She turned her attention to the anima mundi. "I . . . Er . . . Ma'am?"

"As good an address for me as any, I suppose," said the anima mundi. "How are you still yourself, lady of vengeance?"

334 + SEANAN MCGUIRE

"Oh, I found my peace a long, long time ago, but I had flowers to tend to, and bees to care for, so I stayed. It takes more than a little pain and suffering to unsettle me," said Agnes serenely. "I have to go back for Jonah, and the bees."

"Then you'll be returned, as will any others still coherent enough to pose no threat to the living," said the anima mundi. They turned to me. "I can put you and your charge down outside the house, but I can't recover the boy from inside without bringing him here and dropping him back again, and he'll have no means of understanding what's going on around him."

"If you get us back into the daylight, I can deal with Arthur." I tried to sound more confident than I felt.

The anima mundi nodded. "Hmm. There is the small matter of resources. You've done as we asked you, which means the time of moving freely and without restraint is over, unless you agree to enter our service, as we previously proposed."

"Elsie is bleeding to death, Arthur is presumably unconscious at the site of multiple murders, and you want to talk employment?"

"Yes. This seems like a time when you'll understand the urgency of our request."

I glared.

"The crossroads also made sure to back me into a corner, and I spent decades fighting against them," I said. "Be very sure you want to do this."

The look of smug assurance on the anima mundi's face flickered but didn't entirely fade away. "We are."

"All right. I'll work for you the same way I worked for them— part-time. My family comes first."

"The *children* come first," countered the anima mundi. "If you are needed for the care of children, you may always choose them over us. If an adult wishes you, then you will wait until your duties to us are done, and we may call you away at any time."

"Just to be clear. I can move freely between my family members with no restraints when I'm not on a job for you, whether or not they've called for me, and I can go to the children I'm responsible for with no restrictions. What about the sick?"

"Come again?"

"Caretaker ghosts don't just care for children. We take care of the unwell. We nurse them back to health. What happens when one of my people is sick?"

The anima mundi waved a hand. "We classify them as children when they ail. You may go to their side."

It was basically the deal I'd had with the crossroads, with less of a focus on tricking people into selling their futures for a handful of glitter and a promise that would be twisted into a weapon as soon as the contract was signed. I'd enjoyed my brief period of freedom, but if it was this or leave my family undefended . . .

I shrugged. "Deal. Now send us back."

The anima mundi smiled, and nodded in a hard, purposeful gesture, and the farm was gone.

Twenty-Two

"You can't save everyone, baby girl. But when you're lucky,
you can save what matters."

—Eloise Dunlavy

*On the sidewalk outside
a definitively not haunted house,
trying to figure out what happens next*

Elsie didn't open her eyes as she was transferred from the
homestead bed to the cold concrete sidewalk. She just lay there,
silent, still, and far paler than I liked. I stooped to check her
pulse, then turned to Agnes, who was glowing gently beside me.

"Can you stay here for a minute?" I asked.

She nodded, looking confused, and I disappeared.

Elsie was definitely sick right now, so even though she was an
adult, I could be sure the anima mundi wouldn't call me away
while I was in the process of helping her. Less than a second
after I vanished, I was standing in the dark living room of Phee's
boardinghouse, where I put two fingers in my mouth and whistled shrill and loud. It was a whistle designed for summoning
children out of parks and back across fields, and it was only a few
moments before people began popping out of the hall, bleary-
eyed and unhappy.

I focused on Amelia. "You're still here."

"Nowhere else to go," she said uncomfortably.

"How far from here to your swamp?"

She blinked, looking utterly baffled. "About an hour if we drive fast. Why?"

"Because I have a way for you to make up for what you did," I said, and she blinked again, and maybe things were going to be all right after all.

✦ ✦ ✦

Cryptid populations who have to keep themselves apart from humans for whatever reason, whether it be extra limbs, snakes for hair, or skin that would absolutely draw attention in a hospital environment, well, they tend to maintain their own medical services. It's sort of necessary if they want to continue being alive.

Amelia drove a small SUV, and she loaded me and Phee into it before driving to the Covenant house as fast as she could reasonably go. Agnes was still on the sidewalk next to Elsie, who seemed to have grown even paler while I was away. Agnes wrung her hands as we picked Elsie up and loaded her into the back seat, and stayed with me and the car as Phee and Amelia went inside—through the simple expedient of crowbarring the door—and emerged with a blood-streaked, solidly unconscious Arthur. We put him in the back next to his sister, both of them united in unconsciousness.

Amelia held her nose as she got into the driver's seat. She rolled down all the windows, turned on the air conditioning, and then pulled a little box from the glove compartment, smearing some sort of sharp-scented menthol gel under her nose. Her eyes were glassy as she turned to look at me.

"I can still smell her, but I think I can keep control of myself," she said.

"Let me drive," said Phee.

They traded places, Amelia taking the passenger seat with a

grateful nod, while I hugged Agnes and got into the back with the kids.

"Go check on Jonah," I said. "I'll be there soon."

She nodded and disappeared, presumably returning to her anchor. Most ghosts can't move the way I do, but they can always flicker between the locations they're rooted to. In her case, the garden she had learned peace to continue tending was almost certainly one of those locations, and the city hall was another.

I shut the car door, and Phee hit the gas, and we were off.

The next hour was a nightmare in slow motion. Elsie's wound was well tied but still bleeding sluggishly, and the body only has so much blood it can lose before shock sets in and recovery becomes impossible. I didn't know how close we were to that line, only that she should have been given medical care hours ago and not spent that time being possessed and bouncing from one layer of reality to another. She didn't move but continued breathing, and under the circumstances, that would have to be good enough.

Amelia didn't speak apart from telling Phee when she needed to make a turn, just kept her hands pressed flat against the dashboard and breathed shallowly through her mouth, shoulders getting tighter and tighter as the smell of Elsie's blood and the combination of her pheromones mingled with Arthur's filled the car.

Lilu pheromones can become overwhelming in sufficient concentration, causing people to agree to, or do, things they wouldn't have done under any other circumstances. Phee glanced at her, mouth a thin line.

"It's okay, Mia," she said. "We're almost there."

"Not almost there enough," said Amelia. "Left up ahead."

We roared through the night, moving away from civilization, into the true dark of the space between cities, the ancient trees pressing in around us on all sides. Phee turned off on a narrow logging road, heading into the state park that housed the Hockomock Swamp, presumably avoiding any manmade barriers or ranger stations.

Frogs and insects sang outside the car, occasionally broken by the screech of a distant owl. The car began to bounce as we drove over ruts and rocks and breaks in the road, and I understood why an SUV had been important. Anything smaller would have gotten bogged down, if it didn't break an axle. Amelia's barked directions become more common, and we left the main logging road for a series of smaller, narrower paths through the trees.

We hit a particularly large divot and Arthur startled awake, blinking blearily as he turned his head back and forth, trying to figure out where we were. I leaned across the motionless Elsie and set a hand on his arm.

"It's all right, baby," I said. "It's okay. We're almost there."

"'Most where?" he mumbled.

"A place where Elsie can get some medical care, and we can get something with a lot of sugar into you." Sugar helps with shock, in my experience. Maybe that's not scientific or modern, but sometimes you can't focus on being as modern as possible. Sometimes you just do what works, and hope it doesn't kill anyone.

Rather than looking soothed, Arthur looked alarmed. He sat up straighter, blinking faster as he tried to clear his vision. "How?"

"That is a very long story, and trying to explain it all right now isn't going to do any of us any good, but please, Arthur, it's me, Mary. Just trust me when I say we wouldn't be doing this if it wasn't going to help your sister, all right?" I tightened my grip on his arm slightly.

The pressure seemed to soothe him. He stopped shifting in his seat and took a deep breath, clearly forcing himself to relax before he said, "Okay, Mary. If you say so."

"We're almost there," said Amelia.

Arthur stiffened again, narrowing his eyes as he focused on the back of her head. "*You*," he spat.

"Me," Amelia agreed. "I'm sorry about what I did before. Those Covenant people made some big threats against my entire species, and I panicked. Maybe I shouldn't have done that, but I did, and now we're trying to make it right. Can you please try to trust me long enough for me to make it right?"

"I'm keeping an eye on you," he said.

Amelia's laugh was small and bitter. "Don't worry, kid. I'm keeping an eye on me too. Turn right up ahead, Phee."

"There isn't any road there."

"There's a road. Just—come on. You know I know these woods. Turn right now."

Phee turned right, seeming to steer directly into the middle of a patch of old-growth cedar trees. I braced for an impact that never came as we continued smoothly down a better-maintained dirt road. Looking back, I saw that the spacing of the trees formed a perfect optical illusion of impassibility while barely concealing a reasonably clear passage. We rolled deeper and deeper, surrounded by trees, until those same trees began to open up and make room for us, leaving us driving into a meadow of sorts, if it can truly be called a meadow in the middle of a swamp.

It was large, whatever it was, and dominated by a fort that could have been stolen from a period piece about American colonization, even down to the lashed-together log wall surrounding the main structure, cutting it off from easy view. There were a few other vehicles parked outside the wall, and flickering torches set along the top, confirming that people were awake inside.

I would never have known this place existed if it hadn't been directly in front of me. Even from the final road, there had been no indication we were going to find a walled settlement. Phee pulled onto a flat piece of ground and turned off the engine, handing the keys back to Amelia, who looked at me in the rearview mirror.

"Can you and Phee carry her?" she asked. Her cheeks reddened. "I don't want to get her blood on me."

That was less a hygiene concern and more a matter of Lilu blood being an even-more-powerful aphrodisiac than their pheromones. I nodded. The day I couldn't help carry one of my kids was the day I gave up on my position in the afterlife.

Amelia looked relieved and got out of the car.

Arthur was awake enough to walk on his own, with a little nudging, and working together, Phee and I were able to lever Elsie out of the car and hoist her between us, feet dragging on the ground as we walked her toward the wall. Amelia was already there by the time we arrived, talking fast and urgently with the gate guards in a language I didn't understand. Then she flashed us a relieved smile, and we were ushered inside.

The gate slammed behind us like a vault door closing, and there was a finality to it that made me flinch. But we'd come this far, and I wasn't going to give up now. Amelia gestured for us to follow her, and we did exactly that, not looking back.

Never look back when you can help it.

✦ ✦ ✦

The Hockomock Swamp Beastie medical center was located in a low wooden building that looked as old-fashioned and well weathered as everything around it. Once inside, however, we found ourselves in a fully modern clinic, complete with glaring fluorescent lights overhead and uncomfortable chairs in the waiting area. Elsie was whisked away into a curtained area at the back, while I stayed up front with Arthur. He drooped in his seat, hands between his knees and head bowed. I sat down next to him after asking the receptionist—they had a receptionist—for a cup of apple cider, putting a hand on his shoulder.

"Hey, buddy," I said. "How are you doing?"

"He just . . . stepped in and took me over," he said. "I couldn't fight him. It was like my body wasn't even my own anymore, and he said I was barely holding on to it, that it would be easy to stay where he was and push me out just a little bit at a time. He said he could just take over. Was he telling the truth, Mary?"

"Possession isn't easy, and it's not something I've ever really tried to do before," I said. "But I think he might be right that you're not as anchored in your body as someone like Elsie is. You belong here, and you're still my family—I hear you when you call—but you weren't here from the very beginning. I think it's possible that he could have pushed you out, given time. For right now, I'm not going to recommend you go on missions that involve a lot of ghosts. I don't think they're very good for you."

Arthur lifted his head, giving me a plaintive look. "Does that mean *I'm* possessing the original Artie's body?"

"No, I don't think so," I said. "You were built to live there, you're not an uninvited spirit taking over a house that isn't yours. This is your home."

"And you wouldn't make me leave if Artie came back?"

There was fear and hope in the question, enough to make me pause. What *would* we do if Artie started to resurface? He was the boy I'd helped to raise, the one I'd known and loved since he was born. Arthur wasn't an intruder, but he wasn't Artie, either.

My pause must have been more telling than I realized, because he began to pull away. I winced, catching his shoulder before he could slip from under my hand. "If Artie started to recover, we'd find a way to keep you both," I said. "We'd find a solution. Because you're allowed to live as much as he was, and it's not your fault he had to go. But you're not a possession, and you didn't steal anything, and we love you whether or not you're him."

Arthur made a thin choking noise and twisted to throw his arms around me, and I embraced him back, letting him cling to me as long as he needed to.

We were still like that when someone cleared their throat, and I looked up to find one of the Hockomock Swamp Beasties standing there, wearing a white doctor's coat over gray scrubs. "You're here with the, uh, Lilu?"

"I'm her babysitter," I said, standing. I didn't let go of Arthur, just allowed myself to turn insubstantial long enough to pass right through him. "How is she?"

"She was in hypovolemic shock when you got her here; any further delay might have been fatal," said the doctor, sternly. "The bullet went through her shoulder and out the other side; it didn't hit any bones or major arteries. We were able to repair the damage and transfuse her, and she should make a full recovery. Did Amelia tell you how things work here?"

"No," I said, almost too giddy with relief to hear what he was telling me. "Please, just tell us what we owe you, and we'll figure it out."

"Ten units packed red blood cells, and five units saline," he said.

"Done." I could steal them from a hospital, even though neither I nor Arthur could donate. "I assume your community is cross-compatible with human blood products?"

"We are."

"Then it won't be a problem."

"We'll also ask you to replace any medications she uses before we can discharge her."

"Understandable, and of course."

The doctor frowned. "You're agreeing awfully easily for outsiders."

"You saved her. That's all that matters right now. Lilu can't go to human hospitals without causing riots."

"She almost caused a riot *here*. We had to drench our surgical masks in peppermint oil. Two people fainted."

"Thank you for going to all this trouble for us."

He looked at me sternly, searching for signs that I was making fun of him. Then, frowning, he nodded. "She's not awake yet. I'll send someone to bring you back to where she's resting when she recovers consciousness."

"Thank you again."

He nodded, then turned and walked away. I collapsed back into my chair as Arthur wrapped his arms around me, and for a little while, we just held on to each other.

That was really all that we could do.

Twenty-Three

"If everyone's still standing when the dust settles, you've won. You have my full permission to deck anyone who says otherwise."

—Jane Harrington-Price

The Burnside Fountain,
Worcester, Massachusetts
Three days later

The turtle didn't appear to have changed its opinion about the boy and what he was doing since the last time I'd seen it. The look of horror on its bronze face remained comical and unchanged. I studied it carefully, hoping it would reveal something of the sculptor's intent. Instead, it revealed how much nuance could be packed into the eyes of a truly terrified turtle.

"There was something wrong with the person who made you," I informed the fountain.

"I think that's true of most people," said Agnes. I turned. She was on her knees among the flowers, carefully pulling weeds. White ladies can influence the living world a little, but so far as I know, Agnes was the only one who chose to use that ability to tend flowerbeds instead of committing homicides. To each their own, I suppose.

"What does the park service think of you tending the flowers?" I asked.

She looked up, blinking large, luminous eyes at me. "They think that during requisitions season, someone leaves a neat little memo by the phone, listing all the flowers I want them to plant, and beyond that, they don't have to do any maintenance. They never have issues with harmful insects or invasive weeds."

"Huh." I tilted my head, thinking about all the possible implications of a white lady who had somehow rewritten herself into some kind of garden ghost. "I may need to have a word with the anima mundi."

"You do that," she said placidly, and pulled another weed.

I turned to face the city hall, and smiled as a slim figure stepped through the doors—literally, they were closed and locked at this hour of the night, and as a homestead, he didn't have the ability to open them—and started toward me. I waited until he was halfway to the fountain, then waved.

Jonah waved back, and sped up, trotting the rest of the way.

"Hey, Mary," he said, once he was close enough. "Agnes said you wanted to see me?"

"I did," I said. "I have a surprise for you. Come here."

He moved closer, and I offered him my hand. He took it, fingers cool and barely solid against mine, and I squeezed his hand, smiling reassuringly. Then I vanished, pulling him with me.

We reappeared in a dark, quiet hall, concrete floor under our feet and chain-link fencing creating a narrow pathway down the center. Jonah gave me a bewildered look.

"You were asking why the puppies never stay," I said, starting to walk. "They're young, and they don't know how to have unfinished business yet—or all they are is unfinished business. Older dogs are more likely to have unfinished business, but it's usually going to their owners and staying until they're sure they've done their duty properly. They guard until it's time for them to go together." It broke my heart the first time I saw a phantom dog sitting by his former master's feet, patiently waiting for a reunion that might take years to come. It broke my heart, and then it healed it, because how many people could say they knew love that would genuinely endure past death?

"Okay . . ."

"Not all dogs have owners to go back to. And sometimes their unfinished business is being a creature we've bred to want nothing more than to be with us—just being dogs—that never got to know genuine love on an individual basis." We had reached a door. Gently, I tugged Jonah through it to the other side, a large, square room teeming with dogs of all shapes and sizes.

They mostly chose to appear as they had been in the very prime of life, old enough to be past puppyhood's wildness, young enough to run forever. As one, they turned to look at us, noses quivering. Jonah made a small sound of surprise, pulling his hand from mine, and moved to meet them.

I stayed where I was, watching him go. It had been a long few days. Elsie was up and moving under her own power, and according to her doctors, she'd be ready to make the drive back to Portland in the morning, as long as we stopped to rest any time she got tired. It was going to be a much longer drive home. A lot more motels and roadside diners. And I was fine with that, because all three of us were going home. There had been a time when I was less than sure of that.

Aoi and Benedita had been among the ghosts freed by the anima mundi. I hadn't seen Aoi captured, but after everything else, it made terrible sense that they had been. Like Agnes, they were mostly fine after their time in the spirit jars, and had already returned to the club—a little more reserved now, a little more careful with their approach to the dance floor, but free to go about their business. As I had expected, Heitor hadn't appeared in the twilight after his murder. Umbramancers never do.

Chloe and Nathaniel were equally absent. If they'd had any unfinished business worth staying for, they'd been dissuaded when the escaped phantoms shredded them into ectoplasmic flecks. With any luck, they either wouldn't appear at all or, if they did appear, it would be in the province of the anima mundi, where the living spirit of the Earth could explain to them that they didn't approve of their attitudes.

Phee and her boardinghouse seemed to have gotten off as lightly as possible: the Covenant operatives who'd known about her were gone, and while there was some lingering animosity over Amelia handing Elsie and Arthur to the Covenant, it was mostly counterbalanced by the Hockomock Swamp Beasties providing medical care. Phee got to stay open and keep providing help to local cryptids, and I had a new waystation for when I needed to ask the local living about their ghost population.

Many of the jarred ghosts were going to take years to recover enough to settle again, assuming they ever did. Until they were recovered from their ordeal, they were going to stay with the anima mundi, haunting her hollows and filling her fields with rustling winds. It was a sad ending but among the best they could have reasonably expected.

And me? Well, I had a new employer, and moments like this were part of it. Much as the crossroads used to have me watching for petitioners, the anima mundi now had me watching for ghosts who'd settled slightly outside their normal roles, who didn't fit, who needed more. Ghosts like Jonah and Agnes. Call it a form of social work—Jane would be proud, if Jane were still around to be anything at all. But I'd have my hands busy for a long time to come. After I got Elsie and Arthur home, I was coming back here to introduce Jonah to the local ever-lasters and get him settled with some kids his own mental and emotional age.

Too many of the systems that should have allowed the dead to find peace and move on had been disrupted by the crossroads, and I'd been a part of that disruption. Now I was going to be a part of building it all back up to where it was supposed to be, and I was honestly excited about the idea.

Jonah emerged from the pack of spirit dogs with a shaggy mutt that looked like a combination Golden Retriever and Pit Bull Terrier walking along beside him, staring up at him with the loving eyes of a dog that had finally found its boy. Jonah looked at me, almost challengingly, and put his hand on the dog's back.

"His name is Tank, and I love him," he said.

"Then he's yours."

Jonah brightened. "Really?"

"Really. He's been waiting here for you to come and get him." Maybe the ever-lasters would want dogs too, once they knew that dogs were an option. Maybe we could fill their afterlife with wagging tails and understanding eyes, and death would be a little kinder. Because it lasts a long, long time, but the longer I go on, the more I think that love lasts even longer.

I offered Jonah my hand. "Ready to go?"

He nodded, burying the fingers of one hand in the ruff at the back of Tank's neck even as he took my hand with the other. I smiled down at him, then raised my eyes to the wall in front of us.

"Let's go home," I said, thinking of a better future, and we were gone.

Turn the page for a brand-new InCryptid novella
by Seanan McGuire

MOURNER'S WALTZ

Mourner's Waltz

"I never thought I'd have a family outside of the Covenant. I never thought I'd done enough to earn such a gift."

—Dominic Price-De Luca

A small, rent-controlled apartment
in Manhattan, New York

Trying to put together a crib without being seriously
injured—or seriously injuring someone else

I DON'T REMEMBER THIS BEING SO *hard* the last time I did it," I complained, letting the leg I'd been struggling to attach fall back into the pile of pieces that would, if put together in the correct order, form a safe and comfortable crib for the baby I was almost finished gestating. Putting a hand on my protruding stomach, I looked down and addressed it, keeping my tone as mild as I could. Kitty insisted the baby could already pick up on my moods.

"I'm glad I don't have any manual control over assembling *you,* kiddo, or you'd come out with three legs and a handful of missing screws," I said.

As if in response, the baby kicked my midsection. I winced, then chuckled, trying to heave my unwieldy self up from the floor.

The feeling of something moving around *inside* me was never going to be something I was completely comfortable with, no matter what the women in my birthing class said. I knew too much about the things that *could* move around inside the human body, and I'd been studying them for a lot longer than I'd been pregnant. My first thought when a baby started kicking wasn't "Oh, how sweet"; it was "How long do I have before this thing chews its way out of me?"

Not the most maternal way of thinking. But I'd done all right so far, and we were nearly done with this part of our relationship. Soon enough, I'd be able to evict my tenant and gain a roommate.

But first, I had to put together this damn crib. I glared at it as I got my feet under me and braced myself against the bookshelf, making sure I wasn't going to fall. This was the same brand as the crib we'd used for Livvy, and that one had gone together fast and easy.

Fast and easy, and with Dominic holding the instructions.

The thought made tears sting the corners of my eyes. It was an incredibly fast response, grief and hormones combining to flood my system with salt water every time I even paused to think about my husband. Which, since I knew I wasn't an immaculate conception, was pretty much every time I was forced to contend with the reality of my condition.

I got the bulk of my torso balanced correctly above my rump and knees, and pushed away from the bookshelf, taking my first clumsy steps away from the room that would belong to the baby—the baby, and eventually the baby and Livvy, when I was finally ready to bring her home from my parents. The ongoing absence of my daughter hurt in a different way than missing Dominic did—no less potent, but not precisely the same. I knew she was safe where she was, with people who cared for her and had the resources to keep her fed and happy. Whereas I still had times when I'd just go blank and wake up somewhere else in the apartment, having changed rooms while divorced from the flow of time. Once, I'd started a grease fire on the stove without even realizing that I'd started to cook something.

Grief is a nasty predator, and the things it takes away are sometimes worse than dying. I was learning to work around the holes in my memory and my day, and I took my vitamins and ate enough to be sure that I wasn't doing my little passenger any harm. Handling that and taking care of an active little girl at the same time just wouldn't have been possible. There was nothing wrong with admitting my limits.

There wasn't.

I shuffled down the hall toward the front of the apartment. A cup of decaf coffee would help to settle my nerves, even as it upset my stomach. But that's what Pepto-Bismol is for, right?

Pregnancy is a magic opportunity to spend nine months voluntarily living in a horror movie that everyone tells you to treasure and enjoy more than you've ever enjoyed anything else in your life.

I reached the kitchen and pulled down the box of coffee pods I'd scavenged from various offices around the city. Working with—technically for—dragons teaches you a lot about thrift. The dragons respected anything that saved money, and since "walking instead of calling for a ride" was no longer quite as easy an option for me as it had been eight months ago, I was resorting to coffee theft.

Whatever. It wasn't like the high-powered executives whose offices I hit drank the decaf anyway, and I knew for a fact that the unused pods were thrown out at the end of a long day of meetings.

As I was getting the machine ready, a small head poked out of a hole in the wall behind the toaster, quickly followed by the rest of a compact, brown-furred body. The mouse now crouching on the counter in front of me was wearing a necklace of beads harvested from one of my dance costumes. I had little doubt that the beads had come loose on their own, victims of normal wear and tear, or that the mice had since identified and repaired the original damage. Cinderella had it right: if you want true wardrobe management, get yourself a bunch of talking mice.

"Hello," I said, acknowledging the mouse.

"Hail," squeaked the mouse. "Hail to the Arboreal Priestess, for surely she remembers that Caffeine Is Bad for the Baby?"

"Decaf," I said gravely, holding up the pod I was intending to use and tilting it so that she could read the lid.

She studied it with equal gravity, whiskers bristling, and turned so that I could see her own swollen abdomen, which she pressed with her paws in an unnervingly human gesture. The Aeslin liked to send their pregnant colony members to speak with me, believing my attention would bless their unborn pups. I tried not to think about it too hard. It was difficult to see my attention as any sort of blessing these days.

"Acceptable," squeaked the mouse, finally.

"Would you like some?" I snapped the pod into the machine, closing the lid and hitting the button to start the brew cycle. "I'm planning to add sugar and cream to mine."

"I would like that very much," allowed the mouse.

"Deal."

I'm not huge on sharing food, but sharing a cup of coffee with a mouse meant tipping a teaspoon-full into a bottle cap, and honestly, that was cute enough that I didn't particularly mind.

The coffee brewed the way it always did, and I had just finished fixing my cup and pouring a spoonful out for my mousey attendant when someone knocked on my apartment door. I shot it a sour look. If someone was knocking without me ringing them up, they had to be a resident of the building, which meant I couldn't just ignore them and hope they'd go away.

Yes, for the first time in my life, I had a job that didn't include short skirts or impractical footwear. Until I could dance again, I was serving as property manager for one of the investment properties owned by the local dragons: an apartment building on the East Side, rent-controlled, and occupied entirely by cryptids who were either able to pass for humans or had remote jobs that let them pay the rent.

I wasn't the apartment handyman—even if I'd known how to fix a pipe, which I didn't, I was eight months pregnant and no longer on speaking terms with my feet. If this was a problem that needed to be repaired, I'd have to call down and wake our actual handyman.

Sadly, I could understand why they would come to me first. Between me and the handyman, I was the less likely to get upset and take a limb off. I might snarl and mutter, but at the end of the day, I knew my job, and I knew how lucky I was to have it. There's not a lot in the way of career opportunities for former professional ballroom dancers who don't want to go into choreography and can't teach yoga and share their living space with several dozen talking, highly religious mice. Building management for dragons was about as good as it got.

Whoever was outside knocked again. I scowled and set my coffee mug aside, then shuffled for the door as quickly as my scrambled center of balance would currently allow. Even hurrying, they knocked a third time before I got there, and I wrenched the door open with an irritated, "*What?*"

The woman on my doorstep raised an eyebrow, giving me a quick up-and-down glance that took in the sum of me, from my stained tank top to my bare feet and messy hair, in what felt like less than a second. Then she rolled her shoulders in a shrug that looked unnervingly like a prime boxer getting ready to wade into the ring, and said, "They didn't tell me it was *this* bad. Look out, Val, I'm coming in," and she pushed past me into the apartment while I was still trying to come to terms with the fact that she was there, right there, at my door, to judge me.

"Malena." I closed the door as I turned to watch her progress through my space, trying to see it the way she must be seeing it. And to be honest, I wasn't too impressed.

The apartment I was renting from the dragons was palatial by New York standards, with two bedrooms, a living room, and a kitchen, as well as a full bathroom and a funny hall closet that might have been half of a bedroom once upon a time, based on the shape of it. If it had been, the other half was now the property of the adjoining apartment, and it wasn't coming back any time soon. It contained the absolute bare minimum in terms of furnishings—the front room, where Malena was now looking around disapprovingly, had a couch that could convert into a futon, and a surprisingly nice hardwood coffee table that the dragons had scavenged from a street corner, stripped, and refinished into something that would probably fetch a pretty penny at one of the more upscale vintage furniture shops. And that was it.

There was no television, no rug, no shelves of books or other little knickknacks that might prove someone actually lived here. There *was* an empty pizza box on the coffee table: living with Aeslin mice means never needing to worry that leaving food out will lead to cockroaches or other pests. The mice had picked the box completely clean before the cheese had a chance to congeal, and if they hadn't, they would have just viewed any insects the leftovers attracted as extra protein for them to hunt down and enjoy.

Who was I to deny the mice a little enrichment?

"This is fucking *bleak*, Val," said Malena, stopping at the built-in counter between the living room and kitchen. She dropped her duffel bag to the floor as she turned to face me, expression remaining flat and somewhat disturbed, like an older sibling looking in on a younger sibling's room and finding it in a total state of disarray. "Did you forget that humans need to keep their enclosures interesting if they don't want them to turn depressing?"

"Who's the human expert here, Malena?" I asked.

"That would normally be you, but since you're the one acting like you're trying to perform some sort of penance, I'm taking your title."

I sighed. "Can we stop sniping at each other and get to the part where you give me a hug and say you're glad to see me? Please?"

"Sure, Val." Malena bounced back across the living room with a spritely ease that would have been offense in my current condition coming from just about anybody else. She pulled me into a hug, which I gladly returned. She smelled of oil-treated leather and rose perfume, and her embrace was warmer than the human norm by at least five degrees.

I would still have taken her for human if I'd passed her on the street. Malena was a lean, muscular woman of apparently Mexican descent, with rich brown skin and frustratingly lush black hair that currently fell to her shoulders in a heavy wave. I'd seen her shed that hair like an unwanted hat, multiple times, and somehow it always grew back even healthier than it had been before. Just another deeply frustrating benefit of therianthropy.

She let me go and pulled back, smile fading into a look of deep concern. "Seriously, Val, you look like hammered shit."

I pointed at the great dome of my belly. "Hey, I'm pregnant. You can't talk to me like that."

"Really? I hadn't noticed." She folded her arms. "You've been wearing those clothes for at least two days. Three, if the chicken I smell was fresh when you ate it. You're not wearing any mascara, you're not moisturizing, and if you were trying to prove that you're a natural blonde, giving up on the idea of washing your hair does more than just confirm you don't need to get your roots done, so you know. You look exhausted, and like you're doing the absolute bare minimum to keep yourself standing while all this is going on. I know what happened to David. I'm so sorry, Val, I really am. But for your sake, and the sake of that pup you're incubating, I need you to get your head out of your ass and stop acting like you're both dead."

"You done?" I asked.

Malena paused, considering. "Think so," she finally said.

"Great. Who sent you?"

"Brenna Kelly."

That was *not* a name I'd been expecting to hear. I stopped moving and just blinked at her. "What?"

"Brenna Kelly. You know, tall, sexy, dragon princess, always sounds like she's trying to make up her mind whether you're just the cutest little schnookums she ever did see or her next bed-buddy; very blonde, very smart, very scary when she wants to be? That Brenna Kelly."

"*She* sent you."

"Yeah, well, something about the dragons of New York told her you were having a hard time of it, and she doesn't want to have to start working with a new negotiator when her Nest needs another male, and can I just say I'm glad that *my* species has never quite reached that level of endangered? Ugh, imagine needing to *pay* for boyfriends. But yeah, she called me and Pax both, told us you were in a bad way and offered to put us in touch with the Manhattan Nest so we could come and visit you."

"Wait." I turned to look suspiciously at the door. "Pax is here?"

"No, he sends his regards, but one of his wives is on the verge of pupping, and he didn't want to leave her." Malena shrugged. "You know, it's kinda fun—out of the three of us, your species is the only one that doesn't have pups. Isn't that funny?"

"I guess," I said, turning back to her. "I feel like it's probably more a sign that humanity won the linguistics fight in almost all languages, and we got to decide what things were called. But 'pup' is one of the more common terms for baby things, and it's one of the pretty positive ones, too. People like to hear about pups. Speaking of which, weren't you talking about pupping?"

Malena wasn't human, which I'm sure is pretty obvious by this point. She was a chupacabra, a shapeshifting synapsid that hadn't changed in any meaningful way since dinosaurs walked the earth—although I'm sure their "humanoid" form had looked pretty different before they had actual primates to emulate.

It's an interesting question, with the shapeshifters. Most evolved alongside or before humanity. Some, like the chupacabra, are classified as members of taxonomical families that died out before primates really got started. So what did they shapeshift into before we were around? Or have they always turned into things that could pass for human, and *we* were the ones trying to emulate *them* for our own protection? Maybe chupacabra didn't modify their forms to blend among the human population, humans evolved to blend into the chupacabra population.

It's an interesting question, and one that may never be answered, since at the end of the day, it's just not important enough to be worth inventing time travel to figure out.

Malena shrugged. "I negotiated a breeding," she said. "Only one litter, though, and he got raising privileges. So I laid his eggs and I left him to hatch them. When it's my turn to parent, I'm going to opt for live birth."

"It's not all it's cracked up to be," I said, and winced as the baby kicked me, hard, in one of my internal organs.

Malena frowned, seeing my expression change. "What's wrong?"

"Nothing. I just need to sit down." I relocked the door, then shuffled my way back to the kitchen to get my coffee before moving to sit on the couch. "Sit" may be a generous description for the way I basically folded up and collapsed, like I'd lost control of my joints.

I didn't spill my coffee. I still had enough control over myself to manage that, and I was briefly smug about it.

"So anyway, I'm here because Brenna asked me to be, and being a dragon, she followed her asking with an offer, and let's just say you have a full-time companion for the next six months, and I'm going to be able to afford to have that baby sooner than I'd been expecting to," said Malena, walking over to sit more gracefully on the other end of the couch. "You can object, but I wouldn't if I were you. This is the best offer you're going to get, and she wasn't wrong. You need someone to keep you from continuing with"— she waved a hand, indicating the entirety of me—"whatever this is. Like I said, you look like hell. That can't be good for the baby. You humans are pack animals. Where's your pack?"

"I'm fine," I muttered, feeling suddenly and—presumably accurately—judged.

"You're not, though," she insisted. "All primates need to be around other primates, especially when they're gravid. It's part of how you stay healthy. I used to think it was a weakness, but after laying my own eggs and trying to keep myself alive while I kept them safe and waited for my instincts to settle down enough that I could let anyone else near the nest, I think it's an advantage."

"I think being able to lay eggs would be an advantage," I said. "I didn't realize it was something you chose whether or not to do. How does that work?"

"Diet, mostly," said Malena. "And temperature. If you want to lay eggs, you have to force yourself to eat a bunch of bone shards and eggshells, and keep them down after you do. But it's easier to eat solid food when you're pregnant."

"Really?" I chuckled bitterly. "That's another place where humans and chupacabra are different, then. I'm having trouble keeping solids down. My bullet blender and I are basically engaged at this point."

"Good thing I brought my own," said Malena. "I'm a wizard at the all-liquid diet. You just tell me what you want to eat, and what the standard vitamin supplements for a pregnant human are, and I'll make sure you don't miss cooking."

I snorted. "Oh, you should open a smoothie bar with that as the slogan," I said. "Malena's Miracle Mixtures! New on the menu: mashed potatoes and slime."

"I make a really great potato leek soup," said Malena. "Chicken foam optional."

I shuddered, only somewhat theatrically. "Please never say those words in that order again," I said. "Remember, that's another thing about pregnant humans: we have a hair-trigger gag reflex, and I *will* barf all over your shoes."

"You will not!" She held up one foot for inspection, showing me her pristine sneaker. "*Some* of us remember how to wear shoes."

"Yeah, well, some of us can find our feet," I countered. "Just . . . tread lightly on the food subject, okay?"

"Yes, ma'am," said Malena.

Chupacabra aren't true sanguivores—they don't live on an all-blood diet, thankfully—but they do have a species-wide form of gastroparesis, making their digestion slow and making solid foods difficult for them. They excrete an enzyme in their saliva that breaks down most animal byproducts, making it possible for them to survive even when they don't have a blender close to hand.

Once you've seen a chupacabra merrily jam a straw into a tall glass of pureed liver and onions, you get a lot less squeamish about the other things they think of as food.

"Why is it easier for you to digest solid food while you're pregnant?" I asked.

"The hormones we produce make our stomachs work faster, and as long as we don't overdo it, we can handle more in the way of things that take time to digest without making ourselves sick." Malena shrugged. "I don't really understand the biology of it all. I'm sure you do."

"Not without some monitoring in a lab, and maybe a dissection or two," I said, trying to keep my words light.

Malena blinked at me. "Way to escalate, lady. You are *not* dissecting me. But maybe next time I lay a dud, we can discuss egg ownership."

That was more than we'd ever been able to get out of a chupacabra before. "Don't you normally eat those to recover the calcium?"

"Used to. But it turns out that when given the choice, it's easier to add a lot of calcium supplements to your smoothies than it is to eat your own unhatched babies. My grandmother says it's a sign that my generation hangs out around humans too much; we've picked up some of your attitudes, and it was better when we just thought of duds as, well, duds. Eggs that weren't meant to hatch. Only now we get all tangled up in questions about whether or not it's right to eat unhatched eggs, and it sort of sucks."

I blinked. "Huh." Humans place a lot of value on our offspring in part because making human babies is *hard*. We have a long gestation period and lots of things can go wrong while it's happening. It saps nutrients and energy from the mother, and even childbirth itself—relatively easy for most mammals—is fraught with dangers, and can end with both parties heading for the morgue instead of making a happy homecoming. It makes sense that species who take fewer risks during that time would place less importance on the process.

Not on the children themselves, once they exist. There's no known intelligent species that doesn't care about their children. Even the cuckoos care enough to abandon their babies in the best possible situations, trying to set them up to succeed in their brood parasitism. It may not be a form of care that looks super familiar to human eyes, but it's there.

"I thought you were going for live birth next time, anyway," I said.

Malena eyed my belly. "I may be changing my mind about that. How do you *sleep*?"

"Poorly. I have heartburn, like, *all* the time, and I have to pee every half hour or so. And the scary part is, compared to Livvy, this is the *easy* pregnancy."

"Really?" Malena asked, with delighted horror. She sounded like a kid being told a scary story.

"Yeah. With Livvy, I had something called gestational diabetes, which means my body basically forgot how to deal with sugar. I also had the *worst* cravings for, you guessed it, sugar."

"And you don't have that this time?"

"Nope. Turns out that's one of the side benefits of living close to Madhura. I already knew my bread wouldn't mold and my teeth wouldn't decay, but it turns out proximity also makes my body better at dealing with sugar. I'm taking Rochak with me if I ever move out of here."

Malena blinked. "Rochak being . . . ?"

"He's the older of our two resident Madhura. They both look like adults to me, but from the way he and his brother talk, it's pretty clear that Sunil is still considered a child. Two is enough, I don't need to adopt a third, no matter *how* good that makes my metabolism."

Malena blinked again. "And what are Madhura?"

"Oh. Right." There are dozens of species of human-form cryptids, which is a very humanocentric way of looking at it: why should we get to come first, when we've already established that other intelligences evolved before we did? Yet because I'm the one doing the describing, that's the lens I have to look through.

It wasn't a particular surprise that Malena didn't know what a Madhura was. They're a relatively uncommon species in North America, originally from the Indian subcontinent, and they tend to be pretty insular when they do settle here, preferring the company of their hives. There was no specific reason that Malena, as a chupacabra, would ever have encountered them.

"They're sort of . . . bee-people," I said, after a pause to collect my thoughts. "At least, we think they evolved from bees, given various aspects of their biology. That would make them closer to the Johrlac than anything else we know of, but since we know the Johrlac originated in another dimension . . ."

"Wait. We know that?"

"We do." I shrugged. Sometimes I forget that not everyone knows what's considered common knowledge in my family. "They came here centuries ago, after they got chased out of the last dimension they totally screwed up. You remember my cousin Sarah?"

"Vaguely."

"Well, she's a Johrlac, and they tried to turn her into their apocalypse maiden to blow a hole in the side of reality so they could all escape to the next dimension down the line."

Malena gave me a hard look. "You shouldn't say things like that as if they were perfectly reasonable. They're *not* reasonable, in the slightest. Does this have something to do with what happened in Iowa?"

I nodded. "Yeah. Sarah channeled the power the Johrlac gave her, and used it to transplant an entire college campus into another dimension. She took my baby sister with her. That was one of the scariest things I've ever had to deal with. We're still not sure my cousin Artie actually came back."

Malena blinked, slowly. "Your family is . . . a lot," she finally said. "Like, that is almost too much for me to deal with in one sitting, and from the way you said it, it's like a third of the story, tops. Can we get back to the Madhura?"

"Right. Bee-people from India, they look human, they tend to live in family groups called 'hives,' they mostly live on honey and other sweet substances, and their presence slows decay. They're pretty friendly, and most people regard them as harmless. Sunil and Rochak own a bakery near here, where they used to work with their sister. She died. Last time I had a chance to really talk to Rochak, he said they were negotiating with a hive in India to bring over two females of their species as prospective brides. Getting an apartment in this building was part of the negotiating process."

Malena lifted an eyebrow. "Oh?"

"If Brenna sent you to find me, you know the dragons own this apartment building," I said. "It's rent-controlled and reasonable enough that I'm sure it causes them physical pain to think about how much more they could be charging per unit. I'm the only human here."

"How many units?"

"Twenty-three."

"Doesn't that make the place a massive target? I know you're dealing with Covenant incursions out here . . ."

"They've backed off a lot since my sister—the one who went to Iowa—helped my cousin Sarah blow up a big part of their main training facility. I think their numbers took more of a hit than they want us to realize. Even apart from that, this place has been here for ages, and the dragons keep a low profile. I think we're okay, as long as whatever ridiculous system they're using to filter out human applicants without being caught by the city doesn't set off any red flags."

"If you're sure."

I sighed heavily. "Malena, I'm a widow, and I'm eight months pregnant. I haven't been able to dance for months. I'm *exhausted*. I didn't know it was possible to be this tired without being dead. I can't start worrying about whether or not the building is safe, or I'll just give up."

"Aw, Val . . . I'm sorry this is all so hard for you, and I'm sorry about David."

That was the alias Dominic had been using when Malena met him, pretending to be the boyfriend of Valerie Pryor, who had nothing in her life to worry about more important than the question of whether she was going to become America's favorite dancer. I rubbed my stomach, trying to soothe the baby now using my kidneys for soccer practice. "His name was Dominic," I said. "He died trying to keep me and this city safe, and the people who killed him probably never realized that he had been one of their own before we met."

"What do you mean?"

"We never got around to giving you his full backstory before. I'm sorry. It wasn't strictly relevant, and it felt like there was a chance that if I explained too much, you'd stop being willing to help us, and decide you'd be better off leaving us to our own devices. Dominic and I met here in New York. He was in town with a Covenant strike team, assessing the city for a purge. Instead, he found me, and wound up turning traitor to his own people, running away with me, and getting married."

Malena blinked, so slowly and deliberately that I saw her nictating membrane as it slid across the eyeball, giving the gesture an unnervingly reptilian quality. "To his own people," she echoed. "Meaning he was Covenant before he married you."

"Yeah."

"You married a man from the Covenant of St. George."

"Yup."

"And you didn't tell me."

"At first it was to keep you working with us, and then it just never seemed like the right time. By the time he met you, he had well and truly cut all ties with his past. Sarah—that's the Johrlac cousin I was talking about before—"

"I met her once."

"Right, I forgot. Well, Sarah scrambled the brains of his former teammates to make sure they wouldn't know him if they saw him, and he stood back and let it happen, because he wasn't one of them any longer. He walked away from the Covenant. He did it for me." I paused, pressing a hand against the curve of my stomach and looking down at it, at the son he would never have the opportunity to know. "He chose me over everything he'd been raised to believe was true, everything he'd expected to devote his life to, and he never said he was sorry. Not even when we fought, not even when it would have been easy for him to regret his decision. He chose me, and he kept choosing me, and he died because the people who would have known him once couldn't recognize him when he was right in front of them. They slit his throat and let him fall, and he was dead before he hit the ground."

"That sucks, Val, I'm sorry," said Malena, awkwardly.

"Yeah, I'm sorry too," I said, and pushed myself out of the couch, rising unsteadily to my feet. "I'm sorry, and I'm tired as hell. You can sleep on the couch, or I can help you find a place to stay while you're here in town, but for right now, I need to go lay down. I'm exhausted."

"Okay," said Malena. "Just . . . take care of what you need, and I'll take care of myself, okay?"

"Sure," I said, already beginning to shuffle away. "You can eat anything in the fridge. Just don't eat any of the mice, please."

"I would *never*," said Malena, sounding affronted. "We're friends, your weird little rodent roommates and me. I don't eat my friends."

"Cool."

I didn't look back as I reached my bedroom door and let myself inside.

Dominic and I had been living with the dragons in the slaughterhouse Nest, which had been destroyed in an open Covenant offensive. Almost all our possessions had burned up in the aftermath, and at the time, I'd been furious. Now, it seemed like a small blessing. My bed was too big, too empty, and too cold, but all those things were general: none of them were specifically because Dominic wasn't there. He had never slept in this bed, never nestled under these covers or put his head down on these pillows. It was a blank space, a new start for me and our children, and his ghost didn't haunt every single thing I did.

I waddled to the side of the bed and sat, rolling myself into the nest of pillows I had been assembling in my efforts to remain as comfortable as I possibly could when my body was doing its best to rebel against me and snuggling down.

I didn't manage to pull the blanket over myself before my eyes closed and I fell into an almost immediate slumber.

✦ ✦ ✦

"Excuse me, miss, are you free for this dance?"

I put down my glass of champagne—sweet and airy, served in a flute rimmed with frosting and edible glitter—to flash a smile at the handsome gallant who was offering me his hand. His hair and eyes were dark, and I had the distinct feeling that I knew him from somewhere, even though I couldn't have possibly told you his name. Several of the mice who'd been using the table's supply of gingerbread to build themselves a castle swept over and carried my glass away, adding it to the supplies they were stockpiling inside their baked palace.

"I am," I said, and slid my hand into his, and he pulled me to my feet. My clothes changed as we moved, becoming perfectly suited to the waltz the band was now beginning. My dress was a long, shimmering sweep of fondant and gelatin, while my glass slippers were boiled sugar, clear and pure as anything.

He smiled at me, resplendent in his own licorice tuxedo, and together we curved elegantly into the first turn, his hand cupping my waist, my hand resting lightly on his shoulder.

"You look beautiful tonight, Verity," he said. "But where's David?"

I blinked, trying to understand both how this stranger knew

my name and who this "David" could possibly be. We spun around the dance floor, and he frowned, and I ached to see such sorrow on his face, to know that I had somehow been the one to put it there.

"Verity," he repeated, "where's David?"

"I'm sorry, sir, but I don't know who you're talking about," I said. "I know several Davids, but none of them are at the party tonight. Do you mean the man who owns the bodega down the block?"

"No. Silly girl, no." He shook his head. "I mean our son. He'll be out in the world and endangering himself soon enough, but right now, he's meant to be with you, always. Where's David?"

I glanced down at my flat midsection, ringed in sugar and familiar as it had ever been. "I don't know what you . . ." I froze. Oh, I was still dancing, still allowing myself to be moved through the familiar steps and gestures of the waltz, which I knew so well that I could dance it in my sleep, but that was automatic motion, my body operating without my order. What mattered of me was frozen, locked under a veil of confusion so thick that it might as well have been ice.

My partner leaned closer, his lips a hand's breadth from my face as he murmured, "You know what I mean, my sweet girl. You have always known what I meant. It's time for you to wake up now."

"I don't want to," I said. I wanted this. A beautiful ballroom decked in spun sugar and edible glitter, where the mice formed a living centerpiece on every table and my dead husband could lead me around the dance floor, his skin warm against mine, his feet keeping perfect time to the rhythm of the band. I wanted a dream. Reality was too grim, and nothing like I had expected it to be. Reality was swollen ankles and aching kidneys, and loneliness so vast I was afraid it might come alive and swallow the world.

"You have to," he said, and kissed my forehead before shoving me backward, away from him. I stumbled, my heel catching on a fold in the rug, and tumbled into a pool of frosting like quicksand.

The mice cheered as I was dragged down to who-knows-where, and continued cheering as the frosting filled my mouth, as I thrashed and shouted and gagged and—

✦   ✦   ✦

—woke up sitting up in bed, both hands clasped across my midsection, baby still kicking like anything, and the mice still cheering in the distance. That was what had broken through the veils of sleep to wake me, aching eyes and all. I swiped at my cheeks with one hand as I swung my legs around to stand. I'd been crying in my sleep again. That wasn't uncommon anymore. Since losing Dominic, I'd woken up in tears more times than I had bothered to count—although the mice could probably have given me an exact number, if I'd ever asked them.

I had no intention of asking. Some information is good, and some information is a gateway to despair. This seemed like the second kind.

As I levered myself out of the bed, a small voice from the dresser said, "Hail to the Waking of the Arboreal Priestess, although did the Well-Groomed Priestess not once Say, 'Allow the Pregnant Ones to Sleep as much as they may, for they will have Less of it When the baby comes'?"

"You don't need to quote the scriptures at me," I said, somewhat more sourly than the poor mouse deserved. They were just trying to take care of me, in their intrusive little rodent way. "I know them. I've been hearing them my whole life. And this isn't my first baby."

"We are Well Aware, Priestess," said the mouse. "We mean no Offense. We seek only to Advise and Inspire, that the next generation of the Divine may enter the world under the Best of Circumstances."

"Too late on that one," I said sourly, and shuffled out of the room.

Malena was sitting on the couch—again, not still, as the kitchen smelled like fresh-cooked steak and cheesy risotto—with a small army of Aeslin mouse surrounding her. Most were on the coffee table or the couch itself, but a fair number were sitting on her knees and the arm she had draped casually over the back of the couch, all watching her raptly.

"Welcome back, Sleeping Beauty," she called. "Hope you don't mind, but once I figured out you'd be asleep for a while, I went ahead and made with dinner. I figured you'd be hungry when you woke up."

"You figured correctly," I said, giving the air an appreciative sniff. My stomach rumbled rather than revolted, which was a good sign. "That smells amazing."

"Steak, asparagus, risotto. And I have sour cream and butter, and some really nice herb paste that helps it all blend harmoniously."

The rumbling stopped, replaced by the first stirrings of what might be mutiny. "Meaning . . ."

"Meaning I can puree the whole mess and it'll still be delicious. Trust me, and think of it as a really interesting cream soup." Malena smiled winningly. "You need to eat and keep it down, and I am here to help with that impossible combination."

"I don't know . . ." I'd been blending my food into unappetizing pastes for weeks. The thought of having it blended into an *appetizing* paste was less enticing than it was alien and impossible. But she seemed so sure that it was possible, and I was so damn tired of being hungry all the time. "Fine, I guess. But I'm going to try chewing it first."

"Deal," she said, far too cheerfully for my tastes. "And on that note, mice, you've been wonderful company, but it's time for me to feed your divinity."

The mice cheered. They'd been more worried about my inability to eat than I had, which made sense, given how food-oriented they were as a colony.

Malena bounced up from the couch with an ease I envied, after giving the mice a moment to get down from her arm and off her knees. "You really need to go shopping," she informed me, as she waved me toward the apartment's small dining area. It was really just a part of the living room separated by a tiny half-wall, and there was no table there normally, but she had managed to find a folding card table somewhere while I was asleep, and had it set up and waiting for us, along with two collapsible chairs that looked, frankly, like they'd been snatched out of one of the neighborhood dumpsters.

Two plates were already waiting there, each with a small portion of the three parts of what would be our dinner. "If you want to sit and start, I'll go get to blending," she said.

"You don't have a lot of faith in my ability to chew, huh?"

"I have absolutely zero faith in *my* ability to chew. Yours is irrelevant." Malena grinned. "Besides, I want to show off my mastery of the blender. You wouldn't rob a poor sweet chupacabra of her signature joy when she's just come all this way to see you, would you?"

"No," I said, waving a hand for her to get on with it as I sat down at the table and pulled the small plate toward myself. "I'm not waiting for you, though."

"Wasn't expecting you to," she said cheerfully, and returned to the kitchen.

Everything was perfectly cooked, hot and ready and delicious, and I managed three bites of the risotto before I had to admit defeat. Solids and I were still not on speaking terms. "I don't know what you have against chewed food," I informed the dome of my belly, "but you are not going to spend your entire childhood living off of smoothies, so you better get over it now."

"Trying to reason with an unhatched pup is a recipe for insanity," said Malena, walking back into the room with a tumbler in either hand. There was a colorful straw in each glass. She looked at them as she set the glasses down, careful to put the one with the blue straw in front of me.

"What are the straw colors for?" I asked, reaching for my blended dinner.

"Your steak was cooked," she said. "Human fetuses don't react well to raw meat."

"Neither do human digestive systems, under most circumstances," I said.

"I know. You're all vulnerable to parasites and stuff. What is up with that?" She sat down and picked up her own tumbler. "Bottoms up."

"Evolution said we had too much going for us already and didn't need a generalized immunity to roundworm," I said, before taking a cautious sip. Then I stopped, and just blinked at the brownish sludge she'd served me.

"What? What's wrong?" Malena sat up straighter. "I only used things I knew it was safe for pregnant humans to eat, and I got a list of your allergies from Brenna, there shouldn't be any issues—"

"Are you secretly a fucking *Wonka*?" I asked. "I know—I *know*—this is just a slurry of all the things I couldn't bring myself to swallow on their own. But it tastes amazing, and I find that upsetting on a genuinely visceral level. This shouldn't be possible. You know it shouldn't be possible, and I know it shouldn't be possible, and can you stay forever?"

"I was already planning to stay for the rest of your pregnancy," said Malena, easily. "Humans have a gestation period of roughly nine months, and I could use the break."

"What have you been up to?"

"Teaching, mostly. One of my cousins has a dance studio, and he was delighted to hire a reality television star to help guide the kiddos through their first forays into the wonderful world of ballroom dance." She took a sip of her own steak smoothie, and smiled smugly. "Yeah, that did come out good, didn't it? Could use a little bit more rosemary, but I didn't want to get too aggressive with you before I knew where your limits were right now."

"I really do mean it when I say you can stay, but you should be aware that means sleeping on the couch," I said. "I can't offer you my bed—I'm too pregnant for that, no matter how polite it would be. And the second room is going to be the baby's, once he gets here and I finish putting the crib together."

"I thought you humans liked to keep your infants in the room with you immediately after birth."

"Don't chupacabra do that?"

"Fuck, no. The little bastards hatch with a full set of teeth ready to go, and they're fast. No one who enjoys having skin sleeps in a room with a bunch of baby chupacabra."

"I see. Yeah, we like to keep the babies near us when they first come out, and I have a special bassinet for that. But he'll only be small enough to sleep in it for a few months, and then he'll need his own space." Privately, I was glad there was a physical limiter on keeping him in the room with me. I knew myself well enough to know that I'd get way too attached way too quickly if I let myself. For everyone's sanity, I needed him to have his own space.

Malena frowned, cocking her head. "Two bedrooms, and I get the couch while I'm visiting. Where are you planning to put Olivia? Where *is* Olivia?" Her eyes widened slightly, and I could almost see her putting the pieces she had together in the wrong order, leading her toward a devastating conclusion.

We didn't need any misunderstandings. The truth was bad enough.

"She's in Portland, with my parents," I said. "We got her out of the city before Dominic . . . before. They're taking good care of her."

"Don't you think she should be here with you?"

"I don't think *I* should be here with me right now," I said. "If I had a way to birth this baby and hand him to my parents immediately, I'd do it. But I can't. Infants need their mothers, and my boobs hurt, and I'm damn well going to give him everything I can to make sure he has the best start possible."

"Val . . ."

"My name's Verity, not Valerie," I snapped. "My husband died, I'm very tired and very sad, and I don't think I can take care of a baby right now, much less a baby and a small child. If I could, I wouldn't have dragons sending people to make sure I could keep us both alive."

Malena looked at me sadly. It made me want to scream and flip the plate whose contents I couldn't eat into the air. I didn't. I just sat there, shoulders tight, and returned her look with my own, trying to telegraph how much pain I was in without needing to come out and say it.

Instead, she took a sip from her own smoothie, and asked, "When was the last time you had a shower?"

"A week ago." My voice dropped, embarrassment overwriting anger. "I'm too afraid of falling to shower when there's no one else in the apartment."

"Great. So tonight's assignment is to get you clean, and then I'll do your toenails for you, and you'll feel better in the morning."

I blinked. "You're staying?"

"What, you thought you'd get a little bitchy and I'd be out the door? Valerie, *please*. I've seen you after a seven-hour rehearsal, when your feet were on fire and you were muttering about pulling people's spines out through their noses. I'm not Lyra. I know you don't have as much reason to trust me as you did her, but please believe me when I say that I care about your well-being, and while Brenna may have asked me to come, she didn't have a way to force me. I'm here because I want to be."

"Stop it, or you're going to make me cry," I said, swiping at my cheeks. "These stupid hormones have me all over the place."

"I won't tell if you don't." She smiled warmly. "Now drink your dinner."

✦ ✦ ✦

Several hours later, I sat at the card table again, clean and running a brush idly through my hair while Malena unloaded the small dishwasher into the cupboard above the sink. I'd tried to protest her doing the dishes, but she'd ignored me, and ordered me to sit down while she took care of the post-dinner cleanup.

She glanced my way, sliding a plate into the cupboard with the others. "How long's it been since you did the dishes?"

"As long as I could find a clean spoon, I didn't figure it mattered all that much."

"Uh-huh. As I was getting around to earlier, you realize you're going to have to move after the baby comes, right?"

I blinked at her, slowly lowering my brush. "Why? The dragons don't have a problem with infants, and the soundproofing in the walls is good enough that I shouldn't upset my neighbors."

"You can't refuse to bring your daughter home forever, Val. It's not good for either one of you. She knows her father's gone. There's no way she doesn't know. Let her grieve with you. Don't let her think you blame her, or that you're replacing her with the new baby."

"I thought chupacabra didn't do human-style family groups."

"Not with parents, so much, but we have extended networks of older relatives who help to raise and care for the pups as they transition into children. My mother negotiated placement of her eggs with my father's family, and *his* mother handled most of the work of raising me. She liked children, and so did he, and so did his two sisters, and all the other aunties and uncles in our den.

Not all female chupacabra are temperamentally suited to child-rearing. He told me my mother was one of those."

"Okay."

"But when I was eleven, I met her. She recognized the smell of me as being kin, and after she figured out *how* we were related, she introduced me to the pups she'd cared about enough to keep. The ones she'd wanted."

"But . . . didn't you say you'd given your first clutch of eggs to their father?"

"Yes, and I visit them, and he never told them I didn't want them, or that I was never going to raise children of my own. Our ways are our ways. It wouldn't have hurt so much if I hadn't believed that she wasn't suited to parenting. *All* my pups will know the reasons they are where they are, whether they call me mama or amma."

I didn't know for sure, but I could guess that "amma" meant "noncustodial birth parent." I frowned, looking down at my hairbrush.

"Do you really think Livvy will feel like I blame her if I don't bring her home?"

"You sent her away when her father died, and you're keeping her at arm's length. You have good reasons—no one's contesting that—but the timing has got to be eating at her. And you can't ask her to share a room with a newborn baby. That's not fair to anybody involved."

I sighed heavily. "So I have to move."

"Look at it this way—it's not like you've done a lot in the way of nesting so far." Malena shrugged broadly, indicating the barely furnished apartment with the spread of her arms. "And you have enough friends that you can probably get it done same day, if you ask."

"The hard part is going to be convincing Candice to let me out of my lease," I said glumly.

Malena laughed. "She's not letting you out of your lease."

I blinked. "What?"

"A human apartment manager who understands how to navigate human bureaucracy? You're worth your weight in gold to those dragons, and they know it. I'll be surprised if they charge you more for moving into a larger place."

"You'll be surprised if *dragons* want to charge me more."

"I will." Malena looked at me levelly, and smiled. "You've done a lot for that species, and they help their friends. That help may not always take a form humans can easily understand, but it exists. Just call Candy and tell her you need a three-bedroom. Maybe that way I don't have to sleep on the couch until I wind up paying a chiropractor."

There were a few three-room units in the building, and at least one of them was currently open. And because of the quasi-legal way the dragons handled listings, there wasn't a wait list of anything. Actually, the unit had been open for the better part of a month, since the harpies who'd been living there left for Colorado, citing a need for wider skies and fewer power lines. Their chicks were reaching the age where they needed to fly for their physical and mental health. It was a pity; they'd been good tenants.

Candice had mentioned the apartment to me several times when we met about other issues in the building, never with any implication that she was looking for someone to rent it out. I blinked.

"I think she already knows that," I said.

"Does she?"

"Yeah. I think everyone knew it but me." I sighed and looked down at my brush again. "This has been hard."

"I know, Val. Losing someone is always hard. But David wouldn't want you to sit around moping forever. He'd want you to take care of yourself, and take care of the babies he made with you. We live on through our children. Help him stay alive."

"I'll try."

The mice, who had been eavesdropping shamelessly, cheered.

I rolled my eyes. "You sure you won't let me help you with anything?" I asked.

Before Malena could answer me, the phone rang. Part of my rental agreement required me to have a landline the other occupants of the building could use to reach me. I shoved myself out of my seat and waddled toward the sound, waving her off as she leaned toward it. This was my job, and most of the other tenants were understandably anxious when it came to new people in their space. With the Covenant in town and a human in the building, they had good reason to be careful about who they talked to.

I picked up the receiver, cradling it between my cheek and my shoulder. "Hello?"

"Ms. Price? This is Roz, down in unit 1A. There's something wrong with the pipes."

"I'll call the building handyman."

"No, I don't mean— They still work, and they're not leaking, but the water that comes out of them is . . . well, it's moving. I don't think Carl can fix this."

I blinked. "Moving?"

"Yes. Moving, around the bottom of my sink."

"Have you tried talking to it? It could be an undine who got sucked into the city water supply."

"It doesn't seem to want to talk. It tried to grab my hand."

"That sounds . . . bad."

"I'm not a fan!"

I looked to Malena. "I'll be right down. I've got a friend with me. Don't worry if I show up with someone you don't recognize."

"Hurry," she said, and hung up.

I set the receiver gently back into the cradle, looking to Malena. "Looks like we're going to be making a house call," I said.

"I'll get your shoes."

We left the apartment to the sound of the phone ringing again, seeming suddenly ominous.

✦ ✦ ✦

Fortunately, while the dragons had never met a corner they wouldn't happily cut, they actually cared about their tenants and, more, about how their treatment of said tenants would impact their standing in the cryptid community. They could have tripled their passive income from this building by renting to humans instead and treating them the way human landlords would, but they didn't. They kept renting to cryptids, and they kept the rents low, and they made steady, reliable improvements to the building to guarantee their comfort.

All of which was a long-winded way of saying that the building had a working elevator less than ten yards from the door of my apartment, one which was spacious and well-lit enough to be comfortable. I got in, closely followed by Malena, and hit the button for the ground floor.

The doors closed smoothly, and she turned to look at me. "This happen often?"

I shook my head. "Not particularly. Plumbing is Carl's problem."

"And Carl is . . . ?"

"Bogeyman. His apartment's in the basement." It was always dark down there, and distressingly echoey, thanks to the total lack of insulation. Cold, too. Perfect bogey territory, in other words. Sometimes I think they must be doing it on purpose, leading into an Addams aesthetic to convince themselves that they don't mind being reduced to "the monster in the closet" while their close cousins, humanity, have free run of the planet. But if it is a conscious choice, it's not hurting anyone, and I sort of enjoy their ongoing horror-movie approach to life.

"He handles the plumbing?"

"He handles everything that breaks in this building. If he can't fix it, he explains to me why he can't, and I call William. William either authorizes calling outside help, or he sends Candice. When he sends Candice, she spends a few hours with Carl, being convinced that we really need the outside help, and then we call them anyway. The dragons are surprisingly good about paying for improvements to the property. Candice says she's just keeping up their investment, but the elevator is never broken for more than a few hours, and we have some tenants who can't do stairs. I think she cares more than she wants to let on."

"A lot of people care more than they want to let on," Malena agreed.

The elevator dinged, doors opening on the ground-floor hallway. There were five units down here, all of them currently occupied, and the air smelled of roasting chicken and boiled cabbage. Good, clean, apartment smells. I sniffed appreciatively as I waved for Malena to follow me down the hall to Roz's door.

I paused before knocking, glancing back to Malena. "Roz is a lesser gorgon. She knows we're coming, so she should be wearing her glasses, but you need to be chill about the snakes," I said.

Malena nodded.

I knocked.

The door opened a few seconds later, Roz's narrow, worried face appearing in the gap. The snakes atop her head were writhing in agitation, hissing continuously, and some of them flashed their fangs when they saw me, threatening without pulling back to strike. She was wearing her tinted glasses, which would keep her gaze from stunning us, and as soon as she saw that it was me, she stepped back and began making gentle patting gestures at her hair, trying to calm it down.

"Verity! And . . . friend. Please, come in, both of you." She stepped aside, letting us in.

Roz's apartment was one of the one-bedroom layouts, barely

large enough for her two cats to exist without playing out a constant war between themselves. The larger of the two watched us from the dining room table as we entered the apartment, triangular ears pressed flat. Malena looked at the cat and raised an eyebrow. The cat fled for the rear of the apartment, sprinting out of sight in a brown-and-tan blur.

"Bernie!" said Roz, sounding exasperated. She turned to Malena. "I'm sorry. She doesn't like new people very much—or at all—but she's not normally that hostile."

"I'm a chupacabra," said Malena, with a shrug. She glanced at me. "I would normally be a little more circumspect about that, but you're not wearing a wig, so I figured that meant we were all friends here. Anyway, cats don't like chupacabra, as a rule, because we're bigger predators than they are, and they can respect that, while also wanting nothing to do with it."

Something meowed by our feet, and I looked down in time to see a smaller, darker cat rub up against Malena's ankles, tail held at a high, jaunty angle.

Roz coughed to hide her laughter. "You were saying?"

"Cats don't like me," said Malena, sounding faintly stunned. She bent to pick up the darker cat, holding it under the arms, so that its hind legs dangled. It looked at her with trusting green eyes, starting to purr. "I think this one is broken."

"That's Ursal," said Roz. "He likes everyone, has no sense of self-preservation, and likes to pounce on my snakes when I'm laying down. He's going to get himself bitten one of these days." She smiled, leaning over to take her cat back from Malena. He continued purring, even as he balled up in her arms.

"Weird," said Malena.

"Fascinating, but I am ridiculously pregnant, and standing around like this is hurting my knees," I said. "Can you show us the sink?"

"Of course," said Roz. "This way." She waved for us to follow as she turned and walked toward the kitchen, still carrying the world's friendliest cat.

Friendly until she stepped over the threshold into the kitchen. Then Ursal puffed up like he'd been hit with an electric prod, hissing angrily, and jumped down from her arms, following the first cat into the depths of the apartment.

"They don't like whatever's going on with the water," said Roz.

I hadn't even seen what she was describing, and I didn't like what was going on with the water. She led us to the sink and gestured for us to look.

I leaned forward, trying not to get too close. There was something small and gelatinous huddled in one corner of the sink. It was almost clear but had a reddish tint that made the back of my brain itch, like I should know what this was. I frowned, resisting the urge to lean closer.

Malena wasn't that careful. She leaned in, getting as close a look as she could without actually sticking her head into the sink. "You say that came out of the tap?" she asked. "Because if it did, you need to have a serious talk with your landlord about fixing the filters."

"Yeah, we're gonna do that," I said, leaning back a bit. "Malena, maybe don't get so close?"

The gelatinous lump quivered, pulling back on itself like it was trying to gather its strength. Then, with surprising speed, it lashed out at Malena, falling roughly a foot shy of hitting her face.

Her face. Where her eyes were. My own eyes widened as I realized what this had to be, and I grabbed her by the shoulders, yanking her away from the sink. She gave me a shocked look.

"What?"

"That's an alkabyiftiris slime," I said. "They're not supposed to be found this close to civilization, or in urban areas, but that's what it is. I don't know if that's the whole thing, or if it's part of a larger slime, but either way, you *don't* want to let it touch you."

"Why not?"

"Because I'm assuming you don't want to have your body taken over by a caustic slime mold that will gradually consume everything you are, and use you as a vehicle to get at other potential prey. This one has already had something small to eat—that's the reddish tinge in the body. Given its size, probably roaches or maybe a rat or something that didn't know to get out of the way. When these things get big enough, they can eat humans and bears and even moose. And by 'eat,' I mean 'hollow them out and drive them around.'" I shook my head. "We should all get out of this kitchen, and Roz, you want to keep your cats away from the sink. Thankfully, it's small, and the sink is stainless steel, which means it won't be able to climb the sides as easily as it might otherwise. But you need to leave it alone."

"What are you going to do?" asked Roz, sounding horrified. That was probably the appropriate response.

"You're going to stay here, keeping all the water turned off for right now—and I know this is gross, but if you need to pee, pee in the bathtub. We don't know how many of the building's water sources this thing can come in through." I found myself suddenly thinking of all the other tenants, quite a few of whom had children. Children were the perfect vehicle for an immature or fragmentary alkabyiftiris slime. Small enough to take over easily, big enough to open doors and carry the slime wherever it wanted to go.

I shuddered and turned to Malena. "Come on. We need to go talk to Carl."

She nodded and followed me out of the apartment, leaving Roz to wring her hands and eye the sink with justified suspicion.

✦ ✦ ✦

The elevator groaned and complained as it descended the additional floor to Carl's basement apartment, a series of sounds that

I was quite sure Carl himself had orchestrated. The elevator ran smooth and easy throughout the rest of the building, and started behaving like something out of a horror movie as soon as it was asked to go below street level. The lights even flickered.

"Very funny, *Carl*," I said, eyes turned toward the elevator ceiling. The creaks and groans continued.

"Is this safe?" asked Malena.

"Oh, it's safe," I said. "Bogeymen have their ways of rigging technology to discourage people from poking around where they aren't wanted. I'm sure Carl is just trying to enforce some boundaries."

The elevator stopped with a ding, and the doors slid open on a dark hall. I stepped out, every hair on my arms suddenly standing at attention as my mammalian instincts shrieked that I was making a terrible, potentially fatal mistake. I ran a hand along my arm to smooth the hair back down and turned to look at Malena, illuminated by the light from the still-open elevator. She looked as unsettled as I felt. Her hair was spikier than it had been, rearranging itself into scaly plates, and her hands looked like they were beginning to contort into claws.

"Carl's an older man, and a half-transformed chupacabra crashing into his apartment will probably give him a heart attack," I said. "Any outside plumber we call at this hour will charge triple time, minimum, and the dragons will be *pissed*. Think you can try to rein it in until he knows we're here?"

"Did he not hear the elevator?" Her voice was rendered slightly mushy by her now-larger incisors and canine teeth, better suited to a muzzle than her current flat humanoid face. She sighed and shook her head. "I can stop it here. Anxiety shifts aren't a major issue for anyone past puberty."

"Good. This way." I pulled out my phone, turning on the flashlight app, and started down the hall toward the door to Carl's apartment. "There are normally at least a few working lightbulbs around here. I guess he must have taken them out for some reason."

"Okay, so your building handyman has taken out all the lightbulbs, and there's a mini blob monster in the sink upstairs."

"It's not a blob. It's an alkabyiftiris slime."

"Does it have bones or an exoskeleton?"

"No."

"Does it dissolve and devour its prey?"

"Yes."

"'Blob monster' works for me. Only this is a blob monster that likes to carjack its victims before it finishes eating them. Does it like dark spaces?"

"Alkabyiftiris slime is most active at night. It's a sort of slime mold, and it doesn't care much for direct sunlight or really bright lights of any sort."

"Uh-huh. Anyone else here feel like we should turn around and run the hell away, or is it just me?"

Before I could answer her, something shuffled in the hall ahead of us. I aimed my flashlight in that direction, holding it at roughly waist height to avoid shining it in Carl's eyes. Instead, it hit him at his own waist, illuminating brown trousers and an untucked, stained plaid shirt. Streaks of slime gleamed on his clothing, clearly wet. He made a rattling noise.

I raised the flashlight beam, catching a glimpse of his face, complete with white staring eyes like poached eggs, and streaks of slime running along his cheeks and oozing from his ears and the corners of his eyes. He opened his mouth, making that rattling noise again, and I fumbled behind me with my free hand. "Run," I said, softly.

"What?" asked Malena.

"Grab my hand, and *run.*" If she dragged me, I'd be able to move faster, despite the general condition of my legs and feet. "*Now,* please, while we're still ourselves."

"Got it." She grabbed my hand and bolted back toward the elevator. I forced my reluctant body to turn and stumble along after her, fighting gravity the entire way. My hips and back shrieked at the abuse, but I managed to remain upright as she pulled me along, until we were back at the elevator doors, Carl shuffling behind us, Malena hammering her fist against the call button.

I put a hand on my stomach, struggling to catch my breath. Then the doors opened and she yanked me inside. I turned back to the hall in time to see the elevator doors close in Carl's slime-streaked face, shutting him outside.

"Okay," I gasped. "Good thing: I doubt the alkabyiftiris slime knows how to operate the elevator, and Carl wasn't really trying to catch us, which means he's still in there enough to be resisting."

"Is there any getting him back from this?" asked Malena, an edge of panic in her voice that I didn't care for very much. It's easy to panic when you run into something out of a horror movie. All the stories tell us that panic is probably a good idea, and that if we run fast enough, we can get away from whatever it is that's chasing us.

They don't point out that anyone who *didn't* get away won't be writing their story down for others to take notes from, or that statistically, most people who run get chased. I gave Malena a stern look.

"Breathe," I said. "Getting Carl back—no, probably not. He was far enough gone, just looking at him, that he's probably already as good as dead. If we can get him to St. Giles's, they might be able to scrape enough slime out of his system that he'll be able to say goodbye to his loved ones. My concern right now needs to be the rest of the building."

Malena stared at me. "That's *cold*, Val."

"Always take care of the living before you take care of the dead, and if you aren't sure which category someone falls into, always take care of the most people you possibly can." The elevator reached the ground floor and stopped. I leaned over and cracked the shield on the emergency stop before flipping the switch. The elevator alarm began to ring, shrill and insistent.

Malena hissed between her teeth and glared at me. "What did you do that for?"

"I don't *think* alkabyiftiris slime knows how to operate the elevator, but seeing more food could motivate it to learn," I said. "Carl has a lot of prefrontal cortex to consume, and to be quite honest, no one's sure how much the slime can actually learn from its victims, versus how much it can make things seem like a good idea. I'm betting Carl didn't wake up going 'Hmm I should remove all the in-building filters so this slime monster that's eating all my soft bits can spread more easily through the pipes.' Something had to suggest it to him."

"Slime doesn't have a brain. How can it *think*?"

"Science is full of fun little mysteries like that, that aren't actually fun for anyone except for possibly the science itself," I said. "Regardless, we need Carl to stay in the basement. I can lock the stairwell door from here, and the elevator will only be out of commission until I reset the emergency switch, which I can do from the manager's office on this floor."

My feet hurt, my knees ached, and I had never needed to pee so badly in my entire life. I almost wanted to laugh at the dubious look on Malena's face, which seemed to imply that she was surprised I had a solution that didn't require me to climb stairs. Oh she of little faith.

"Okay. So what are we going to do now?"

"Back to Roz's apartment. Come on." I started waddling down the hall, pausing halfway there to lock the door leading to the basement stairs, then continuing onward to Roz's apartment. Malena paced me, patches of black and orange scales appearing and disappearing on her arms as her body attempted to shift under the stress.

Roz opened the door almost as soon as I finished knocking, the snakes on her head hissing wildly. About half of them were looking back toward the kitchen, while the rest focused on us as the intruders into their territory.

"Hey, Roz," I said.

"How's Carl?" she asked.

I shook my head. "He probably encountered the slime somewhere down in the sewers, and carried it back here before he knew he was infected. He's not dead yet, but we're not getting him back without a miracle that I doubt even the Caladrius at St. Giles's can pull off. But he doesn't appear to have succeeded in spreading the slime to anyone else yet. How's your sink friend?"

"Still stuck. I managed to put the plug back in when I saw it moving that way. I stopped the slime with a ladle so I could reach in without getting tagged."

"And you're *sure* it didn't touch you?"

She nodded. "I like to think I would have noticed if it had."

"All right. You're a lesser gorgon, yes?"

"Yes. You knew that. It's on my rental application, and I know you have copies of those. Why?"

"I just wanted to be absolutely sure." There are three known varieties of gorgon. Only the greater gorgon can actually petrify with a glance—stories of the other varieties doing that exact thing are exaggerated, and probably spread by the gorgons themselves, because it makes them sound far more terrifying if they can *all* turn you to stone with a look. The venom in their hair can do a lot worse, regardless of species.

But lesser gorgons *can* paralyze people. It's just more like the biotoxins found in some algae. So paralytic shellfish poisoning, contracted ocularly. Which is a terrifying-enough concept, and really doesn't need the additional horror of turning into stone as an inescapable secondary consequence.

Roz looked uncertain. "Well, you can be sure now. Why?"

"Carl has been infected by the alkabyiftiris slime. It's advanced enough that it's visible to the naked eye, and I don't think he's going to get better. I'd ask if you were willing to let your hair bite him, but we don't want that stuff getting on your teeth. Which leaves eyes. If we all go down to the basement and Malena lures him out, you can look at him without your glasses. That should paralyze him. Then we wrap him in a tarp and tote him over to St. Giles's, in case they can help him after all. The slime has infiltrated a lot of his body. Probably most of it, by percentage. But I'm not a doctor, and maybe there's something they can do."

"And if there's not?" asked Malena.

"Then they stand a better chance of stabilizing him while they contact his family than we do," I said. "I'll call the dragons from the hospital, get them to send someone over here and flush the pipes. Clearing out an alkabyiftiris slime that isn't inside a body is pretty straightforward, or we'd have a lot more issues with the stuff. We'll just kill it, and alert the bogeyman and hidebehind communities, so they can go looking for the source."

"You've thought this through."

"My family's dealt with this stuff before," I said, grimly. The mice performed stirring recreations of the time we'd almost lost Grandma Alice to alkabyiftiris slime, and they had always terrified me when I was a child.

"I don't know," said Roz. "If something happened to me, the cats . . ."

"How long will the cats survive if we don't do anything and the slime takes you?" I asked. "It hollows out smaller animals and abandons what it doesn't eat in relatively short order. It can go through a rat in an hour." Or a mouse, in less time, according to the account of the slime's attack on my grandmother. "A cat might take it two or three."

Roz stiffened, snakes writhing in agitation. "I'm coming," she said. "You can stop saying terrible things."

"I just need to swing through the office so I can reset the elevator, and we'll head down," I said. "Roz, you stand behind Malena. She's going to shift and go corral Carl. Malena—"

"I got it," she said, holding up hands that were already starting to twist into something between a lizard's hand and something you'd expect to see on a horror-movie werewolf. The combination should have been silly. It managed, somehow, to be anything but silly, scales and skin coexisting in a terrible blend.

"Great," I said. "Come on."

We left the apartment in a ragged line, me at the front—which made sense, since I was the one with the keys to the office—Malena in the middle, and Roz bringing up the rear. We quickly became a line of two as Malena kicked off her shoes and scurried up the wall, keeping pace on the ceiling. I glanced up.

"That's creepy, you know."

She shrugged, which was impressive, given that her hands were still flat against the ceiling. "Tell it to the evolutionary pressures that decided I needed to be able to run straight up a sheer cliff face," she said, words only slightly garbled by the size of her teeth.

"If I ever get the chance, I will."

We reached the office, and I unlocked the door to let myself in and head for the breaker box on the wall. Three of the five lines on the office phone were lit up and flashing red. I glanced at them and winced. Hopefully, people were just calling to let me know that something was funky with the water, and so they weren't touching or drinking it. Hopefully, this wasn't me standing at the doorway to an outbreak that would wipe out half of the building and leave the dragons blaming me for the sudden drop in rental income.

(Even if Candy tried to blame me, William would probably talk sense into her. It was a sheer stroke of luck that I even knew what alkabyiftiris slime was: most possible apartment managers would have been as out of their depth as Malena was. Alkabyiftiris slime is one of those things that sound incredibly badass and dangerous, but is actually ecologically fragile, and tends to prompt vigorous extermination campaigns whenever it comes into contact with a sapient population. Some people believe it may have been one of the inspirations behind *The Blob*, and I wouldn't be surprised if that turned out to be the truth. When your existence is enough to inspire a horror franchise, you're not going to have an easy time of cohabitation with the rest of the world.)

Leaving the lights to flash to themselves, I opened the panel on the wall and flipped the switch to reactivate the elevator, then slammed it shut again and hurried to the door as fast as my swollen ankles would allow. Looking out, I saw the elevator doors already starting to slide closed.

"Malena!" I barked.

She whipped around, following my line of sight to the elevator. Hissing, she scurried along the ceiling and shoved one clawed hand into the opening before the doors could finish closing.

Dinging in inanimate confusion, the doors slid back open.

"Good job," I said, and waddled out into the hall, heading for the once-more-open elevator. Malena scurried inside, still on the ceiling, and Roz moved to stand behind me. "Everybody ready?"

"Are we allowed to say 'no'?" asked Malena.

"Nope," I said, and hit the button to take us to the basement once again.

✦ ✦ ✦

This time, the immediate darkness of the basement was less "a bogeyman lives here" and more "be afraid, be very afraid." I pulled my phone out and activated the flashlight, scanning to be sure Carl wasn't waiting to seize us as soon as we stepped into the open. The light found a few pale streaks of slime, but nothing more immediately alarming than that. I lowered it, stepping back.

"Malena, Roz, you're on," I said.

They moved into position, Malena scurrying out onto the hallway ceiling, Roz reaching up and removing her glasses. She kept her eyes fixed steadfastly forward as she did so, asking, "Are you sure this is going to work?"

"Absolutely," I lied. There was no point in shaking her faith in me now, not when it was too late for us to turn back. She stepped out of the elevator. I stepped up to the threshold, where my presence would keep the doors from closing again. If things went unexpectedly sideways, my corpse would have the same effect.

Malena quickly vanished into the dark, claws scraping on the concrete, and then her voice drifted back to us. "What did you do, break all the bulbs with a broom handle? I thought a handyman would be more handy than— Oh, don't you spit at me, you filthy bastard. None of this is your fault, but that doesn't mean I want you spitting at me."

She came scurrying back, eyes tightly closed as she retraced her steps, and I whistled, giving her something to follow to the elevator. She ducked gladly inside, huddling in a corner, and said, "Val? I need you to look and be sure he didn't actually spit on me."

I looked up. There was blood on her scaled hands, probably from the broken light bulbs, but nothing else gleamed like it was wet or slimy—or covered in spit. I exhaled, shoulders relaxing slightly.

"You're fine," I said. "We'll get the doctors to look at your hands."

"Thank you," she said, huddling deeper into her corner, until it seemed like she was trying to compact herself into a black hole. "He's coming."

"You got his attention?"

She gave me a withering look. "No. He was spitting at me for fun."

Something scraped against the hallway floor. I turned, watching the snakes on Roz's head writhe in agitation, and kept watching as the worn, wet-looking figure of the building handyman shambled into view.

His eyes were still entirely white. That didn't mean he couldn't see us. Sarah's eyes were frequently solid white, and she could see just fine. Cataracts could interfere with vision without cutting it off; was alkabyiftiris slime inside the eye like a living cataract? What would happen if Roz paralyzed the slime without paralyzing the host?

He shuffled closer. Roz took a step forward, turning so that there was no chance he could miss meeting her eyes. She took a slow breath, then hissed like the large serpent she almost was. His head canted slightly to the left, turning toward her like a flower turns toward the sun.

What happened next would have been comical if it hadn't been so damned terrifying. His whited-out eyes widened fractionally, expression going from one of slack disconnection to confusion and even a sliver of fear. He began to shamble faster, moving toward her with singular purpose. The slime that was oozing out of his nose and the corners of his eyes ran thicker, tinted with red and seeming to writhe on its own as it escaped his body. Then, with a sharp upward jerk like someone touching a live electric wire, he just . . . stopped. His limbs stopped moving, and his eyes stopped twitching, and he pitched forward to land face down on the concrete hallway floor.

"Is it over?" asked Roz anxiously. She took a step toward his motionless body. "Can we be finished with this awful, nasty, scary thing now? Please?"

"Roz, move back," I replied, eyes on the floor, where the slime that had escaped Carl's body before it fell was pulling back, oozing together to form a larger puddle. It was about a foot away from her toes, and if it managed to acquire enough mass, it would easily be able to surge forward.

It wasn't super acidic, to chew through her skin in an instant, but skin is an imperfect barrier, because the people who have and care for it are imperfect hosts. More, Roz had two cats. The odds were good that there was a break in the skin somewhere on her feet or ankles, an ingrown toenail or a little scratch that she had barely even noticed happening and was now blissfully unaware of. If the alkabyiftiris slime touched unbroken skin, it could be washed easily away. If it found a break . . .

Once it got inside the body, there were very few options. Most involved having access to a sorcerer, and we currently didn't, in New York. Maybe Dr. Morrow would be able to help—Caladrius are supposed to be able to heal all illnesses. That was what we were counting on, with Carl. He was chewed up enough that I didn't expect him to make it, assuming he was even breathing after getting a clear look at Roz's eyes. But if anyone could save him, it was Dr. Morrow.

Roz began walking backward, apparently taking my tone for the warning that it was. She didn't stop until she bumped into the wall next to the elevator doors, and I saw her raise her hands, putting her glasses back on, before she turned to face us. "What?" she asked.

"You froze the slime that was inside him and connected to his eyes," I said. "You didn't freeze the slime that was already out. It couldn't 'see' you, because it didn't have any ocular pathways to send the message along. You almost stepped in it."

"Oh." Roz blanched, which was an impressive sight, since the snakes atop her head also paled in the process. "That could have been bad."

"Yeah, it could have," I agreed. "Malena, can you come down from the ceiling?"

There was a thump as she dropped down behind me, horror-movie-style. I was getting awfully tired of people doing things horror-movie-style around me. I was definitely in the mood for a few things done period-romance-style. Or maybe light-afterschool-drama-style.

Beggers can't be choosers, I guess. I fished my cellphone out of my pocket. "One of us watches that pool of slime at all times," I said, indicating the larger puddle that had escaped from Carl. It was continuing to pulse, but looked otherwise harmless.

That was a lie. Pretending to be harmless is how those things get you.

"What are you doing?" asked Roz.

"Normally, the solution for alkabyiftiris slime is 'cleanse it with fire,' so I'm calling the dragons," I said, and lifted the phone to my ear.

In the dark, unpleasant basement, alkabyiftiris slime dripping down the walls, we waited.

✦　✦　✦

"—going to have to pay the plumber *triple* time to get the filters back in place when there's a chance of alkabyiftiris slime in the water supply," ranted Candice, pacing back and forth in the manager's office and glaring at me like I had done all of this just to frustrate her.

I didn't care. I was sitting *down*, in the glorious old armchair we kept in the manager's office for potential tenants. It was an unpleasant shade of cat-shit brown, and had that distinctive rotting-fabric smell that all old armchairs seem to acquire, no matter how well they've been cared for, and in that moment, it was my favorite thing that had ever existed. I wasn't sure how I was going to get *out* of it, since my feet had declared their independence from the greater state of Verity and my knees no longer believed they had any responsibility to bend, but that was a bridge I would cross when I got to it. For right now, everything was right with my world.

"I had no way of knowing that Carl had encountered the stuff,"

I said, keeping my voice level and calm, and not allowing myself to whine the way I wanted to. By this point, I felt like I had definitely earned my bed, a pint of Ben & Jerry's, and maybe a foot rub, if I could talk Malena into it.

But no, she was off helping several dragons transport Carl's tarp-wrapped body to St. Giles's, while Roz sat in her apartment with a fortifying shot of brandy and thought about rental applications for properties that didn't have blob monsters incubating in the basement.

Good luck with that, Roz. Finding someplace rent-controlled that would let her have two cats and wouldn't mind the part where she wasn't actually human was going to be a tall order, and I didn't expect her to be moving out any time soon.

"You knew what it was," said Candice. "That implies familiarity. How did you not pick up on the signs?"

"Okay, first, alkabyiftiris slime moves fast. He probably picked it up two days ago at most, which brings me to second, why are we wasting time with this instead of notifying the underground communities of the threat? They need to know, Candy."

"I already asked William to send word," she said. "They'll listen to him more quickly than they would listen to me."

"Tell them—okay, this will sound silly, but—tell them they need to pour a mixture of white-wine vinegar and baking soda anywhere they think the slime may have accumulated. It's weak without a host, and that mix will clean it out. Fire is also good, if they have a site they feel like they can burn. We'll probably be dealing with small outbreaks for a few months, while it burns out the roaches and rats it's currently hiding inside. They won't last long. It's going to be looking for larger hosts, because anything else will just fall apart."

"We know all that," she said. "What we still don't know is how you missed Carl bringing it back here. I hired you to keep this place safe."

"No."

"What do you mean, no?"

"I mean, no. You and Willam hired me because I knew how to negotiate with the human world, and I know enough about the Covenant that I can help protect your tenants from *that*. I never agreed that I'd be protecting them from absolutely everything the world could throw at them. Roz called me, I came. I identified a threat, and I helped to deal with it without anyone else getting hurt. And I did it all while I was eight months pregnant and my ankles felt like they were literally on fire. I think I did pretty well!"

I didn't realize I was going to shout until I was already shouting, and then, it felt good enough that I didn't feel bad about it. I stopped and glowered at Candice, who looked briefly stunned.

"We'll need to hire a new handyman," she said. "I'll have the applications sent to your apartment for review."

I blinked. "Can I suggest candidates?"

"Of course."

"Malena."

"The chupacabra?"

"She's good with her hands, she can stick to walls, and there's nothing in this building that's going to freak her out. I can't guarantee how long she'll be in New York, but she may want to check out the local dance scene, and I can promise she'll have more opportunities here than she does back in her home town."

"If she wants to apply, I'll give her the same consideration we grant to anyone else."

"Good. And if she gets hired, she can help me move."

"Move?"

"I'm going to need to relocate to one of the available three-bedroom units. The baby's almost here, and it's close to time to bring Olivia home from my parents. So I need to be in a larger space."

To my surprise, Candice actually smiled at that. "I was wondering how long it would take you to get around to making that request. You need your daughter, and our daughters have been asking when she'll be coming back from her trip. They miss her."

"I miss her." I missed her so much that I couldn't let myself think about it too clearly. Admitting how much it hurt to have my child far away from me would mean looking critically at all the places I was bleeding inside, and that was the sort of accounting I just wasn't ready for. Not yet. Maybe not ever.

"Good. You should."

"Thanks."

Candice shrugged. "What? It's true. We've allowed you to wallow in grieving for this long because you're a gestating mammal, and gestating mammals are irrational. William said so. But it's been months. It's time for you to start moving forward, and caring more about Olivia than you do about your grief."

"I'll try. You'll let me know when there's a prognosis on Carl?"

"I will," she said, and that was it. Candice sighed and started to turn away, then looked back at me, blinking. "Why are you still sitting there?"

"I don't think I can stand up anymore," I admitted, and shrugged.

Candice groaned.

✦ ✦ ✦

It wasn't until Malena came back and helped me out of the arm-chair that I was able to return to the safety of my own apartment. She took one look at my ankles, swollen, angry things that they were, and bypassed the couch to drag me directly to my bed, where she brought me my toothbrush, toothpaste, and a small Tupperware bowl to spit into. I glared at her even as I started brushing my teeth.

"I'm pregnant, not an invalid," I said.

"Mm-hmm," she replied, agreeably. "Very pregnant, which means I get to bring you things, and you don't get to hit me. Bad for the baby."

Several mice, watching this from atop the dresser, cheered. I switched my glare to them. They cheered again.

"Be quiet or I'm borrowing one of Roz's cats," I said.

More cheering.

I sighed, looking back to Malena. "I'm not winning this one, am I?"

"Nope," she said, unrepentantly.

"Will you apply for the handyman position?"

"And get my own apartment, away from the cheering throng? Already did."

I smiled. "Good. I'm glad you're here, Mal."

"I'm glad I'm here, too. You needed somebody."

She was right about that. No matter how much I wanted to pretend that I was an island unto myself, I needed people, and if I currently didn't feel like I could lean on my family, well.

That's what friends were for.

Price Family Field Guide to the Cryptids of North America

UPDATED AND EXPANDED EDITION

Aeslin mice (Apodemus sapiens). Sapient, rodent-like cryptids which present as near-identical to non-cryptid field mice. Aeslin mice crave religion, and will attach themselves to "divine figures" selected virtually at random when a new colony is created. They possess perfect recall; each colony maintains a detailed oral history going back to its inception. Origins unknown.

Basilisk (Procompsognathus basilisk). Venomous, feathered saurians approximately the size of a large chicken. This would be bad enough, but thanks to a quirk of evolution, the gaze of a basilisk causes petrification, turning living flesh to stone. Basilisks are not native to North America, but were imported as game animals. By idiots.

Bogeyman (Vestiarium sapiens). The thing in your closet is probably a very pleasant individual who simply has issues with direct sunlight. Probably. Bogeymen are close relatives of the human race; they just happen to be almost purely nocturnal, with excellent night vision, and a fondness for enclosed spaces. They rarely grab the ankles of small children, unless it's funny.

Chupacabra (Chupacabra sapiens). True to folklore, chupacabra are blood-suckers, with stomachs that do not handle solids well. They are also therianthrope shapeshifters, capable of transforming themselves into human form, which explains why they have never been captured. When cornered, most chupacabra will assume their bipedal shape in self-defense. A surprising number of chupacabra are involved in ballroom dance.

Clurichaun (Clurichaun sapiens). Supposedly, clurichaun are fairies, related to leprechauns, and prone to all the nasty stereotypes you can think of for the Irish. As we've never seen any indication that "fairy" is anything aside from another way to classify cryptids, and clurichaun are very real, we're not sure how much credence to place on their theory. Clurichaun are virtually immune to all forms of poison, including the mild recreational ones, leading to them developing a reputation for being great drinkers.

Dragon (Draconem sapiens). Dragons are essentially winged, fire-breathing dinosaurs the size of Greyhound buses. At least, the males are. The females are attractive humanoids who can blend seamlessly into a crowd of supermodels, and outnumber the males twenty to one. Females are capable of parthenogenic reproduction and can sustain their population for centuries without outside help. All dragons, male and female, require gold to live, and collect it constantly.

Ghoul (Herophilus sapiens). The ghoul is an obligate carnivore, incapable of digesting any but the simplest vegetable solids, and prefers humans because of their wide selection of dietary nutrients. Most ghouls are carrion eaters. Ghouls can be easily identified by their teeth, which will be shed and replaced repeatedly over the course of a lifetime.

Hidebehind (Aphanes apokryphos). We don't really know much about the hidebehinds: no one's ever seen them. They're excellent illusionists, and we think they're bipeds, which means they're probably mammals. Probably.

Hockomock Swamp Beasties (Hockomock Gigantopithecus sesquac). We are currently consulting with the doctors associated with the only known colony of Hockomock Swamp Beasties to better classify them; for the moment, it seems most likely that they're relatives of the Sasquatch, North America's most widespread known primate. Hockomock Swamp Beasties possess skin closer to that of a manatee or hippo, allowing them to remain submerged for long periods without wrinkling or risk of infection. They are otherwise well aligned to other known hominids.

Huldra (Hulder sapiens). While the Huldrafolk are technically divided into three distinct subspecies, the most is known about *Hulder sapiens skogsfrun,* the Huldra of the trees. These hollow-backed hematophages can pass for human when they have to, but prefer to avoid humanity, living in secluded villages throughout Scandinavia. Individual Huldra can live for hundreds of years when left to their own devices. They aren't innately friendly, but aren't hostile unless threatened.

Jackalope (Parcervus antelope). Essentially large jackrabbits with antelope antlers, the jackalope is a staple of the American West, and stuffed examples can be found in junk shops and kitschy restaurants all across the country. Most of the taxidermy is fake. Some, however, is not. The jackalope was once extremely common, and has been shot, stuffed, and harried to near-extinction. They're relatively harmless, and they taste great.

Johrlac (Johrlac psychidolos). Colloquially known as "cuckoos," the Johrlac are telepathic ambush predators. They appear human but are internally very different, being cold-blooded and possessing a decentralized circulatory system. This quirk of biology means they can be shot repeatedly in the chest without being killed. Extremely dangerous. All Johrlac are interested in mathematics, sometimes to the point of obsession. Origins unknown; possibly insect in nature.

Laidly worm (Draconem laidly). Very little is known about these close relatives of the dragons. They present similar but presumably not identical sexual dimorphism; no currently living males have been located.

Lamia (Python lamia). Semi-hominid cryptids with the upper bodies of humans and the lower bodies of snakes. Lamia are members of order Synapsedia, the mammal-like reptiles, and are considered responsible for many of the "great snake" sightings of legend. The sightings not attributed to actual great snakes, that is.

Lesser gorgon (Gorgos euryale). One of three known subspecies of gorgon, the lesser gorgon's gaze causes short-term paralysis followed by death in anything under five pounds. The bite of the snakes atop their heads will cause paralysis followed by death in anything smaller than an elephant if not treated with the appropriate antivenin. Lesser gorgons tend to be very polite, especially to people who like snakes.

Lilu (Lilu sapiens). Due to the striking dissimilarity of their abilities, male and female Lilu are often treated as two individual species: incubi and succubi. Incubi are empathic; succubi are persuasive telepaths. Both exude strong pheromones inspiring feelings of attraction and lust in the opposite sex. This can be a problem for incubi like our cousin Artie, who mostly wants to be left alone, or succubi like our cousin Elsie, who gets very tired of men hitting on her while she's trying to flirt with their girlfriends.

Madhura (Homo madhurata). Humanoid cryptids with an affinity for sugar in all forms. Vegetarian. Their presence slows the decay of organic matter, and is usually viewed as lucky by everyone except the local dentist. Madhura are very family-oriented, and are rarely found living on their own. Originally from the Indian subcontinent.

Manananggal (Tanggal geminus). If the manananggal is proof of anything, it is that Nature abhors a logical classification system. We're reasonably sure the manananggal are mammals; everything else is anyone's guess. They're hermaphroditic and capable of splitting their upper and lower bodies, although they are a single entity, and killing the lower half kills the upper half as well. They prefer fetal tissue, or the flesh of newborn infants. They are also venomous, as we have recently discovered. Do not engage if you can help it.

Oread (Nymphae silica). Humanoid cryptids with the approximate skin density of granite. Their actual biological composition is unknown, as no one has ever been able to successfully dissect one. Oreads are extremely strong, and can be dangerous when angered. They seem to have evolved independently across the globe; their common name is from the Greek.

Sasquatch (Gigantopithecus sesquac). These massive native denizens of North America have learned to embrace depilatories and mail-order shoe catalogs. A surprising number make their living as Bigfoot hunters (Bigfeet and Sasquatches are close relatives, and enjoy tormenting each other). They are predominantly vegetarian, and enjoy Canadian television.

Tanuki (Nyctereutes sapiens). Therianthrope shapeshifters from Japan, the Tanuki are critically endangered due to the efforts of the Covenant. Despite this, they remain friendly, helpful people, with a naturally gregarious nature which makes it virtually impossible for them to avoid human settlements. Tanuki possess three primary forms—human, raccoon dog, and big-ass scary monster. Pray you never see the third form of the tanuki.

Ukupani (Ukupani sapiens). Aquatic therianthropes native to the warm waters of the Pacific Islands, the Ukupani were believed for centuries to be an all-male species, until Thomas Price sat down with several local fishermen and determined that the abnormally large great white sharks that were often found near Ukupani males were, in actuality, Ukupani females. Female Ukupani can't shapeshift, but can eat people. Happily. They are as intelligent as their shapeshifting mates, because smart sharks is exactly what the ocean needed.

Wadjet (Naja wadjet). Once worshipped as gods, the male wadjet resembles an enormous cobra, capable of reaching seventeen feet in length when fully mature, while the female wadjet resembles an attractive human female. Wadjet pair-bond young, and must spend extended amounts of time together before puberty in order to become immune to one another's venom and be able to successfully mate as adults.

Waheela (Waheela sapiens). Therianthrope shapeshifters from the upper portion of North America, the waheela are a solitary race, usually claiming large swaths of territory and defending it to the death from others of their species. Waheela mating season is best described with the term "bloodbath." Waheela transform into something that looks like a dire bear on steroids. They're usually not hostile, but it's best not to push it.

Yong (Draconem alta aqua). The so-called "Korean dragon" shares many qualities with their European relatives. The species demonstrates extreme sexual dimorphism; the males are great serpents, some easily exceeding eighty feet in length, with no wings, but possessing powerful forelimbs with which to catch and keep their prey. The females, meanwhile, appear to be attractive human women of Korean descent, capable of blending easily into a human population. Unlike European dragons, their health is dependent on quartz rather than gold, making it somewhat easier for them to form and maintain their Nests (called "clutches").

Playlist

"High School Is Killing Me"	*Nerdy Prudes Must Die*
"Journey to the Past"	*Anastasia*
"Hey Friends"	Ludo
"Forever and a Day"	Ally Rhodes
"People Like Us"	Matt Bomer
"Moving on to Gone"	Gin Wigmore
"Good Night Sweet Girl"	Ghost of the Robot
"Jane's A Car"	*Nightmare Time*
"FM Radio"	Dar Williams
"I Am the One Who Will Remember Everything"	Dar Williams
"Trouble"	P!nk
"Dead Flowers"	Miranda Lambert
"Ghost"	Red Molly
"Death Danced at My Party"	Talis Kimberley
"Puppeteer"	*Epic*
"How to Save a Life"	The Fray
"Keep Breathing"	Ingrid Michaelson
"Misery Loves Company"	Emilie Autumn
"Dragging the River"	Idgy Vaughn
"Locked Out of Heaven"	*Glee*
"The Web I Spin for You"	*Nightmare Time*
"Fall Down"	Shawn Tutt
"The Witch in the Web"	*Nightmare Time*
"Save Me from Myself"	Marla Sokoloff
"Secret Worlds"	The Amazing Devil

Acknowledgments

Mary's second outing as our narrator is finished, and I hope you're as pleased with it as I am. I adore Mary as a point-of-view character—working through and with her really drives home a lot of the commonalities we find in our various family members, and why they are the way they are. When you're raised by someone as sarcastic as she is, it rubs off a bit. I love the lens she provides me for viewing the rest of the family, and the way she puts them properly into context.

So, the elephant in the room: this is the first InCryptid book to be published by Tor Publishing, after thirteen volumes with DAW Books. The change has been a lot to adjust to, but very smoothly facilitated by helpers on both sides, and while I'm going to miss everyone at DAW, I'm very excited to be embarking on a new adventure with everyone at Tor.

I am still in Seattle, still happy with my house and my community, and with my local game store (Zulu's Board Game Café, I love you so). As I write this, we're still in the middle of a global pandemic, and that makes me even more inclined to feather my nest and work on loving where I live. I hope you're still all okay with the decision not to include COVID-19 in the InCryptid setting. There was just no logical way to make it work, and unlike the real world, fictional realities *do* need to hang together narratively. Even ones as ridiculous as this.

It's mid-2024 as I'm writing this, and despite what I said above about the global pandemic, I've done my share of traveling. A trip to the Library of Congress to spend a day being Very Fancy Indeed, some long, lazy days in my swamp, and a lot of trail searches for toads. I've continued to keep and breed fancy praying mantises, and have expanded to two new species, ghost mantises and giant rainforest mantises. It's very engaging.

And now, gratitude time. My first and biggest thanks go to my agent, Diana Fox, who remains my staunchest advocate, and utterly willing to ride into battle for my sake, championing me and this series with endless poise, grace, and vicious firmness. She handled the entire transition between publishers, and it was a complicated process. I appreciate her more than words can say.

Thanks to Chris Mangum, who maintains the code for my website, and to Tara O'Shea, who manages the graphics. Alec Fowler has joined our team to manage website updates and get things all into the modern world, and I am so very grateful. Thanks also to Terri Ash, who is no longer the "new" personal assistant, but is still at the party—if you email through the website I just mentioned, she's the one who'll send your mail on to me. She's essential, and I am very glad she's here.

Thanks to the team at Tor Publishing Group for their part in this transition, and to our new team, including Oliver Dougherty, my new editor, who has done a remarkable job of stepping into an ongoing series without getting bowled over.

Cat update (I know you all live for these): Thomas is a fine senior gentleman now, and while he has a touch of arthritis, his sweaters help to keep him warm, and I've set up cat stairs all over the house so he can still come and go as he pleases. Megara remains roughly as intelligent as bread mold, and is very happy as she is—this is not a cat burdened by the weight of a prodigious intellect! Elsie is healthy, fine, and very opinionated, and would like me to stop writing this and pet her. Tinkerbell is a snotty little diva who knows exactly how pretty she is, and Verity would like to speak to the manager. Of life. (If that all seems familiar, it's because it is. The cats are stable, which is wonderful.) Kelpie is absolutely massive, and growing by the day. Her primary purpose is being very long, and she's really good at it.

My mother has a new cat. Hercules (her older boy) sadly passed away of congestive heart failure, and she now has Muffles, a younger sibling of Tinkerbell and Verity, who keeps Tink company and keeps her from eating us all in our sleep.

And now, gratitude in earnest. Thank you to everyone who reads, reviews, and helps to keep this series going; to Kate, for picking up the phone when I call her in a panic; to Phil, who knows what he did; to Shawn, for being the best brother a girl could possibly want; to Chris Mangum, for being here even when it's inconvenient; to Wing Mui, for keeping me socializing outside my head; to Manda Cherry, for a heated car seat and a wonderful friendship; to Crystal Fraiser, for regular company and grilled cheese; and to my dearest Amy McNally, for everything. Thanks to the members of all four of my current ongoing D&D games. And to you: thank you, so much, for reading.

Any errors in this book are my own. The errors that aren't here are the ones that all these people helped me fix. I appreciate it so much.

Let's go home.

About the Author

Beckett Gladney

SEANAN MCGUIRE is the author of the Hugo, Nebula, Alex, and Locus Award–winning Wayward Children series, the October Daye series, the InCryptid series, and other works. She also writes darker fiction as Mira Grant. McGuire lives in Seattle with her cats, a vast collection of creepy dolls, horror movies, and sufficient books to qualify her as a fire hazard. She won the 2010 John W. Campbell Award for Best New Writer, and in 2013 became the first person to appear five times on the same Hugo ballot. In 2022 she managed the same feat again!